Praise for *New York Times* bestselling author Lindsay McKenna

"A treasure of a book...highly recommended reading that everyone will enjoy and learn from."
—Chief Michael Jaco, US Navy SEAL, retired, on *Breaking Point*

"Heartbreakingly tender...readers will fall in love with the upstanding hero and his fierce determination to save the woman he loves."
—*Publishers Weekly* on *Never Surrender* (starred review)

"McKenna skillfully takes readers on an emotional journey into modern warfare and two people's hearts."
—*Publishers Weekly* on *Down Range*

"...Packed full of danger and adventure. Fans of military romance will appreciate the strong female characters, steamy sex scenes, and details of military life."
—*Booklist* on *Taking Fire*

"This was a beautiful and heartwarming story. Grayson and Skylar are an awesome alpha pair."
—*Night Owl Reviews* on *Wolf Haven*

"Readers will find this addition to the Shadow Warriors series full of intensity and action-packed romance. There is great chemistry between the characters and tremendous realism, making *Breaking Point* a great read."
—*RT Book Reviews*

LINDSAY McKENNA

Night Hawk

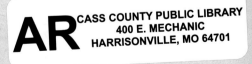

HQN™

ISBN-13: 978-0-373-77995-6

Recycling programs for this product may not exist in your area.

Night Hawk

www.HQNBooks.com

Printed in U.S.A.

To the best editors I've ever had:
Alicia Condon, Tara Gavin and Linda Curnyn.
From the "good ole days" where we kicked butt
and took names in the romance world of publishing...
taking romance at Silhouette to new heights! Creativity!
Thinking outside the box! We, and so many others,
changed the course of romance publishing. Many thanks
to my wonderful readers for showing us the way!

Dear Reader,

I love what-ifs because they lead me down some interesting, twisted, turning paths. In *Night Hawk*, you will meet former Delta Force sergeant Gil Hanford, who went into the US Army at eighteen.

Gil met and worked with Sam Morrison. Sam was married to US Army Apache combat helicopter mechanic Kai Tiernan. Gil fell in love with Kai but, respectful of their marriage, he kept his distance. It was a painful time for Gil because he saw how unavailable Sam was to his wife, Kai. He could only sympathize with their plight.

Sam is killed in a firefight, and Gil is there when it occurs. Feeling grief-stricken, wanting to console Kai, he goes to her to offer his condolences. They end up in one another's arms for five days, dealing with conflicting emotions. On the morning of the fifth day, Gil is ordered out on an undercover op. He thinks it's for a few days, but it ends up being two years.

Kai is left without her husband and without Gil. She never finds out what happens to Gil. Thinking he's used her to soothe her grief, Kai goes back to Wyoming and drifts from one ranch to another. Few ranchers are willing to hire a woman to be a mechanic.

Finally, four years later, she ends up at the Triple H Ranch near Jackson Hole, Wyoming. It's only half a day later that she meets the ranch foreman: Gil Hanford...

Join my newsletter to get all kinds of exclusive information given to subscribers only, giveaways and my latest books coming out at lindsaymckenna.com!

I hope you enjoy *Night Hawk*.

All the best,

Lindsay McKenna

NIGHT HAWK

CHAPTER ONE

KAI TRIED TO get her heart to stop pounding so hard in her chest. She sat in her Ford pickup in front of the Triple H Ranch, rubbing her damp palms against her jeans. This was the twentieth ranch she'd traveled to in order to apply for a job as a mechanic and wrangler. She'd been to six ranches in South Dakota, ten in Montana, two in Idaho, and now Wyoming ranches didn't look like they were hiring, either. Worse, she was a fine mechanic due to her US Army time as an Apache helicopter repairer, but the listless economy was stopping any new hires. Plus, she was a woman and the ranch owners just rolled their eyes when she said she was a mechanic.

Kai could fix anything. You name it, she could handle it. She knew being a woman brought prejudice to the table. And ranchers tended to be conservative, old guard and even outright Neanderthal in their view of women. She'd had one rancher nearly fall off his chair in his office laughing hysterically when she said she was a mechanic.

Hell, it was tough enough getting out of the military after enlisting at age eighteen and separating from the Army at twenty-eight because of downsizing. She thought her job rating would make it easy to get hired. In the military, women did so-called men's work, and no one thought anything about it. But they sure did out in the civilian world, she was discovering.

Kai wiped the dampness off the top of her lip, taking a quick glance around the ranch. There was an opening for a mechanic and wrangler. She was a perfect fit for it. The owner, Talon Holt, was the contact. Would he laugh her out of his office, too?

Money was tight. Kai didn't have enough left, after buying the tools she'd need and her wrangling gear, to try to rent an apartment in Jackson Hole—*if* she got the job. She'd already cased the town, looked through the rentals in the newspaper and found exorbitant demands for a small one-bedroom apartment. It was sticker shock. Yes, she had savings. Yes, she could pay that kind of highway robbery, but she was counting on a bunkhouse where she could live, instead, until she got her feet under her. Her goal was to eventually buy a house.

Looking around, the main ranch home was built of cedar and two stories tall, a silver sheen to its aging wood. The roof looked new. There was a white picket fence, recently painted, surrounding it. It was June first and Kai knew Wyoming winters hung around forever. She saw someone had bravely planted flowers in beds along the inside of the fence in hopes they could survive and struggle to stay alive in the near freezing temperatures that occurred at night. As she gazed out beyond the graveled parking area, she saw a number of rusted pipe fences that were in sad shape. This rancher would need a welder. She knew how to weld. That would be a plus, something she could tell the owner in hopes of him hiring her.

Kai sat there, feeling her stomach knot. Desperate for a job, her hope long since fading, she didn't want to apply for government assistance. It just wasn't somewhere she wanted to go, and she fought the idea. Swallowing, her throat dry, she closed her eyes, knowing she couldn't go home. Home to Cody, Wyoming. Home to her father's ranch, the Circle T.

Her father had disowned her when she joined the Army at age eighteen. He favored her older brother, Steve, over herself. He'd written her out of the will when she left for the Army. And he never believed a woman could run a ranch, so he'd left it to her brother when it was his time to die. At age 59, Hal Tiernan was the same gruff, terse, mean son of a bitch he'd always been. Kai had been an unwanted addition to her father's life. He doted on his son and barely tolerated her because she was female. He called her Troublemaker.

Rubbing her dark blue long-sleeved blouse that was feminine looking but functional, her heart ached for what she wished might have been with her broken family.

If her mother, Olivia, hadn't died when Kai was eight years old, things might have turned out a lot different. Kai was in constant touch with Steve, who loved her fiercely, begging her to come home. But home to what? Hal verbally digging at her on a daily basis? Making sniping remarks because she was a woman? He looked at all women as useful only when they were pregnant and barefoot. That was her father's favorite saying. Kai didn't know how her mother, who had been a high school principal, tolerated that kind of shit from him. She certainly didn't. And that was why he called her Troublemaker. He never called her by her real name, only his nickname for her. Kai hated it.

She pulled herself out of her pain. Opening the door, she climbed out, her cowboy boots crunching across the graveled driveway to the gate of the picket fence. Kai heard a dog barking but couldn't see it. Walking down the red-tiled sidewalk, she liked the wide, U-shaped porch that surrounded three-fourths of the house. There was a large, dark green porch swing in one corner and it looked inviting. A person could sit in it and look out over the lush swales and small hills of green grass that grew thick and abundant all around her.

Her boots thunked hollowly across the cedar porch. She saw the screen door was open and knocked loud enough so that someone would hear that there was a visitor. Heart pounding, Kai removed her dark blue baseball cap, nervously running her fingers through her short auburn hair.

A blond-haired woman in her late forties, who was very thin and frail looking, walked slowly down the foyer. She wore a bright apple-green-colored knit shawl around her shoulders, jeans and a pink sweater.

"Hi, I'm Kai Tiernan," she said. "I've got an appointment with Mr. Holt for a job interview at one o'clock."

The woman smiled and pushed open the screen door. "Nice to meet you, Kai. I'm Sandy Holt. Come on in. I'll let my son, Talon, know you've arrived. Make yourself at home."

Kai smiled and nodded, noticing Sandy moved at a halting pace. She appeared very ill, her skin not a good color, but her blue eyes were alert and the smile on her lips was genuine. Stepping into the foyer, she waited for the woman to guide her. She smelled bread baking in the kitchen and her mouth watered. Her mother used to bake bread and it brought back poignant memories. There were also other wonderful fragrances, apple pies baking. Her heart ached because she remembered her mother baking pies just like these in the kitchen of their ranch home. It brought back so many good but sad memories.

"This way," Sandy invited. "Sorry, I'm a little slow…"

"No worries," Kai replied gently. "Do you need some help?" She offered her hand.

Sandy shook her head. "No, but that's sweet of you to ask." Her face took on a wry look. "As it is, Cass is like a mother hen and I'm his chick. I'm lucky I got to answer the door before he could race to get to it, first."

"I heard that, Sandy," Cass called. "You must be feeling better because you were faster to answer that door than I was."

Kai saw a tall, sandy-blond-haired man with glinting blue eyes poke his head around the corner of the kitchen entrance. He was wearing a red apron around his narrow waist. He wore jeans, cowboy boots and a dark brown shirt with the sleeves rolled up to his elbows. His hair was rather longish, but she could see his ears and the nape of his neck. There was something about him that alerted Kai. She'd swear he'd been in the military. It was nothing obvious, but frequently she could meet someone and tell if they had been in or not. It was the way they carried themselves and that rock-solid confidence they had about themselves.

"This is my broody hen caregiver," Sandy dead-panned, weakly lifting her hand toward him. "Cassidy Reynolds, although we all call him Cass, meet Kai Tiernan. She's here for a job interview with Talon in about ten minutes."

Cass grinned and came around the corner, holding out his large, work-worn hand toward her. "Hey, nice to meet you, Kai. Can I get you anything to drink while you're waiting?"

Kai gripped his hand. The man was definitely ex-military, no question. He was probably about six foot two, with powerful shoulders, his forearms thick with muscle, telling her he worked hard. She saw some bits of flour spotted across his shirt. "Nice to meet you, Cass. And no, I don't need anything to drink, but thank you."

"Ah," he said, giving Sandy a wicked look, "she's just like you. Kai has this look on her face of *what is a man doing in a kitchen and wearing, of all things, an apron?*" He released her hand and chuckled. "Just FYI, Kai, I do the cooking around here five days a week. And—" he gave Sandy a warm, teasing look "—I take care of this headstrong, wild filly, plus I'm the operating officer for this ranch."

"Wow," Kai said, put at ease by Cass's easygoing nature, "you're a multitasking guy if I ever saw one."

Sandy chuckled and shook her head. "I'm going to the living room to sit down. Come join me, Kai?"

"Yes, ma'am," she said.

"Don't 'ma'am' her," Cass warned gravely. "Things around here are loosey-goosey. No one stands on much protocol."

"Good to know," Kai murmured, giving Cass a

grateful look. Already, she liked this ranch. Sandy worried her, though, and now she knew Talon Holt was her son. Was he like his mother? She didn't know but hoped some of her DNA had made its way into him. Cass was a man in the kitchen. So maybe Talon wouldn't think it odd she was a woman mechanic. Here at this ranch, they seemed not to care what the gender was as long as they were good at what they were doing. Mentally, Kai crossed her fingers.

Kai didn't have long to wait for Talon Holt. She heard a man come in the screen door, the clacking of paws indicating a dog with him. Sitting on the couch, she saw a beautiful Belgian Malinois dog enter the room. His alert cinnamon eyes instantly settled on her. The intelligence in the dog's gaze was apparent and Kai lifted her chin, seeing the owner come in right after him.

"Zeke, sit," he ordered the dog.

Instantly, the dog sat.

"I'm Talon Holt," he said, glancing at his mother and then at her. He took off his black Stetson. "You must be Kai Tiernan?"

Kai instantly stood. "Yes, sir, I am. Nice to meet you, sir." She saw the tall man with black hair and gray eyes, grimace.

"Stand down," he said with a slight smile. He crossed the room and shook her hand. "No need to say 'sir' to me."

Zeke whined.

Talon looked back and pointed at his mother. "Zeke, guard."

Sandy made an unhappy noise. "Now, Talon. I do

not want that dog herding me around like I'm a sheep to be taken care of. Really!"

"No," Cass boomed, coming into the room, handing Talon a cup of hot coffee, "she has me. Let the dog go out and smell the flowers that you're trying to grow."

Grinning, Talon nodded. "Kai, one second? I'll be right back."

Kai nodded, fascinated with the family dynamic. Unlike her own, no question. Sandy was the matriarch. Cass was protective of her, for sure. And as Talon turned and gave the dog a hand command, Zeke leaped up, tongue hanging out of his mouth, and ran down the long cedar hallway toward the screen door ahead of him.

Cass handed Kai a cup of coffee. "Might as well be relaxed. Come on, I'll show you to Talon's office. That's where he'll interview you."

Grateful for Cass's warmth and thoughtfulness, she followed him out of the massive living room and kitchen. It was an open-concept area. Down another hall, Cass led her into a small office. There, he gestured to a chair in front of a massive oak desk that looked to her to be at least a hundred years old. She sat, holding her coffee between her hands.

Cass hesitated at the door and said, "Now, just be yourself. And don't call him 'sir.' He was in the military, but he's out now. Okay?"

"Yes, si— I mean, yes, I'll remember."

Cass nodded and said, "You've got mechanic's hands."

Dumbfounded, Kai stared up at him.

"I was in Special Forces, a sergeant," he said. "I

was the mechanic in our A team. You can always tell someone who works around equipment."

"Really?" she asked, still in shock that he could tell by just looking at her hands.

"Sure," he said, "short, blunt nails, calluses on the insides of your fingers, and the skin around your nails is darker, indicating oil or other fluids you've been handling." He grinned. "Hey, be proud of it. I tried to talk Talon into letting me go finagle those sick pieces of equipment in the barns, but he needed me because I'm good at numbers." He laughed.

A little shaken, Kai wondered what kind of ranch this was. Talon had been in the military. Cass had been an Army Special Forces operator. She was a vet. Did he hire vets? Her hopes rose sharply. Kai heard the thunking of Talon's boots along the hall. Her heart rate went up. Setting the cup on the desk, she pulled out her résumé from her pocket and unfolded it, placing it on the desk where he would sit. What would he think?

"Cass make you at home?" Talon asked, entering the office and quietly shutting the door.

"Yes, s— I mean, yes, he did. Thank you."

Talon hooked his Stetson on a peg behind the leather chair and sat down, scooping up her three page résumé. "I've been anxious to see you," he admitted, glancing up, the paper in his hands. "Good mechanics are rare as hen's teeth. And when you answered the ad and sent me an email, telling me you had been a mechanic in the Army, I was very interested. Let me read this for a moment?"

Kai sat there trying to relax. Talon Holt was as tall as Cass and he walked like he'd been in the military, no question. His gray eyes were darker colored than hers. She remembered her father hated her eye color, accusing her mother of it being her fault that she had been born with the god-awful color. He didn't like the light gray color because he constantly told her he felt as if she had X-ray vision and was looking straight through him. That it made him feel damned uncomfortable.

Kai watched Talon's expression closely. The man homed in on the résumé like a laser-fired rocket. Kai could literally feel the shift of energy around him, that sudden focus. She gulped once, realizing that her dead husband, Sam Morrison, who had been a Delta Force operator, had that same kind of intensity, that same telltale energy about him. It was a mark of an operator. And Kai had known enough of them at Bagram in her many tours at that Afghanistan Army base to recognize one when she saw one.

Was Talon Holt an operator, too? Shaken by the synchronicity, if that were true, Kai felt her hopes rise a little more. If he was, he'd speed-read it, memorize it and have it locked permanently into his brain. That's the way operators were. She waited, barely breathing. Hoping against hope. Finally he looked at her after rapidly skimming the three pages.

"I like that you were an Apache helo mech. Only the cream of the Army crop of mechanics get that important position. Were you the only woman?" He smiled a little.

"No, s— No, I wasn't. In my squadron, we had four women. The rest were men."

"I see you had six deployments to Bagram. You were kept busy."

She nodded. "Well, if I wasn't on Apaches, I and a few others were sent over to work on Black Hawks and MH-47s for the Night Stalker squadrons located there with us."

"Yes," he murmured, "I'm a little familiar with Bagram."

Kai was dying to ask him what branch of the military he served in but didn't dare. That would have been inappropriate.

"So," Talon said, holding her stare, "if you were being asked to work on other birds then, you were a multi-engine qualified mechanic. They don't let mechs work on anything but what they're trained in on."

"That's correct. I was multi-certified." Kai saw a pleased look come to his face. He didn't hide how he felt. If he was an operator, usually they had a game face on and no one knew what they were thinking or feeling. Maybe Talon Holt wasn't an operator, after all.

"I see here you were born in Cody, Wyoming? That your father owns the Circle T?" Talon cocked his head, studying her. "Why aren't you home working for your parents instead of applying here for a job?"

Her throat tightened for a moment. Yeah, Talon was an operator. They had an unerring ability to home in on the exact issue that needed to be revealed and investigated. She told him the least she could, keeping out the fact she had a permanent rift with her father. His expression became sympathetic when she told him her mother had died when she was eight years old.

"That had to be tough on you," he murmured. "And you have an older brother?"

"Yes. Steve works at the Circle T." Her hands grew damp. "My father didn't need a mechanic. I needed to expand my horizons and stay in my MOS after I separated from the Army. That's why I'm applying for a job here."

Rubbing his shaven jaw, Talon regarded her for a moment, the silence thickening in the office. "And you grew up helping to repair tractors, trucks and hay balers?"

"All of those," she said, "and more."

"Did your father think it odd for a girl to be a mechanic?"

Shrugging, she said, "He did, but I persevered." Because she would work with her brother, Steve, who taught her everything that her father refused to teach her about fixing equipment.

"What are you looking for, Kai?"

The question caught her off guard. It was a thoughtfully posed question, without rancor. She saw kindness in Talon's gray eyes, his face fully readable. There was a gentleness around this man despite how tall he was. Holt wasn't pretty-boy handsome—he was deeply tanned and tough looking. For a moment, a man from her past, Gil Hanford, came to mind. He'd been a Delta Force operator and Sam's best friend. Kai quickly slammed that door shut in her memory— too much grief and loss came with it. Moistening her lips, she answered honestly.

"I wanted a family. The military was my family for ten years, but they were downsizing and a lot of us were being let go when our enlistment expired." She opened her hands. "I love people, children and animals. I like being part of something greater than myself. I was hoping to find a ranch owned by a long-time family and become a part of it."

He glanced at the résumé. "You're a widow?"

"Yes. My husband was a Delta Force operator and was killed in action in Afghanistan five years ago."

"I'm sorry," Talon said, meaning it, giving her a frown. "Are you in a relationship right now?"

"No."

"How do you see yourself fitting in around here?"

Kai was shocked at the kind of questions Talon was asking. No one had ever asked her questions like this. "I'm a good mechanic. And I'll be responsible for keeping all the equipment up, running and perform routine maintenance on them. Then, when I'm not busy with equipment, I'd like to be a wrangler. I can do anything asked of me because on my father's ranch, I did everything. I like working. I like being out in the weather. I don't mind dog work because I always take personal pride in the job I perform."

She saw his eyes twinkle. Kai didn't know if her answer meant he was pleased or not because his expression gave nothing away.

"What if," Talon said, setting the résumé aside, "our ranch manager asks you to go work on the employee house we're building presently? Do you have any house building or construction skills?"

"I helped my father with roofing, drywalling, painting, laying wood floor, tiling, plumbing and electrical. My weakness is carpentry, like making window openings and setting one into it. I hate hanging doors. I'm not very good at it, although I know I can be if asked to do something like that." She saw a slight smile come to his mouth.

"You are a jack-of-all-trades and that's what we need around here." Talon settled back in the squeaky chair. "I like your résumé, Kai, and I like your can-do spirit. We're trying to hire military vets here at our ranch. They're the hardest-working group I know of. They're responsible, disciplined, enjoy being a team member and they're the most organized group that I know of. Around here? We work dawn to dusk every day. You get weekends off. I'll give you two weeks vacation each year. The bad news is that we can't pay you as much as you're worth right now, because this ranch has had nine years of disrepair. It means you won't be able to make the money you're worth for two years. We have a business plan and Cass has a math degree. He's got us on track financially speaking, and everyone around here is busting their butts to make it happen."

"I'm okay with less money for now," Kai said. "And you're ex-military like me. I know you'll give me raises when you can and I'm fine with that. I just want to fit in. I'm looking for a new family, I guess."

He smiled a little. "You're good. I was in the US Navy. As you've probably already seen, the Holts are a pretty laid-back, easygoing family. Only my ranch foreman is pretty crusty and uptight, but he's good at what he does. The other thing is, we'll give you a room here on the first floor of our home. We're in the process of building the employee house, but it won't be ready until next June. We've only got so much money to buy items for the construction phase of it right now. We're working to enclose it before snow flies in late August."

Nodding, her heart was racing, but it was with joy this time. "I know I'll love working here, Mr. Holt."

"Call me Talon," he said, sitting up in the chair. He rested his arms on the desk. "The wranglers' lockers are located in the big red barn, next to the tack room on the main floor. Just grab one and put all your gear in there." He looked at his watch. "My wife, Cat, is a paramedic. She works at the local hospital three days a week. She'll be home at 5:00 p.m. We'll eat at six sharp, in the kitchen. Cass is a helluva chef. The guy missed his calling and he should have gone to chef school. He'd probably have his own TV show by now." Talon grinned. "We're lucky to have him."

"Your mother seems to really like him. He's very kind and gentle with her."

Talon lost his smile. "My mother's just gotten through her last round of chemo and radiation. This is her second go-around with breast cancer."

Kai winced. "Oh, no…" She saw the pain in Talon's darkening gray eyes. He loved his mother very much.

"There may be days," Talon said more softly, "that me or the foreman might ask you to do a little caregiving for her instead of being out riding fence. Would you be up for that?"

"Of course. I like Sandy. She's very kind." *Like her son*, she thought. The joy bubbling through Kai was fierce, like a tsunami, and she tried to keep a serious face because of the worry she saw in Talon's eyes. "I see you have a dog. He's beautiful."

Talon grimaced. "You need to know that he's a US Navy SEAL trained combat assault dog. Zeke and I were together for three years before we both got wounded in a firefight. I'll make sure to introduce you to him so he knows you're a friend of mine, not an enemy to bite."

Her eyes widened. "You were a SEAL?" She saw his face turn grim and she saw anguish in his eyes for a split second, and then it was gone.

"Up until about nine months ago," he said gruffly. "I came home to take care of my mother and get our ranch back on its feet."

Nodding, Kai felt the sting of tears in the back of her eyes. "I would never have thought you were a SEAL."

He smiled a little. "No?" He rose and pushed the chair back.

Kai stood. "Operators wear game faces. You don't."

"My wife is teaching me to let that be a thing of the past." Talon opened the door for her. "Go into the kitchen and ask Cass to show you to your bedroom. He'll get you squared away. And then, take your wrangling equipment to the locker in the barn. By that time, my foreman should be back from his run to town. If you happen to run into him, introduce yourself. If not, you'll meet him tonight at dinner."

"Good enough," Kai murmured. Her voice lowered with feeling. "Thank you for giving me a chance, Talon. I promise, I won't let you or your family down."

He patted her shoulder. "I believe you, Kai. Welcome home."

CHAPTER TWO

GIL HANFORD DROVE in with the flatbed truck filled with sixty bales of straw for the horse stalls on the Triple H Ranch. It was midafternoon as he backed the truck up to the graveled slope that led up to the main red barn. The huge doors were slid open at both ends to allow a breeze through the massive three-story building. He was hoping that Talon Holt had hired someone to do this kind of work, leaving him free to do other more important things to get this broken-down ranch back online.

He thought he spotted someone near the lockers, but the shadows were deep inside the barn because no one had turned on the overhead lights. Could be Cass. But, God knew, his duties were stretched thin, too, which is why his boss needed to hire another wrangler. *And soon.*

As he backed the truck up into the wide concrete breezeway, ten wooden box stalls on one side and the tack room and wrangler locker area on the other side, he did spot someone standing in front of an open locker. Unable to get a good look at him because he was backing up the truck, Gil's hopes rose. All he saw was the backside of the person. Had Talon hired a wrangler?

Turning off the engine, Gil climbed out of the cab

and shut the door. The whicker of several horses in nearby box stalls greeted him. He inhaled the scent of the alfalfa and timothy-grass hay stored up on the second floor above them. It was a good, clean smell, one he grew up with on his father's ranch near Billings, Montana.

He felt his left knee gripe, a war wound that had gotten him released from Delta Force and the Army a year ago. His kneecap had been broken during a firefight and he'd been airlifted out by medevac to Bagram, undergoing immediate stabilization. And then he was flown by an Air Force C-5 to Landstuhl Regional Medical Center in Germany, for the surgery. The best orthopedic surgeons in the world were there and Gil was grateful they were able to save his kneecap.

Now, it got grumpy if it was in one position for too long. Moving his leg and flexing it, the stiffness dissolved. Pushing the brim of his tan Stetson up on his brow, he wanted to see who else was in the barn. As foreman, it was his job to know where his people were at all times. He had responsibility for the day-to-day operation of this teetering ranch that was struggling to make a comeback.

Gil smiled to himself as he walked casually around the end of the truck stacked five bales high with straw to be used for the box stalls. Getting this job three months ago had been a godsend for him. And, like this ranch, he was making a comeback, too.

Gil saw whoever it was place a big toolbox into the large locker. Damn if that backside didn't look familiar. His eyes narrowed. The person had short red hair, built small for a man. He halted about six feet from the unknown wrangler who was crouched down, pushing the toolbox into the locker.

"Excuse me," he rumbled.

The deep, male voice caught Kai by surprised. She didn't mean to gasp. As she stood and turned, her eyes widened, her mouth dropping open. It was Gil Hanford! For a second, Kai felt dizzy, as if someone had hit her in the head and she was staggering from the blow. And then her heart ripped with such pain that she took a step back, hitting the locker door with her back.

Instantly anger surged through her, along with a tangle of confused feelings that tightened in her throat. "Wh-what are you doing here?" she managed in a shaky tone, disbelief in it.

Gil scowled, staring down at her. "I might ask you the same thing," he growled defensively.

Touching wisps of auburn hair across her brow, Kai tried to get herself under control, the shock of meeting him nearly overwhelming her. Gil had been her husband's best friend, both Delta Force operators and on the same team. She saw his blue eyes grow to slits, felt his gaze rake her like invisible talons from head to toe. Feeling vulnerable, stripped emotionally, rage rolled through her. "I was just hired by Mr. Holt," she snapped, her voice wobbling with feelings that threatened to swamp her. And yet, her heart, pounding as it was, wanted a redo of this conversation. She saw regret, sadness and defensiveness in Hanford's eyes. Oh, he had his operator's game face on, for sure. She knew it well. Too well. "What are you doing here?" she demanded, hard anger in her tone.

Gil put his hands on his hips, staring at her. "I'm the foreman."

Kai closed her eyes for just a moment, opened them, feeling the air sucked out of her lungs. "Y-you work here, too?" No! That wasn't possible! This couldn't be happening! Her mind worked at the speed of light. Her heart expanded with traitorous emotions, wanting Gil. Again. God, she could not go there! The bastard had walked out on her after five days of the most wonderful loving she'd ever experienced with a man. Gil had left suddenly without explanation, never to return. She hadn't seen him for four years.

Anger flowed through Kai. Gil had used her as a convenient sex partner to bury himself in to get rid of his grief. His brother Rob, a Delta Force operator with another team in Afghanistan, had been killed. Gil had seen his brother's body to the morgue at Bagram and then looked her up.

Touching her brow, Kai saw his generous mouth moving into a resistant, thin line. She remembered that mouth. Far too well. The pleasure he'd given her. Kai had never known such tenderness and vulnerability in a man until Gil had walked into her life for those five days. She'd been a widow for a year. When he reappeared, he said he needed her. Silly her. She'd believed him and they had ended up in a five-day sexual feast that was the best thing that Kai had ever encountered with a man. Yet, on the sixth morning, when she awakened, Gil was gone. No note. No explanation. No email. No...nothing. She wished she could have forgotten him, but she never had.

And now, he was towering over her, all six feet of him, broad, capable shoulders beneath a white cowboy shirt, a black leather vest stretching across his powerful chest. His Levi's were worn and dirty, but from Kai's view, his strong, hard thighs were just as beautiful now as they were when they'd captured her legs and held her in place to give her the most incredible pleasure she'd ever had.

And then, he'd run. Kai had never felt so used by a man. Now, the bastard was standing there, defensive, bristling, and she could feel the energy pouring off him toward her. She was only five feet seven inches tall. She wasn't short, but she wasn't Gil's height, either.

What would he do? Try to get her fired? Invent some lame excuse to let her go? Would he do that to her after what they'd shared? She searched his eyes, which were now a darker, stormy blue. Kai could feel how taut and upset he was. It felt as if they were two boxers in a ring sizing each other up, looking for weak spots, a place to get in and punch, taking the other down.

Her heart said it shouldn't be like this. That Gil was a man of honor, like his best friend, Sam Morrison. Why had he walked away from her like that? Kai knew Gil well because Sam and he were on the same team. They had been like inseparable brothers. Maybe she didn't know Gil at all. And he'd already proved to her that he would use her and then run.

Kai wasn't about to let him scuttle her or get her fired. She glared up at him. "And what are you going to do about me being here?" Standing tensely, her fingers curved into her palms, her adrenaline flowing through her, she saw his eyes soften for a moment. And then that implacable hardness returned. She hated the game face an operator wore!

"If Talon hired you, I'm not getting in the way of his choices."

Kai didn't believe him. Her nostrils flared. "You're a good liar, Gil. I have no reason to trust you." She saw him take a step back, rage in his face.

"I'm good for my word, Kai. If Holt hired you, then I'm okay with it."

Kai saw what she thought was hurt in his expression for a moment. Gil was struggling to get that game face back into place, but her sharp words were like a slap to his face and he was reeling from it. "You'd better be," she muttered. Jamming her finger down at the wooden floor between them, she said, "I got this job fairly. And, unlike you, I don't run."

Gil lifted his lips away from his clenched teeth. He stared grimly at her. "Go about your business," he snapped. "Has anyone given you a tour of the ranch yet?"

Breathing hard, Kai rasped, "No."

"I'll get Cass to do it," he snarled over his shoulder as he turned and walked away.

Kai's knees felt like jelly. She heard the hard thunk of his boots on the floor of the barn and then caught sight of him as he walked with determination down the slope toward the main ranch house.

Dammit! Sagging against the locker, she pressed her hands to her face, trying to steady her breathing. Of all the things that life could throw at her, she never thought she'd see Gil again! He'd disappeared like the black ops soldier he was.

Hands falling from her face, Kai knew she had to

get herself together. Her heart stopped racing and her breathing began to settle down. God, she had to sit at the family dinner table with that bastard! How far away could she get from him? Her mind raced with terrible possibilities. Gil was the foreman. He could make her look bad. And if she did, Talon Holt would fire her and she'd have no job.

Slowly putting the rest of her gear in her locker, Kai closed it, resting her head against the metal door. Should she tell someone? Talon Holt? This was so messy. Would Gil be mature about it? Let bygones be bygones? Not pick at her? Make her life a daily, miserable existence?

Standing, she pulled the baseball cap from her back pocket and settled it on her head. Right now, Kai wished she had a friend she could confide in. Just to be able to talk this out because it helped her to figure out what to do. Kai didn't want to feel drawn to Gil. But she was, dammit. Her stupid heart was pining away for him even now! She remembered his kisses, his strong arms around her, cherishing her as if she were the most precious being on the face of the earth.

Guilt warred within Kai. Sam, her husband, had been an operator who couldn't remove his game face. He never told her how he felt. He never cried. Sam hated to see her cry and would always plead with her to stop because it tore him up so much. Even though she loved Sam, Kai had never been able to get past those horrifically tough walls surrounding him. Sam never let her in. There was only one-way intimacy in their relationship, and she felt as if she were slowly dying emotionally, never fed by Sam in return.

Kai looked around. Just the soft snort of the few

horses in the box stalls made her feel better. The scent of alfalfa hay was like perfume to her nostrils. She wished she could erase those five days with Gil. Until he showed up at her small barracks room, she had thought he was just like Sam: implacable. Unreachable. But he hadn't been. She'd seen the devastation in his face, his eyes red rimmed, seen the rawness, the terrible grief over his younger brother's death hours before. He had met her in the lobby and told her he needed to talk with her. She'd taken him up to her room to speak in privacy.

Talk had turned into an unexpected arousal when Kai had spontaneously kissed him in her room. That kiss had thrown them into each other's arms. To this day, Kai couldn't figure out why she'd agreed to go with Gil to the conjugal building on base reserved for married couples. He was black ops, so he knew how to work the system to utilize the facility. Gil had gotten them a large, beautiful suite with a real bed.

Kai drew in a ragged breath. She would never forget the tears falling down his stubbled cheeks, the utter vulnerability in his eyes as he stood in her room allowing his grief to surface. And when she'd come into his arms and kissed him, everything changed in a heartbeat. She thought the kiss was to soften his grief over his brother's death. Oh, she'd always thought he was a ruggedly handsome man. Every woman who laid eyes on Gil stared longingly at him, lust and interest in their eyes.

He wasn't pretty-boy handsome at all. Just the opposite—a kind of rough-hewn face, intelligent, hard blue eyes that missed nothing. His nose was hawkish, mouth wide, his lower lip fuller than his upper one. It was his square face and that granite-looking chin that Kai should have read differently.

Worse, she had no idea that Gil was drawn to her until she'd kissed him. And then she corrected herself: all he'd really wanted was a woman, any woman, to bury his grief in. She was just a convenient receptacle, was all. *Nothing more.* Gil had proved that by walking out of her life after five days and never contacting her again.

Why did she want to cry, then? Why did she still feel such gutting loss over his running out on her? Before, when she was married, Gil was the epitome of decorum around her. He never once flirted with her or indicated in any fashion that he was drawn to her.

Then why had he sought her out after handing off his brother's body to the morgue on base? Hell, Hanford had all kinds of women groupies on base. Every operator did. Women just fell over themselves, salivating to get one of those badass warriors in bed with them. Kai had never been like that. In fact, she didn't like operators precisely because of their cocky arrogance, the alpha-male attitude dripping off them like honey. Sam had to court her a full nine months while they were stationed at Bagram before he'd ever gotten her to fall in love with him.

He was the light brother to Gil's dark brother. Sam had blond hair, green eyes and a killer smile that made her melt. Gil had black hair, blue eyes and was the quiet one who said little. Sam was always a big, immature kid if he could get away with it while Gil was always the mature, responsible adult. Sam always smiled. Gil rarely smiled. Sam would play jokes. Gil never did.

It bothered her to this day why Gil had come to her barracks, asking for her. She knew he had other women on base and used them. But it was a two-way street and Kai didn't draw a judgment on it. Whether there was a war going on or not, men and women had libidos, and that was that.

She wandered down the breezeway, checking the horses in the box stalls. They were friendly, big quarter horse types, coming to the front and thrusting their soft, velvety noses between the iron bars or the door to try to smell or touch her outstretched fingers. She called to each one, seeing their name carved on the front of their stall. The big gray horse, she thought, was probably half Thoroughbred and half quarter horse. All of them were geldings. There was a horse for each of the wranglers, including Talon Holt.

Worrying her lower lip, Kai walked out the other end of the breezeway. Down below the gravel slope were five pipe corrals of varying sizes. They were in terrible shape. The other barn, painted green, was about one-third smaller than the red one where she stood. The second barn sat at the opposite end of all the corrals, facing her. The Triple H was a big ranch. The doors to the green barn were slid shut. Probably all the equipment needed to run the ranch was parked in there. It would be her new home.

"Hey," Cass called, striding down the passageway toward her. "Gil asked me to show you around. You up for the five-cent tour, Kai?"

Kai smiled, liking easygoing Cass. His blond hair was thick and slightly wavy, hanging around his ears and nape, making him look like a scruffy dog. But he was clean shaven, and even though he was damned tall, muscular and powerful to her, his perennial smile made her feel better. "Sure. Can you spare the time?"

Cass pulled his black baseball cap out of his back pocket and pulled it on. "Yeah, no problem. I've got dinner in the oven, got the apple pies out to cool and presently have six huge Idaho spuds baking in the oven. I'm all caught up."

"You really do like to cook?" she asked, falling into step as he cut his stride for her, leading her down the slope toward the pipe corrals.

"Yeah, love it."

"How long have you been here?"

"Hmm," he murmured, rubbing his shaven jaw, "about as long as Gil. I'd say three months."

"How did you get a job here, Cass?"

"Well," he said, giving her a wink, "I knew Talon from our days as operators. He was a SEAL and I was in Special Forces, but we often worked together out in the field in Afghanistan. He saved my ass a couple of times, and I saved his. Of course, he had his combat assault dog, Zeke, so he was double-barrel trouble to the enemy."

Kai warmed to the man. "My run-ins with spec ops guys was like running into you," she admitted, giving him a shy smile. "I always like the Special Forces A-teams. They were really friendly and outgoing compared to the Delta guys and the SEALs."

Cass drawled, giving her a wink, "Our jobs were a lot different from SEALs and Delta Force types. We speak the language, go into a village, try getting them some organization, help, education and medical support. We aren't the game-face types like Gil and Talon are. Although—" he brightened "—Talon is really working on opening up. I think a lot has to do with him being recently married to Cat. You'll meet her in about an hour," he said, looking at his watch. "The guy's completely smitten by her. Talk about a SEAL biting the dust," he said, and chuckled. "All good, though. Talon's learning to lighten up, be a little more accessible than SEALs usually are. Love is a good thing, you know?"

Kai nodded, feeling an ache center in her heart. She thought she knew what love was with Sam Morrison. But she hit a brick wall with her husband emotionally, and she was with him only three months out of every year of the three years they were married. If he wasn't in direct combat for six months, he was out training somewhere on the globe for another three months. And then, they had three months with each other. It had never been enough for her. "I was married once," she admitted to Cass. He was someone who inspired immediate trust. And she liked his openness and warmth. He was like sunshine. Gil was like a damned dark moon. So closed up. Full of secrets. Full of toxic emotions he'd never unloaded, just like Sam. Why couldn't she have been drawn to someone like Cass? He was an open book in comparison.

"You said you were in the Army," Cass said. "Are you divorced?" And then he held up his hands as he slowed to a stop at the first pipe-rail corral. "Hey, if I'm getting too personal or nosey, just tell me it's none of my business."

Kai nodded. She moved her fingers lightly across the rust on the top pipe rail. It flaked off, dropping on her boots below. "I don't mind confiding in you," she said, looking up at him. He was now serious and she felt his full attention on her. "I was married three years to Sam Morrison. He was a Delta Force sergeant." Her voice got a little choked up. "He was killed in a firefight in Afghanistan." She saw his eyes go kind with sympathy. Shrugging a little, she said, "For the most part, I'm over it."

Placing his hand on her shoulder, he said, "I'm very sorry, Kai. That's rough."

"Yeah…it was for a while," she admitted, needing his kindness. After hitting a wall with Hanford, some of her hurt and fear dissolved beneath Cass's warm care. Now Kai saw why Sandy Holt was responding so well. Cass was sunlight and he just seemed to have a knack for penetrating her darkness, her grief and pain. She looked up at him. "Were you a medic?"

"Yeah," he said wryly, removing his hand. "I was a great mechanic in my team, which was one of my skills, but my official MOS was as an 18 Delta combat corpsman."

"You have a nice bedside manner," Kai admitted.

"I'd like to think I do," Cass said. He gestured to the corrals. "Let me give you an idea of our work week. Every Monday morning we sit down in the kitchen with Gil and Talon. They hand out our assignments for the week. That way, everyone stays on the same page and we're like a well-oiled, coordinated team. I think next week Gil is looking to start wire brushing this rusted pipe. Once the rust is removed, we'll move on to a metal paint to coat it and then a second coat over it."

Wrinkling her nose, Kai said, "I sure hope I'm sent to fix machinery," and she grinned. Wire brushing was labor intensive on the wrangler's part. It was hard on shoulders, joints, arms and hands. She heard Cass chuckle.

"I'll bet you are. Come on, let's go over to the green barn. That's where all the equipment is kept. None of it is working, by the way."

Rubbing her hands together, Kai grinned. "Good, that means Talon will let me do what I'm best at— being a mechanic."

"Gil's the one who decides," Cass said, walking her around one corral.

"Once he gives out assignments, can you get him to change his mind?"

Cass shrugged. "He's a pretty set dude. Even Talon can't get him to do some things. But, hey, he's the foreman for a reason. Right? And he came from a big Montana ranch near Billings, so he knows what he's doing."

There was so little Kai knew about Gil. Oh, she knew his body, but God, they didn't talk about much during those five incredible lust-filled days. They had come together like two lost souls, hurting, full of grief, lonely and needing love. Maybe not love, Kai self-corrected. Maybe just horny as hell after no sex for a year after Sam's death. And she knew for men, at least most of them, when they had sex, it did not equal emotion or love, like it did for a woman. Each gender came to the bedroom with different perspectives, expectations and realities, and suffered from different outcomes. That's why Gil had walked away. For him, it was just sex. Relieving himself. For her, it was an entirely different experience; there were emotions and heart involved with him that she'd never realized until that moment. Kai wondered if she lived a life with blinders on all the time.

She pulled herself out of her rumination as Cass pushed hard and the huge hanging door grudgingly slid open. He walked in and turned on the overhead lights. What she saw was farm and ranch equipment with a lot of dust on it.

"Uh-oh," Cass teased, leaning against the door opening, arms across his massive chest. "I see that look in your eye. Mechanics get a gleam that's unmistakable. I'll bet you're just dying to get your hands on these metal monsters." He chuckled, his grin widening.

She walked over to the John Deere tractor. All four tires were flat. Kai had a keen eye and swept over it from stem to stern. "You're right," she confessed with a laugh. Cass made a lot of her fear over what Gil might do to get rid of her dissolve. Once she started to work on these machines and showed Talon how quick and good she was, it wouldn't matter what Gil said. Talon would keep her over any protests he made.

Remembering Gil's face, that hurt that had crossed it when she'd accused him of trying to get rid of her, made Kai hesitate in her cruel judgment of him. He had always been a man of impeccable morals and values when she knew him. He was always respectful toward her, protective when Sam was away on a special mission and she was stationed at Bagram. If Gil and the rest of his team came in for a brief R & R between missions, he would always come to see her. Ask how she was. Did she need anything? That was how Delta brothers took care of their own. Not that many wives of a Delta operator were at Bagram. She was the only one.

Gil would escort her to the chow hall; they'd eat, talk about Sam and herself. Gil never once talked about himself. Kai had thought he was a closed book to the outside world. She was sure within the Delta Force brotherhood, he was much more open and forthcoming. Never once did Gil let on he was attracted to her. And then, Kai grimaced, Gil had clearly shown her, without a doubt, that all he wanted from her was sex. Instead of a one-night stand, it had developed into a five-night stand. How could she have been so blind? So stupid?

"Hey," Cass called from the door, "I need to get back to the house. About time to set the table and start getting stuff ready for our 1800 chow hall."

She grinned, liking his dropping into military lingo. "Everything in the kitchen smelled so good when I first arrived, I can hardly wait to eat tonight."

Cass let his arms fall to his sides. "Don't come late. It's a food fight every night," he warned her with a wicked grin.

She laughed, knowing he was teasing her. Cass was so easy to read in comparison to Gil. Moving between the hay baler and the tractor, and checking out the horse and cattle trailers, Kai knew she had her work cut out for her. Every tire would have to be replaced. That was a lot of money. Pulling out her notepad and pen, she started making notes on each machine. Moving between them, Kai got lost in the needs of each one. When she looked up later, she saw a tall, very well-built, black-haired woman coming her way. She was wearing jeans, a red long-sleeved tee and cowboy boots. Kai went out to the front of the barn to greet her.

"Hi," Kai said, holding out her hand, "I'm Kai Tiernan."

"Cat Holt. What are you up to?" she said, and shook her hand.

"Just taking notes," Kai said, gesturing toward the inner barn. She liked the tall woman. She had slightly curled black hair that lay like a cloak around her proud shoulders. It was Cat's blue eyes, large and sparkling with life, that drew Kai. "Are you just getting home from the hospital?"

Cat moved into the barn with her. "Yes." She rubbed her long, slender hands. "It's Friday. I have the whole weekend at the ranch and I can hardly wait to throw my leg over my horse and start riding some fence." She grinned over at Kai. "Maybe you'd like to join me? Get a feel for the rest of our ranch?"

"I'd love to," Kai said eagerly. There was an earthy warmth to Cat Holt and her smile was often, her eyes also kind looking, like Cass's eyes. But then, they were both medical people and they couldn't be in a service field career like that without a lot of compassion in them.

"Cass said that he'd lost you to the depths of the green barn," Cat told her, walking among the equipment. "He said you had that gleam in your eye."

Chuckling, Kai said, "Guilty as charged. My hands are positively itching to get started on getting these beasts up and running."

"Well," Cat warned, sliding her fingers over the John Deere tractor's fender and gathering lots of dust on them, "our budget can't handle all the repairs. I'm sure Gil will give you the go-ahead, most likely, on the tractor, because we really need it in service now."

"I grew up on a ranch and I helped my dad with the accounting books," Kai told her as they left the barn. "It's a balancing act, for sure."

Cat nodded. She pushed the large door shut and locked it. "Monday morning at nine o'clock, there's a meeting in our kitchen. Cass always makes cinnamon rolls, which draws every wrangler on the ranch." She laughed. "After everyone gets their quota of cinnamon rolls, Talon and Gil will go over the week's assignments."

"I love cinnamon rolls. Nothing like a hot one coming out of the oven. It sounds like you're really organized." She walked down the slope with Cat. Above them the sun was in the western blue sky. It was beautiful here and Kai was so grateful to have landed a job at this ranch. If only Gil weren't here. And every night, she'd have to sit at the same table and eat with him. Her stomach tightened. Kai was already losing her appetite. When Gil put on that game face, he was a tough hombre and nobody cracked that steel facade of his. No one. Except her. During those nights of endless pleasure with him. Then, she'd seen the real man beneath it, and he had taken her breath away.

CHAPTER THREE

THE LAST PLACE Gil wanted to be at dinner was with the Holt family. He'd always looked forward to it up until tonight. Dammit, Kai was here. He was still reeling from meeting her in the barn earlier. The family sat down, Sandy at the head of the table, Cass to her right, Kai opposite him and, thank God, Talon and Cat and himself at the other end of the long trestle table. It could easily seat fourteen people for the holidays.

Gil had breathed a deep sigh of relief when Cass asked Kai to sit opposite him. Actually, it had been Sandy who requested her presence there, a good sign she liked Kai. Who wouldn't? There was some quiet table talk, some laughter and smiles, but Gil felt like hell. He stole a glance in Kai's direction. His whole body tightened in memory of her in his arms. Jesus, he'd never forgotten those torrid five days with her. Not that he'd tried. The look on her face when she realized it was him was one of mixed emotions. He'd seen Kai's shock, hurt and then anger come to her face. Kai could never hide how she felt. It was one of the many things that drew him to her. Unlike himself, who was so stove up that even Cass teased him about never smiling or being more robot than human.

Gil wanted to be close to Kai. Smell her scent. Touch her skin. He remembered all of her. Every scent, every small cry of pleasure, that husky voice of hers afterward, when they were both weak and sated with one another.

He passed the glazed carrots to Cat, who thanked him. Gil wasn't sure who was more miserable right now: Kai or himself. But for different reasons.

When the thick slices of pot roast came his way, he took an ample amount. Working ten hours a day meant loading up on protein and carbs. The huge Idaho baked potato on his plate was slathered with cheese, crumbled bacon and heavy dollops of thick sour cream.

Earlier, everyone had gone to their respective rooms, taken turns in the bathroom on the first floor, cleaning up, getting a shower and putting on a set of clean clothes before dining. Gil swore he could smell the scent of orange shampoo that Kai had used in her hair. Those thick auburn strands gleamed beneath the hurricane lamp chandelier that hung high above the long table. She looked beautiful in a pale pink sweater, a set of pale blue slacks and sensible leather shoes. The small pearl earrings adorned her delicate lobes, and he sharply remembered tasting, teasing and kissing each of them and her sensual reaction. Kai looked fragile and that hit Gil hard. The strained expression on her face was his fault. Damn, he hadn't handled that meeting today worth shit. He hadn't meant to get angry at her, but it hurt when she accused him of running. Well, he had. But she didn't know the rest of the story.

Gil covertly watched her as she passed Talon a bowl of thick brown gravy, which he poured across the slabs of beef. Kai was shy, but she'd always been that way. Her mouth stirred him, and Gil inwardly groaned. Just the dainty way she ate, that full mouth of hers lush with promise, sent streaks of heat into his lower body. Harshly, he told himself there was no way to rebuild the broken bridge that loomed like the Grand Canyon between them. She saw him as an irresponsible bastard who had taken advantage of her and given nothing in return except to disappear out of her life. *Dammit.*

Sandy Holt gave Kai a gentle look as she nibbled haphazardly at the food Cass had put on her plate. "Kai? Tell us about your family. Where do they live?"

Kai blotted her mouth with the pink linen napkin and told them. She looked at all of them as she spoke and tried to avoid Gil's stormy, narrowed look, her voice faltering slightly.

"And how many in your family?" Sandy inquired.

"I have one older brother, Steve."

"Did he go into the military like you?"

Kai shook her head. "No, he loved ranching and Dad wanted Steve to stay there to teach him how to run it."

"Well," Sandy said, patting her arm in a motherly fashion, "you served your country and we're all grateful for your service. You need to know that."

Gil saw a faint blush touch Kai's sloped cheeks. The ache in his chest intensified. Even though she did a man's job, she was excruciatingly feminine. Oh, he knew she wore her hair short, but hell, with the heat in Afghanistan, over a hundred degrees every day in the summer, he didn't blame her. There was a wishful part of him that wondered what her auburn hair that glinted with gold and burgundy beneath the lamplight would feel like as he sifted his fingers through those strands once more. He remembered those silky textures and he felt himself hardening. Not what he wanted at a dinner table.

The woman had always made him want her from the moment Sam had introduced Kai proudly to him. It was the darkest, deepest secret he'd kept from his best friend. And Gil would never have told Sam that he wanted Kai for his own. That just wasn't going to happen. He'd loved Sam like a brother and they'd gone through many years as operators, saving one another's ass. Even today, when he thought of Sam, he missed him. And he was glad he'd never given one hint of how much he desired Kai. Neither of them knew his secret.

"Gil?"

He looked up, jerking out of his dark, heated thoughts. Sandy smiled sweetly at him. "I'm sorry. What did you say?"

"I asked if you were going to take Kai around our ranch tomorrow. You know? Ride the fence line? Let her get a feel for our place?"

"Oh," Cat said enthusiastically, "I had already asked Kai if she'd go for a ride tomorrow morning with me."

Gil felt relief. He wasn't prepared to spend quality time with Kai. Not yet. "That's fine, Cat," he told her. "I got a lot to do Saturday morning." Gil glanced up to see the look in Kai's large gray eyes. She was relieved, too. Obviously, she wanted nothing to do with him. His heart twinged with guilt. And gutwrenching regret.

Zeke whined. He lay on his doggie bed in the living room, his black ears perked up, eyes shining hopefully at the group sitting at the table.

Kai turned and looked at the beautiful seventy-pound male dog. She looked over at Talon, who was scowling in Zeke's direction. "Is he begging?"

Grumping, Talon said, "Yes. My wife made the mistake of giving him a piece of her sandwich at noon one day here at the table and he's never forgotten it. So now—" Talon gave his wife a wry look "—Zeke sits on his bed and whines dramatically from the living room, hoping to snag someone who has a soft heart who will give him some food."

Cat smiled and gave her husband a teasing look. "I don't know why you don't let us spoil Zeke. You said yourself he's been happy since coming home. And so are you, hmm?"

Talon nodded. "*You* make me happy. Zeke is on his own."

The table rolled with chuckles.

"I know what will get Zeke's attention," Cass said. "Get him a playmate."

Talon groaned. "Zeke doesn't know how to play, Cass. You of all people should know that. He's a trained combat dog. He doesn't know what it means to relax and play."

Cass shrugged easily. "So? Un-train him. Get him a puppy playmate. I'll bet he's lonely. Or—" he gave Talon a wicked look "—how about a nice female Belgian Malinois girlfriend? I'll bet Zeke will forget all about scraps at the dinner table. And, hey! How about a litter of puppies?"

The table burst out into good-natured laughter.

Even Gil grinned a little and shook his head. "Cass, you're a rebel at heart. Always stirring up trouble."

"Thank you," he said. Turning, he checked Sandy's dinner plate. "Now, Sandy, you have to finish off those last two pieces of beef."

Sandy gave him a stricken look. "I'm just not hungry, Cass. Let's give them to Zeke."

Talon gave his mother a panicked look. "Mom…"

"Well, maybe not Zeke," Sandy said quickly, seeing her son's consternation. Giving Cass a pleading look, she said, "I've finished everything else. Isn't that good enough?"

"That's true, you did, and I'm proud of you," Cass murmured. "But protein is going to build your muscles back, Sandy. You said to me this afternoon you longed to go ride a horse. And I'll go out and saddle two horses and we'll do just that after you get that muscle back." Cass picked up her fork, spearing one piece of meat and holding it up to her lips. "This is the way to do it. Just think of meat as a fast way to throw a leg over that horse you're dreaming about riding."

Sandy wrinkled her nose, surrendered and delicately took the proffered meat off the fork he held.

"Great," Cass praised her, spearing the last one. "Just one more?"

Gil hid his smile. Cass could charm anyone into doing anything. Special Forces operators knew how to manipulate, that was for damned sure. He saw Sandy give him a sour look, pout, but then reluctantly take the last bite of meat from the fork. Cass knew nothing about cancer or the journey she'd been on twice now until Talon had hired him. Gil could starkly see what the treatment of chemo and radiation did to the

woman. Sandy was in a very fragile condition and
Cass had been a brilliant hire, but then, Talon had
worked with him in Afghanistan and knew his stellar
qualities. And Cass had been a good choice because
Sandy was tired of feeling bad and depressed due to
the chemo and radiation treatments. Every time Cass
gently cajoled her, Sandy brightened a little because
she was one of those women who would turn themselves inside out for a man who had kindness in his
soul. And Cass, being a medic, was the perfect foil.

Gil's heart jolted as his gaze drifted to Kai, who
had a concerned look on her face for Sandy. Yeah,
she wore her heart on her sleeve, too, even though
Kai wasn't a medic. He remembered she'd rescued
an Afghan puppy who was barely six weeks old,
found a glass baby bottle with a nipple and fed it
milk from the chow hall. She'd loved that little puppy.
And then, six months later in a mortar attack, it got
killed. He learned about it when he'd sought her out
after Rob had died. She'd cried over the loss of the
puppy. There was always nothing but loss in Afghanistan, he thought grimly. That country took everything
away from everyone. Even his brother. Her husband,
Sam. He hated the place.

Just the softness in Kai's face, how relaxed she
looked, grabbed at Gil's heart. He remembered that
look and it was starting to make him ache for her in
his arms again.

Kai was easily touched by everything. And it was
all there in her expression. He wished he could be like
her instead of being so damned emotionally locked
up. Kai had sucked the poison out of him, the rabid
grief eating him alive after his brother Rob had died

in that firefight. Her care, her nurturing, her maternal abilities, had withdrawn those toxic emotions from his soul and she'd healed him with her tenderness, care and love in those five days.

Scowling, Gil felt guilt eating him alive. Kai was at this table. With him. Jesus, he wanted to apologize, to tell her he was sorry for what he'd done to her. But there were no second chances after his actions. That sent a pain so deep into his heart, his soul, that he couldn't suppress it even if he'd wanted to.

"Talon," Cat said, "have you paired Kai with Zeke yet?"

"No," he muttered, finishing everything on his plate. "I'll do that after dinner."

"I love dogs," Kai told them wistfully, turning and giving Zeke a warm gaze.

"Well," Talon warned her, "he's not your average, friendly, lick-your-hand dog. He was highly trained for three years before he was given to me to go into combat with. He takes delight in bringing down Taliban, crunching bones and keeping them in one place until we can get there to flex cuff them."

Cat gave her husband a pleading look. "Darling? We're at the dinner table?"

Kai saw Talon blush, his cheeks turning ruddy. "My fault," she told everyone in apology. "I did see combat assault dogs at Bagram from time to time. And you're right, Talon, they aren't your next-door neighbor's dog."

"Well," Sandy piped up, "I would love Zeke to have a mate! I'd love having puppies around here. Wouldn't that be wonderful?"

Groaning, Talon shook his head. "Mom, you don't

know what you're asking. Zeke's breeding is as a highly aggressive guard dog. He'd throw puppies just like him and most people don't know how to deal with that kind of energy and focus. They wouldn't make good house pets, believe me."

"Maybe," Cass suggested, giving Sandy a warm look, "get him a male puppy friend? Someone he can bond with, then?"

Talon shrugged. "I've seen combat assault dogs out in the field when another male dog comes around them. They chew the hell out of them and damned near kill them. They're very territorial. Zeke will be the same way."

Sandy frowned. "Do you think he'd kill a little male puppy, Talon?"

"I don't know, Mom. He might. I was never in villages where there were scruffy mutts around he could interact with. Zeke's focus was on chasing Taliban down in the valleys and up into the mountains."

Kai gave Sandy a kind look. "Do you want a dog of some kind?"

"We used to have a beautiful golden retriever when Talon was growing up. Goldy was her name. My first husband, Gardener, had bought her as a pup for me on our first wedding anniversary. Goldy just doted on Talon after he was born. And I love all animals, so yes, I think I'd love to get another golden retriever."

Talon put his head down, paying attention to the food on his plate.

Kai smiled gently and touched Sandy's hand. "Maybe it will happen someday."

Cat chimed in, "I'd love to have a second dog around here, Talon. Zeke always goes with you, wher-

ever you are. He's *your* dog. Couldn't we have a general dog that just hangs around, licks our hands and
is happy to keep us company? And he could stay with
Sandy. I don't see a dog hurting her recovery."

Talon gave everyone a distressed glance. "Maybe.
It means I have to take time out of my schedule to get
Zeke familiarized with another dog in order to see
how he reacts to him."

Cat gave him a happy smile. "That would be wonderful! I'd just love to have an ordinary dog around
here, someone you could go riding with." She glanced
at Sandy. "Why, maybe even have that dog stay in
your bedroom at night when you sleep. Keep you
company."

Sandy glowed. "I'd like that a lot. Goldy lay on
the rug at the end of our bed. And in the morning,
she would wake us up by licking our hands or faces
or whatever she could reach." She smiled fondly over
those memories.

Gil could tell that Talon had lost the battle and the
war. His boss was grimacing as he ate, saying nothing,
keeping a low profile. It was obvious Talon wanted to
please his excited wife, her eyes shining with the possibility of a puppy in the house. And Talon's mother
looked at her son with the same expectation and joy.
Talon was gruff, but the women in his life ruled him.
And maybe, Gil thought, that's what love did to a man.
It made him want to keep the woman he loved happy.
In this case, Talon had two women to keep smiling,
for different reasons.

"Maybe," Talon grunted, "I'll get Zeke around
some dogs in the coming weeks when I get a chance.
I'll see how he reacts. If he seems okay with them

and isn't too territorial, then Mom, you can have your puppy." And then he looked at his wife. "*One* dog," he warned Cat. "You and Mom are gonna have to share it. Okay?"

Cat grinned happily. "Fine with me. Sandy? You okay with that?"

"More than fine," Sandy agreed, giving her son a grateful look. "Thank you, Talon."

IT WAS GIL'S job to get Kai settled into the ranch routine. On Saturday morning, he got up at six o'clock. He opened his bedroom door and saw Kai's door still shut across the hall. Usually, on Saturday, everyone was up by seven getting breakfast. He heard some noise out in the kitchen and thought Cass was up, preparing the breakfast for the family and wranglers. As he walked across the living room, his heart shrank. It was Kai. He halted for a moment and stared at her.

Kai was wearing a bright orange long-sleeved tee that complemented her auburn hair. Gil felt his lower body stir as his gaze moved down to her fine butt and those long legs encased in a pair of Levi's. She had on a pair of work boots, not cowboy boots. And she was busy dumping some cereal into a bowl at the counter. Mouth tightening, he had to make this work. He was her boss, regardless of their jaded past with each other. Last night at the table, she'd patently ignored him. Of course, he'd ignored her, too. Gil didn't blame her for her reaction to him. He could feel a lot of rage simmering just beneath the surface of Kai and it was all aimed at him.

"Morning," he growled, long before he reached the kitchen. Gil didn't want to scare the hell out of Kai. He saw her jerk her head in his direction. Those beautiful dove-gray eyes of hers widened in surprise. And that soft mouth he had never forgotten about compressed. And then her fine, arched brows drew downward.

"Morning," Kai muttered defensively. She turned her back on him, pouring the cereal into her bowl.

Gil needed to eat something before he started the day. And whether he liked it or not, he headed into the kitchen and worked around Kai. Already, her posture had gone from relaxed to tense. Her shoulders had come up, as if expecting a blow. Pain drifted through him. It was the last kind of reaction he wanted from her. But he'd earned it in spades. Moving past her, he walked over to the cupboard where all the dry cereals were kept and opened it.

"You finding everything you need in here?" he demanded brusquely, hauling down a box.

"Yes."

Her voice was clipped. Gil winced internally. He set the box on the drain board, a good three feet away from Kai. He saw a dark blue neckerchief around her slender neck. She wore no makeup, but being on a ranch didn't invite cosmetics and wearing perfume. Still, her profile was clean and beautiful. Grabbing a bowl from another cupboard, he watched her pour milk into the bowl. Her hand trembled ever so slightly. He could feel the tension amping up between them. It was up to him to try to smooth things over the best he could.

"Need sugar?" He pointed above her head toward another cupboard. "Cass keeps a sugar bowl up there."

"Thanks."

Gil took his huge bowl, twice the size of Kai's,

and poured half a box of the cereal into it. Today was going to be a work-heavy day and he needed the extra calories. He watched Kai retrieve the sugar bowl. When she was done with it, she pushed it a little in his general direction. Well, she might be pissed as hell at him, but she wasn't beyond decent human thoughtfulness. A part of him breathed a sigh of relief. He watched her pick up the cereal bowl and go to the table and sit down. Thank God, she sat at one end. He'd sit at the other, giving her all the space he could.

KAI SAT AT the end of the table where Sandy had sat last night. Her stomach was tied in knots, literally. All her hunger had fled when Gil had unexpectedly arrived. She had hoped to avoid him, but here he was. Trying to ignore his recently shaven square face, those hard, intelligent blue eyes meeting hers, she'd felt an emotion that had just floored her: desire. Of all things!

After sitting down, she quickly started eating, knowing that today Talon expected her to make an assessment on all the machinery. They had talked last night during dessert. He wanted her opinion on every piece of equipment, what it would take to get it up and running. She had her job cut out for her today.

Watching covertly, she gazed at Gil's broad shoulders and long, powerful back. Why couldn't she get the past out of her memory? How she'd felt that masculine power, felt his tenderness despite his size and weight. Never would Kai have thought a man could be as gentle, as loving, as Gil had been with her.

Tears burned in her eyes and Kai made a soft, frustrated sound in her throat, forcing herself to eat quickly. She had to get out of here! Get as far away from him as she could. But Kai knew that because Gil was the foreman, he would always be around her. She wasn't sure she could handle it, but she needed this job so desperately. And she loved all the other people here on the ranch. It was such a whiplash and shock for her to see him once again.

She averted her eyes as Gil turned and walked casually to the table. To her relief, he took the other end of it and sat down. She could feel the man's energy all the way down the table! In the kitchen, she had inhaled the sage soap he'd used, and then that achingly familiar masculine scent of Gil, like a sexual aphrodisiac to Kai, had entered her nostrils. And damn her, she'd inhaled it like a starved beggar. Of all things!

She kept eating as fast as she could, gulping down her food, willing it to disappear as fast as it could. There was no way she wanted to spend any time with this bastard.

"We need to go to the equipment barn," Gil told her, lifting his chin and staring down the table at her. "I need to get a detailed list from you when you're done with your inspection. Then, Talon will decide what gets fixed first."

Nodding, Kai swallowed hard, holding his gaze. She remembered his eyes and how they would darken as he'd loved her. How they would lighten when he was honestly relaxed, which wasn't often, as a field operator. But he had with her, in her arms, beside her after making such wild, hungry love with each other. "That's fine," she said, frowning. She hoped he wasn't going to hang around her, working with her. That wasn't something she could tolerate, because the anger and hurt over his walking out on her was

boiling just beneath her surface. And she had to keep
this job. If she rounded on Gil, took him to task, he
could get her fired just like that. Insubordination toward a superior.

"We'll go over things after breakfast," he said casually. "And then I'll leave you alone. Come to me
with the list once it's finished."

"I can do that." Relief sped through Kai. Was Gil
reading her mind? Did he see the expression on her
face and figure out she wanted him the hell away
from her?

"Good," he muttered.

Kai stood up, her bowl empty. As she walked toward the kitchen, she said, "I'm going out there now.
I'll see you when I get done with that list." She saw
him give a brisk nod but not look up. *Good.* Drenched
with tension and the urge to run the hell out of the
house, Kai forced herself to act normal. Not scared.
Not angry. She knew during the first month of working here, Talon would be assessing her closely to see
how she fit in with the ranch team or not. And more
than anything, Kai wanted to integrate. She had loved
the warmth and camaraderie at the table last night,
despite Gil's dark, quiet presence.

She rinsed her bowl out and placed it in the nearby
dishwasher. After washing her hands, she quickly
dried them off. Walking out into the foyer, she grabbed
her green baseball cap off a wooden peg and left the
house.

The air was chilly. A lot more than she realized.
Turning, Kai went back inside. As she walked through
the living room, she felt Gil's gaze on her. Refusing to
look or tell him why she was back, she hurried to her

room. She retrieved her new Levi's jacket and pulled it on. Patently ignoring him, she left, glad to be away from him.

The sky was pink on the horizon, along with a band of gold. The sun was just about to rise. She saw the light frost on the plants in the flower beds as she opened the gate and then shut it. Her breath was white vapor as she walked around the ranch house and down a gravel path toward the green barn in the distance.

There were no cattle at the ranch yet. She'd heard Talon say something to Gil about going to look at buying a bull and thirty Hereford cows, but that was all. The ranch was quiet, as if it were still slumbering. Kai could see the amount of work ahead of everyone. Her boots crunched on the gravel as she made her way past the rusted corrals. The sky was now a pale blue. In the distance, she could see the sharp, teeth-like Tetons with a thick white coat of snow on the upper half of their blue granite slopes. The song of several robins and a cheerful cardinal picked up her spirits. The farther away from Gil that she got, the happier Kai felt. He was her past. And that's where it was going to stay.

CHAPTER FOUR

KAI HAD PUSHED the big green door on the barn wide open to allow maximum light into the area. The sun came over the horizon and rays shot into the area, lighting up everything so it was easy to see the equipment.

Trying to still her angst over Gil coming out at some point, she busied herself with her notepad and pen. Every piece of machinery in this place, including the floor, was dusty and needed a good sweeping. Each one needed a full, thorough assessment by her.

Above her, the cooing of mourning doves soothed her tightened stomach. Kai kept glancing down the graveled slope of the barn, expecting to see Gil coming her way. The morning was near freezing and she was glad she had on thick, warm leather gloves. The cooing made her look up. She spotted a nest high in the rafters of the third floor where the doves were more than likely sitting on a clutch of eggs. She remembered the dove hunting that took place in Wyoming every September, hating it. She loved the gray doves whose beautiful sounds always filled dawn and dusk. Kai didn't like killing anything if she could help it. Another strike against her, because her father was an avid hunter.

Walking to the red barn, she opened the locker and

carried her toolbox over to the green barn. There was a set of lockers there, and she chose one and placed the box down beside it. Opening it, Kai dragged out a few tools and had everything she needed to start the inspection on the green-and-yellow John Deere tractor. She wished she had a bucket of water, a washcloth and a dry towel to take the worst of the thick layer of dust off the big machine, but that would have to wait.

"Find what you need?"

Kai gasped, jerking up and whirling around. Gil stood there, the sunlight backlit around him, darkening him. "God!" she whispered, her hand flying to her throat, "you scared the hell out of me!" Kai reminded herself he was black ops and, of course, she wouldn't hear him approach her.

"Didn't mean to," Gil growled unhappily, apology in his tone.

Heart pounding, Kai didn't want to be this close to Gil. He was a big man, thickly muscled, hard and powerful. She saw his eyes narrow upon her and then felt a bolt of heat from her breasts down to her lower body. *Damn.* The man could incite her body from simmer to boil in a split second. Scowling at him, she muttered, "Yes, I have everything I need."

"Good. Let's check this tractor first."

Alarm spread through her. "I thought I was supposed to do this on my own." Gulping, Kai just wanted to be left alone, not have him underfoot. When she saw him stare down at her, she snapped, "I know my job. You had something else to do? Right?"

Gil pushed up his Stetson with his gloved hand. "Did you get enough sleep last night?"

His growly demand only made her more surly.

"That's none of your damned business!" She was breathing hard, her chest rising and falling beneath her denim jacket. His full mouth compressed into a hard line, his blue eyes glittering. She felt as if she was in combat mode with him. Well, wasn't she?

Gil held up his hand. "We need to talk this out, Kai."

Her nostrils flared with anger. "Yeah, you're years too late!" Her hands fisted and unfisted at her sides. And, dammit, her voice was wobbling and she tried to shove down the nest of snakes in her gut crawling up to choke off her voice. "There's nothing to talk about! You left. End of story!" Her breathing was rapid and choppy as she glared at him, hunched, as if getting ready to fight. But he wasn't her enemy and Kai knew that. For a moment, the hardness melted in his face. His mouth softened a little as her voice grew strained with tears. Kai wasn't going to cry! She was so angry at Gil that she wanted to slap his arrogant face. But there was no arrogance in his expression right now. His blue eyes were murky looking and it probably meant he was emotionally upset. Well, so was she!

Gil took a step back. He closed his eyes for a moment, then lifted his head and held her mutinous glare. "I didn't know you were hired," he admitted wearily.

"Yeah, and I bet if you had," Kai said angrily, "you'd sure as hell have told Talon to pass on me. Wouldn't you have?"

She saw the confusion in his face. Oh, Kai knew Gil could come clean and take off that damned game face he wore the way Sam had. But where Sam couldn't let down his game face, she knew Gil could do it. And to her surprise, he was allowing her to see him. That shook her because she didn't expect it. Especially right now. She saw him struggling, his expression ravaged.

"No," he breathed in a gruff tone, "I would not have said anything to Talon. I know how good you are."

She straightened, throwing back her shoulders, battling tears she refused to let fall. "I'll bet."

"I owe you an explanation."

"Ya think? Gee, Gil, it must have been one helluva shock to you to see me here, huh? I'll bet you thought life was rosy here on the Triple H until I stepped back into the picture." Kai jerked off her gloves and threw them down on top of her metal toolbox. "Well, I don't like this situation any more than you do. But you know what? I earned this position here at this ranch!" She jabbed her finger down at the wooden floor. Her voice was trembling with anger. "And you aren't going to take it away from me! I'm damned good at what I do! You just need to stay as far away from me as you can get." She pushed her fingers through her hair, glaring at him. "I don't intend to tell anyone about us if that's what got you worried. You go your way. I'll go mine. I want nothing to do with you." Her voice cracked. "Do you understand me, Gil? Do you?"

Gil nodded. "I'm sorry, Kai. It shouldn't have happened. I know that now." He gave her an apologetic look.

"If you think I'm going to stand here and listen to why you screwed me for five days and then left me without a word, you can forget it," Kai whispered unsteadily. "You've hurt me enough, Gil. I was still hurting from Sam's death. And then you walked in, devastated, asking for my help." Kai choked, "You used me, Gil! You bastard! You used me!"

Wincing, Gil rubbed his jaw and his mouth tightened. "That's not true, Kai—"

"Get out of here, Gil. Leave me alone! I'll do my job and I'll do it well. You'll have no reason to worry I'll do anything less than that."

He stared at her, the whiteness in her face and the rage in her gray eyes making him wince. Gil knew better than to try to pursue any conversation with Kai right now. Hell, he deserved her rage. Every bit of it. "Okay," he growled, "you'll get your wish as much as possible. When I need to see you or talk with you, I will. Let's keep it civil and we'll just make the best of it."

He stalked out of the barn, the thudding of his boots echoing throughout the building.

With a little sob, Kai turned away, a hand pressed against her mouth. She bent over, tears rushing down her drawn cheeks. She tried not to cry, but it was four years' worth of hurt, grief and a broken heart that had built up within her. She crouched down by her toolbox, wanting to hide, her shoulders shaking violently as she sobbed into her hands, trying to stop the sounds from being heard by anyone. Her nose ran, and her tears flooded across her face. Damn Gil Hanford! The bastard knew when to take off his game face and look vulnerable. That is what had tricked her into feeling sorry for him, feeling… Oh, hell, feeling things she had felt guilty for feeling to this day.

Sam had been dead only a year. She'd grieved deeply for him, cried often and felt torn in half by his loss. But when Gil walked in, his eyes raw with grief and with tears in them, she had opened her heart and her arms to him. Because he'd been Sam's best friend. And Gil had turned them into lovers within two heartbeats, his mouth curving powerfully across hers, taking her, making her body suddenly bloom beneath his life-altering kiss. No one had ever kissed her like Hanford had. No one. Not even Sam...

Kai finally dropped to her knees, rocking back on her heels, letting the flood of weeping sweep through her because she knew it was better to get it out than let it sit like a toxic waste dump inside her.

GIL TRIED TO steady his twisting emotions roaring through him. Dammit, he'd caused Kai to cry! He'd stood at the opening of the barn, halting, turning around, wanting to go back to her and explain everything. Take the responsibility for his actions. But when he heard her softened sobs, Jesus, it felt as if the invisible claws of a bald eagle had ripped into his chest and clutched his writhing heart in its sharp talons, shredding it. And he couldn't go back in there to hold her like she deserved. Like he wanted to. This was such a FUBAR. Rubbing his chest beneath the black leather vest he wore over his dark green cowboy shirt, Gil wavered.

Just hearing Kai sob like a lost child, the sounds muted, almost unheard, tore him wide-open. His straight black brows drew downward and he felt miserable for her, not himself. Anything she had to dish out was his to take. Wiping his jaw, he sadly turned away, knowing that if he walked back in there to comfort her, Kai would lose it completely. The devastation in her face, the unconcealed hurt in her eyes, made him bleed.

As he slowly walked down the slope, he searched frantically to somehow fix what he'd destroyed within Kai. She hadn't deserved this in any way. She'd been a loyal, loving wife to his best friend, Sam. And Gil had seen the love she had for Sam in her beautiful gray eyes. And how many times had Gil ached to see her look at him that way? Rubbing his chest again because the agony bursting through his chest made him feel miserable, Gil knew what he'd done to her had been wrong. It had been utterly selfish.

He slowed his walk, not wanting to reach the ranch house just yet, his mind and heart back in Bagram where Kai was stationed. She didn't know how much he looked forward to seeing her when he and his Delta team came off a mission. He would always walk over to the Apache hangars, look her up and casually ask if she'd go to chow with him. He would see her eyes widen a little, a sudden smile blossom on her lips when she'd spot him. And she always was eager to go eat with him.

Did Kai know how much he looked forward to those special times? To hear her talk, hear her dreams, hear her getting over Sam's death.

That's what they shared between them: Sam Morrison. He was a larger-than-life Delta Force operator. The perfect poster child for the shadow warrior group, the best the Army had. Gil recalled the first time Sam had accidentally run into Kai. It was in an Afghan village. At Bagram, Kai worked with a group of Army people who had started a charity for the children of the Afghan villages. She was with a group of volunteer medics, the only female in the group. The medics, all men, couldn't talk to the mothers or little girls, but Kai could because she was a female.

Gil remembered going into the village because they were looking for a Taliban suspect who had run and hidden in it the night before. They'd tracked him by infrared scope on their rifles. Often Taliban would hide in villages to throw them off the trail. Gil couldn't get Kai out of his mind, his heart or his body after seeing her there. Sam Morrison was leading the team and spotted her. And he reacted the same way toward her, telling Gil he was claiming her.

Well, Sam had claimed Kai. The guy knew how to turn on the charm Gil never possessed. He watched his best friend sweet-talk innocent Kai. And she was naive at that time. Hell, she still was. Innocent in the sense that she was an idealist. She didn't see the bad in life. She always saw the good.

Gil was privately jealous of Sam for getting to her first. He'd been so powerfully attracted to Kai that he couldn't explain it at all. He'd lain awake in his tent at Bagram, unable to erase her from his thoughts or, worse, his heart.

Every time they came back to Bagram, Sam would go directly to Kai. And Gil ached to be the one who went to her, instead. But Sam was his brother-in-arms. They had each other's backs. He would never betray Sam to get to Kai. *No way.* There was honor in him although as Gil slowly walked by the rusted corrals, he admitted sourly that his morals and values had gone to hell when he'd lost his brother Rob. By that time, Kai had been a widow for a year. Gil had stepped in to be an emotional support for her after Sam was killed.

It was his duty, his moral obligation, to be there for Kai. To let her weep unashamedly on his shoulder, clinging to him, the raw sounds of grief tearing out of her. And he'd held her, patted her back, whispered gruff words, trying to make her feel better.

And sometimes, after a good cry and they were sitting out in back of one of the hangars, Kai would talk to him. She never, ever suspected he ached for her, wanted her for his own, dreamed of her in his arms, in his bed. And Gil never gave her pause to think that he was anything other than Sam's brother who was there to help her through the transition of losing her husband, his best friend.

Gil could never tell Kai how much he looked forward to coming off an op, landing at Bagram in an MH-47 Chinook flown by Night Stalker pilots and looking her up. Just to be with her. To see her face, those haunting, large gray eyes of hers, to watch how her mouth flexed when she talked, to hear what was bothering her or what had made her laugh. She had been an oasis in the desert of his heart. Gil could never explain why he was so powerfully drawn to Kai. And he never did. It was just there. In his face. In his dreams. In his heart and memory. In his soul.

Mouth quirking, Gil headed past the rusted corrals and knew he had to meet everyone else. By that time, Sandy was up and puttering around. It didn't take much to know that Sandy was drawn to Cass. The Special Forces operator had a way with people, no question. And in the three months that Gil had been at the ranch and knew the situation with Sandy's health, he'd seen Cass put at least ten pounds on her skinny frame. Sandy would eat for him. Gil knew Cass was more than a little drawn to Sandy. He wasn't sure she was aware of it, however. She was in a struggle for her life and when that happened, a lot of nuances slipped unseen beneath the bridge of normal awareness. Still, the warmth that existed between the two of them was real and Gil liked to sit at the table and watch the dynamic. Sandy deserved some breaks in her life. She'd had two husbands die unexpectedly. And from what her son, Talon, had told him, she had loved each of them with her whole heart.

In a way, as Gil opened the picket-fence gate to the ranch house, he saw a little of Kai in Sandy. She had loved Sam with everything she had. And she had been true and loyal to him. Gil's conscience needled him as his boots rang hollowly against the cedar steps leading up to the massive ranch house porch. He wanted to turn around, walk back to that barn and hold Kai. Just stop the pain she was feeling because of a situation he had no control over. He had been shocked at the depth of her anger, the depth of hurt he'd caused her.

Taking off his hat, he opened the door and stepped into the foyer. There was conversation and laughter coming from the large kitchen down the hall and to his right. His heart twinged. Settling his Stetson on a peg, he halted for a moment, trying to get his strewn emotions collected. No one knew what had happened between him and Kai in the barn. He had to appear as if nothing was wrong. But the truth was that his whole life was in chaos for a thousand reasons. And it wasn't Kai's fault. It was entirely his.

KAI AVOIDED LUNCH with everyone. She had a protein bar she kept in her toolbox, and she kept working out in the barn instead. The day had warmed up, the air fresh with a scent of pine drifting fragrantly through the barn.

As she went to each piece of equipment, she cleaned it up. It was a lot of work, but it made her feel better under the circumstances. Gil was like that dust that had collected on the metal surfaces of the machines. She had never forgotten about him, his kisses, his crying in her arms, as if his entire world had been torn up and would never be the same again. It had turned her grieving heart inside out. She'd never heard a man cry before and it had stripped her emotionally in ways she could never describe, except that it was an agony that tore her up, made her want to hold him, give him safe harbor from his brother dying unexpectedly in combat.

She heard someone walk into the barn around one in the afternoon, and instantly Kai went on alert. Was it Gil? Looking up from where she stood, she saw it was Cat Holt. She wore a black baseball cap, a pale yellow tee with short sleeves and Levi's.

"Hey," Cat called, lifting her hand, "we missed you at lunch. Everything okay?"

"Fine," Kai answered. She washed her hands off in the bucket of clean water and wiped them down on the sides of her jeans. "I know we were supposed to go riding today, but I'm really focused on getting this list of repairs done for Talon. You okay with that?" Kai liked the tall, well-built woman. She was in good shape and Kai knew from Cass that at one time she'd been a firefighter in the Jackson Hole Fire Department until she injured her knee.

"Sure, no problem." Cat came over and smiled.

"Wow, you're really making all this stuff sparkle and shine. You didn't have to do that, Kai. You know that, don't you?"

Shrugging, Kai smiled a little and ran her hand over the hay baler. "Can't stand to see equipment dirty like this."

Cat leaned against the baler. "Know what you mean." She looked around the barn, cooing sounds echoing every now and then. "The Triple H was in the Holt family for a hundred years. Sandy got breast cancer at age forty and, sadly, she had to sell the place to get the money to pay off her medical bills."

Kai wrinkled her nose and took a break. "That's horrible."

"The worst," Cat agreed softly. "I've known Sandy since she first contracted breast cancer. I was working at the fire department then as a paramedic. We became good friends and I'd drop over to that small, awful apartment, which was all she could afford. She loves reading, so I'd read to her, share lunch with her and try to get her to eat."

Kai felt warmth flow through her heart as she studied Cat. "And you knew her for how long before Talon got home?"

"Five years," Cat murmured, smiling. "I kinda knew Talon from the photo scrapbook that Sandy showed me. I knew just about everything about their family, the love she had for her two husbands who both died unexpectedly."

"And Cass told me that her breast cancer had returned." Kai felt badly for the woman. Cancer scared everyone.

Nodding, Cat said, "It did. Talon had gotten wounded

nine months earlier, and so did his dog, Zeke. He was coming home after he got discharged from the hospital, to take care of her."

"And is Sandy's cancer gone yet?"

"It is. But she's got an aggressive kind and I worry." She nibbled on her lower lip. And then her eyes sparkled. "But I think with Cass coming into her life, it's helping her to rally."

Kai smiled a little. "I think they like one another. Don't you?"

Cat chuckled. "Just a little. Cass is forty-nine and Sandy is the same age. They're good together. He can get her to eat and has actually helped her gain back some of her lost weight. That's a miracle in and of itself."

"I feel love is the greatest healer of all," Kai said quietly, holding Cat's worried look. "I mean, I don't know if there is love between them or not, but loving care makes the difference." She ought to know. She'd reached out, opened her arms to Gil, who was clearly suffering and in anguish, and helped him. She saw Cat's face soften and become pensive.

"Love is the greatest of healers. You're right." She lifted her chin. "My husband was very wounded in so many ways as a SEAL operator. He came home to a mess with Sandy. She'd given up hope and refused any more treatment to stop the return of her cancer. He was dealing with a lot. I just happened to walk into the picture at that moment."

Kai studied Cat, the silence ebbing gently between them. "But you fell in love with Talon?"

"I did, but I didn't want to. I'd screwed up my life, too. I didn't want to involve Talon in it."

"I think life is messy at best," Kai muttered distastefully.

Laughing a little, Cat nodded. "No argument there. The good news is that we're starting to get a workable foundation under us to bring the Triple H back into great shape."

"Gil said the ranch went into a state of disrepair for nine years."

'Yeah. Easterners bought it, one after another playing cowboy, and they knew nothing at all," she said grimly, wrapping her arms around her chest. "I can't tell you how many times Sandy cried over the guilt of having to sell their family ranch for her medical bills. It was a horrible, stressful burden on her."

"Guilt is a bitch," Kai agreed, just as grim. "But she's better now? Coming back home?"

"Yes. The doctors cleared her a month ago, proclaimed her free of cancer. Again." Cat shook her head. "I just keep praying it stays away this time."

"Don't you think that the shock of having to sell her ranch brought it back a second time?"

Giving her a searching look, Cat said, "Funny, I always thought the same thing. I mean, I never talked to Sandy or Talon about it."

"But you're a paramedic. You see how shock devastates a person on every level."

"Yes, it does. You're pretty sharp and observant, Kai."

Grinning a little, she wiped her hands on a rag. "I see patterns in people's lives. I look for cause and effect."

"Hmm, well, that's not a bad way to approach it. Sandy was always weighted down by the loss of their ranch. I saw her at least three times a week and she always talked about it. Cried over it. She couldn't let it go."

"How did you get the ranch back?"

"Miss Gus, over at the Bar H, which is next door to our ranch, bought it back for Sandy. She's eighty-five years old and a matriarch here in the valley. Gus is tough, no-nonsense, but that old woman has a heart of gold. All she wanted in return for buying the ranch back for Sandy was a twenty-year lease on two hundred of the five hundred acres we have on this ranch."

"Wow," Kai murmured, "that's incredible. She must be very rich, then?" Because Kai had seen other ranches for sale in the valley in the local newspaper and they were going for millions of dollars.

Cat nodded. "Yes, she is. I hope you get to meet her soon. She's a love. Feisty. Tough but fair. She worked hard for every penny she has. Gus usually drops over to see Sandy at least once a week." With a grin, Cat added, "And she's always snooping around to see what else we've done to get the ranch online."

"Well, it's sort of her investment, right?"

Chuckling, Cat eased to her feet. "Right. She and Sandy had been ranch neighbors ever since Gus came here from across the state. So when Sandy got ill, lost her ranch, Gus decided to try to get it back for her. And, eventually, she did." Opening her hands, Cat gestured around the barn. "So here we are. We're putting our money to good use, thanks to Cass. He's a brilliant math guy and he also works with Griff McPherson, who is married to Val, Gus's niece. Griff has an MBA from Harvard and sometimes he and

Cass get together to go over the business plan for our ranch. We're really lucky to have both of them."

"Well," Kai said gently, "I think Sandy is lucky to have Cass."

"Oh, Cass loves being Sandy's keeper. Talon and I both feel that sooner or later, love is going to blossom between them."

"It looks like it has already."

Shrugging, Cat said, "Sandy's fallen in love twice, Kai. And each time, she married that man. And then, she lost him. Gardner died when Talon was ten. And then she met Bradley Holt, and he died unexpectedly in a car accident. I don't know if she has enough of her heart left to fall in love again. She hasn't said anything to me, but I can see it in her eyes. She's afraid to fall in love a third time."

"Because she's afraid she'd lose Cass like the other two men?"

"Bingo," Cat said. "Cass knows her history. I pulled him aside when he first came and gave him the lowdown. He's just naturally a caregiver besides being a brainy dude. Never mind he was Special Forces. The guy rocks in my book and I love him like a big, hairy, fuzzy brother." She grinned. "Cass grows on everyone."

Kai smiled. "I liked him from the moment I met him." She crossed her fingers and held them up. "Let's hope Sandy gets through her fear of loss and lets Cass into her heart. I feel if she does, she won't have any more bouts with cancer. Love heals."

CHAPTER FIVE

ON MONDAY, KAI had driven into Jackson Hole to the John Deere store to pick up the items she'd need to repair the Triple H's tractor. They'd had their 9:00 a.m. meeting and Gil had given her permission to go into town and get the items she needed. As she walked in, she saw a number of shiny new green-and-yellow tractors.

Seeing a sign that said Repair, she headed across the waxed white tiled floor toward the opened window. As she did, she spotted a man in a white cowboy shirt and dark brown slacks talking with a John Deere salesman on the floor. He had looked up as she entered, his dark brown eyes assessing her intently for a moment. Kai felt the power around the man, a sense of control and of his importance. He was dressed like a rancher, not a businessman, but she spotted a gold Rolex watch on his thick wrist peeking out from beneath the white cuff of his shirtsleeve.

If she hadn't been so focused on getting parts for the tractor, she might have taken another look. He was a good-looking man, wearing a brown Stetson on hair of similar color. She liked that he stood tall and straight. Why she was even vaguely interested in him made her snort softly to herself. She had enough problems with Gil Hanford shadowing her life at the ranch right now. Still, she felt the stranger's gaze linger on her as she stopped at the open window.

Kai knew Talon wanted her to get replacement parts for the tractor but if she could get, for instance, a rebuilt carburetor for the tractor instead of buying a new one, that would save them money. Talon was up on equipment and that shouldn't have surprised her. Talon went over each item she'd found that needed to be replaced. He'd given her the name of Joe Hoskins, who repaired tractors for John Deere in the town. The balding man of sixty came to the window and smiled at her.

"What can I do for you, missy?" He placed his long, gnarled, darkly tanned hands on the opened door that served as a Dutch door to the repair department.

Kai smiled and introduced herself. "Joe? Do you have any of these items that are rebuilt and not new? I'm the mechanic for the Triple H and money is tight." She liked his dancing hazel eyes and his quirky smile. The man, when he smiled, had two front teeth missing.

Joe studied the list. "Hmm, well, I can get half of this list on rebuilt. That's a mighty old tractor, missy." He looked into his repair room, which was filled with long rows of equipment on each shelf.

Kai grimaced. "I know it's old. Do you have any parts here for it?" Kai knew from studying the tractors online that they were evolving remarkably from their forebears into electronic and computerized whizzes. The engines had changed and their old model was most likely a dinosaur to Joe.

"Well," he murmured, "I don't think so...but lemme go look..."

Kai stood at the window, her mind running over where else she could find the parts she needed.

"Got a little problem with your tractor?" a male voice inquired from behind her.

Turning, Kai looked up. It was the cowboy who had been talking to the salesman on the floor earlier. She smiled a little. "Just got an old tractor that needs some parts," she explained. When he smiled, his whole face changed.

"I'm Chuck Harper," he said, offering his hand to her. "I own Ace Trucking at the west end of town."

Kai took his hand. It was the hand of a man who worked. She felt the calluses as she slid her hand into his. "Kai Tiernan. Nice to meet you."

Chuck released her hand and looked toward Joe. "My trucking company has a very large state-of-the-art mechanical and repair shop. I heard Joe say your tractor was pretty old. Chances are he won't have the parts you're looking for." He studied her with curiosity. "Are you working for someone around here? It's kind of odd to see a woman with an equipment list in her hand instead of a grocery list."

She felt his interest in her as a woman, mentally rejecting it. Harper was either in his late thirties or early forties. He was deeply tanned, his face long, with crow's-feet at the corner of both his eyes. There was alertness in them. This man didn't miss much. "I was just hired by the Triple H. They needed a mechanic."

"Oh, yeah," he murmured. "That ranch is broken."

"Well," she said, "it's coming back. The Holts are putting their love into it, breathing new life into it." She saw him smile a little and she could feel his interest growing in her. Man-to-woman interest. Glancing down, she saw no wedding ring on his finger, but that meant nothing nowadays. If he owned a trucking company, chances were he was fairly well-off money-wise and was married. Probably had a couple of kids, to boot. She was *not* interested.

"You're a dreamer," he teased, his teeth even and white as he smiled down at her.

"No, I'm a realist. The people I work for are like me. We know hard work will bring the Triple H back to her feet."

Shrugging a little, Chuck said, "In my book, that's dreaming. But hey, I wish you all luck. Here comes Joe…"

Turning, Kai saw the older gentleman come back with her list.

"Sorry to tell you, Kai, but none of these things are carried by our company anymore."

Feeling down, Kai said, "Well, do you know of a parts dealer around here?"

"Naw, the only thing you can do is maybe call the John Deere dealer in Idaho Falls, Idaho. It's the nearest large city to us," and Joe pointed northward. "It's a three-hour drive one way." He reached down and pulled a business card from a tray. "Here's their number. They might have something, but that tractor of the Holts is really out-of-date."

"I know it is," Kai said, taking the card and tucking it into her pants pocket, "but it's still a good, hardworking machine. It has a lot of years left in it."

Joe gave her a slight smile. "They make Deeres to last forever."

"You know," Chuck said, moving closer to her, "I have a complete repair facility. Do you know how to rebuild a motor? A carburetor?"

"I do. Why?"

"Well," Chuck said, "I'd be happy to take you over there to check out our repair shop. If you bring in what you need repaired, I have the tools, the machinery and other items you need to do it. Now, I wouldn't charge you anything but a fair hourly rate to use my equipment. If you needed spare parts, my man, José, could probably find the things you need in our spare parts department. Why don't you come over with me? Check it out? Might save you the loss of a day having to drive to Idaho Falls and back."

The idea was tempting. Kai said, "Let me call Talon Holt. I need his permission. Could you give me an idea of costs?" She liked that Harper was willing to help her, but it wasn't lost on Kai that he liked her, either. Right now, as bruised as her heart and ego were from the blowout with Gil, it was nice to be appreciated by a man. Especially someone like Harper, who appeared to be kind and thoughtful.

Chuck took a piece of paper from Joe and scribbled down the rates and handed it to her. "I'll wait by the door," he said. "Let me know what Holt says."

"Thanks," Kai murmured, pulling out her cell phone.

GIL WAS COMING down the porch steps from the main ranch house near four in the afternoon when he saw Kai drive in. She parked her truck with the rest and climbed out. He saw her wrestle with a large cardboard box that was obviously heavy. He met her halfway.

"Let me take that for you," he said gruffly, reaching out for it.

Kai scowled. "I got it." She glared up at him.

Gently, Gil eased his hands around it. "Let me help you, Kai."

Her heart twisted and Kai didn't want him touching her, so she released the box to him. Why was she still so drawn to him? Why? It frustrated the hell out of her. "They're parts. I need to take them to the green barn."

"Okay," Gil said, turning and beginning the walk around the ranch house. "Were you able to get the John Deere parts you needed?"

Kai fell into step with him, keeping plenty of room between them. "No. But I met a really nice guy, Chuck Harper." Instantly, she saw Gil's face go hard, and his gaze snapped to hers. He halted abruptly, staring down at her.

"Harper?" he snarled.

Shaken, Kai said, "Well…yes. Why?" She saw blackness in Gil's eyes and it bothered the hell out of her. "I called Talon Holt about this hours ago," she began defensively, her chin jutting out. "He gave me permission to use Ace Trucking's repair facility to make the parts I needed for the tractor. Why?"

Gil compressed his lips, staring at her. "Stay away from the bastard. You hear me?"

The snarl in his voice tore through her. Confused, she muttered, "What are you talking about? The guy was nice. He offered me his facility so I could make the parts I needed for the tractor. Talon approved the payment and I wrote him a check afterward. Why are you looking at me like that?" Her heart rate ramped up and she could feel the sudden tension gathering around Gil. He was acting as if he was about ready to go into a firefight. She'd seen and felt that same kind of energy around Sam anytime he was threatened. Why the hell was Gil threatened by Chuck Harper? Or was he angry at her? Jealous? Either way, Kai felt her stomach knot. Her hands curved against her Levi's as she stared him down.

Cursing softly, Gil said, "Let's get these parts to the barn. I'll fill you in there."

Kai almost had to run to keep up with his long, swift stride. In no time, Gil had placed the cardboard box on the table where she had her toolbox. He turned, pushing up his Stetson.

"Harper is a bastard," he growled at her. "Did Talon know who you were dealing with?"

Struck by the ferocity of his words and the way his body had tensed, Kai muttered, "Yes, I told him. Why the hell are you acting like this, Gil? I didn't do anything wrong!"

"Dammit, I'm not angry at you, Kai." He took a swipe at his jaw, looking out the barn door as if he was trying to put the right words together. "Where did you meet Harper?"

Scowling, she told him. The look in Gil's eyes was glittering and she could feel his sudden, almost overwhelming protectiveness cascading around her. She remembered that sense of safety and protection in his arms. He was an operator, and he protected his own.

Just as Sam had once protected her. In as few words as possible, she told Gil where she'd met Harper and their subsequent conversation.

"He's not to be trusted. I don't care how damned nice he was to you, Kai."

She stared at him, mouth dropping open. "What is this, Gil? I just saved this ranch a lot of money by arranging to use his facilities to fix that tractor." She saw him scowl, his game face in place. Kai hated that unreadable expression. She had hated it on Sam, too. Black ops men were screwed up so damned badly in her opinion precisely because they sat on their emotions to do their jobs. And Gil was looking like that right now.

"Harper is a bastard in the finest sense of the word," he gritted out.

She snorted. "I know a bastard when I see one, Gil."

The muscles in his jaw ticked. "You're new to this area, Kai. You don't know the lay of the land yet. If you don't trust my assessment of Harper, just go to Gwen Garner at the quilt shop in town. She'll give you a fair readout on him."

A little unnerved because she saw something in Gil's eyes that set her on warning. Was he jealous of Harper? That couldn't be! Searching his eyes, there was worry in them. For her? Why? Gil didn't even like her! She was a burr under his saddle by being here. So what was his angle at getting all huffy, protective and upset that Harper had done something decent for the ranch? "When I get time," she said, turning and walking out of the barn. Let him stew in his own juices. Kai was confused by the raw care burning in his eyes for a second in the barn. There was no way Gil cared for her. No way in hell!

As she quickly walked down the gravel slope, Kai couldn't contain her emotions. She knew that look in Gil's eyes. She'd seen it the night before he left her and walked away. The sense of protection had surrounded her as she lay in his arms and he had gently moved several tendrils of her damp hair away from her brow. Kai hadn't known she could fall so hard for anyone as she did Gil. It had never happened before or after him.

One kiss!

Just that one haunting, searing kiss as his mouth took hers with desperation had turned her world upside down and her life inside out. Her knees had weakened and he'd literally swept her into his arms, holding her tightly against him, ravishing her mouth, his other hand holding the back of her head as he plundered her lips, her heart and her soul. It was as if a lifetime of need and hunger had been built into his one life-changing kiss with her. Kai got in that instant how much he had desired her over the years and, even more poignant, how much he needed her right then. The feeling that washed over her was if he didn't kiss her right now, he'd die. It was that intense. That soul-rocking. Without thinking, Kai touched her lips with her fingertips, that branding kiss always with her. No man had ever kissed her like Gil Hanford had.

Anguish rose in Kai, tearing at her heart, turning it into bloody ribbons that made her want to gasp because the hurt, the fact that he'd left her, was still too much for her to deal with. She slowed her walk, wrapped in the misery and rejection by him. Kai thought she'd suffered when Sam died. But, in truth, what Gil had done to her was far worse. His kiss had been like a telepathic transmission to every possible level of herself. As he had taken her into his arms, capturing her against his tall, strong body, the scent of sweat and dust stinging her nostrils, she'd felt a man in such utter distress and sheer need of her alone. And her heart had opened fully to him, trusting him with herself. She had given. And he had taken.

End of story.

It hurt to breathe for a moment as Kai pushed herself to walk toward the ranch house. It was almost dinnertime. She needed to take a shower and change into some clean clothes beforehand. Unable to shake off that shield that surrounded her, Gil's protectiveness, she made a noise in her throat, disgusted with herself. How her stupid, blind heart could react to his look of concern for her made her angry and confused.

GIL TRIED TO ignore that Kai wore a pale pink blouse and loose white trousers to dinner. Her hair had been recently washed, the gold strands gleaming among the burgundy beneath the light above the table. He heard people talking, some laughing, but none of it really registered. His heart ached so damned bad he didn't know what to do to stop it. Maybe kiss her. Yeah, he wanted to kiss the hell out of Kai.

He covertly watched as she nibbled disinterestedly at the homemade lasagna Cass had made for them tonight. The scent of garlic and butter on the French bread complemented the meal. Her mouth was one of the most delicious parts of her body and Gil could feel his lower body stirring in memory. She had kissed him so passionately, giving her heart, her trust, to him without question. His brows drew down. Four years later he was seeing the results of how his life had screwed both of them over. Kai was more beautiful, more mature, than before. And she hated him.

From Gil's perspective it was obvious Cat and Kai were going to become close friends. They smiled and laughed often as they chatted. Sandy was looking a bit better, he supposed, because Cass was like a harpy eagle getting her to eat protein, and the nutrition was working. Sandy's dark hair was usually thin and hanging around her nape, but tonight it was pretty. He wondered if Cat had fixed her hair. Sandy was a beautiful woman and he secretly envied Cass because Gil knew the man was attracted to her. But Sandy seemed to be unaware. Or maybe she was ignoring Cass? Like Kai ignored him?

After dinner, the table cleared, Talon asked Gil, Kai and Cass to remain. Cat brought over fresh cups of coffee for everyone and then retired to the living room with Sandy to watch the news on television.

Talon brought over the notes Kai had made and laid them out in front of himself. He glanced across the table at her. "This is pretty remarkable, Kai. You've cut the repair bill in half on the tractor."

Kai felt heat in her cheeks. "Thanks, Talon."

Gil growled, "It might save us money, but I don't like Kai being around the likes of Harper."

Talon nodded. "Yeah, this isn't the best of all worlds," he agreed. Giving Kai a look of concern, he said, "Did Harper bother you while you were over at his place?"

"No. He introduced me to his repair boss, José, and I never saw him again."

"I don't like it," Gil muttered, giving Talon a hard look.

Kai shook her head. "What is everyone talking over my head about?" She gave Talon a frustrated look.

Cass, who sat next to her, said, "Harper is a woman chaser, Kai. He's got a seriously bad reputation in town."

"He didn't come on to me. He overheard me talking to Joe at the John Deere place." Kai saw Gil give her a look of disbelief, but he kept his mouth shut, his large, callused hands clasped tightly on the table.

Talon moved his fingers through his short hair. He stared at the bill. "She's saved us a helluva lot of money. And every penny counts."

"Not at her expense, it doesn't," Gil growled in warning, looking each man in the eyes.

Kai's skin ruffled beneath his growl. He sounded like a pissed-off grizzly. She refused to look at him, again feeling that intense sense of protection suddenly blanketing her. It almost felt as if he was staking or claiming her! Thinking she was imagining things, she said quietly, "Look, I'm twenty-nine years old. I can take care of myself. We need that machinery shop that Harper's got. He said I could come back at any time if I wanted to rebuild something. He'd charge me a fair-market price." She gave Talon a pleading look. "I only got two pieces of machinery fully vetted today. There's eight more pieces of equipment out there. And I think you can tell from how much repair has to be done to bring that tractor and baler back to life we need what Harper is offering us. I think it was nice of him to do it."

Talon frowned.

Cass moved uncomfortably around in the chair, his gaze moving to Gil.

Gil's mouth flattened, his knuckles whitening as he looked at Talon, waiting for an answer.

Studying the list, Talon rubbed his brow as if he had a headache coming on. He studied Kai. "Okay, judging from what you saw and did today, do you think the other pieces of equipment need as much rebuilding?"

"I haven't really done any kind of inspection to honestly answer that, Talon." Kai opened her hands. "But just seeing these two, the amount of rust, the amount of metalwork and welding it will take to re-place badly rusted areas, yes, I think it's going to be a pretty good estimate of what's to come."

"And you work with metal?"

"Of course," Kai said. "If we had to replace a fender or some metal skin that took a bullet hole in an Apache, it was up to us to fix it. I'm good at weld-ing, Talon. I'm qualified in specialty metals. I can do all this for you. But I need a good machine shop to do it in. And Harper runs a clean place and he's got all the latest equipment to make my job easy and fast."

Talon glanced at Gil. "Is Harper the only game in town?"

"Unfortunately, yes."

"And the next closest machine shop would be Idaho Falls, Idaho. That's a six-hour round-trip and that doesn't account for the time Kai would have to spend at a machine shop," Talon said.

"I know for a fact what he charged us today is about one-third less than what a regular machine shop would charge us," Kai pointed out.

"Cass?" Talon held up the paper toward him. "Have you seen this yet?"

"No," he said, taking the papers and quickly parsing the numbers. His brows moved up. "Well," he murmured, looking at Talon, "Kai is right—these numbers are lower than normal."

"Because Harper wants something in return from you, Kai," Gil ground out.

All heads turned toward him.

There was no mistaking Gil's words or his barely closeted anger. Kai shook her head. "I think all of you are going overboard," she stated flatly. "Harper did not accost me this afternoon. I worked with José. I never saw him again." She saw Gil grit his teeth. The man was jealous as hell.

Cass sat there scribbling some numbers on the back of one of her notebook pages. "Boss? If we assume each piece of equipment is going to need this kind of do-over, then we'll easily save one-half of what was going to be spent on those repairs. That's a considerable sum when you look at the totals here."

Kai couldn't stand being near Gil anymore. He felt like a nuclear power engine that was about ready to explode. "Look, Talon, when you guys figure out what you want to do, let me know? I'm tired and I'm going to bed. Good night…"

GIL WATCHED KAI walk away, the soft sway of her hips reminding him starkly of far too much from their past. He swung his head toward Talon. "You cannot let her do this. You know Harper is into the sex-trafficking trade and drugs. There are two women he was dating and both are gone. Disappeared without a trace. Do you want to guess where they probably ended up? In some Eastern European slave trader's hideaway to be sold to the highest bidder."

Talon held up his hand. "Look, I'm aware of the gossip about Harper. No one's proved anything, Gil. At least—" he sighed "—not yet."

"What if one of us went with her?" Cass asked, giving the two men an inquiring look.

Talon's mouth quirked. "Like any of us have time to babysit her for fear Harper will steal and sell her?"

"Look," Cass said reasonably, opening his hands, "why not go talk to law enforcement? The sheriff's office is in town. Talon? You could swing by—"

"I'll do it," Gil muttered. "No one is handling this except me." He gave Talon a look of warning.

Shrugging, Talon said, "Fine by me. I'll tell Kai to not go back there until you've talked to the sheriff's department about Harper."

Gil rose. "She needs to be protected from that bastard," he growled, and left.

Cass gave Talon an amused look. "Did I miss something here? Or did your SEAL nose catch it, too?"

"What?" Talon asked.

Cass sat back in the chair, rocking it on its two hind legs, hands resting on his thick thighs. "I might be wrong about this, but I sure think there's something simmering between Kai and Gil. Did you pick up on it?"

"No," he muttered, rubbing his face. "I'm so damned

busy trying to coordinate everything else, I'm probably missing a lot."

Cass smiled a little. "She's a pretty lady. I'm surprised she's single."

Talon shook his head. "She was married to a Delta Force operator for three years until he got killed in a firefight."

Brows drawing down, Cass said, "Yeah, she told me earlier about it. Probably why she's still single."

"Well," Talon said, standing, "I wonder if Gil knew her husband. Maybe there's a connection there you're picking up on."

Cass grinned a little as he rose. "What I felt was definitely interest on Gil's part toward her. He's like a nighthawk around her."

Talon shook his head. "A nighthawk is the wrangler who protects the herd during the night from all kinds of danger. Gil is protective of Kai. You have eyes in the back of your head, Cass. You always did."

Giving him a wicked look, Cass slid the chair up to the table. "Yes, and I can count how many times we saved your sorry ass out on an op, too, because of it."

A sour grin edged Talon's mouth. "Can't deny it, bro. I'm going to spend some time with my mother and then I'm hitting the sack."

"Yeah," Cass grumped good-naturedly. "All I have to look forward to is swimming in red and black numbers in my office for a couple of hours now."

Talon looked over his shoulder. "Better be more black than red," he warned him.

"Doin' my best, boss," Cass teased. "We're slowly eking toward the healthy side of the business ledger. Rebuilding an empire takes time."

CHAPTER SIX

TALON HOLT SAT with Gil in his office at the main ranch house. Both were grim. Talon said, "Look, we know that Chuck Harper is being watched by the FBI and ATF for drug running. So far, no one has caught him at it." Pushing his fingers through his dark hair, he added, "Deputy Sheriff Cade Garner is someone I trust, Gil. You haven't been here long enough to know that, but if he suggests that someone escort Kai over to the Ace Trucking machine shop, we need to do it."

"You won't get any argument out of me," Gil said, feeling relief start to trickle through him. He would talk to Garner soon. Until then, Gil had made a decision that someone would always be with Kai over at Harper's machine shop. He had her back. "It's going to be a balancing act. Needs at the ranch versus needs of machinery being available so we can use it. Right now, I need a horse trailer. And we don't have one that's safe enough to use." He saw his boss sit back in his chair, nodding. "You need to tell me what repair should be first."

"On another issue, we need to buy a horse for Kai," Talon said. "Slade McPherson, Griff's twin brother, owns an endurance-racing horse ranch on the other side of Jackson Hole. Cass has allotted us fifteen hundred dollars for the animal. Can you take Kai over after setting an appointment up with Slade? Let her see what's available and then you need to get him to agree to our money limit."

Gil had never met Slade McPherson, but he knew his twin, Griff, who he respected and admired. The man had an MBA, along with horse sense and hard work combined. He was bringing the Bar H back to life. "I'll see what I can do." He knew the worth of the horses he had bred and trained.

"Then," Talon said, talking more to himself as he looked up at the copper ceiling that had been imprinted with hundred-year-old patterns from the past, "get Kai to look over all the equipment. Have her make up a complete repair list. Tell her the double-wide horse trailer has to supersede the tractor for now. If push comes to shove, we can always ask Slade to deliver the horse here and he will. But we need that trailer as bad as we need the tractor."

"And who do you want to go with her to Ace Trucking?" Gil wanted it to be him. He saw his boss's expression pinch.

"Whoever is available at the time. Hell, it will be Cass, you or me. Any way you cut it, she's got a black ops guy at her side. I don't think Harper will try anything."

"You want us to pack a weapon?"

Talon nodded. "We all have a license to carry a concealed weapon. I don't trust Harper. At all. But I sure as hell like the prices he's giving Kai. If we don't use his services, that means we're wasting a day driving to and from, plus, if Kai can't finish everything off at another machine shop in Idaho Falls, we have to pay for her food and hotel bill. And we're paying one-third more in costs. It mounts up in a hurry."

Gil understood Talon's position. He knew from his own father always battling the accounting ledger that keeping a ranch in the black was the toughest thing to do in the world. And right now, the Triple H was in the red. Cass had a good, solid plan for the ranch, but it was slow going. Rome wasn't built in a day, he reminded himself. So Talon was going to be damned conservative, and Gil didn't blame his boss for wanting to use a nearby facility and save money while he was at it. He just didn't want to put Kai at risk. But neither did Talon. Gil could see he was morally wrestling with the situation. In one way he knew he was putting Kai in a potentially dangerous situation. On the other hand, all three of them were well-trained operators and would be packing a weapon in case shit happened.

"Do you think Harper would try anything while she was in his facility?" Gil wondered.

"No, I don't. And that's the only reason I'm willing to even consider this idea. Harper is known to be very low-key. He doesn't want trouble. There's been enough of it of late and Cade thinks that he knows the FBI is following him. He employs only Latino workers. Cade thinks most of them are illegals. But the other agencies that usually swoop down and find them are pulling back. The FBI is trying to insert someone into the trucking company, but they know Harper is watching closely."

"Sounds like a standoff of sort," Gil agreed.

"If you can ask Kai to focus on that horse trailer and tell her why, I'd appreciate it."

Gil rose. "I will."

THE LATE-MORNING sun felt good coming into the back of the green barn where Kai was working. She was dusty from taking a broom and putting a bandanna around the lower half her face to start sweeping off the thick dust on every piece of machinery. There were clouds of dust hanging in the air, sparkling as it hit the shafts of sunlight piercing through the barn.

She lifted her head and saw Gil coming up the gravel slope. For a moment her heart pounded. The fear of having to confront him and then fight back her desire for him always left her exhausted afterward. His face was set and shadowed, the sun at his back. He was so damned good-looking to her. He always had been.

Going to meet him at the front of the barn where there was less dust in the air, she pulled the handkerchief off her face, broom in one hand. Kai longed for some kind of truce between them. But how could there be? Gil had not told her why he'd left her. Not said one peep. He had apologized, she reminded herself, when they'd had it out in the barn the day after her hiring. And he'd looked so damned sad, as if he were going to cry or something, but he always tried to hide it from her. She'd been brimming over with anger, and having gotten it off her chest now Kai wanted a truce, maybe.

"How's it going?" Gil asked as he drew up to her, keeping a good six feet between them.

Wrinkling her nose, Kai said, "I couldn't stand how dirty everything was." She internally tensed, unsure why Gil was here. There was no reason that she could think of. And she didn't want another argument with him. Searching his blue eyes, she saw worry in them, not anger or defensiveness.

"If we had more hands, I could get someone in here to do it for you. Like it should be."

Her stomach began to unknot. For the first time, this was the Gil Hanford she knew from her past. He'd put his hands on his hips, shifting his weight to one leg more than the other. His face was relaxed looking, too. Some more of her sagged in quiet relief. "It's okay. I'm good at cleaning up situations." She managed a sliver of a smile.

"You are very good at everything you do."

Praise riffled across her. She almost asked Gil if he'd gotten a decent night's sleep, remembering the tense discussion at the dinner table last night. "Thanks, it's nice to hear it."

"Talon's happy with you, and that's all that counts."

Gil wasn't happy she was here, but she bit back the words. To say that would be to stir the tension that flowed between them. "What do you need?"

"Talon wants to get you a horse. Slade McPherson has some for sale on the other side of town at his ranch. I was wondering if you were at a place where you could stop for a couple of hours?"

A horse! Her heart sang. Kai felt giddy. "Sure. That would be a lot of fun to go look at horses." She saw a slight curve of one corner of Gil's mouth, his blue eyes lighter. Was he happy? It felt like it. Far better than being at odds with him.

"Let me go get cleaned up? I look like a dust bunny."

Gil gave her a slow inspection from head to toe. "Yeah, a little. Go ahead. I'll meet you out front in the company truck in twenty minutes?."

Heat soared through Kai and she felt her breasts tighten beneath his heated gaze. That look wasn't impersonal. Her mouth went dry. God, was it possible he wanted her? Man to woman? The realization was like a bolt striking her and Kai inwardly floundered. Her heart was doing a happy dance. Her memory sourly reminded her of the hurt he'd caused her. "Sure," she murmured, setting the broom inside the barn. "Twenty minutes."

KAI WAS UNEASY riding with Gil so close to her in the cab of the truck. They had a good twenty miles together. She sat with her hands in her lap, tense. Gil seemed relaxed in comparison. The scenery was rich and green, the valley blooming to life after eight months of hard, cold winter. She enjoyed the patchwork quilt of small farms on the left. To her right rose a rocky hill and cliff.

"Does Slade have quarter horses?" she wondered, wanting to break the silence.

"No. He's got endurance horses. Talon was telling me Slade has a sunbonnet paint mustang stallion called Thor. His stud has won every endurance event in North America. Jordana McPherson rode Thor to victory two years ago. Slade got gored in the thigh by one of his ornery bulls and couldn't ride him in the event, so she did and won."

"Is she an endurance champion like Slade?"

"No. She's an ER physician." Gil slowed the truck down as they began to enter the traffic going into Jackson Hole. "They met about a year earlier. She'd come from back east and loved endurance riding.

Bought a nice endurance horse from him and I guess they fell in love."

"That's nice," Kai said softly. "I like to see people who are happy in relationships."

"Well," Gil said, "we have one and a half at the Triple H."

Kai tilted her head and gave him a look. "One and a half? What are you talking about?"

Opening his hand for a moment on the steering wheel, Gil said, "Talon and Cat are happily married. Granted, they're newlyweds. And then you have Sandy and Cass."

"You think they like one another?" She saw him slant a partly amused glance in her direction before returning his attention to the traffic in front of them.

"Cass was married once, from what he told me one time. His wife died of breast cancer about seven years ago. They had no children."

Frowning, Kai whispered, "Oh, God, that's awful. He always seems so upbeat and happy."

Snorting, Gil muttered, "He's a friggin' Special Forces guy. They're all like that. The meet-and-greet boys."

"Still," Kai said stubbornly, forcing herself not to look at Gil, "he's suffered a lot."

"No question."

"But, you think Cass likes Sandy?"

"Oh, I think it's mutual. Everyone else does, too."

"They both deserve some happiness."

"Yes."

Compressing her lips, Kai tried not to feel good about talking in a normal tone of voice to Gil. She still had a lot of anger inside her. And he'd never given her an explanation of why he'd deserted her like he did. "Then these horses that Slade has… Are they all mustangs?"

"No, he breeds Arabian blood with mustang blood. I guess it's pretty successful conformation because Talon was telling me Slade has box office business and can barely keep any horses up for sale. He's even selling to Europe and to the Middle East, now."

"That's amazing. I know nothing about endurance riding. All I know is getting on and off a horse to fix fences."

Gil grinned a little. "That's it in a nutshell. Talon was saying he has a nice half mustang, half Arabian mare he thinks might suit you." Shrugging, he added, "But it's up to you, Kai. You're the one who has to ride the horse. If you don't like her, Talon has a couple of other places we can go to look to buy you one."

Excitement wound through Kai. "I like the fact she's a mare."

"I don't."

"You wouldn't. You're not a woman. Growing up, I always fought my dad on this very point. I insisted on having a mare to ride, not a gelding."

"Mares are cranky, hard to manage and get the geldings stirred up when they're in heat," Gil muttered.

She laughed outright, unable to help herself. "Gee, does that mean once a month you're going to view me like that, too?" She saw Gil give her a sour grin.

"Not exactly."

"Your argument is lame to me," Kai said, still smiling. She lost herself for a moment in his eyes. There was warmth and heat in them—for her. It was unmistakable. She couldn't let this happen again. Her smile faded. "It doesn't bother me that she's a mare. I'm more interested in her conformation and her legs." And then Kai saw a gleam come to his eyes, but Gil didn't say a word. He didn't have to. She knew he was a leg man, pure and simple. Well, amend that: ass and legs. But there wasn't any part of her he hadn't lavished and worshipped.

Wishing she could forget those heavenly days that suddenly plunged her into hell, Kai felt longing. It was so deep within her that it caught her off guard. Longing? For Gil Hanford? She had to be crazy!

IN NO TIME, they were at the small horse ranch. There was a single-story ranch house, a nice pipe oval corral between it and a three-story barn. Excitement started to bubble within Kai as she eased out of the truck and shut the door. In the arena was a very tall man, square face, and short, dark brown hair beneath a black Stetson he wore.

"That's Slade," Gil told Kai. He saw her nod. The unexpected and shared laughter between them had caught him completely off guard. It reminded him sharply of the time he'd spent with Kai. They couldn't get enough of each other. They'd had hungry sex, fallen into one another's arms afterward, exhausted, and then they'd slept for a while. Hungry upon awakening, they'd eat and then they'd start all over again.

Gil couldn't understand how starved they were for each other. It was mutual. It had been unbelievably good and satisfying. Kai was so sweet and funny when they'd awaken. She had a wonderful sense of humor and she would tease him until he'd start to laugh. Gil had never laughed so much in his life. Kai had handed him a lifeline when he was going down for the count. She had pulled him up, helped him stand again, recapture a sense of himself without all the heavy grief over Rob's loss that had been eating him up alive. Every time they'd made love, a little more of that monster weight had dissolved. Kai had healed him.

As he cut his stride for her sake, a few feet between them, Gil risked a glance down at her. She wore her green baseball cap and her sunglasses were perched up on top of the bill shading her gray eyes. Her mouth was softened at the corners and he felt himself going hard. Kissing Kai's mouth had been the most right thing he'd ever done. The way she kissed…

Groaning internally, Gil had to stop thinking about the past, about Kai, about what they had. Yet, when he saw that diamond-like sparkle in her eyes as they approached the closed gate to the arena, he ached to have Kai look at him with that same desire once again.

Gil halted beside Kai. In the center of the arena Slade had a beautiful young mare, a pinto with white and chestnut markings all across her compact, strong body. He heard Kai make a soft sound in her throat as she curled her fingers around one of the pipes, watching the horse move at a slow canter in a wide circle around Slade. The mare had a long tail, caramel and cream, flowing like a flag across her rump. Her mane was a combination of dark sienna, caramel and cream, and was equally long. Gil could see the dished face on the mare and as she came cantering around toward where they stood, he grinned.

"She's got two blue eyes," he told Kai. "Beautiful."

Kai gasped. "She does! Oh, my God! She's gorgeous!" Kai twisted a look up at Gil. "Is she the mare that Slade wants to sell to us?"

Nodding, Gil hitched a hand up in hello to Slade. "I think so."

Slade gave a low, one word command of "whoa," and the mare sank her hind legs down beneath her and slid to an immediate stop. Her fine, thin ears twitched between Slade and them as they quietly entered the arena. Kai was enraptured by the pretty paint mare standing and languidly swishing her tail. She looked toward Kai, ears forward, her blue eyes large and alert. Gil grinned to himself. Yeah, these two were made for one another.

His gaze moved appreciatively and knowingly over the mare's conformation. Mustangs had Arabian blood in them already, and she was small, maybe 14.3 hands but for Kai's height and weight, the paint mare would be a good fit for her.

As Gil approached, he took Slade's gloved hand and shook it. "Nice to see you again. This is Kai Tiernan. She's looking for a nice mare we can purchase and ride over at the Triple H."

Slade nodded to Kai. "Miss Tiernan."

"Call me Kai," she said, gently laying her hand on the mare's sleek white-and-chestnut neck. "She's beautiful. Does she have a name?"

"Mariah," Slade said. He smiled a little. "She's five years old and my wife Jordana had her eye on her as an endurance horse." Slade came around, handing the longe line to Kai. Running his hand across her short back and well-muscled rump, he slid it down below the hock, asking the mare to lift her leg, which she did. "You see this scar here? Across her pastern? A year ago she got tangled in some barbed wire and damned if I know where she found it because we use only piping at the ranch. Anyway, she cut herself. The vet came out and stitched it up and said about a quarter inch of the tendon was cut into."

Kai leaned down, studying the old scar on the mare's fine leg. "But she wasn't favoring it now when you were longing her."

Slade gave her a pleased look and released the mare's leg. He straightened. "No, she's fine now. It's just that as an endurance horse, which is much different than what a ranch horse does, it could cause her lameness or other problems down the road."

Kai gazed up into the mare's curious blue eyes as she seemed to be listening to the conversation about her. "So you've had her for a year. Has anyone been riding her?"

"Yes, my wife uses her around here." He swept his hand toward the fifty acres that had two pastures with about ten Herefords apiece in them. "Mariah is as sound as a dollar."

Gil saw the desire in Kai's eyes. She had completely fallen in love with the pretty little horse. And the mare was nuzzling her cheek, smelling her, like two girls having a chat. "Kai brought her saddle. We'd like to get her saddled up and give her a test ride," Gil told Slade.

Slade nodded. "Of course. I have her snaffle bit hanging over there. And a blanket."

Kai smiled. "She's so beautiful, Mr. McPherson."

"Call me Slade. And, yes, she's a delicate little thing."

"Does she have any bad habits?"

"I don't have horses with bad habits. I train every

one of them myself. They're trained with firmness and love."

As if to verify that, Mariah nudged Slade's left upper arm.

Kai laughed. "She's smart."

"She's got Arabian blood in her, that's why," Slade said, patting the mare's neck fondly. "And she's sharp. Misses nothing. She's a quiet horse, but has a big heart and will do anything you want. Her sire is Thor, my sunbonnet stallion. She's got his heart. And she's got endurance to burn. She'll outlast every horse you have at your ranch."

Kai smiled and clucked to Mariah, leading her over to the bridle and bright red wool blanket. Gil walked on the other side of the mare.

"I'll get your saddle," he told her.

"Thanks," she called.

In no time, Kai had the bridle on the mare, who took it without a fuss. Slade stood back and would occasionally murmur something, giving her some bits of information as Kai took the dandy brush and quickly brushed the mare's back and withers down. One did not put a blanket on a dirty back of a horse. Brushing was a must because it would keep grit from digging into the horse's skin and rubbing it raw, thereby causing a saddle sore. She saw Gil give her a pleased look, admiration in his eyes for her knowledge of horses. It made her feel good.

After Kai placed the red blanket over Mariah's back, Gil lifted her Western saddle into place and gently placed it on her back. Kai gave him a silent look of thanks and quickly cinched up the saddle, making sure it was not too tight and, therefore, uncomfortable for Mariah.

"Take her around in the arena," Slade suggested, leaning against the fence, his arms across his massive chest. "We'll stay here and watch you two get acquainted."

Smiling, Kai nodded. She led the horse to the center of the arena, quietly placed the reins over the mare's head and mounted.

Gil had never seen Kai ride. She had swung her leg expertly over the quietly standing horse, and now her long legs wrapped around the barrel of the mare. She sat straight, her shoulders back as she squeezed the horse with her calves and urged it forward into a walk along the pipe fence. He liked the way Kai's hips moved back and forth in the ancient rhythm between horse and rider. The mare's ears were constantly moving back to listen and be aware of Kai on her back, and then moving forward, her blue gaze alert for what was out in front of them. The mare was dainty, with slender legs and small feet, much like Kai.

"They fit each other well," Slade told him.

"Yes," Gil said. For the next fifteen minutes, he watched Kai put the attentive mare through her paces at a walk, trot and canter. Not only that, he was surprised but pleased to see Kai knew how to ask a horse for a flying change of leads. When a horse moved in a circle one way, the inside leg was to take the lead to keep the horse balanced. Many horses wouldn't do it under saddle and had to be trained. It was obvious that Slade had trained the mare well because as she did figure eights in the arena, the mare would automatically shift front legs and take the correct lead.

Gil could feel his lower body stirring as he watched Kai take the mare into a canter. Most people didn't know how to ride a three-beat canter, but she sure as hell did. There was no daylight between her butt and that saddle as the horse kept a nice, rocking canter around the arena. He saw the delight in Kai's face. She was smiling and her cheeks were blooming with a flush that made him ache. If only he'd been free to do things differently in the past, but he hadn't been. Just seeing her smile, seeing her fluid body move in concert with the horse, was sensual as hell. Beautiful.

"They work well together," Slade noted.

"Yeah, like they were made for one another," Gil agreed. He watched Kai bring the mare down to a walk, lean forward and pet her enthusiastically, praising her. The mare liked it, snorting, curving her neck and prancing a little beneath Kai's low, excited voice.

"Arabians are sensitive," Slade said, gesturing toward Mariah, who was now dancing a little, showing her own brand of happiness with Kai. "They pick up on a rider's emotions in a heartbeat. I think she'll work well with Mariah because she's sensitive, too."

Gil nodded, his heart and memories in the past. With Kai. In her bed. Loving her, listening to her sweet cries of pleasure, feeling that sinuous body of hers creating a firestorm of need within his. Pulling himself back to the present, he asked, "What are you asking for this mare?"

"Three thousand. If she didn't have that tendon issue, I'd get five times that amount for her."

Gil nodded. Slade could have sold her as a brood-mare for a high price, but he was willing to sell Mariah as a working horse for Kai. Talon had given him a check for fifteen-hundred dollars. He knew the strict budget the Triple H was on. "It's a fair price."

"I was going to ask five thousand," Slade told him, giving him a glance. "That's a fine mare. Her legs are damn near perfect, plus, she could be a broodmare someday. She'd throw nice babies. I've spent a lot of time training her and she's push button to ride."

Gil wouldn't argue with Slade. He knew the time it took, the patience, the love, to make a good riding horse. "Three is fair. Can I give you a check for half of it and you take my credit card and run the rest?"

Slade nodded. "Sure. Let's go do business in my office."

CHAPTER SEVEN

KAI COULD BARELY contain herself on the way back to the Triple H. "Mariah is beautiful!" she bubbled, as she turned to Gil, who was driving. "She's so responsive. I love that in a horse!"

"She's a nice animal. Moves well," Gil agreed. He glanced over to see the joy shining in Kai's gray eyes. He'd only seen her happy like this once before, this kind of infectious display. With him. Those five lost days.

He'd never seen her this happy with Sam, although, to her credit, his best friend was closed up tighter than Fort Knox, unable to show much emotion to anyone at any time. Whatever Sam had been before training, his emotions got trained out of him along the way to becoming a Delta operator. Somehow, Gil had been able to span the bridge at both ends and put on his game face when he needed to but also be able to remove it. Many operators couldn't do that.

"I think we are going to get along just fine." Kai grinned over at him. "Now, I can hardly wait to go ride fence line with her."

Gil wished with all his heart that Kai would look at him like she was looking right now. "Well, for the moment, Talon needs you working on equipment, not riding fence line," he said.

"I know. And I will." Kai rubbed her hands together, excitement in her low voice. "But that doesn't mean that on weekends I have off I can't ride her around the property and get familiar with it. Maybe do a little fence repair along the way." And then she added, worried, "I mean, if you'll let me." He was, after all, her boss. And Kai didn't want to be overstepping her bounds with him.

Shrugging, Gil said, "This coming weekend, I was going to ride the southern leg of the property. Griff McPherson called me the other day to say that there were three thousand acres of grassland going up for sale next to the Triple H. He thought we might be interested in acquiring it. We need it if we're going to run cattle."

Nodding, Kai lost some of her ebullience. "Sure, I'd like to ride out and see it."

Gil heard the lack of enthusiasm in her voice, saw her eyes lose that gleam of happiness. Yeah, riding with him would be a real downer. He got it. "It could be a way to introduce you to the ranch," he said. More than anything, he wanted Kai with him, not against him. Gil knew he didn't deserve a second chance with her; nor did she look as if she was going to give him one anytime soon.

"Sure," Kai mumbled. "I haven't seen hardly any of it."

"No," Gil said, trying to sound lighter, "you've been stuck in the green barn since arriving here." Today was Thursday. "You think you'll get that tractor online pretty soon?"

"Count on it. I've got everything on my list to be

repaired. I plan to fire it up later today and see how the engine behaves."

"Good," he said. "Damned hard to have a ranch without a working tractor."

She smiled a little, looking out the window, appreciating the mighty Tetons that rose out of the floor of the valley, clothed in white snow at the tops of the peaks. "I loved using the tractor on our ranch. Every chance I got from the time I was twelve years old on, I wanted to drive it."

Gil heard the sadness in her voice. "What's the deal with your father? I don't understand why you didn't go straight home and work on your family's spread." Granted, his question was personal, but it ate at Gil wondering why. Something wasn't right and he'd felt it all along.

When he glanced over at Kai, he saw pain banked in her gray eyes, her whole body going still. Whatever her answer, it couldn't be a good one.

"I just never got along with my father."

"Why?" He held his breath for a moment because Gil knew this was very personal. Kai had never talked about her life before being in the Army. He should have been a helluva lot more sensitive toward Kai when they spent those days together. He was too busy using her as a place to hide, to heal, and it had been completely selfish and one-sided on his part. Regret flowed through him. Kai had been unselfish, giving, loving and she was perfect for him. To this day, she did not know he had coveted her when he first met her with Sam.

"My dad prefers sons to daughters," she admitted

quietly. "Steve, my older brother, is the apple of his eye, not me."

Gil scowled, slowing down as they hit the long hill that sloped down into Jackson Hole. "Why?"

Shrugging, Kai said, "He thinks all women are helpless. That all they're good for is being barefoot and pregnant."

Brows lifting, Gil muttered, "Yeah, ranchers tend to be ultraconservative about men and women's roles on a ranch, but not all of them. How did you take it?"

"I didn't." Kai grimaced. "My mom died when I was young. She was a brilliant woman, a high school principal. But she had a weak heart."

"I'm sorry," Gil said, meaning it, giving her a concerned glance. The hurt in Kai's eyes tore at him. "I didn't know." How had it affected Kai? To lose a parent at such a young age? Especially her mother. He wondered if her choice of careers, mechanics, had been molded by her father's needs at the ranch. Gil knew from his own ranching days with his parents struggling to make ends meet, everyone worked hard, long days. Just because Kai was a girl didn't mean her father didn't utilize whatever skills she had.

"It's not something I talk too much about," Kai admitted quietly, stealing a look over at Gil. He looked sad. For her?

"Did your father get over her death?"

"No. Not to this day. That was part of the problem. When Mom died, my dad just kind of curled up and died in front of our eyes. He couldn't cry. He couldn't… well, get out his grief, I guess. Steve was eleven and I was eight. I was hurting so much, so lost, that he became like a parent to me instead of my dad. Steve would hold me when I would cry. I couldn't cry in front of my father. He threatened to beat me with a belt if I did. I'd run off to the barn, climb up to the haymow area, hide and sob until my throat ached. Steve would always find me... He'd come and hold me, rock me, tell me it was going to be all right."

Gil felt anguish stir in his chest. He could picture Kai as a lost little girl of eight, hurting, wanting her mother. "I hope I meet Steve someday. He sounds like a good man."

"Oh," Kai murmured softly, smiling a little, "Steve and I are thicker than thieves. I love him so much. He grew up into such a good person, Gil. He does right by others, but he suffers so much under Dad."

"What do you mean?"

"Dad gave Steve the ranch in the will. Ever since Mom died, he turned angry, impatient, and he took it out on the two of us."

"What did your father do?" Gil asked, his voice grim. Some ranchers believed if you spared the rod, you spoiled the child. His gut tightened. He didn't want to think that Kai had been physically punished. His hands tightened around the steering wheel as they began the slow drive through busy Jackson Hole.

"Oh," Kai said wryly, "he picked up his belt to beat me one time because I talked back to him. Steve was there and put himself between me and Dad. He told him to beat him instead, that I was a girl, and it was wrong of him to hit me."

"I like your brother even more, now."

"Steve took the beating. My dad made me watch." She closed her eyes. "It was awful. He raised thick, red welts all over Steve's butt and legs. I cried."

"That son of a bitch."

Her eyes widened as she regarded Gil's low snarl. There was such a sense of protection radiating off him right now toward her, it was palpable. Kai swallowed against a tightening throat. "Well, it was the last time dad beat either of us. Steve stood there, bent over, gritting his teeth, his hands braced against his knees. He never cried out once. He just took it."

"What happened after that?" Gil demanded darkly, making the wide turn that would lead them into the south end of the town and out of the major traffic congestion.

"My dad just kind of shrank and went away. He… just went away, Gil. I don't know how else to say it. Being older now, I can look back on that time and realize what really happened. When I lost Sam, I died inside. I wanted to hide. I now realize that my dad loved my mom so much that it wounded him in a way I couldn't possibly understand as a child. And Steve couldn't, either.

"That first year after Sam was killed was hell on me. I was emotionally numb. I felt like I was caught in some kind of between-the-worlds feeling and I just wasn't fully present in either one of them." She sighed. "My dad had done the same thing. He was grieving. He didn't have anything else left over to give to us. It was all he could do to struggle day by day, to keep the ranch going."

"He did the best he could. At least he stopped taking it out on you and your brother." Gil's mouth curved downward. He'd been there when Sam was killed in that firefight. He'd been wounded himself, unable to be there to support Kai as much as he'd wanted to. And he'd been too much of a coward once he'd gotten out of the hospital and back on deployment in Afghanistan to go see her. He knew Kai was based at Bagram. But he was still hurting so much from the loss of Sam that he couldn't trust himself emotionally to be around her.

Just glancing over at Kai, the sadness in her expression, his heart wrenched in his chest. Gil knew he should have been there for her. Much later, he did visit her, but by then, she was over the worst of Sam's death. He had been an emotional coward.

"Dad ignored us from then on," Kai said. "I was such a sensitive little thing growing up. All I did was cry after Mom passed away. Poor Steve…" She smiled fondly, picturing her strong, tall, older brother who had gray eyes and black hair. "He never told me to stop crying. He knew intuitively when I was going to bawl my eyes out and he'd take me to the barn. We had a special place by that time, where he'd take me so I could sob and make all the noise I wanted and no one would hear us. He was so good that way… still is to this day."

"Is he married?"

"No. He should be," Kai said, "but he keeps telling me the right girl hasn't come along yet. He's so handsome, so good. He's the kind of man I've never met."

Gil flinched inwardly. He should have been more caring, more focused on Kai during those days, not trapped in his own pain, guilt and grief. "You deserve a man who can hold you when you want to cry," he said gruffly, his focus on the traffic. In truth, Gil didn't want to look over at Kai. He was afraid of what he'd see in her expression. The revulsion. The disgust.

"Steve keeps telling me not to give up hope," Kai admitted, staring down at her clasped hands. "I keep telling him I want a guy just like him. He's so kind, so sensitive and, yet, he's a man and does a man's work. I don't think there's another guy like him on this earth. Whoever he falls in love with is going to be the luckiest woman alive. I'm almost jealous."

"He's thirty-one now?"

"Yes, he is. I warned him time's slipping away. Part of it," she admitted, giving Gil a glance, "is that my father is ill. He got prostate cancer when Steve was twenty-five. The doctors are saying he doesn't have much longer." Her voice trailed off. "Steve and I think it's because dad could never let go of his grief over my mom's death. He never talks about any of it. Steve helped me get through it."

"Steve was able to cry?" Gil remembered how many times after making love to Kai, the sobs tore out of him whether he wanted them to or not. Having sex with her made him completely vulnerable. He'd always trusted Kai with himself and she did not disappoint him. Gil imagined she held him in her arms and rocked him just like Steve had once held her as a child and allowed her to cry out the loss within her soul. He sure as hell had given his soul to Kai. And she had been there for him, caring for him, whispering sweet words of comfort, her hand stroking across his hair, his shoulders, being present and a witness to his grief and loss of Rob.

Laughing a little, Kai said, "Oh, yes. I'd start bawling in his arms and pretty soon, he'd join me. By the time we got down with our cloudburst, our shirts were soaked with our tears. I never thought of Steve as being weak. I was glad he could cry. It helped me. It helped both of us to slowly heal from the loss of Mom."

Uncomfortable, Gil wanted to say more, wanted to pull the truck over and talk with Kai. Talk like they had when they were together. Nothing had been off-limits between them at that time. He could tell her anything and she'd absorbed it, no judgment, no censure. She'd just listened. "Was Steve a good listener?" he wondered.

"Yes. He is to this day."

"Do you stay in close touch with him?"

"I talk to him weekly. We can lean on one another and I trust him with my life."

Again, Gil felt his heart twinge with anguish. Kai had trusted him that way until he'd broken her trust. And her heart. He swallowed hard, his throat tightening. "I'm glad you have him in your life, Kai."

"Me, too," she said softly, leaning her head back, eyes closed. "I couldn't have gotten through Sam's death without him. Steve was there for me. He was there at Arlington Cemetery for Sam's funeral with me. I cried so hard and he stood there and just held me." Struggling, her words were strained. "I don't know what I'd do without Steve in my life. It's like he carries around a box of bandages and tissues, and whenever I get hurt, he's there for me." Her voice grew fond. "I told him he had to get tired of always taking care of me when a crisis hit, but he just laughed and said he wouldn't have it any other way."

Gil dragged in a slow, ragged breath. They were outside city limits now and on a four-lane road, heading down toward the Triple H. "I hope to meet him someday. Thank him."

"I'm trying to talk him into visiting, but with Dad ill and him having to keep the ranch going, I don't think it will be anytime soon."

"Maybe you can visit him?"

"I don't know… When I left the ranch at eighteen to join the Army, my dad disowned me. He said a girl had no right to join the military. That it was the wrong place for any woman. That a woman should get married, settle down and have children."

Wincing, Gil muttered, "Your dad is a real throwback to the nineteenth century."

"Ya think?"

He grinned a little, meeting her amused gaze for a moment. Kai's gray eyes were so large and shining with life in their depths. He wished he could see them grow stormy looking, because they became that way when he was making love to her. "How long does your dad have?"

"The doctors give him six months, but you know doctors. It's a guess. Dad is stubborn and he's strong in spirit. He's fighting the cancer, but it's still spreading."

"How are you taking all of this, Kai?" Because Gil could see the heartbreak ahead for her if she didn't get square with her father before he passed on.

"As well as I can. A part of me wants to drive over to see him. But we can't talk. He always gets upset with me. He yells. He accuses. I—I can't take that, Gil."

Gil nodded. "My dad," he began awkwardly, "was a tought man, too." He glanced over at her and saw surprise flare in her eyes. He had never spoken about his family, but something was forcing him to reach out to Kai, to try to help her, in his own obtuse way, get through what he knew was coming for her to deal with. "He was always hard on Rob and me. But he didn't believe in physical punishment if we screwed up." He saw Kai nod, understanding in her eyes. "My mother, Janet, was the other strength in our family. When Wayne, my father, had a heart attack at forty-nine, he nearly died."

"That should be no surprise," Kai said. "You black ops guys nearly all had some kind of near-death experiences. And it does change you. I know when Sam got wounded and nearly died a year after we were married, I saw a huge change in him."

"There is a change," Gil admitted in a gravelly voice. "And you're right, it does. Forever."

"Is your dad alive today?"

"No," he said hesitantly. Gil gave her a look of apology. "Rob died. And then I was called out on a long-term op over in Pakistan with my team. I was ordered deep undercover for what was supposed to be one year. It ended up being a three-year assignment. After that mission was completed, before I was coming back stateside, my father had a second heart attack. I had to fly home to be with my mother, to support her. My father never recovered fully from the first heart attack and the ranch was going down because he could no longer manage it and the wranglers he'd hired. When I got there, things were a mess. My father died a week after I returned home." He took a long breath and added, "I took a medical discharge from the Army because my mother needed me there to get the ranch back on its feet."

Kai stared at him, her lips parting. "Y-you were undercover for three years?"

He heard the disbelief, the sudden emotion in her voice, knowing Kai was calculating his suddenly being missing in action in her life following their five days together. "Yeah," he rasped. "It was impossible for me to contact anyone," he said, and held her widening gaze. "I'm sorry I couldn't contact you, Kai. I wanted to, but I couldn't. I'm more sorry than you'll ever know. And then, my father dying, our ranch teetering on the edge of bankruptcy...well, I had to go home. I had to save the ranch and help my mother. It took me time to get that ranch back on stable footing. My mother met a nearby rancher and they fell in love. I was able to leave the ranch in good hands with her." He saw the words hitting Kai like bombs raining down on her.

Gil hadn't meant to talk today about why he'd left her. When they talked, there had always been an ease between them. And it had magically happened just now. He saw the shock in Kai's expression, her lips parting, putting his unexpected absence in her life all together. Damn, he wished it had been someplace else other than in a truck when he had to drive and concentrate on the road ahead.

To hell with it.

Gil pulled the truck over on the berm and placed it in Park. He turned, elbow on the steering wheel, the other across the back of the seat as he held Kai's stunned look. "I didn't mean for all of this to come up right now," he said. "I was trying to find a way...a time when you weren't pissed off at me, Kai, to tell you why I never came back into your life. I tried once out in the barn last week, a day after you arrived at the ranch, and that didn't work. Until the deep undercover work our Delta team was ordered to undertake was completed, I could not break cover and make a call or send an email to anyone. We were in the Swat Valley of Pakistan, one of the worst places on earth, hunting down HVTs, high value targets. Because of our looks, the fact that we all spoke Pashto and Urdu, we could fit into the population. That mission was beyond top secret."

He saw tears gathering in her eyes, her lower lip trembling. "As much as I wanted to contact you, I couldn't." He opened his hand on the steering wheel. "Believe me, I wanted to, Kai. I didn't mean to leave you in the lurch, not knowing anything. But every man who was chosen for this mission was single. The Army didn't want anyone who was currently in a present relationship. They had no idea how long it would last and we didn't, either. They wanted men without attachment and who spoke the local languages." His voice lowered. "And one of those men was me..."

Gil gave her a searching look, a lump forming in his throat. "I'm sorry as hell to this day, Kai, that I walked out of your life and never returned to it. I wanted to, but too many things happened in between that were out of my control." Anguish filled his words. "I'm so damned sorry I hurt you like this. I never meant it to happen. I'd rather take a bullet than have done this to you."

Kai sat there, staring at him, shock rippling through her. She saw the raw, abject apology in Gil's weath-

ered face, the deep regret in his blue eyes, heard it in
the heaviness of his unsteady voice. "I was confused,
Gil," she began hoarsely. "I didn't understand why you
left me without even a note. Nothing…" Kai swallowed
hard.

How badly Gil wanted to reach out to her, touch
her hair, stroke her shoulder and give her some kind
of solace. "I got a call from the CIA, and I went outside the room where we were, to answer it while you
were still sleeping, Kai. They ordered me on a flight
out of Bagram an hour out, and they didn't allow me
to say anything to you. I wanted to—I argued with
them about it—but they ordered me to keep my mouth
shut. I'm sorry." Sorrier than she would ever know.

"Okay, what about later? When you came out of
Pakistan on that mission? Why couldn't you contact
me then? Why did you leave me hanging, Gil?"

He avoided her sharpened gaze, the emotion trembling in her voice. "Because by then, I knew how
much I'd probably hurt you and you'd never want to
see my face again. There wasn't anything I could do
or say to make it right between us, Kai. And there was
no way that you would forgive me for doing what I
did to you…"

"Jesus," Kai muttered, rubbing her face. She stared
at him. "So you just gave up on me? On us?"

The raw hurt in her voice made him wince outwardly. "I never meant to hurt you, Kai. You have
to believe that. I know it doesn't prove out, but you
understand Delta Force takes on these types of deep
undercover black ops."

"Yes," she muttered, "I know that." She stared at
him. "You just figured that whatever we had for those

five days was it? That there wasn't something more serious between us?" She choked, fighting back tears.

Giving a shake of his head, Gil said gruffly, "Try to look at it from my side, Kai. You were a widow for a year. I needed you… After Rob got killed, I was in shock. I know it's not an excuse for what I did, but I needed you. I needed…" His voice dissolved. Giving her a pleading look, he whispered, "I know what I did was wrong. I don't know how you had the strength, the care, to take me in when I showed up at your barracks at Bagram. I know you were still grieving the loss of Sam. I don't, to this day, know why I came to you. But I'm grateful for the love and care you gave to me when I was the most down in my life. Rob was like the other half of me. We got through the first eighteen years of our life by leaning on one another because our father was more tyrant than parent. We relied so heavily on one another and when he got killed, well, I fell apart." Gil stared at her, his voice charged with barely held feelings. "And I showed up and I asked for your help."

Bitterly, Kai looked at him. "And I gave you everything I had, Gil. Everything. I never asked for anything in return. I knew you were hurting. I knew what losing someone you loved was like two times over. It was easy for me to extend myself to you."

"I had no right to come to you like I did," Gil admitted heavily, holding her tearful gaze. "None." He saw her battling the need to cry, saw that backbone of hers, the internal strength that had always been there, that had drawn him to her from the beginning. Kai might cry, but damn, she'd held him like an oak in the greatest storm of his life after he'd lost Rob. She'd been steady, strong and constant, holding him, allowing him to weep out all the anguish and pain over losing his brother. Never once had Kai wavered. Gil saw the strength in her face. She was part strength, part delicate, but that didn't mean she was fragile. No, Kai was a beacon who drew him to this day. It was a secret that would go to his grave. Gil could only imagine what it would do to Kai if he spilled his torn heart out to her now. She'd been hurt too badly by him to ever think he could walk back into her life, to ask forgiveness and love him.

"I'm sorry, Kai. I know I apologized before, but you need to hear it again."

"Did you mean to walk away from me eventually, Gil?" she cried softly, searching his face.

Closing his eyes, Gil gripped the steering wheel until his knuckles whitened. God, he wanted to tell her the truth. But he knew she'd never believe him. And even if he spilled out how much he'd always loved her, she'd have assumed he was jealous of Sam for taking her away from him; that all he lusted after was her body, not her. Not her heart, which, God knew, was so large, nurturing and maternal. Kai had kept him together, knitted him back into coherency, after the grief overriding him in every possible way. He had not been able to cope with it alone, that much he knew deep in his gut. Gil never realized what grief could do to a person, never really understood it until Rob had suddenly been ripped out of his life, forever. And it was Kai's strength and her beautiful, giving body, as well. Gil had always felt a deep connection with Kai. It was sex, of course, but much more than that. Something…precious. Fragile. And he'd destroyed it.

His throat ached with tension as he slowly opened his eyes and stared at her, the silence thickening in the cab between them. "I was hurting so much, Kai— you were the only one I wanted to turn to. I needed you. I knew, somehow, you'd be strong, when I was weak." That was the truth. Gil couldn't stand to tell her a lie—that he'd used her, that she meant nothing to him. Because nothing could be further from the truth. God, he'd ravaged her life enough already. The torture he saw in her face, the tears brimming in her eyes as she angrily fought them back, hacked into his chest.

"Were you ever going to tell me the truth, Gil?" Kai waved her hand angrily around the truck cab. "Or was this a slip?"

"No, I was going to talk to you, Kai. I tried at the barn, but you weren't ready to talk with me. You deserved that much from me, at least. I was just trying to pick a time when things between us weren't like a war going on, is all. I hadn't meant to bring it up today, but it just happened…"

Rubbing her wrinkled brow, she whispered, "Just get me home, Gil. I—I can't discuss this anymore with you. It's just too much to take in…"

CHAPTER EIGHT

KAI TRIED TO focus on getting the tractor to work. Gil had dropped her off at the main ranch house. He looked miserable. She felt miserable. As she double-checked her work from one end of the John Deere to the other, her heart was in free fall.

She should have felt some relief that he'd been called on a top-secret black op. Kai understood what that meant: no communication between Gil and those he loved or who were in his life. When she was married to Sam, he sometimes went on deep undercover ops and she wouldn't hear from him for two or three months at a time. It had been a terrible stress, not knowing.

So why did her heart ache so much? Why did she feel sudden elevator-like sensations of joy crashing up against her grief? Was his explanation enough? That he honestly thought she would be angry and never want to see him again because he had disappeared out of her life? Kai knew there was no real connection other than those five blissful days with Gil. She'd never known he was personally interested in her before that. Not once. He had always been respectful of her, but had never given her an indication of anything more until that afternoon he appeared at her barrack's doorsteps. And he'd looked so devastated that it had made her automatically reach out to him. At that time, Kai had no idea where it would take them.

It just happened.

Moving the damp cloth across the seat of the tractor one more time, Kai stood still, feeling her way through what had happened. Okay, so she'd wanted Gil to kiss her that day he appeared at her barracks. She didn't know who was more surprised when she'd initiated that first kiss between them. Gil's suffering triggered her own grief where Sam was concerned. His ability to cry for Rob's death. It was so confusing. Gil was there, a fellow Delta operator, Sam's best friend. And when their kiss escalated, Kai suddenly found herself wanting Gil in every possible way. They were like two lost, hungry animals that had somehow run into each other by accident, and they couldn't resist one another. It was that powerful. That life-changing.

"God," Kai muttered, rubbing her brow where a headache was forming. Why had she lost her sense? She had never done anything like that in her life. She'd been utterly loyal to Sam. In her previous relationships, they were long-term and she'd never strayed to another man.

But Gil had walked into her life and turned it upside down. Moving the cloth slowly over the seat, she tried to think her way through the why of it. Had Gil been a replacement for Sam in that blinding moment? That she was missing Sam so much, the loss so great? A last goodbye to her warrior husband? Had Gil needed sex in order to get through the shock and grief of Rob being killed?

Kai knew that the pressures on the operators were

tremendous. She was no stranger to being around Delta guys. Those that were single were always looking for a woman to bed. And when Sam came off an op, he was more than hungry to have Kai in bed. As if...as if sex were some kind of mediator, a way to take the edge off his anxiety, the pressures and stresses of undercover work.

She just didn't know, because Sam was so closed up. No matter how many times Kai had tried to talk to him after they made passionate love, he couldn't get out of his self-imposed shell.

Kai dragged in a ragged breath, stuffing the cloth in her back pocket. She'd had no idea that Gil was unlike Sam. At least, in bed and afterward. He was able to talk, to share, to be emotionally honest in some ways. Some men never cried. Gil could cry. He had been incredibly tender with her and Kai felt like a goddess being worshipped by him. The look in Gil's eyes totaled her emotionally. As if...as if he were in love with her. At the time, Kai was so lost in Gil she wasn't thinking straight at all.

Her mouth compressed and she hauled herself up into the seat of the tractor. Had what she seen in Gil's eyes been love? Or just the way he was with any woman he bedded? Kai didn't know. She never got a chance to find out. Resting her hands on the black steering wheel of the tractor, Kai desperately tried to sort it all out. Gil had looked honest with her earlier in the truck. But she knew men could lie. And lie well. Somehow, her gut told her Gil wasn't lying to her at all.

If he'd come home and his father had had that second heart attack and died, she could understand him taking a hardship discharge to go home and help his family. He was the only son left. It was his responsibility to help his mother and the ranch.

Her fingers curved around the steering wheel. Had Gil ever thought of her after that? Even if he thought she might be angry, had he missed her? Today Kai hadn't seen in Gil's eyes the look from years ago, but, God, four years was a long time. And how did she know he wasn't in a current relationship? She'd never asked him.

Above all, the pain in her heart did not diminish, but at least, her anger was no longer as virulent. Kai reached for the key and turned it. The tractor's engine turned over and in moments fired up. She focused on it instead of her own miserable state. Kai saw movement out of the corner of her eye. It was Cass coming into the barn. He grinned and threw her a thumbs-up as the tractor purred to life.

The noise reverberated inside the barn. Kai smiled and raised her hand as Cass came around the front of the tractor. In the past three days, a service truck had come out and replaced the two huge tires in the rear and replaced the two small ones in the front. She had made the necessary part. Kai made a signal that she was going to drive the tractor out of the barn and Cass nodded, standing back, still giving her a proud smile.

It felt good to have at least one piece of equipment working. Kai released the brake and drove the tractor at a low speed out of the barn and down the sloping gravel ramp. It was late afternoon, the sky cloudy, as if it might rain later on. Kai saw Talon Holt on a big gray gelding come riding up from the pasture. She waved to him and brought the tractor to a stop on the flat, placing it in Park. The engine sounded good and it was galloping along, not missing a beat. She'd done the timing right and felt good about her skills.

As Talon rode up, she turned off the engine.

"Hey," he called from his horse, pulling it to a stop next to where she sat on the tractor, "that sounds awfully good." Giving the tractor a once-over, Talon nodded to her. "Nice work, Kai."

"Thanks," she said.

Cass walked up, putting his hand on the fender of the tractor. "She's got magic, Talon."

Kai saw the hope in Talon's eyes. She knew how much it meant to keep the equipment up and running. On the front of the tractor was a front-end loader as well as a posthole digger in the rear. "Everything works on it," she said. Talon leaned back, his hand on the rump of his gelding.

"Great." He looked over at Cass. "You can get to work tomorrow morning when you have time, and take that dirt and start putting it down by the pond."

"Can do, boss." Cass gave Kai a merry look. "Engine sounds like it's running real smooth. Nice work, Kai."

"Thanks, Cass." Kai patted the tractor. "It's a good, heavy-duty tractor."

"What's next?" Talon asked her, sitting up, standing in the stirrups for a moment before settling back down in the saddle.

"I think you wanted that horse trailer fixed next?"

"Yeah," Talon said, wiping his sweaty face with his gloved hand. "Before, I wanted the horse trailer first because we needed it to go pick up that horse you wanted from Slade. Then I changed my mind and decided we had to get that tractor running first."

Kai nodded. "Without a tractor? A ranch is pretty much DOA." She smiled. "I can wait a few days before picking up my new horse."

"Gil said she's a nice-looking mare. You happy with her?"

"I fell in love with Mariah. She's a gorgeous horse. Wait until you see her." She saw Talon smile a little. Buying a good ranch horse wasn't inexpensive. Talon could have bought a much cheaper horse, but it wouldn't have been as well trained, which could cause the rider problems. Kai liked that Talon did the right thing for the right reasons. "Thank you," she said, her voice lowering with sudden emotion. She saw Talon nod in her direction.

"You told Slade we'd pick her up in a few days?"

"Yes. I should be able to have the trailer ready in about two days if everything goes according to plan."

"Great," Talon said. He pointed to the gray, churning sky above them. "Let's put the tractor away in the barn."

"You got it," Kai said, turning the key. The tractor chugged to life. Talon backed his gray gelding out of the area and Cass moved aside to give her room to drive the tractor around and head for the barn. She felt no small amount of pride as she drove it up into the barn once more. This time, Kai put the tractor in another area, where it would be easy for Cass to reach and drive out the next morning.

THE EXCITEMENT AT dinner that night was infectious. Kai was getting praise from everyone at the table for the tractor working. It was almost like Christmas, and she felt good, felt like she'd finally proved she was of value to the ranching family. Sometimes, she'd catch Gil looking at her. This time, it didn't bother her as much. She saw an unknown emotion in his eyes and was unable to translate it. He was more relaxed than she'd ever seen him since coming to the Triple H. The tension in the lines of his face were no longer in evidence, either. Maybe getting this off his chest had helped him. She wasn't sure about the information for herself. It still left a gaping hole in her heart. Why?

"Guess who's coming to Sunday afternoon dinner?" Sandy asked everyone. She beamed. "Gus, Val and Griff are coming over. I invited them because we haven't seen them in a month."

"Yes," Cass said, looking at Kai, "you'll finally get to meet Miss Gus. She's a force of nature," he said, and chuckled. Everyone at the table nodded their heads in unison as they ate the chicken and dumplings that Cass had made for dinner.

"You'll like her," Cat assured Kai. "Gruff but fair. She's really a teddy bear in disguise, so don't let her scare you."

"I think," Gil said to no one in particular, "once they find out how good Kai is as a mechanic, they're going to try and steal her away from us."

Sandy frowned. "They wouldn't do that, Gil."

He shrugged and gave Kai a warm look. "Well," he hedged, "I think once Griff finds out, he'll more than likely get down on his knees and beg her to come over and tinker with their equipment on her days off."

Kai felt heat come to her cheeks. Gil's praise meant

more to her than anyone else's and she didn't know why. "How do you feel about that, Sandy?"

"Good mechanics are hard to find," she agreed. "And when word gets around in the valley how good you are, I'm sure that on weekends, if you wanted, you could loan yourself out to other ranches. It's a great way to make some extra money."

"That sounds good," Kai said, "because I'm saving to buy a house."

Talon groaned. "Save a *lot*, then, because real estate prices on anything in this valley are sky-high. It took Cat seven years to save enough for a down payment on a home." He grinned at his wife. "But I got lucky and took her off the market before she did that."

Cat gave her husband a tender look. "Yes, you did, but you also gave me my house with a white picket fence, too."

Kai sighed. "This is a gorgeous house, Cat. You have to be happy with it."

"I am," Cat murmured, smiling at Talon. "But it's the guy I married that really makes everything work for me around here."

"You're really lucky," Kai said, meaning it. And she was happy for the newly married couple, love in their eyes for one another. And then, something jolted through Kai as she studied the look in Talon's eyes. It was the same look Gil had given her when he was with her. Her heartbeat tripled for a moment as the shock bolted through her. Did Gil *love* her? The thought was stunning and she felt herself skidding down a slippery slope, unsure what to think about it. Yet, that look in Talon's eyes was the same as what she'd seen in Gil's eyes earlier. How was that possible?

"Lucky?" Cat smiled a little, cutting into one of the huge dumplings on her plate. "I call it a lot of hard work. When I met Talon, I was drawn to him but I didn't want to like him. Or," she added wryly, casting a look at her husband, "fall in love with him. I had a lot of baggage and I was truly gun-shy of men at that point in my life."

Zeke whined from the living room, his eyes on Cat, his tongue hanging out, thumping his tail.

Everyone snickered at the table, all eyes going toward Talon.

"Zeke," he growled.

The dog instantly obeyed and lay down on his large, comfy dog bed.

Cat laughed. "When are you going to give into him, Talon?"

"Never," he groused, stabbing at a piece of chicken on his plate. "He's not a house dog. He's a combat assault dog."

"Maybe," Sandy said more gently, reaching over and touching her son's arm, "he wants to change, too. Look at you. You did. Didn't you?"

"I guess I have," Talon hesitantly admitted.

"Dogs can change," Cass added. "I just think you need to work with him daily, Talon. Get him more acclimated."

"Besides," Sandy said, excitement in her tone, "when we buy a golden retriever puppy, we want Zeke to like him, not tear him apart."

"I don't think Zeke would hurt a puppy," Talon defended. "He's just not used to having other dogs around him, is all."

Cass murmured, "Well, you'd better start getting

Zeke up to speed then, bro. Because I think Sandy is serious about buying a puppy sooner, not later."

Talon gave his mother a look of consternation. "Really, Mom?"

"Well," she hedged, "I get lonely in here during the day." She gave Cass a fond look. "And you really need Cass working, not babysitting me."

"It's not babysitting you, Sandy," Cass corrected gently. "I enjoy your company."

Sandy colored a little. "Well," she said, paying attention to her plate, working to clean it up, "I know how much Talon needs you as a wrangler. If I had a puppy, she could keep me company. I'd have someone around while all of you are out working."

Kai saw Talon grimace, keeping his head down, eating. "Talon? Would it take a lot of time to get Zeke used to being more of a house dog?"

"Yeah," he muttered, "it would."

"There's a golden retriever breeder in Jackson Hole," Sandy said hopefully, giving her son a pleading look. "There's a new set of puppies that are almost six weeks old and the woman, Judy, told me there's a runt in the litter, a little female. She said she'd sell her at a good price because she's the runt. I thought Cass might drive me over there next week sometime and I could look at her."

Kai saw Talon realize he wasn't going to say no to his mother. She saw the frustration in his eyes and also the wish to make his mother happy, too. But it was time that was causing Talon's knee-jerk reaction. "Could I help retrain Zeke? I mean, I don't know about how to handle an assault dog, but could Zeke come and be with me in the barn while I work on equipment? Kinda get him used to being around me and the stuff we do? Would that help?"

Talon gave her a grateful look. "Yes, that's exactly what Zeke needs. He needs to be socialized in the different ranch settings. If we put his dog bed out there, he could stay with you. You know the commands for him and he'd obey you."

"I'd make sure he had a big bowl of water," Kai promised. She smiled over at Zeke, whose black ears were up, listening intently to the conversation in the dining room. It was as if he knew they were talking about him.

"Would you?" Talon asked, relief in his voice. "Because right now, I'm out on the fence line. We got so many posts that are rotting that need to be replaced. With the tractor online now, Cass could come and help me by driving it around and we could start setting a lot of them. I can't have Zeke with us because he's not used to working around the machinery. And if you could sort of babysit him, that would be a lot of help."

Kai shrugged. "Sure, I'd love to. I love animals and I think he's so beautiful." She saw the worry in Talon's eyes dissolve. "He won't be in the way. And I can get him used to the equipment, walk him around it, and he can stay with me while I'm repairing something. Get used to the different sounds, sights and smells."

"That's perfect," Cat said, smiling at Kai. "Are you sure you don't mind?"

"No, because it gets kinda lonely out there working by myself," Kai admitted. "I'm used to working around a team of men and women, so having Zeke with me would be nice. I can talk to him." She smiled.

"Wonderful," Sandy said, giving Kai a look of

thanks. She turned to her son. "Talon? Then are you all right with Cass taking me to look at this little puppy next week?"

"Sure, Mom," he said. "Cass can arrange it."

"I'm not certain of the price," Sandy hedged, giving Cass and Talon a worried look. "She said most puppies are a thousand dollars or more."

Kai saw the worry in Sandy's eyes. She glanced apprehensively over at Cass.

"Listen," Cass soothed, placing his hand on Sandy's arm for a moment, "we'll find the funds." He grinned slightly over at Talon. "I always build a little rainy-day money into the accounting books, anyway. I don't think you need to worry about that. Okay?"

Kai saw the gentle look Cass gave to Sandy. She saw the woman's eyes grow moist. If anyone hadn't realized how important it was to Sandy to have a puppy, they did now. The whole table grew quiet. Gil was exchanging looks with Talon and Cass. Cat was wiping her eyes. Kai felt her throat tighten.

Zeke whined.

Talon rolled his eyes. "That dog, I swear, understands every word we're saying."

The table broke into hearty laughter.

Kai happened to glance to her right, where Gil sat at the other end of the table. He was looking at her. His eyes were warm with unknown emotions and it sent heat tunneling through her. She'd seen that look before, and this time it shook her. There was pride in his look but, also, a tenderness that made her heart swell with need—for him.

Quickly looking away, Kai was confused. Her body wasn't, that was for sure. She felt a gnawing ache in her lower body. Disconcerted, Kai tried to ignore it and him. But it was impossible. Gil's presence at the table was like sunlight to her, lifting her, making her want things she couldn't have.

Cass gave Sandy a look of praise. "Hey, you get my world-famous bread pudding dripping with warm caramel sauce for dessert. You cleaned up your plate."

Sandy smiled, her whole face suffused with pink. "Well, if I'm going to get stronger and I have a puppy who will want to run around with me, I need to eat."

Kai smiled to herself. Cass had a way with Sandy and the woman was gaining weight. Now, if she got her puppy that would make her want to live even more, to do the things that she used to do. Kai's heart moved with so many emotions for the woman who was battling to live. She saw Cass rise, take Sandy's plate and give her a smile that told her a lot. She wondered if Sandy was falling in love with Cass, because the ease between them was so real and obvious to everyone at the table.

There was a lot of love at this table, Kai realized. It was clear Talon worshipped Cat. And vice versa. They were a strong team who worked together and worked off each other's strengths not their weaknesses.

As Kai got up and helped Cass clear the table and dish up the dessert, she wondered if Sandy realized the man really did love her. It was in his eyes for all to see. And the way he touched her sometimes sent an ache through Kai. She remembered that kind of loving touch. And she wanted to feel it again. But it hadn't been Sam who had touched her like that. It had been Gil. He had been able to show her, without any hesitation, how much he cared for her. Kai didn't want to use the word *love*. It wasn't possible to fall in love in five days, was it?

And it couldn't be love because Gil had never returned to her. As she brought over the bread pudding that Cass had drizzled with warm caramel sauce, her mind was on Gil. On herself. And that chasm still stood between them. Cass had made Sandy a smaller dessert, wanting her to eat all, not part, of it. The other slices were huge in comparison, but the rest of them were out working from daylight to dusk.

When she served Sandy, the woman smiled her thanks. Giving Cat hers, she grinned. And when she gave the third plate to Gil, the serving was twice the size of Cat's dessert.

"Thanks," he murmured, looking up at her.

Kai's heart twisted. His blue eyes were banked with that same warmth and it made her feel so damn good. It made her feel wanted. By him.

Quickly leaving the table, she went back into the kitchen to bring over the rest of the desserts for them. Shaken by the low, smoky timber of his voice, her body was taking off on its own even though her head warned her that too much from the past stood in their way. Kai couldn't place her heart before Gil again. There was no guarantee that he wouldn't walk off and leave her again. Granted, he'd had good reasons for disappearing from her life before. But the hurt, the loss, had totaled her.

"Oh," Sandy said, "this is delicious, Cass." She turned and looked up at him as he returned to the table and sat down at her elbow.

"Like it?"

"I love it!" Sandy said, eating it enthusiastically.

There were general mumblings of agreement and happy sounds from everyone else at the table, their mouths full.

Cass chuckled. "Well, you remember you told me that you like peach brandy, Sandy?"

"Yes."

"I put a little into the bread pudding. Figured it would give it a bit of oomph."

She radiated with pleasure. "That was so smart of you!" She reached out, gripping his hand next to his plate for a moment. "You're so thoughtful. And you're right, it gives the bread pudding a wonderful, zesty taste."

"Just don't get drunk on it," Cass teased, squeezing her fingers gently and then releasing them.

Kai smiled, enjoying the tasty dessert. The look in Sandy's eyes was clearly filled with love for Cass. Did she realize she was falling for him? Did he? Love was such a fickle thing, she thought as she ate the bread pudding. Sam had loved her and she had loved him. But she'd never seen in Sam's eyes the appreciation and genuine love that shone in Sandy's and Cass's eyes. Frowning, Kai began to wonder what kind of love she had shared with Sam. There were so many kinds she was discovering. She thought she knew what love was. But maybe she didn't.

It was clear Talon loved Cat and vice versa. It was so obvious and everyone could see it. And now she thought she saw that same emotion shared between Cass and Sandy. If anyone deserved happiness, it was Sandy. And she could see that Talon was not unaware of the relationship that seemed to be blossoming between the two of them. In fact, if she didn't misread

Talon's expression, he seemed relieved and grateful that his mother had a man in her life once again.

With Cass being here, Sandy was rallying daily, gaining weight and getting stronger. Love did that, Kai realized. She felt so happy to be here with this extended family. It was something she'd missed growing up. And it fed her soul in a way that she was starving to have filled. And here, at the Triple H, she'd found it. Kai never wanted to leave. She knew she was a good mechanic and she was already proving her worth to all of them. In some ways, it felt like a huge, happy family without drama and tension, which is what she and Steve had grown up with.

CHAPTER NINE

ZEKE WAS RIGHT at home with Kai the next morning. It was Saturday and the ranch was buzzing with everyone working.

After bringing out Zeke's dog bed and the bowl of water, Talon had given her some instructions and then left her with his dog. Further, Zeke had his favorite ball, a green rubber one, and she could throw it for him, much to his delight. When she needed a break, Zeke was a great excuse to get out of the barn and into the morning sunshine for fifteen minutes or so. The dog enjoyed it as much as she did. It was a win-win.

In the distance, she could see Talon and Gil starting to replace the many rotten fence posts in the nearest pasture to the ranch itself. Cass was driving the newly fixed tractor and using the posthole digger on the back to drill down into the dark, rich Wyoming soil to make a deep hole for the new, treated post. The three men were down to T-shirts and jeans, working hard. Kai knew how tough it was to pull out a post. All the rotted wood had to be dug out of it, the hole then redrilled with the drill rig on the back of the tractor. Then, gravel had to be shoveled at least a foot into the hole, known as a French drain, to help the water drain so it didn't destroy the timber as quickly.

Cat came riding up on a bay gelding, her chaps

on, her Stetson in place. "Hey," she called, pulling her horse up at the entrance to the barn. "How's Zeke doing?"

Wiping her hands on a damp rag, Kai came out from the back of the barn. She gave Zeke a hand signal to come with her. He instantly leaped to his feet, moving to her side, panting and happy, tail wagging.

"We're doing fine," she said, smiling and stopping at the edge of the barn. She patted Zeke's head. He sat down like the gentleman he was, watching Cat. "What are you up to this morning?"

"Oh, going to the south side of the property. I thought you might like to go with me?" She pointed toward the other barn. "You can ride Cass's horse, Shorty, if you want? Or are you at a stopping point with that trailer?"

"Actually," Kai said, "I'm almost done. Could Zeke come with us?"

"Sure," Cat said, running her fingers gently down her chestnut horse's neck. "Come on, it will do you good to get out. Zeke, too."

In no time, Kai had Shorty, who was a very tall sixteen-hand-high sorrel gelding, saddled. Zeke was beside himself, trotting along at her side, ears up and alert. Kai could see the look in the dog's eyes. He was happy. Given that Zeke was a dog used to a lot of heavy exercise, Kai knew he was glad to get out and stretch his legs. Talon would sometimes take him with him but not often. The work around the ranch wasn't always suited to a dog like Zeke.

The morning was clear and brisk, and the horses were prancing a little, anxious to stretch their legs, too. She and Cat rode side by side beyond the green barn and onto a trail between two fenced pastures. The land was rolling, heavy with rich green grass cattle would go crazy over. Yet, they had no cattle on the land yet. If they didn't get all the fences and posts fixed, cattle would easily push through them and run away.

Kai enjoyed the sway of Shorty beneath her. Zeke moved ahead, lunging and jumping playfully through the grass, snapping his jaws at the long strands. Soon, his entire chest was dripping wet from the dew clinging to the blades. He was one happy dog.

"So," Cat said, giving her a smile, "are you liking being here with us?"

"I am. I was thinking the other night at the dinner table that it felt so good. I didn't have that kind of experience at my dad's ranch, so this is really special for me."

Cat nodded. "I missed the closeness, the warmth we have in our home, too," she admitted. "And Sandy is where she needs to be. Losing this ranch to pay her medical bills, I think, did her more harm than good. I think losing this place broke her in a way cancer never would have."

Grimly, Kai said, "It shouldn't come to this, Cat. A person shouldn't have to sell their house, their soul, to pay those damned medical bills. It's just wrong."

"Don't get me started. I was here and met Sandy before she sold the ranch. I saw what it did to her."

"Good thing Cass is here now, though," Kai said. She saw Cat nod and smile.

"I was telling Talon last night when we were in bed that I think they're falling in love."

"I saw it, too," Kai said, sighing. "It's wonderful to see two people fall in love with one another."

Cat led them past the fences and down a sloping hill where the grass was knee-high. "I think Sandy's afraid."

"What do you mean?" Kai saw a fence down below them. It had to be the end of their ranch's property.

"Sandy married Gardner when she was eighteen. At twenty, she had Talon. And then he died of a sudden heart attack when Talon was ten. Sandy then met Brad Holt and they fell in love two years later. He was a wonderful stepfather to Talon." She frowned. "And then he died when Sandy was thirty-six, in a car accident. A year later, Sandy contracted breast cancer. I honestly believe the shock, loss and grief just hit her so hard."

"To be able to love twice in your life is really lucky," Kai said. "And I've seen a lot of people get ill a year or two after some horrible event occurs in their life."

"I'm a paramedic and I know I'm supposed to be objective about medicine, but our hearts and our emotions dictate how healthy we are or not."

"And then Sandy had to sell the ranch?"

Cat nodded, pulling her horse to a halt near the fence line. "Yes. And then I saw her really go downhill. She lost hope because she lost the family ranch. It was such a tough time for her. There's about fifty people, all women, in Jackson Hole, who gathered around Sandy to help her through all her stresses."

"You were one of them."

Cat smiled a little. "Yes. I used to go over to her apartment, when I got lunch from the fire department, and read to her. Her eyes were really bad at the time due to the chemo, and she loved reading but couldn't.

I took up that duty and I spent a lot of quality time with her."

"It's easy to see you two get along," Kai said. Zeke came up and sat down in front of her, his eyes dancing with light and joy. Kai gave him the signal to guard them. Instantly, Zeke leaped up and made a huge semicircle where they were standing, taking in half of the hill above them. Kai smiled, knowing the dog was happy to be doing what he did best.

Cat craned her neck, looking down the fence line. "I've always loved Sandy. I just didn't know that someday, I'd meet her son and fall in love with him. And now she's my mother-in-law. I love how life turns out, sometimes."

"Talon clearly loves you so much. I see it in his eyes when he looks at you," Kai said.

Cat turned in the saddle and studied her. "Do you see the way Gil stares at you?"

Swallowing, Kai gave her a startled look. "What are you talking about?"

"Gil really likes you." Cat dismounted and grinned over at her. "What? You missed it?"

Kai dismounted and held the reins of her horse and followed Cat long the fence line. At every post, Cat would push and pull on it to see if it was stable or rotting. About every third post was rotten and needed to be replaced. "I never saw it," she admitted, feeling a little panic.

"Talon saw it and so did Cass. They asked me if there was something special going on between the two of you." Cat pushed up the brim of her hat, bending down and studying the five strands of rusted barbed wire, tugging at one strand with her gloved hand. It broke instantly and dropped to the ground. Cat cursed softly and straightened.

Kai hesitated. She had no one to talk to and Cat was very easy to relate with. She was someone Kai trusted. "It's not that simple," she said, and she told Cat the whole story as they slowly walked the fence line for nearly half a mile. By the time the fence headed upward, back toward the ranch, Kai was feeling drained by sharing so much. She saw Cat listening closely, but she said little, just absorbing her words. Finally, they turned and headed up the hill, testing each post as they went.

"God," Cat said after Kai finished, "that had to be a huge shock to you when Gil left."

"It was. I had no clue what happened."

"Talon was a SEAL and he did a lot of undercover work like that, too. Not for years at a time, like Gil did. He said because of the type of missions he was on, it could last weeks, even months. And he couldn't email Sandy and let her know anything he was up to. It about killed him. He hated being out of touch with her when she was going through that first round of chemo and radiation for her breast cancer."

"I can't even imagine what Sandy went through. I'm sure she needed to hear from Talon," Kai said, walking through the long, tangled green grass. The horses would lean down, grab a bite and keep on walking. "With Gil and I? It about killed me when I never heard from him again. I thought the worst. I didn't know he'd been unexpectedly ordered undercover."

Cat gave her a sympathetic look. "Maybe both of

you were suffering so much that you and Gil needed one another. You'd lost Sam. He'd lost Rob."

"I thought about that," Kai admitted. "It's still so confusing to me. I mean, I'm not the kind of woman who just lets a man walk into her life like Gil did and then take me to bed. And it wasn't for one night. It was five days."

"Sometimes," Cat said, halting and studying Kai, "humans need one another. It isn't right or wrong. But when we're lonely and we're hurting, human connection is what helps heal us. Helps us move forward."

"Gil was devastated losing Rob," Kai admitted. "I never met Rob. But from time to time when Gil was with Sam, he'd proudly talk about his younger brother. It was clear he loved him a lot."

Cat put her hand on Kai's shoulder, looking deep into her eyes. "Do you think Gil loves you?"

Stunned, Kai stared up at the woman. "What? I mean…no, of course not! I was married to Sam. Gil was his best friend. And he was always respectful around me. He never… I mean… Gil never said anything—nor did he show me that kind of interest, Cat."

Quirking her lips, Cat said, "You met Gil when you met Sam, right?"

"Yes."

"Is it possible Gil fell in love with you at the same time, but he never said anything about it because you and Sam fell in love?"

Kai chewed on her lower lip, staring down at the grass for a moment. "I—I don't know, Cat. I honestly never thought about it in that way."

Cat rubbed her shoulder. "Then why would Gil

come to you when he needed someone so badly? He could have tied one on and gotten drunk. He could have had any woman he wanted at Bagram. Why did he come specifically to you?"

Helplessly, Kai whispered, "I don't know. I don't have an answer, Cat."

"Did you like Gil?"

"Well, sure. He was Sam's best friend and they were thick as thieves. They were like brothers."

"Talon has told me quite a bit about the brotherhood that black ops guys have. I don't think Gil would ever let you know how he felt toward you, because of his love and respect for Sam. He'd never encroach on Sam's territory with you. These guys have a very strong honor code of ethics among themselves. If an operator has a girlfriend or wife, the rest of them respect that relationship and they don't hit on that woman. Instead, they support her as a friend. And it remains a friendship at all times."

Rubbing her brow, Kai said, "Yes, all that's true." She searched Cat's face, holding her blue gaze. "Do you know if Gil had a significant other when you knew him in Bagram?"

Shrugging, Kai said, "No. Sam said he was a loner, that Gil one time told him that when the right woman came along for him, he'd know it. I mean, yeah, those guys had their pick of women for a night in bed. You know how they fall over themselves when they know the guy is black ops. The danger. The risk."

Chuckling, Cat said, "Yeah, Talon told me about the women who would swarm the SEALs at local bars in Coronado. That they wanted to bed them to brag that they'd done it."

Wrinkling her nose, Kai said, "That's not something I'd do. You wouldn't, either."

"No," Cat agreed with a slight smile. "Do you know if Gil was engaged or had someone special back home?"

"I have no idea."

"But he came to you when the chips were down, Kai."

"I was available. I was at Bagram, and so was he. I was convenient. Only I didn't figure all this out until afterward."

"I've only known Gil for three months, but he doesn't seem like that kind of man to me, Kai. He's got honor, his word is his bond and he's responsible."

Sadness and conflict moved through Kai. "Do you know if he's going with someone here in Jackson Hole?"

Cat walked slowly up the hill, testing the posts. "Not that I know of. Talon has never mentioned it to me. Gil is at the ranch most of the time unless he's forced into driving to town for stuff we need here at the ranch."

Zeke trotted over when Kai called him. He was panting, his pink tongue hanging out the side of his mouth. She pulled the green ball out of her coat pocket and he instantly focused on it. Kai threw it for him and the Belgian Malinois took off like a shot, bounding through the grass, charging after it. The dog snapped it up, lay down and started avidly chewing on it between his paws.

Cat came over and watched Zeke for a moment and

then turned her focus to Kai. "Given all that's happened between you, I can't imagine how tough it is for you to handle this situation, Kai. I mean, what are the odds of the two of you ever meeting up again?"

"I know," Kai muttered, shaking her head. "I'm still getting used to it."

"You didn't look uncomfortable at the dinner table."

"I hid it."

"Gil did, too, because I sure didn't have a clue. Neither did Talon."

"Good, because I love having dinner with all of you and I'm going to live my life even if Gil is here. I'll get along with him and I'll respect him because he's the foreman."

Cat started walking the fence line again. Kai walked with her horse, who was eagerly grabbing and munching grass by the mouthful. "You're a professional," Cat said, complimenting her. "And, hey," she said hopefully, "maybe you two will bury the hatchet and over time actually get to like one another again."

Kai nodded but said nothing. Zeke came running toward her with the green ball in his mouth. She ordered him to sit down and to give her the ball. Zeke did. She put the ball away and then ordered him to guard them. The dog then made a huge circle around them and remained alert. Cat had warned her that while riding fence line, moose and grizzly would often plow through it in search of food. The moose loved traversing from the forest service land, cutting through the ranch to get to Long Lake, which was part of the Bar H ranch. Kai was glad that Zeke was out there taking care of them.

"How ARE YOU and Zeke getting along?" Gil asked, coming into the barn. The noontime sun was overhead, the temperature in the low eighties.

Kai looked up from working on the horse trailer. Her heart sped up. She hadn't expected to see Gil today, thinking he was with Talon and Cass pulling rotten posts along the fence line once again. She was kneeling down by a tire she'd just put on. "Oh…fine." He stood tall, his face relaxed, but she could see the interest in his eyes. For her? Cat's discussion with her yesterday had shaken her up. Kai hadn't slept well. Motioning to the corner where Zeke lay on his bed, she added, "I think he's happy out here."

Gil sauntered over, looking around. He saw she'd removed both tires. "Let me help you," he said, picking up the second new tire.

Kai got up, moving away to give him room. He was a big man and she didn't want to be that close to him. Being near Gil made her ache to be even closer. She knew it wasn't his fault. "You don't have to do that. I can swap out tires."

He gave her a patient look, and one corner of his mouth lifted slightly as he pushed the tire onto the axle. "I know, but it's always nice to have a bit of help every now and again."

She pushed her dirty hands down the sides of her jeans. "Thanks…" Kai felt nervous, as if on new ground with Gil. The easiness of his smile softly touched her pounding heart, made her feel things she hadn't ever felt. And that confused her even more. What was it about Gil that he influenced her this way? This morning he was wearing a red bandanna around his neck, a white cowboy shirt and jeans. A pair of heavy-duty leather gloves hung out of one of his back pockets and he put them on. He carried a Buck knife on his black belt. Whether she wanted to or not, she watched him handle the tire easily.

His forearms were covered with a sprinkling of dark hair, the muscles moving and tightening as he got the tire anchored to the axle of the trailer.

"There," he said, pleased. Gil stood, brushing his gloves together.

"Thanks." She gestured to the other side. "The trailer's ready to go. I was wondering if we could pick Mariah up today sometime. Or I can go over and get her myself?" She could smell the sage soap on his flesh from the shower he'd taken this morning, along with his sweat. It was a fragrance to her and she felt herself stirring, and Kai groaned inwardly. The look in Gil's eyes was without rancor, unlike the other day. His mouth drew her. She remembered how powerful and crushing his kisses could be, sweeping her off into another realm. But she also remembered how tender his mouth became when teasing her sensitive skin behind her ear, the nape of her neck and... Kai dragged in a breath, forcing herself to hold his gaze.

"We're busy with posts and postholes until dark. If you want, you can go pick her up."

"Great, I will."

"Do you have a box stall ready for her yet?"

"No. Gotta do that first." She saw him study her and it made her breasts tighten beneath her black tee. Thankfully, she wore a sturdy cotton bra, because she felt her nipples responding to his look. The energy around Gil felt completely different from the tense discussion they'd had in the truck days earlier. Maybe he'd forgotten all about it. She hadn't. Kai felt as if Gil wanted to say something, but he didn't.

"I'll see you tonight at dinner," he said, turning and leaving.

Kai felt bathed in Gil's energy and it always lifted her, made her feel better. Hopeful, maybe. But there was nothing hopeful between them. Cat's words bothered the hell out of her. She knew the woman was wise beyond her years and had a very calm, settling influence on everyone. In a way, Gil did that for her, too. And it mystified Kai. But it had always been that way from the time she'd met him so many years ago. Sam was hyper and intense. Gil was solid and low-key, so much more like Cat. The look in his blue eyes just now tore at her. Kai swore she could feel that Gil wanted to tell her what was in his heart. It was so real she could feel he was going to say something important.

Wiping her hands on a nearby cloth, Kai muttered to herself and got busy going to the red barn to choose a box stall for Mariah. In a way, she wished Gil was going with her. Whether she wanted to admit it or not, she wanted his quiet, calm company. Life was not easy.

SLADE MCPHERSON SHUT the trailer door on Mariah, who was standing quietly in the trailer. "Okay," he told Kai, "she's ready for her new home." He pulled out some papers from his back pocket, handing them to her. "Tell Gil the receipt is in there for Mariah. I'll be sending in her papers to the registry and you should get them in about six weeks. Any problems with this little mare, you call me, okay?"

Kai took them. "I will, Slade." She thrust out her gloved hand and shook his. "Thank you for everything. Mariah is just so beautiful. I can hardly wait to throw a leg over her."

Grinning, Slade tipped up his Stetson. "Tell Gil he made the right choice, will you? I think you and Mariah are well paired."

Getting into the cab of the truck, she watched Slade casually walk toward the large barn where he kept his prize endurance horses. She opened up the papers. Her eyes narrowed. The price for Mariah was marked as three thousand dollars. Stunned, Kai looked up, frowning. Talon had given Gil a check for fifteen hundred dollars, the most he could afford to buy her a horse. She pulled out a second set of papers, a credit card receipt. It was in Gil Hanford's name and it was for fifteen-hundred dollars. Down below, Slade had written "final deposit on Mariah."

Her heart started to pound as she realized what Gil had done. Slade had wanted three thousand for the mare. Swallowing, she felt tears burn in her eyes. The numbers on the credit card receipt blurred for a moment. Gil had used his own money to help buy this horse for her.

Why? Oh, God. Why?

Her heart trembled in her chest and so many escaping emotions of loss, love, grief and need swept through her. What had Gil done? And why? She wiped her tears off her cheeks, but more fell. Feeling Mariah moving around in the trailer, wanting to go, she quickly started up the truck and slowly pulled out of Slade's graveled driveway.

Kai couldn't let this go. She wondered if Gil was

going to hand Talon the receipt that said fifteen hundred dollars on it, making Talon think that was the cost of the mare. Was this another secret Gil was going to carry? How many secrets did the man have? Black ops men were known to carry so many of them. Was he going to say anything to her about this? She got a feeling Gil would never mention it to her.

Sniffing, Kai grabbed a tissue from the glove box as she drove out of the ranch driveway and onto an asphalt road. Wiping her nose, more tears fell. Why the hell was she crying? What were Gil's intentions by doing this? Was he trying to say he was sorry by helping get Mariah for her? Or was it out of guilt? Or a combination of both? Or something else?

Kai hated confusion more than anything else in her life. She always wanted clarity and transparency, not these damned black ops secrets.

She didn't know whether to be angry with him or hug him. Gil had seen how taken she'd been with Mariah. The mare was easily worth more than three thousand and Kai knew Slade was probably giving them a good deal; one struggling rancher to another. Her heart expanded with such a keening desire for Gil that it almost avalanched Kai. There was no way to deny any longer that she was attracted to him. She always had been, but when married to Sam, she'd thought nothing more of it. In fact, Kai thought that because Sam and Gil were like inseparable brothers, she would like Gil as much as she liked Sam. But her heart and mind never went beyond that point. Sam had been her life, her love.

Rubbing her cheek free of the last of the tears, Kai braked at the stop sign, looked both ways and then slowly pulled out onto the main highway that would take them into Jackson Hole. Somehow, Kai had to get Gil aside tonight after dinner and have a private, serious talk with him.

CHAPTER TEN

"CAN I TALK to you, Gil?" Kai tried to keep her voice neutral and low as everyone left the dinner table. He had taken a shower before dinner and she inhaled his clean scent. Tonight, he wore a red polo shirt and tan chinos, looking more like a civilian than a cowboy. It was the first time she'd seen him not in Western clothing. The polo shirt looked almost too small for him, accentuating the breadth of his powerful shoulders and massive chest. There was nothing small or weak about Gil. There never had been, but tonight her lower body tightened. Unhappy about her physical reaction to him, she saw his blue eyes narrow briefly on hers as she caught his attention.

"Sure. Where do you want to go?"

"The porch?" Because Kai knew that it was her night off from helping clear the table. That duty fell to Cat. And rarely did people go to the porch after a meal. Her stomach fluttered and she was more than nervous. In her pocket were the receipts that Slade had given her.

Gesturing, Gil said, "Sounds good. After you?"

Always the gentleman. Kai walked in front of him and she swore she could feel the heat of his gaze on her butt and legs. He had loved every part of her. In truth, he'd loved her so thoroughly, so well, that she'd felt guilty comparing Sam's skill with his. Gil had loved her until she couldn't remember her name. No man had ever taken her to the pleasure heights that he had. And he'd taken her with him. She wasn't second in his book when it came to loving someone. She self-corrected: Women called it *making love*. Men called it *sex*. That was so cold, clinical, and without any human feelings, intimacy or tenderness from her perspective to just call it *sex*.

Gil leaned ahead across her and pushed open the screen door for her.

Kai barely turned her head, nodding thanks to him. Outside, the sun was very low on the western horizon behind the ranch house. The sky had fluffy clouds here and there, growing darker in the East with the coming veil of night approaching within a couple of hours. Nervously, Kai motioned to the swing at one end of the porch. "Do you want to sit there?"

Gil said, "I helped build, paint and put it up. One of the first things I did when I got the job here."

"It looks strong and sturdy," she said, sounding inane. How would Gil react to those receipts? What would he say? Would he get angry at her like Sam did when she questioned him about something he didn't want to talk about? Kai was within her right to demand an explanation. Pure and simple. And she didn't want to embarrass Gil in front of anyone else. This was between them. The swing had light green cushions on the seats. Gil had made the swing with an arc of rays that reminded her of the sun on the back. It was beautiful and yet utilitarian. She moved her fingers down one of the thick chains, choosing one side of the large swing.

Gil took the other end, leaving room between them. The swing creaked in protest when he sat down.

"What do you want to talk about?" he asked, holding her gaze.

Kai pulled out the two receipts. "Slade McPherson gave these to me today when I went over to pick up Mariah. He said to give them to you and that's what I'm doing." Her cold, damp fingers touched his warm, dry ones as she transferred them to him.

"Oh," he murmured, "the receipt on Mariah. Thanks." He started to stuff them in his pocket.

"Aren't you going to check them out?" Kai demanded in a low voice, watching his face.

"No, I know what they are."

Was Gil trying to avoid talking about this? He acted as if nothing were wrong. Kai watched him stuff the receipts into his pocket.

Kai frowned. "I looked at them, Gil." She pinned him with her gaze. His face changed a little, as if surprised. Her voice faltered as she said, "You paid fifteen hundred dollars of your own money in order to buy Mariah for me." Her hands closed into small fists on her thighs. "I want to know why."

Gil took a deep breath and steadily held her gaze. "Because I know you liked the mare," he said gruffly, becoming tense. "I wish Slade hadn't given you those receipts."

"Well, he did." Kai forced her hands to relax and unfist. Right now, Gil looked as if he had been caught with his hand in the cookie jar. His cheeks had turned ruddy. And he was damned uncomfortable. "That mare cost twice as much as Talon was willing to pay," she said quietly, not wanting anyone to overhear their conversation. "She's a fine horse with excellent conformation and even at three grand, she's a steal. You and I know that." She pointed at the pocket that held the receipts. "I can't let you do this, Gil. That's a lot of money. I'll pay you back out of every check I get." She saw him suddenly go thunderstorm dark, his eyes flashing with anger as he sat up.

"You'll do no such thing," he growled. "I took care of it. It shouldn't matter to you how that horse got paid for."

Sitting straighter, lips tightening, Kai held his glare. He was really upset. She felt it, heard it and saw it. Why? "Is Talon going to pay you back, then?" she demanded, keeping her voice firm but low.

"No."

She stared at him, the silence brittle between them. "No? Well, what is this, then, Gil? I don't know what to think. How about you tell me why?"

Gil looked away for a moment, gathering his thoughts, taming his sudden emotional reaction to being found out. Kai had caught him red-handed. Dammit! Swinging his head toward hers, he said, "Because you needed a good horse. And you're right—Slade gave us a deal on that mare. He knows the Triple H is struggling. He did right by us."

"I could easily have gotten a decent enough horse that would have cost half that," Kai said, feeling suddenly emotional and her stomach tightening. Damn him! Gil wasn't going to tell her the truth. He was giving her words, not reasons. "You knew that, too."

Gil pushed his fingers through his short black hair. "You liked that mare. You two complement each other in height and weight. She'll be a good mount for you, Kai."

Her heart was beating hard now, the adrenaline pouring into her bloodstream. Kai felt she was in a battle of words with Gil. She could see the set quality to his mouth, that warrior side of him starting to raise its head. Both were breathing a little raggedly now.

Trying to keep from curving her hands into fists, she whispered angrily, "That's not the real reason, dammit!" She took a look toward the screen door halfway down the porch. Kai wanted no one walking in on their conversation. She saw Gil's brows draw down. And she saw emotions in his eyes. He had never hidden how he felt at any time he'd been around her when she was married to Sam. Or that time he came and asked her for help. And up until just now, he'd purposely kept his feelings hidden from her. But there they were: easy to read. She saw anger in his eyes. And frustration.

"Well?" she goaded. "Want to tell me the truth?"

"I always tell you the truth," Gil snapped roughly.

Snorting, Kai's voice quivered. "Sure you do! You left me after being with me for five days with no note, no explanation, no nothing. I realize you told me you were ordered out on an unexpected op, but you could have left something behind to let me know why you left without saying goodbye." Her voice rose. "So much for truth, right, Gil? Or maybe by just leaving without saying goodbye, that *was* your truth?" She felt his anger surge, but all he did was stare at her with that hard look he possessed. Her emotions were bleeding out of her and Kai was barely able to control them at this point.

"I told you why I had to leave you, Kai. Do you think I wanted to do it that way? Did you think I wanted to leave you?" He snapped his mouth shut and stood up, the swing rocking. Gil walked several feet away from her, his hands tense at his sides. His nostrils were flared, his chest rising and falling sharply as he turned on his heel, staring down at her. "I wanted to give you something to… Oh, hell, I don't know."

Her throat ached with tears as she stared up at Gil. He stood so tensely, his eyes flashing with frustration. "This makes no sense to me!" Kai cried out softly. Her mind spun with his blurted admission that he hadn't wanted to leave. The words had come out with such emotional force that she felt slammed by them. She saw the rawness, the grief and desire in his eyes for just a moment when he'd spoken those words, and then it disappeared. In its place, a game face she couldn't begin to interpret.

"Stop manipulating me!" Kai hissed, standing.

Gil's head snapped up. His eyes widened. "Is that what you think I'm doing?" He moved toward her, a foot separating them. "Do you think I'm deliberately trying to hurt you, Kai? Is that what you think?" Gil breathed roughly.

"I don't know what to think! What man doles out fifteen hundred dollars of his own money like this?" Her chin jutted out and she was damned if she was going to be intimidated by Gil. "Are you trying to buy me? Do you feel sorry for me? Guilty? Just why the hell did you do it?" She punched him in the chest with her index finger. "Tell me the damned truth for once!"

Gil backed off. He turned and walked to the railing, leaning his hips against it, his arms across his chest. "It was a chance for me to…say I was sorry for the way I left you, Kai," he admitted in a growl. "It didn't work out the way I wanted. I didn't know I was going to be called out of the blue for that op. I knew I'd hurt you and you were the last person on this earth I'd ever wanted to hurt." He looked to the left, trying to think through the haze of emotions whipping through him.

"So," Kai rattled, "this is your way of fixing our past? Give me a gift? Call it even. Is that it?"

He glared at her. "Dammit, Kai, you can be hardheaded sometimes."

"I don't want your sympathy, Gil. I will pay back every penny of that money you spent to buy Mariah. I will not have this standing between us. I just won't!" Then she choked, her voice breaking. Tears jammed into her eyes. Kai refused to cry. She would not cry in front of Gil Hanford!

"Son of a bitch!" he snarled, stalking down the porch, his shoulders hunched. He turned around, moving to where she stood. "I get that you're angry. You have every right to be, Kai. But you know how ops work. Once I'm committed, I'm incommunicado. I had no idea it was going to last so many damned years. I knew it would tear you up. Hell, I was torn up. All I could hope for when I got called out on that mission was that you would understand. I was hoping it wouldn't last as long as it did, and I could come back and explain. To apologize."

Kai wavered. The anguish in Gil's lowered voice vibrated through her, stirred her up even more until she wanted to burst into tears. But tears were not going to get this fixed between them. "Well, it didn't happen. Did it? And I will pay you back. You can't tell me not to." She saw his face suddenly lose that mask, saw the bleakness, the grief and regret in his eyes as he stared down at her.

"Look," Gil began wearily, shaking his head, "I did it to make you happy again, Kai. That was all. I saw what I'd done to you when you arrived here. I wanted to fix it. I remember... Hell... I remember how much you smiled and laughed before. And when you found out I was here, all I saw every day was woman burdened with grief and sadness." Gil's voice was hoarse with emotion. "And that's the God's truth— I just wanted to see you smile like you were smiling when you rode Mariah around in that ring." He straightened and seemed to struggle to get a hold of his escaping emotions. "Please, accept it as a gift to make you happy. That's the bottom line on why I put in the money to get Mariah for you. I swear it." Gil drilled a look into her widening eyes that were moist with tears.

"I think I've said enough," he groused, unable to stand her tears right now. "Good night."

Kai stood there, feeling as if she'd gone through a tornado. Only it wasn't fierce winds buffeting her. It was Gil's emotions rupturing her whole world. She heard the screen door close. The place was suddenly quiet. His presence, that sunlight of him, was gone. Slowly, Kai let her drawn-up shoulders sag. She stumbled to the swing and sat down, her hands pressed to her face, trying to sort out what had just happened.

GIL COULDN'T GO to sleep. He lay in his bed, naked, a sheet up to his waist, his hands behind his head, staring up at the darkened ceiling of his bedroom. Right across the hall was Kai's room. Aching to go in there and tell her how long he had loved her, had never stopped loving her, and trying to sort out the mess, needled the hell out of him. Gil knew it wasn't that easy. He'd messed up too much and had not gone to find Kai after returning home.

His mouth compressed as he stared into the darkness, the window open, and he could hear the crickets singing outside it. Maybe it was a stupid, knee-jerk decision to put his own money into the ranch till to buy Mariah for Kai. She interpreted his honest gesture as somehow manipulating her. Damn, he didn't manipulate people at all. Why couldn't she see his gesture for what it was? All he wanted to do was make her happy. To see her smile once more.

A ragged sigh eased between his lips. His heart hurt like a son of a bitch. From the first day Sam had introduced Kai to him, Gil had felt his heart tearing a little more every day. He'd been completely enamored with her. She was shy then, not as confident as she was now, and Sam was highly protective of her. But all operators were like that with their women. Still, Gil remembered how he'd felt hit hard in the chest by simply meeting Kai, shaking her hand, being respectful toward her.

And then, because they were based at Bagram, Sam would often invite Gil along when the two of them went to the chow hall. Gil never said much. Being drawn powerfully to Kai was a deep secret known only to him. He was truly happy for Sam, who had a lot of emotional issues he sat on, never releasing them. He ignored them. And Kai was so open, vulnerable, and able to share her emotions with Sam.

His friend had courted Kai for nearly a year before asking her to marry him. And Gil had been their best man at their wedding. It was a bittersweet moment for him. One look at Kai and Sam, and Gil couldn't go there. It was clear they loved each other. And he was honestly happy for both of them.

When Sam was out on an op, Gil would always drop by and take Kai to the chow hall if she had time. Delta men took care of their own. If a husband was away and a Delta team member was around, he'd go over to help the wife. He remembered every last damn one of their talks. She'd never realized the emotional beggar he was, lapping up her smiles, her laughter, the way her eyes danced with so much life. Kai fed him on every level, even though she never knew it. Gil was old enough, mature enough, to appreciate Kai and his position with her. He never once made a move toward her. Never spoke of his growing love for her that he couldn't stop from taking root in his heart.

Wiping his face, Gil sat up, the bed creaking beneath his weight. When his bare feet touched the coolness of the floor, it was grounding to him. He sat staring out the window, the curtain drawn back. He heard the click of the clock up on the mahogany antique dresser. Outside, he could see the blackness of the sky and the thousands of stars twinkling within its velvet embrace. He reran his words to Kai out on the porch. Jesus, every time he got around her, his emotions started unraveling. And he didn't think clearly when that happened.

Gil didn't want to go into operator mode with Kai.

That meant stuffing his emotional reactions to her down until only his sharp mental alertness remained. He'd never been able to do it with her. And to see how shattered she was, how shaken by the fact he'd paid for half her horse, jolted him.

First of all, he was pissed that Slade had given those damn receipts to Kai. Secondly, if he'd thought Slade was going to do it, he'd have picked up the phone and told the rancher to mail the receipts to him.

Gil hadn't wanted Kai to know what he'd done. His gesture of goodwill had backfired on him. Badly. And now, she was more wary, more distrusting of him than ever. *Dammit.*

He slowly stood and padded over to the window, searching the dark, silent heavens. Gil never expected to see Kai again. He thought he'd purged her from his heart. But how the hell did he know she'd show up here? And she looked so much more beautiful than he recalled. Mature. Graceful. And, God, how he wanted her. Gil was still reeling from the fact he saw Kai every day. He wanted to see her more often but knew his presence was rubbing her emotionally raw. Now he was beginning to understand how deeply he'd devastated Kai by not leaving any message behind.

He'd thought about it. Almost done it. But what the hell could he say to her? *I'm off on an op. I don't know how long I'll be gone. Oh, by the way, wait for me because I love you?*

Shaking his head, Gil knew that Kai was completely unaware of the love he held for her. And then, when he'd told her he needed her in the lounge of the barracks after Rob had been killed, she'd opened her arms to him. Gil hadn't expected that. He didn't know what he'd expected, really. But not that. Kai had held him strong and close to her, initiating the kiss with him that had blown him wide open. Gil didn't even realize he'd come to Kai's barracks, that was the depth of his shock, how emotionally dazed he was from Rob's death.

Running his hands over his face, Gil felt hamstrung. Kai's kiss had dismantled him. At first, it had shocked him, but then her mouth was so warm and tender against his that every fail-safe mechanism he'd ever put into place to respect her because she was Sam's woman, dissolved. He was hurting too much not to accept her charity. But it had turned into far more than that. By the time the kiss was finished, they were both heavily aroused, wanting sex with one another, and Gil had taken her to a conjugal unit on base. And they'd had five of the most powerful, beautiful days of Gil's life. No one had loved him like Kai had. Even now, he could feel the whisper of her lips against his nape, the shivers of fire radiating outward from wherever her lips had glided across his taut flesh.

To this day, Gil didn't know why it had happened. He knew what he'd gotten out of it. Kai had healed him to a point where he could focus on being an operator. He wasn't sure what she received out of their exchange. Afraid to ask Kai, Gil feared that she felt used and manipulated by him because he'd left without any explanation. God, why had he done that? Why hadn't he followed through and penned a note? *Just a note.* But it would have been a love sonnet to Kai, him spilling out the years of love he'd held for her while she was married to Sam. He wasn't sure she would accept his love. And although they'd shared great sex, no mention of that word ever came up in that time frame. Not once. So Gil was afraid to say he loved Kai.

He hadn't known how long he'd be gone. His CO was saying a year, more or less. He thought it would be a short op and he'd return to Bagram, find Kai and continue where they'd left off after apologizing for not leaving her a note of some kind. And he had planned on telling her everything at that time, how he'd always loved her.

But that didn't happen. He was gone for years. Undercover. Out of touch. Now Gil understood the full impact of how it had affected Kai. Of his not leaving something behind to thank Kai for who she was, for what she had done for him, and how grateful he was for her generosity of heart. He'd been so damned stupid. But he was messed up and not thinking clearly at all. Gil thought he'd be back sooner and he'd have that serious conversation with Kai. He'd worried how she felt about those five days so often when he was undercover and uncertain when he'd be home. Did she feel as if he had blindsided her? Taken advantage of her as a recent widow, one year out from losing her husband? Taking advantage of her grief? Was that why she was so upset and angry with him? Even her questions on the porch reflected her belief that he was using her.

Jesus, nothing was further from the truth. Gil wanted to love her, never use her. But how was Kai to separate all of this out if he wasn't being fully honest with her? Right now, Gil felt that if he told Kai the truth, she'd not believe him. She'd scoff at him. Hurt moved through him, deep and eviscerating, into his chest. He rubbed the area with his hand, scowling. How to undo the past? How to get Kai to realize he really did love her? It looked like a Gordian knot to Gil and he had no real plan on how to proceed to untie it.

Turning, he slowly padded to the bed and lay down, his arm across his eyes, in a quandary. His mind whirled with options, strategies and possible ways to reach Kai. She did not trust him. That was the real issue here. And Gil wasn't sure whether she'd loved him at all. Or if she had, it was dead by now, because he'd killed it with his unthinking actions. Trying to see himself through her eyes, he realized he'd really screwed up by telling her not to pay back the money he'd put out on Mariah. That took control away from Kai. Damn, he had gotten so tangled up in his own emotions, the fear of losing her, that he'd lost his usual logic and clarity.

The tears in Kai's eyes tore at him like nothing else ever would. He had been mentally asking her not to cry out there on the porch. She had come so close…so close. Because, Gil knew, he'd have swept Kai into his arms to hold her if she had started to cry. He couldn't stand to see a woman or child crying. It did terrible things inside him and he would lose his composure. All he wanted to do was absorb her pain, take it away from her and ease her years of burden and anguish.

They had cried together a number of times during that time together, clinging to each other, their sobs indistinguishable. It always happened after they had made love; as if the orgasms, the climax, exposed their raw human vulnerability. Never once had Gil felt apologetic for crying in Kai's arms. Each time, after they had wept, they held one another, the quiet descending around them, like healing balm. Then they would go to sleep. And then one or the other would wake up, and they would make hungry love all over again, unable to get enough. Each time better than the last. Each time his heart opening so damn wide he didn't know it was possible to love Kai as much as he did.

His heart throbbed with silent anguish. If he crowded Kai, confronted her, she'd retaliate. She was a strong woman with a backbone of steel. He knew that because when he'd broken over Rob's death, it was her who put him back together again. And Gil would be forever grateful for her compassion toward him. He still didn't know why she'd done it; he was too afraid to ask her. Right now, he needed to treat Kai gently, not lose his composure. Somehow, he was going to have to restrain himself, not keep losing it around her because he so desperately loved her. Every time he tried to stop the erosion between them, it caused the reverse.

Gil knew there was nothing fair in life. He'd blown his chance with Kai four years earlier. Now, it looked like the cosmos was giving him a second chance and he was handling it very poorly. Dragging his arm off from across his eyes, he stared up at the ceiling again, wishing it would speak and give him some good advice on how to get Kai back.

Not that he'd had her in the first place. He never had. The throbbing in his chest never went away. And to see Kai so upset and sad took another pound out of his anguished heart. It wasn't her fault. It was his.

CHAPTER ELEVEN

THE LATE JUNE sunlight was bright as Kai pulled the ranch truck into the Ace Trucking terminal. It was a huge, busy place, with uncounted numbers of eighteen-wheelers either arriving or leaving with their cargo from the long, U-shaped docking platform.

Kai knew she wasn't supposed to be here without someone from the ranch, but it was going to be a quick stop to pick up a few items from the repair shop. She parked in the employee area and hopped out of the truck.

The June weather was in the eighties and she relished the warmth, removing her sunglasses and pushing them up on her baseball cap. Kai quickly took the concrete steps to a door that read Office. She always checked with either the office assistant, Sue, or with Chuck Harper himself, if he was there. Kai felt it was only respectful to let them know she was there and to ask permission to walk through the building to reach the machine shop.

She pushed open the door, a bell tinkling to alert people inside that she'd come in. Sue wasn't at her desk. Chuck came around the corner and she said, "Hi, Mr. Harper."

"Chuck," he said, returning her smile. "Where's

your ranch guy today? Usually you stop in here with one of them in tow," he teased.

There was nothing to dislike about Harper as far as Kai was concerned. He'd always been nice to her. Today he was dressed in a pair of dark brown trousers, a white pressed shirt, the sleeves rolled up to his elbows. "Oh, this is just a quick stop. I just wanted your permission to go the machine shop and buy a few items."

Chuck nodded. "Sure, you know the way?"

"I do."

"You look pretty today, Kai." He gestured and said, "I like your hair in a set of braids."

Grinning, she said, "It keeps my hair out of the way." She saw warmth in his eyes and that simmering male interest in her. Gil had been adamant about not trusting the man, but he was easy on her eyes and he was always a gentleman around her.

"Do you ever go riding?" he asked.

"When I get the chance. Why?"

"Well, I was thinking of taking my trail horse up the slopes of one of the Tetons. There's a beautiful waterfall about halfway up, a real nice place for a picnic. Are you interested? I have a second horse, a nice gelding, you could ride."

She hesitated. Harper was tall, muscular, and he was a handsome man. From Gwen Garner, who owned the quilt store in town, Kai had found out that he was divorced with no children. "That sounds like fun. Pack a picnic lunch? I can bring my camera. I love taking landscape photos." She saw him give her a pleased look.

"Sounds perfect. Why don't I meet you here Saturday morning about nine o'clock at the terminal? We'll make a day of it. The trail we'll take is about five miles up into the mountains, pretty steep, but the horses will have no problems negotiating it. Want me to surprise you with a picnic?"

"Sure," Kai said, liking the idea of being surprised. She really thought Gil had gone overboard in telling her not to trust Harper. Lifting her hand, she said, "I gotta go. I'm on a short turnaround…"

He nodded. "Get going. See you Saturday."

KAI WAS PUTTING the finishing touches on the stock trailer when she saw Gil Hanford walk into the green barn. Since their confrontation two weeks ago, he'd pretty much stayed away from her. Her heart beat a little harder as he rounded the equipment she was working on. She saw wariness in his blue eyes. At least he wasn't wearing that damned game face she hated so much, the one that made him completely unreadable.

She was kneeling by the axle and stood up, wiping grease from her hands onto a cloth she held.

"How are you doing, Kai?" Gil halted near the stock trailer, putting his hand out on one of the horizontal metal rails. He hungrily absorbed her braids, thinking how girlish it made her look. But that wasn't a bad thing in his book, it was a good one.

"Great," she said, trying to sound even and unruffled. Gil always made her body take off, the memories downloaded, and it drove her crazy. She saw his face was set, but she didn't pick up any anger around him. Not that Gil was ever angry. Except when they argued. She quickly wiped her hands off and dug into her pocket. "Here," she said, stepping toward him, thrusting a wad of bills into his hand. "First payment I owe you for buying Mariah." She saw a muscle leap in his jaw, but his expression didn't change. Gil was trying as hard as she was to make this a pleasant exchange, not have it deteriorate.

"Fine," he said, tucking the money into his pocket. "I'll keep a ledger if you want. It will help you and me keep track."

"Yes, I'd like that. Thank you." Kai saw so much in his eyes. There was sadness, most of all. The urge to step forward, slide her arms around his shoulders, startled her. "What did you want?"

"Just came to see what kind of progress you had on the stock trailer, was all." He moved his chin toward the barn door opening. "Slade McPherson has a bull for sale and Talon wants to buy him. When this trailer is ready to go, we can pick him up."

"What kind of bull?"

"Hereford. Slade has some of the best breeding lines in the valley."

"Do we have a pasture with decent fencing to keep him there?" Kai wondered.

"That's what we've been working on for the last couple of weeks—the pasture for the bull. All the rotten posts have been replaced." He smiled a little. "You've had your head down into this equipment and haven't seen the progress we've made."

That was true. "Which pasture?"

"Talon divided off a hundred acres into one twenty-five acre parcel as a pasture for the bull. The other seventy-five acres will be for cows, once he purchases them."

Frowning, Kai muttered, "He'd better put up some serious fencing then. I've seen bulls plow through five strands of barbed wire to get to the cows like it was nothing."

Gil nodded. "Yes, I've discussed it with him. Talon's having Cass erect an inner electric fence with enough voltage to make even a bull think twice about trying it. He should have that finished by tomorrow."

"I've been missing a lot," Kai muttered, looking out of the barn fondly, wishing she could go saddle up Mariah, slap on a pair of chaps, leather gloves and ride fence.

"I know you have," Gil said. He cleared his throat. "Would you… Saturday? We could go riding down to those areas and I could show them to you?"

She saw the nervousness in his eyes, which was completely unlike Gil. A part of her did want to go with him. "Oh," she murmured. "I can't. I have something going on Saturday." Kai didn't want to tell him that it was going on a trail ride with Harper. He'd hit the proverbial ceiling and get angry. Not to mention overprotective.

"Oh…you do?" Gil searched her face. "Ranch business?"

"No, personal." That's all she was going to say, but judging by the look on Gil's face, he wanted to know a whole lot more.

"I see."

Shrugging, she said, "Maybe Sunday I'll saddle Mariah and take a trot down to the area. I'll just have to see what all is going on." She grabbed the greasy rag. "I've got to get back to work."

"Right. Okay, let us know when the stock trailer is ready to go."

Kai saw concern in Gil's face. She saw him wrestling with her answer. He was surprised. Curious. And maybe a tad jealous? The emotions in his expression were many and she didn't try to sort them out. Above all, Kai felt concern on his part. Why the hell did she feel so guilty about not telling him the truth? There was nothing between her and Harper. All she wanted was to go out and have some fun, maybe laugh a little and break the tension of being at the ranch all the time. Her heart twisted in her chest. As much as Kai tried to tell herself that Harper would lift her spirits, she knew that wasn't true. Gil did, though. If they could just get off this tightrope together.

KAI MET CHUCK HARPER right on time Saturday morning. He was standing by a big Dodge Ram truck that had a double horse trailer behind it. This time, he was dressed in Levi's, a black Stetson and a dark red cowboy shirt, sleeves rolled up. There was a pair of thin deerskin gloves tucked in his belt. Today, he truly looked like a cowboy. She noticed he wore snakeskin boots, which were very expensive. She smiled as she came up to the rear of the white horse trailer.

"Beautiful day for a ride, isn't it?" she said.

"Very," Chuck agreed. He smiled and placed his hand on the rump of a black stallion. "This is my Arabian stallion. Used to belong to Curt Downing before he was killed. He's an endurance champion and I'll be riding him today." He walked over to the other horse, a buckskin with a gold coat, black legs, mane and tail. "This is Dusty. He's a fine trail gelding and is well trained. Did you bring your own saddle?"

"I did," she said, pointing toward her truck.

"Let me get it for you," he said.

Kai opened her mouth to protest, but he was already striding in that direction. The code of the Old West was at work. Her mind automatically slid to Gil. He would have done the same thing. She couldn't explain why she was thinking of Gil right now. At the breakfast table, he was quiet as usual. Cass was the chatterbox, always inviting Sandy, Cat, her or Talon into an interesting conversation and enlightening topic. He was an extrovert, no question.

Kai had pretended not to see the worry, the question, in Gil's gaze when she'd excused herself from the table and gone to her room to pick up her red down vest and her saddlebags, which contained water and protein bars. She always rode with water and food. Plus, she'd tucked her cell phone into her front pocket. Saying goodbye to everyone, she'd told Cat she'd be back by five o'clock that afternoon.

Chuck placed her saddle carefully into the front area of the horse trailer. "Okay, ready for an adventure?" he asked, walking her to the passenger side of the truck.

"I am." She climbed in and he shut the door.

On the way through Jackson Hole, Chuck asked her a lot about where she was born, her family, and how she became a mechanic. Kai didn't mind giving him some information but certainly not in-depth. She barely knew him and was careful with strangers.

In no time, they were out of the town and climbing the long hill that would take them ten miles farther to the entrance to Grand Teton National Park.

Kai relaxed in the cab, feeling the warmth of the morning sun through the windshield. She had laid her head against the seat, her eyes partly closed. Maybe she'd dozed because when she heard the truck hit gravel, she sat up. Rubbing her eyes, she looked around.

"Where are we?"

"In the park." Chuck pointed to a turn up ahead. "We go to the left. That will take us to a big parking lot where we'll unload the horses. It's called Lupine Trail. Did you have a good nap?"

A little embarrassed, Kai said, "Yes, I did."

"They must be working you too hard at the Triple H, huh?"

Kai rubbed her eyes and appreciated the beauty of the meadow on their left and the evergreen-clothed slopes of the Tetons. Up above at ten thousand feet, the blue granite flanks were covered with snow. "We all work from dawn to dusk. I just haven't been getting good sleep at night, is all." She didn't say why. Gil's words kept rolling around in her head, coming up for view. He wanted to make her happy. Why? Out of guilt? Payment for their prior fling at Bagram? She wished he wasn't so obtuse sometimes and would simply tell her the truth.

"Well, today's trail ride ought to fill you with energy," he promised, parking the truck. "Let's go have some fun."

* * *

GIL WAS DAMNED moody when he saw Kai walk into
the living room at four-thirty that afternoon. All day,
he'd worried about her. She came in, smiling and telling everyone hello.

Cass was getting ready to put food on the trestle
table and nearly everyone was gathered in the living
room, chatting. It was Gil's turn to set the table tonight. Kai's hair was mussed and her eyes were sparkling. What had she been doing? Where had she gone?
Gil wanted to ask but knew where that would lead.
Besides, it was none of his business.

As Cass called everyone in, Gil spotted Kai hurrying from the bathroom, rubbing her hands dry on
her Levi's. Just the sweet sway of her hips in the
loose-fitting jeans made his lower body tighten. She
had unbraided her hair and pulled it back into a po-
nytail, making her look like the casually elegant
young woman that she was. Everyone took their allotted places, with Gil at one end and Sandy at the
other. Cass had made a crowd favorite, macaroni and
cheese. There was a huge salad and toasted French
bread slathered with butter and garlic.

Sandy beamed. "Guess what I did today, Kai."

Kai lifted her head in her direction while she
spooned the macaroni and cheese onto her plate.
"What?"

Sandy smiled broadly at Cass. "I took my first
horseback ride today! Cass saddled the horses and
off we went."

Grinning, Kai felt joy thrum through her. Sandy
looked so alive, so happy. "That's wonderful! Where
did you two go?"

"Oh," Cass deadpanned, "that's top secret." He gave Sandy a burning look that no one could misinterpret.

Chuckling, Kai said, "The fact you rode a horse is a huge achievement, Sandy. Congratulations. How are your legs feeling?"

"Oh, pretty rubbery and pretty darned sore. You know it takes about three days of riding to get your legs in condition."

Kai nodded. "I know what you mean." She had ridden for three hours with Chuck and the insides of her thighs were feeling tight, too. She saw the pleased look on Cass's face as he put the food on Sandy's plate. If Sandy were allowed to serve herself, she'd place one third that amount on it. Cass had figured that out real quick and he placed healthy dollops of everything on her plate, instead. Everyone knew she was expected to eat all of it. And, really, in the three weeks that Kai had been at the ranch, Sandy had probably gained another five pounds. Her face was starting to fill out so she didn't look so gaunt. Her eyes were sparkling with such happiness that Kai felt it burst through her chest.

"Hey," Cat piped up, pouring the vinaigrette on her salad, "guess who's coming to dinner again on Sunday? Miss Gus, Val, Griff and their baby girl, Sophia."

"Good," Gil said, giving Cass a dark look. "Maybe we'll get something like roast turkey or a big pot roast?"

Cass smiled. "Now, now, Gil, I know you prefer meat and potatoes, but I make well-rounded, healthy meals for everyone here."

"Yeah," Talon said, giving a sly grin to Gil. "You'd eat those two food sources every day if given the choice."

"I'd live off them just fine," Gil growled. "What's for dinner tomorrow night, Cass?"

"Actually, Miss Gus sent Griff over late morning with half a lamb. So, we'll have lamb, couscous, curry salad made of apples, raisins and cranberries."

"Thank God," Gil groused, "real meat."

Everyone chortled.

"You're such a growing boy," Cat taunted Gil.

Kai smiled, loving the teasing around the table. She felt so happy here, a part of a big, extended family of sorts. There was no fighting. No sniping. No one being a drama king or queen. Just hardworking, good, solid people. Her kind of people. She slipped Gil a look. His brows were down and he was giving the casserole a deadly look, as if it weren't enough to make him feel full no matter how much of it he ate.

"Hey," she said to him, "can I take you up on that ride down to the area where you guys have been working?"

"Sure," he said. "You can see our new bull."

Cass grunted. "Mean son of a—" He grimaced, watching his language because Sandy didn't like it used at the table. "Well, he's a mean mother." Cass threw a thumb toward Gil. "When we were offloading him from the stock trailer, he tried to hook a horn into Hanford there. Lucky for him, he moved faster than the bull did."

Kai sucked in a breath, fear stabbing through her. She stared at Gil. "Are you all right?" Even her heart was beating harder in her chest. She saw him nod.

"I'm fine. Cass blows stuff out of proportion," he grumbled, embarrassed by everyone looking worried. "It's a bull. That's what they do."

Kai reached out and touched his lower arm. Instantly, the muscles beneath his skin grew rigid. His head snapped up in her direction. She met his blue gaze. "*You* be careful. You take too many risks."

Cat said, "I second it." She looked around the table. "All we have at this table are operators. All they know how to do is take risks."

Sandy said, "I'm in total agreement." She shook her finger toward Gil. "And we aren't making too much of this. Slade warned you ahead of time that he was a mean bull. And Slade ought to know. He got gored by the bull's father a couple of years ago. Jordana, his wife, saved his hide."

Gil groaned. "Ladies," he pleaded, "we're all okay."

"Well," Sandy grumped at him, "Slade told you to watch him the first couple of days. He's a fence charger."

"I think he'll leave the fences alone," Cass said smugly. "We've got one-thousand-volt electric wire five feet away from the fence line."

Kai grimaced. "My dad had a Hereford bull we called Boulder. He went through electric *and* barbed wire fences without blinking an eye. No matter how high the voltage."

Sandy sighed. "I just think you boys should be keeping a close eye on him for a while. And be on your toes."

"Yes, ma'am," Gil said, smiling a little but being respectful.

"How close did you come to getting gored?" Kai asked him.

"I don't know," he said, shrugging it off.

"It tore his Levi's," Cass told her.

Gasping, Kai gave Gil a shocked look. "Seriously? He did?"

Gil gave Cass a deadly look. And then he turned his attention to Kai. "It's just a pair of Levi's."

"Are you bruised? Did his horn tear open your skin?"

"I'm *fine*," Gil grumbled, paying attention to his food.

Talon chuckled. "You can always tell an operator. So long as he can crawl, he's fine. Never mind he's had two legs shot out from under him. He'll tell you he's okay or fine."

That got a big laugh out of Cass and a grudging grin tugging at Gil's mouth.

Sandy said, "When Gil came in, Cass patched him up. I didn't get to look at it because they went into the bathroom."

Kai gave Cass a one-eyebrow-raised look. "Tell all, Cass. I'm *all* ears. Maybe I can squeeze the truth out of you because Hanford, here, is buttoned up."

Talon snickered and kept his head down, eating.

"Just one big bruise on the outside of Gil's thigh. About four inches long. No broken skin. Just a topical rash from the fabric is all."

"There," Gil said archly to her. "Do you feel better now? I told you I was fine."

Kai shook her head. "Men…"

Cat finished off her salad. "Yeah, operators. There's

never been a more closemouthed bunch than them."
She gave Talon a narrowed look, including him in
her statement.

"I'm eating," Talon said.

"You need to keep an eye on that bull," Sandy
warned all of them, her voice firm.

Kai agreed wholly with her. It blew her away that
Gil, Talon and Cass just shrugged it off. She knew it
wasn't dinner-table talk, but one of her father's wranglers had been working with a vet to vaccinate the
bulls on their ranch when a bull hooked him through
the chute with his horn and gutted him. She had only
been ten years old when it happened. Her brother,
Steve, had been there with her. She'd promptly thrown
up in reaction to seeing it. Luckily, the vet was there
and was trained as any medical physician and he'd
saved the wrangler's life.

The horror of that moment had never left Kai.
She'd run from the corral into the house to her room
and cried wildly. Her father never came to see if she
was all right. But Steve had. He was as shaken by the
accident as she was.

"We'll be watchful when we go check on the bull
tomorrow," he promised her.

Kai saw the concern in Gil's eyes and knew he was
worried for her. It should have been the other way
around. He'd already gotten a taste of the bull's lethal personality. "Okay," she murmured. "What time
do you want to go?"

"After breakfast?"

"Sure," she murmured, "that sounds good."

"I want to ride tomorrow," Sandy told Cass.

"Okay," he said. "After I put the leg of lamb in the oven, we'll take a short jaunt as far away from that bull as we can get. Fair enough?"

Sandy rolled her eyes. "Oh, I don't want to be near that beast! They're a ton of meat with horns. I've seen them do so much damage in the past."

Talon nodded. "My Dad, Gardner, got a horn in his butt. The bull lifted him off the ground with one head toss. When my dad landed, the bull gored him."

"Good place to get gored," Gil said, seriously.

"Guys," Sandy pleaded, "can we change the conversation?"

Both men winced, got guilty looks on their faces and an apologetic nod in her direction.

"Well, let's talk about Miss Gus coming over again," Cat said, excited. "She said she had some good news for us. The last time she said that, she'd bought the Triple H back and put it in Sandy and Talon's names."

"I wouldn't get my hopes that high," Talon intoned drily.

"Gus is like Christmas every day of the year," Sandy said softly, smiling. "She's a Mrs. Santa Claus. And she doesn't have to bring anything except herself to our home. She's a gift to all of us with her wisdom and experience. Last time she was here with Val's family, she brought us a huge five-pound box of chocolates. And you know how long that lasted, huh, guys?"

The men shot guilty looks toward Cat because they'd eaten the lion's share of the chocolates, leaving a lot less for the women of the ranch. Cat had chewed them out royally for that one. It was Talon who'd come the next day with a one-pound box of chocolates for Sandy, his wife and Kai, to make up for their greedy chocolate heist. All was forgiven, but Cat wasn't going to let them forget about it, either.

"Yes," Talon said, "well, we did give you ladies a box of chocolates to make up for us taking more than we should have from that five pounds Miss Gus had brought for all of us."

Cat eyed him, stared challengingly at Gil and then over at Cass. They all gave her weak smiles, chastened.

Talon tried to change the course of conversation, saying, "Miss Gus is eighty-five years old. I hope I'm as spry as she is when I hit that age."

Cat grinned. "I can just picture you at that age, Talon. You'll still be riding your horse."

"Well," Talon said, "Miss Gus was riding a horse until she broke her leg a few years ago, and she was past eighty. She's one tough ol' bird, and we all love her."

That brought an instant nod of agreement from everyone. Kai had met Gus when she and her family visited a couple of weeks earlier. Everyone always spoke highly of her.

"I just find it incredible," Kai told Sandy, "that she bought the Triple H back and gave it to you and Talon. I mean, that's a *lot* of money."

"She has a lot of money," Talon said. "But that doesn't define Gus. She's got a heart as big as Wyoming and she likes doing good deeds for others who deserve it. Plus—" he looked fondly down the table at his mother, who was cleaning up her plate "—she and my mom go back decades because their two ranches butt up against each other. She's a good neighbor," he said solemnly.

"I can hardly wait to see her again," Kai said, feeling exhilarated. She loved to be around people of action, and Miss Gus sounded like she'd invented the word.

CHAPTER TWELVE

KAI WATCHED GIL rise from the table. Although he tried to hide it, he was stiff and his right leg was sore where the bull almost gored him. She sat there thinking about the possibilities if he had been gored. Unable to wipe out her childhood memory of her father's wrangler being gutted by an angry bull, she watched as he moved with a slight limp out into the hall. She heard the screen door open and close. Worried, she excused herself and left the table.

Unsure, Kai hesitated at the screen door. The evening sky was cloudy and it looked as if it might rain. Off in the distance, she could hear thunder rolling somewhere north of them. The air smelled of rain coming their way. Stepping out, she looked to the left and saw Gil slowly sitting down on the swing. Now she saw the pain in his face since he wasn't inside where he had to hide it. She remembered that afternoon he'd appeared in her barracks, so devastated and vulnerable. He had been shaken, honest and didn't avoid how he felt.

"Could you use some company?" she asked, hesitating halfway to the swing. She saw Gil's head come up, as if he weren't aware of her at all. The pain was probably so great he was focused on that.

"Sure. Come sit down."

She gave him a worried look as she drew near. Kai could see the Levi's material around his outer right thigh was pulled taut from the swelling of the leg. Sitting down a foot away from him, her lips thinned. "That looks pretty bad, Gil. Are you sure you shouldn't have it seen by a doctor?" The urge to reach out, touch him, nearly drove her to do it. Every time she got near Gil, she seemed to stop thinking and all she wanted to do was touch him, kiss him, hold him and have him hold her. The need never went away in her.

He grimaced and slowly moved the injured leg and stretched it out. That relieved some of the pressure and pain. "Cass is the best. He said I had a hematoma. That's not a regular bruise. The bull's horn broke a more major vein in my leg somewhere and it's swollen because of the amount of blood gathering in there. It has nowhere to go but outward." Gil gestured to the huge knot of swelling.

Without thinking, Kai lightly grazed the area and it sent pleasant shocks up through her fingers. She needed to touch Gil. "This looks really bad." Kai felt him tense when she unexpectedly touched him. Looking up, she could see dullness in his blue eyes. She knew that look. She'd seen it the first day he'd come to see her. Pain. A lot of it. Only then, it was emotional pain. This was physical pain. But she also saw something else and recognized it instantly: that look of a hunter wanting her in every possible way.

"I need to get some ice on it and reduce some of the swelling," he muttered, putting his hand across the back of the swing. "Stop being a worrywart."

She smiled a little unsurely, meeting his gaze. She

felt so tentative with Gil. He'd reacted powerfully to her grazing fingertips. Kai hadn't meant to do it, but she felt they were like two magnets being drawn together no matter what she tried to do to fight the attraction. Her heart stretched toward him. She could almost feel it. Right now, Gil was vulnerable with her. He didn't try to put his game face on as he had during dinner. It made the need for him that much deeper, haunting her, the past overlaying the present.

"Can you get hurt by a hematoma?" she wondered, forcing her hands to stay on her knees.

"Yes, I suppose you can," he groused. "You worry too much, Kai. I'll be fine."

Wryly she gave him a glance. "Said the operator to the world around him. You Delta boys always downplayed your physical injuries to everyone."

Shrugging, he said, "All true. But I'll be fine, so wipe that frown off your brow." He reached out, moving his thumb gently across her forehead.

For a second, Kai froze. His touch, the roughened quality of his thumb smoothing her brow, sent shock waves of pleasure and hunger down through her. She swallowed convulsively, aching to kiss him. She held his blue gaze, feeling awash in arousal as he removed his thumb. Her skin skittered with licks of fire spreading outward, making Kai want to touch Gil much more. All over.

In that moment, something fell into place for Kai. Whatever the connection between them, it had never died. And now, so many years later, it was burning bright and strongly between them once more. Her heart was wide-open to Gil, crying out for his caress.

How badly Kai wanted to kiss this man. Her lips tingled in memory of his mouth upon hers.

"Can I get you a bag of ice to put on it?" she wondered, feeling too drawn to Gil right now. She was confused by the attraction between them. Nothing was ever clear in their relationship.

"No, don't bother." Gil's face softened a little. "You always were a little mother to everyone, Kai. Really, I'll be fine."

Kai stood. "No, I'm getting some. I'll be right back."

GIL STARTED TO protest but swallowed it because he saw the set of Kai's jaw. He knew what that meant. God, his leg was throbbing, but so was his erection that pressed insistently against his zipper. The woman inflamed him and Gil couldn't do anything about it. He wanted to do something. He wanted to take Kai to bed and love the hell out of her. It seemed like an impossible dream to Gil. Yet, tonight, he could tell she was genuinely concerned about him. Where had that come from? Had they somehow buried the hatchet between them? Was she trying to start all over with him? Leave the past where it was because it could never be changed?

Cursing softly, he hadn't meant to reach out and graze Kai's skin. But dammit, when her fingers had barely brushed his swollen leg, an ache ten times more powerful entered his heart and then tangled his lower body. Gil hadn't ever expected Kai to show him this kind of care. Her anger and hurt from the past had fueled their relationship up until now. His brows drew downward as he tried to sort out why. Had his brush with the bull gone beyond her anger toward him? Was he seeing a deeper part of her? Dragging in a ragged breath, Gil sat back, staring sightlessly off into the distance, feeling his way around that possibility. Kai's reaction to his injury was real.

He didn't have time to think any more about it because Kai returned with a gallon-sized ziplock plastic bag filled with ice cubes. She sat down near him and he could smell her womanly scent along with the fragrance of the orange-scented shampoo she'd probably used on her auburn hair. Gil saw real concern in her eyes.

"Can I gently place this on your leg?" she asked.

Gil couldn't handle Kai touching him again. His erection would kill him if she did. Taking it out of her hands, he said, "I'll do it. Thanks." He settled it against his leg, holding it in place. Kai was worrying her lower lip. She always did that when she was troubled about something. Sam used to share her quirks with him when they were out in the field. Gil got to know a lot about her without seeing it for himself. Her hands were restless on her lap, as if she wanted to do something more. "Feels good. The ice, I mean."

She nodded. "Good."

Cass stepped out on the porch and sauntered toward them. "Hey, how's that leg doing, Gil? I just had nurse Kai in the kitchen hunting up some ice."

"It's fine," he grumbled, scowling.

Kai snorted. "Come here, Cass. Come and see for yourself. It looks awful. It's so swollen." She got up and gestured for him to sit down and examine Gil's thigh.

Gil rolled his eyes.

Cass gave him a sour grin and sat down, removing the ice, moving his hand lightly over the area.

"Well?" Kai asked, looking over his shoulder. "Is something wrong? Shouldn't Gil be going to the hospital?"

Gil was about to speak, barely getting his mouth open.

"Yeah, this doesn't look good, Gil. It's pretty swollen." Cass looked up at him. "Let me call Jordana. She's the ER doctor at the hospital. I don't know if she's on duty over there or not, so I'll try and get her at home."

"I'll be fine," Gil said, not wanting to go to a damned ER.

Cass stood up, placed the ice bag on his leg and pulled his cell from his pocket. He gestured for Kai to sit down with Gil. "Keep that bag of ice on it," he told her.

"Jordana is Slade McPherson's wife," Gil said. He put his hand over the ice bag, making it clear he didn't want her touching him. His jeans were stretched and his erection was throbbing right along with his leg, but for very different reasons.

"Yes," Kai said, "everyone says she's wonderful." Anxiously, she tilted her head, listening to Cass talk to Jordana. He talked in medicalese she couldn't understand.

Cass turned and held the phone away from his ear. "Jordana wants to know if you're experiencing any numbness above or below that swelling," Cass said.

"Yeah, there's numbness," he muttered.

"Where?"

"I can't feel anything between here and my knee."

Kai gasped and jerked a look up at Gil. "And you didn't say anything? Gil Hanford, you could be dying!"

"He's not dying," Cass said soothingly, relaying the information to Jordana.

Gil gave Kai a glance. "It's all right."

"I'm no doctor," she said strongly, emotions coloring her voice, "but even I know numbness is not a good sign, Gil." She glared at him. "You're so damned stubborn! You just hold everything inside you! You should have at least told Cass this, never mind me," she said, and jabbed a finger into her chest.

Gil reached out, his hand closing over her knotted hands in her lap. Her skin was cool to his touch. She was so small in comparison to him. Squeezing them, he rasped, "I'm not dying, so just relax, okay?" Gil didn't want to release her hands. He saw the shock on her face by his move. Damn, but her skin was so soft beneath his hard, callused fingers.

Releasing her, he saw Kai's cheeks flood pink. And damned if he didn't see something else in her eyes. Longing. For him? No. That wasn't possible. She was angry and hurt by him. His mind spun with the realization she *liked* him touching her. His heart exploded with new, intense yearning. Groaning inwardly, the pressure against his erection amped up. The woman could turn him from zero to sixty in a heartbeat.

Cass nodded and signed off the cell. Turning, he said, "Partner, I need to take you to the ER. Jordana thinks that the blood vessel that got broke by the bull has put too much blood into that area. It's pressing up against a major nerve that goes all the way down to your heel. She's gonna have to put a big needle in there and drain most of it off to get sensation back in your leg."

"Hell," Gil grumbled, glaring up at Cass. "Why can't I just wait and see? Let me sleep on it. See how it is tomorrow morning."

Cass grinned and tucked his cell away. "Because by tomorrow morning your leg will probably be numb all the way down to your toes. Remember? Blood congeals? And then it hardens to a degree and sits there waiting for the body to clear it over weeks or months of time. The larger the hematoma, Gil, the more blood has spread into the surrounding tissue." He made a gesture for him to get up. "Come on, I'll drive you to the ER and get this over with. Once she's sucked out the blood, you will feel a helluva lot better than you do now."

"I'm going with you," Kai said, standing, glaring down at Gil, just daring him to say no.

Cass nodded. "Fine by me. I'll go get the truck and bring it around. Can you tell everyone else what's going on, Kai? Meet you guys here in about five minutes? Let's roll."

Gil cursed to himself, slowly standing. Putting pressure on that leg made the pain even worse, and he could no longer disguise it and had to limp a little. It hurt his pride.

Cass grinned and shook his head. "You're one tough hombre, Hanford." He took the steps, walking out toward the picket-fence gate.

Kai had disappeared inside. Unhappy, Gil hated to be made the center of attention. He limped down the stairs and out the gate, the bag of ice in his hand. Despite what was going on, he liked touching Kai's hand.

He'd seen the yearning in her widening gray eyes, swore he saw arousal in them. Could their battles with each other be over? Did he honestly have a chance to mend fences with her? Gil had never expected to see what he saw in her eyes just now. It threw him good, and his mind spun, looking for reasons, trying to understand the change in Kai.

He had no idea where Kai had been all day, but he'd had a gnawing worry in the back of his mind about her. Gil wasn't about to ask her where she went, although he didn't have a good feeling about it. That, he knew. It bothered him a hell of a lot to think she might have met a man and spent the day with him. Jealousy ate at him. He shouldn't be jealous but, dammit, he was.

He saw the white ranch truck pull up in the driveway. The screen door opened and closed, and Gil turned to see it was Kai. She was genuinely worried, her slender brows drawn together. His heart opened and he was secretly glad that she was coming along. Maybe his injury was an opportunity in disguise. Maybe...

JORDANA MCPHERSON SMILED over at Gil, who sat on the gurney in the ER, the curtains drawn around his cubicle. "There, all done," she said, pulling off her gloves and dropping them in a nearby receptacle. "How does it feel now?"

The nurse took a tray bearing the container of the blood she'd drawn off and the hypodermic needle she'd used to reach the area of the bleed.

"Better," he admitted. Gil had had to climb out of his Levi's earlier and Kai had excused herself and left the cubicle until the nurse had draped a paper over his lower legs, leaving an opening where Jordana could suck the blood out of the hematoma area. Kai had come back in when he'd called her. Cass had to almost cut the Levi's to get it past the swelling on his thigh. Almost. Gil bore the pain to save his Levi's.

Giving a brisk nod, Jordana viewed the area. "I think the bleed has clotted off, Gil. But I'd like you to hang around here another hour." She gestured to the area. "Keep ice on it in the meantime?"

"What if the bleed has not clotted?" Kai asked the doctor, standing near the gurney and Gil's shoulder. He was in a semisitting position.

"Well, that's what we have to watch for," Jordana told her. "If it hasn't clotted, then we have a fairly major vein that is torn and can't close itself off."

Cass roused himself from leaning against the other side of the gurney at Gil's other shoulder. "It means, more than likely, Jordana is going to have to put him in surgery to repair that vein because it can't do it by itself. He'd be losing blood slowly over time, but the worst is that more blood pouring into that area means more pressure on that nerve again, which may continue to numb his leg."

Kai nodded. "It doesn't sound good." She gave Gil a concerned look. He was pissed off and uncomfortable. He reminded her of a snarly grizzly bear who had just come out of hibernation. Gil had never liked people fussing over him. It just wasn't an operator's way of living. They worked hurt all the time and never complained.

Jordana patted Kai's shoulder. "We'll know in an

hour. Why don't you go with the nurse? She'll get you a big bag of ice that you can lay across Gil's leg?"

"Okay," she said, following the blond-haired nurse out of the cubicle.

Jordana waited until Kai left. "Gil? I know it's not lost on you about your injury. If I recall, you're former Delta Force. Right?"

"Yes," he muttered.

"If you'd have told Cass here about the swelling hours earlier, it might have helped."

Gil cut Cass a dirty look. He was grinning, enjoying Jordana chewing his ass out. "I hear you, Doc."

Patting his lower leg, Jordana shook her head, giving him a grin of her own. "Okay, tough guy, you get to sit here whether you like it or not until we see if your leg is going to swell up again."

"Thanks," he grumbled, trying to sound halfway grateful for her help.

Cass was chuckling, his hand against his mouth.

"Later, guys," Jordana said, then pushed the curtain aside and disappeared.

"Well," Cass murmured, grinning broadly, "that went well, didn't it, Hanford?"

"Shut up."

Snickering, Cass said, "I think I'm gonna make myself at home in the visitor's lounge. I think you need Kai in here, not me. I'll come back in an hour and check on you." He lifted his hand and left.

"You do that," Gil growled, unhappy. He had been alone for about five minutes when Kai slipped back into his cubicle, a huge ice pack in her hands. He promptly lost his growliness as he saw her face. She looked stressed and, worse, he saw what he thought was moisture in her eyes. Why? This wasn't some life-and-death emergency. He wasn't going to die. Why was she taking this incident so hard?

"Here," she said, handing him the large ice pack. "The nurse said to just lay it on top of your leg."

"Thanks," he said, putting it on the area. He watched her fret for a moment, restless and distracted. "Are you okay?" he demanded. Gil wanted to grab her by the upper arm and pull her over to his gurney. She looked distraught.

"Uh...yes, I'm okay. Just—" Kai opened her hands "—upset, I guess. That's all."

Gently, Gil said, "Come over here." He held out his hand toward her. He didn't think for a moment she'd take it, but that at least she'd come closer to him. Wanting to hold her because he suddenly remembered that expression on her face. Kai had looked devastated like this after Sam had been killed. He didn't understand why she was reacting so violently to his injury. It was a pain-in-the-ass kind of injury, nothing to write home about, but she was taking this too hard. Or maybe to heart?

Kai turned, stared at his open hand. She wrapped her arms around herself and moved about a foot away from Gil. "What?"

Dropping his hand, he searched her moist gray eyes. "Look," he began, keeping is voice low and calm, "I'm really all right." He gestured to his leg where the ice pack lay on top of it. "I've been hit and been wounded a number of times a lot worse, Kai." She wouldn't look at him, and he saw her lower lip tremble for a second. *Dammit*. Forcing himself not to open his arms and haul Kai against him, he rasped, "Why the tears? There's nothing to cry over, Kai."

She sniffed and quickly wiped her eyes, giving him an embarrassed look. "Sorry. It's just that…well…it just brings back a lot of memories…"

Her voice was riddled with emotion. Gil gritted his teeth for a moment, making the connection. "When Sam died?"

Giving a jerky nod, Kai moved restlessly around the cubicle, her arms wrapped tight around her body. "It just hit me out of nowhere, Gil."

He sat there, trying to understand. "But I'm not Sam. And I'm nowhere near dying." And then it slammed into him like a runaway freight train: Kai cared for him. Sure, she might be reacting from the past, from losing someone she loved, but this was here and now. Gil wiped his mouth, scowling, watching her move slowly around the cubicle, never making eye contact with him. The anguish he saw clearly in her expression tore at him. Shock rolled through Gil as he rapidly put all the pieces together. He ached to take Kai into his arms, his heart swelling fiercely in his chest over the realization of why she was really upset. Gil wasn't sure she even knew why from the way she was behaving. Or maybe she was and she was just as shocked by the stunning revelation as he was? That there *was* something still between them? Something good?

For a moment, Gil wanted to shout in triumph. But he could be wrong about her reaction, so he tabled it. "Does this happen often?" he asked her.

Kai halted, staring down at her boots. "Not often," she admitted, her voice hollow.

"I know it takes years to get over a death, Kai."
He'd never gotten over her, or what he'd done to
her. God, how he wanted to make up for it, to give
Kai happiness because Gil knew he could. Sam had
treated her poorly in his estimation. He'd been a cold
robot. Sam had never been able to let down and be intimate or allow his emotions out of that box he stuffed
them in.

Sometimes, when he was with Sam and Kai,
he'd see the sadness in her eyes when she looked at
her husband. She was rarely animated or emotional
around him, and Gil knew that was because Sam
wasn't able to share how he felt. Many times over,
he wondered what kind of intimacy Sam was able
to achieve with Kai. He saw their marriage as a mis-
match and in that three years they'd been married,
he'd seen Kai shrinking away a little more each time
he saw her. As if Sam's inability to let down and be
emotional with her was killing her a little more every
time he was able to come home and be with her. Sam
had been so damned locked up. And Gil had to stand
aside, saying nothing.

He was not going to force Kai not to show her emotions to him. She had to be feeling strongly about him
to want to cry. His heart turned to mush because he
loved her so damned much. This was the first time
Gil had any inkling of her feelings toward him other
than anger. And by him trying to minimize his injury, he was sure it was jogging Kai's memory of how
Sam had treated her. Gil didn't want to go there. "You
could help me if you want," he said. He wasn't going
to throw this opportunity away, betting that Kai's reactions were because she cared for him.

Kai turned. "How?"

He gestured to his leg. "Would it bother you to massage my lower leg? I think it would help." Hell, Gil didn't know if it would or not, but he was dying to have her hands on him. And it would give Kai something to do, something positive that she could be part of his healing team, of sorts.

Instantly, Gil saw her face brighten, as if he'd just thrown her a life preserver. Wincing inwardly, he realized that whatever was going on here, it was about them. Not Sam. Not her marriage to him.

"Sure," she said.

Gil moved the paper aside, exposing his hairy lower leg. He saw her give a quick swipe of her eyes and she came around to that side of his gurney. The moment she laid her small, cool hands on his leg and gently moved them from below his knee to his foot, a startling arc of fire sheeted through Gil. Trying not to overreact, he lay back, closing his eyes.

"That's great, Kai. Feels good." Hell, he felt guilty, lying, to get her to touch him. But as he opened his eyes, studying her profile as she focused on his leg, he saw it was helping Kai a lot. Doing something when you were upset usually was good, and he saw it was working for Kai.

"I'm not hurting you, am I?" she asked, glancing up at him.

"No…it feels better." He tapped the ice pack. "It's helping up here." That was a lie. The look of hope burning in Kai's gray eyes would make Gil lie to God himself because he saw her rallying. She'd felt helpless and cut out of the loop. Like Sam had so often cut her off from himself. A warm feeling moved through

Gil. It was a white lie, he convinced himself. Her fingers were strong, but she was moving them gently against his flesh. And, dammit, his erection was growing. *Again*.

Grimly, he reached for a blanket sitting on a nearby tray and dragged it across his hips so it wouldn't become obvious. There was no zipper and tough Levi's material to stop it from showing. Gil didn't want Kai to see it. Everything felt so tentative with her, but he silently watched her throw herself into massaging his lower leg. And, damn, it felt good. When her fingers began to push and knead his foot, he groaned. He couldn't help it.

"Damn, you're good at this," he murmured. When she glanced up, he was glad he'd lied. Kai's cheeks were turning pink. Was she remembering the times when she'd massaged his back and legs? Her touch had always been healing. Right now, it was sending flames up his leg, directly to his erection, and he kept the blanket in place, hiding it.

"Thanks. I just want you to get better, is all."

Hearing the slight tremble in her voice, Gil said less gruffly, "I'm going to be fine, Kai." And then he teased her a little. "Were you always like this? Taking care of everyone else in your family?" He saw her full mouth purse for a moment and then a faint curve at one corner of her mouth.

"I guess so." She managed a one-shouldered shrug. "Steve always called me Little Mother. If I wasn't taking care of a sick chicken, a kitten or a horse, he said I wasn't happy. He thought I'd go on to become a nurse someday."

Gil nodded. "Was your mom like that?"

"Very much so."

"I guess it was kind of tough growing up without your mother around to sort of guide you?"

"Probably," Kai admitted, kneading his thick, hard calf gently between her fingers. "But I was always that way."

"It's a nice way to be," he said, watching her expression bloom with happiness. Gil felt good being able to make her feel better. He'd give his right arm to make that happen. And her fingers were working magic on him. Because Kai didn't know medical stuff like a Delta operator did, he had tricked her, but he didn't feel bad about it because now her anxiety was remarkably reduced. White lies were okay in his world. They hurt no one and often helped. More than anything, he felt such a powerful wave of love for her roll through him. Gil had to clench his jaw to stop from telling her how much she had always meant to him.

CHAPTER THIRTEEN

"TELL ME MORE about your growing-up years," Gil urged Kai. She continued to gently massage his lower leg, and he could see her shoulders beginning to lose their tension. He was discovering something else about her and it made him feel good. When she was upset he could get her to focus on helping in some way, and then she ramped down. It made him feel like a miner who had just found a placer gold nugget in a stream.

"Not much else to tell," Kai said, her mouth quirking downward.

"Humor me?" Gil said, adding a pleading look to go with his request. Kai's gaze was haunted looking again. Why?

"I've told you a lot of my history. I have one brother, Steve. He's two years older than I am. My Dad favors him over me because I'm female. Steve has been like an oak in the storm of our lives. He's a good person and I love him very much."

Frowning, Gil said, "You said you contact him weekly, right?"

"Yes. He fills me in with what's going on." Kai raised her chin and looked at him. "Being disowned by my dad means I can't cross the ranch property line."

"It's crazy to do that to you." Gil saw the anguish in her eyes. Her hands stilled for a moment over his leg.

"He's a caveman throwback," Kai muttered, forcing herself to focus on Gil's limb. "Because Mom died when I was eight he got it into his head that all women were weak. He wanted me to stay at the ranch and cook and clean for them instead of going into the Army. I wasn't going to stay there and be a servant. There was more to me, Gil, than just washing dishes and pushing a broom around. He got pissed because I was leaving and told me if I left, he'd disown me."

"Damn, I'm sorry, Kai. No parent should ever do that to their child."

"Yeah, well, my dad believes women should be seen, not heard. And I have a big mouth on me when someone starts to push me around. I don't take it. So what if I'm shorter than Steve and I'm not as strong as he is? I did all the ranch work Steve did, but my dad still considered me weak." Bitterly, she added in a whisper, "He might as well have added the word *useless* while he was at it."

For a moment, Gil saw tears in her eyes. Just as quickly, Kai swallowed and they were gone. "Maybe he was threatened by you because you were strong and self-sufficient, unlike your mother?"

"I don't know what was going on in his mind. He wrote me out of his will and Steve gets everything. I don't blame Steve. God, he does the work of two men. My dad needs to hire another wrangler, but he's cheap and so Steve picks up the slack. My brother always sounds so tired when I call him."

Rubbing his jaw, Gil studied Kai. "Was your father hard on you?"

"He has no feelings," she said wearily. "I never saw my father cry except once, and that was when Mom died. He beat the tar out of Steve when he was seven and told him that men didn't cry."

"How did your father relate to you, then? You were his daughter." Gil saw her roll her eyes.

"I was an afterthought in my dad's world. I had to fight to learn everything I did about ranching. Steve was the one who taught me what I know. My dad refused to, said a girl should know her place." Her voice dropped with barely veiled anger. "I never knew my place as far as he was concerned."

"Can you go home and visit Steve?" Gil searched her misery-laden face. His stomach tightened with hurt for Kai. No one had protected her. No one except her brother. He felt anger stir deep in him for the father who reminded him in some ways of Sam. He wondered if Kai had married a man like her father in some respects: cold, emotionally unavailable and unable to be intimate. That old saying held some truth to it.

"No. My dad told me I couldn't step foot on the ranch ever again. He means it, Gil."

"That's crap," he muttered angrily. "You're his only daughter."

"He's not exactly what I'd call a stellar parent. I do go visit Steve once a year. I drive close to the ranch, stay off the property, and he drives out to meet me. We go into town and I stay at a motel for a couple of days. It's fun catching up with him. Steve needs someone to talk to, Gil. My dad is rough on him, treats him like a slave, like he's less than dirt. I've told him he should leave the bastard and let him stew in his own juices."

"You think he might?"

"No." Kai sighed. She turned and spotted some hand lotion on the steel counter and picked it up. Squeezing some into her palm, she rubbed her hands together and then began to massage his leg once more. "He feels guilty."

"What do you mean?"

"Steve feels like he let me down. That he didn't take good enough care of me. My dad was always telling Steve it was his job and responsibility to take care of me."

"But he was only two years older than you." Gil rapidly made a calculation in his head. Steve had been ten when his mother died, a very fragile age for a child trying to grow from boy to man. Gil could only imagine the struggles Steve had with his own grief, and then dealing with Kai's grief, plus suddenly having total responsibility for her. Now, he was beginning, perhaps, to understand some of the sadness he had observed in Kai since coming to the Triple H. Maybe it wasn't about being around him, after all. Maybe it was the silent cross she bore regarding her family and her remote father. It made him feel even more protective of her than ever.

"I know," Kai said softly, frowning. "Steve is sensitive, like me. We both took after my mom so far as I can remember. It was brutal for Steve. He wanted to cry over Mom's passing, but he held it in. We helped each other through that time…"

Hearing the pain in her low voice, Gil held on to his building anger for her damned father. "It's good that you have one another." He wondered if Kai had gone home after Sam had died. "Is Steve ever going to get married?"

Shaking her head, Kai said, "No. Steve doesn't want to bring a woman to the ranch with our dad there. He saw what he did to me. He doesn't want to put another woman in his crosshairs."

"So Steve has more or less surrendered his life to running a ranch?"

Her hands stilled on his leg for a moment and she said in a strained voice, "Yes. I wanted to go home, to make my peace with my father before he died, but he rejected my request."

"Jesus," Gil muttered, running his fingers through his hair. "What the hell is the matter with him?"

"I don't know. Steve's upset about it, too. The stress he's under with Dad dying, being part-time caregiver and trying to keep the ranch running properly, has really worn him down. After I left the Army, I wanted to go home and help Steve. But when he talked to Dad, he said no. He said—" Kai shrugged weakly "—he never wanted to see or talk to me again. That I was dead to him."

Gil couldn't stand it. "Come here," he said roughly, sitting up, leaning forward and hooking his hand beneath her upper arm. The surprise on her face as he gently tugged her toward him was evident. The tears in her eyes tore at Gil. "Just let me hold you, okay?" he growled, dragging her into his arms, enfolding her against his chest, her head coming to rest on his shoulder. The gurney stood in the way between them, but Gil didn't care. He was driven like an obsessed man to do something…anything…to give Kai a little comfort. A little love that her damned father had never given her.

Gil thought Kai might pull back or fight him, but she didn't. It was as if this was exactly what she needed as she surrendered fully to him. The orange scent of her hair mingled with the fragrance of her skin. Gil inhaled deeply, remembering her special scent, her body, her kisses…her unselfish heart when she gave him everything when he'd needed it the most. Her breasts were soft against the span of his chest, her arm sliding around his torso, tightening. He could feel the beat of her heart against his, the soft silk of her hair sliding against his chin.

Closing his eyes, Gil felt an inner tremble, the memories of loving Kai coming back so powerfully. Kai rubbed her cheek against his shoulder, his skin tightening.

"Now, you listen to me," he growled softly, holding her close. "You're the finest woman I've ever met in my life. You give so much to so many, Kai. You never ask anything for yourself in return. Your father is a sick man to think he could ever throw someone like you away." He felt tears hit the backs of his eyes. Swallowing against a lump, he muttered, "I know I don't deserve someone like you, but you need to know you saved my sorry-assed soul when I walked into the barracks and asked for you. Anyone who has ever been touched by you, Kai, knows you're someone special." He pressed his mouth against her hair, the memories sweet and intense. How badly Gil wanted to love Kai, to give back to her. Knowing how much her father had stripped from her young, innocent heart that only knew how to love, sickened him on a new level.

Wanting to pull her away just enough to tip up her chin and curve his mouth against hers almost overwhelmed him. Gil had to keep his wits because his whole body was unraveling in memory of their time together.

"Okay?" he demanded gruffly, giving her a small squeeze to emphasize his words. He felt her give a jerky nod. Kai had rested her brow against his neck and jaw, clinging to him. As if she were a scared child seeking a safe harbor. An intense sense of protection toward Kai overwhelmed Gil. He wished things were different. Right now, all he could offer her was what she was willing to accept from him. He was sure Kai wasn't entertaining loving him. With a ragged sigh, Gil reluctantly eased her away from him, their eyes meeting. Hers were a soft gray, moist, raw with vulnerability. He managed a faint smile for her benefit.

Releasing her, he nudged a few strands of her hair away from her temple. For some reason, Kai was allowing her hair to grow. It made her look even more beautiful. Dragging his gaze from her soft, parted lips, he barely stopped himself from leaning forward to take her.

Giving him a grateful look, Kai backed away, touching her reddened cheek. "Y-yes, I'm okay. You're the one who is hurt. I should be asking you that."

Gil wondered if Kai had developed that kind of response because when she was hurt, her father never cared enough to find out how she really was. "There are all kinds of injuries, Kai. Some are seen. Some aren't." He searched her eyes, lost in their velvet quality. "Thank you for all you've done for me. Never forget that. Okay?" He dug into her gaze, making the point. He now realized that by him leaving her without a word, he'd been like her coldhearted father who had emotionally abandoned her at eight. The awareness staggered Gil and, more than ever, he was incredibly sorry for his stupidity in not at least penning a note to her before he left. He hadn't been thinking right, lost in grief over Rob's death, lost in her, the bright, wonderful emotions she'd brought to life within him. But that wasn't an excuse for his behavior or his poor decisions.

His mother had raised him to be better than that. Filled with sorrow, Gil added gently, "Listen, I'm here for you. Do you understand that? I know I screwed up with you before. No one, believe me, is sorrier than I am for what I did to you. From now on, let's just allow that chapter to be closed, because we can't change it." Gil reached out, barely brushing Kai's pale cheek. "Tonight, we start a new chapter. I'll be better at being accountable to you. I won't ever leave you in a lurch again, Kai. I promise you that," he rumbled, meaning every word of it.

Kai gave a nod and sniffed. "I'd like that, Gil. You're right—the past is done and gone."

But not forgotten. Gil bit back the words as he studied her in the lulling silence. Nothing in the world existed in that moment except Kai with her gray eyes, black pupils large with a rim of color around the outer edge. The way her soft mouth parted, the look of hope in her expression, totaled him. "Okay," he said thickly. "I want that, too."

God, if only he could share his love for her. If only Kai knew. He felt as if his heart wanted to tear out of his chest. All he wanted was Kai. All of her and that beautiful, selfless heart. Gil had seen Sam slowly kill Kai's heart over the years. How many times had he wanted to step in and shake some sense into Sam? Didn't he see by him being emotionally distant that Kai was like a plant dying from lack of water? But he never had.

Not until they'd come together like oil and water; lust, sex and his love for her all turning into a starving hunger for each other. Gil had always thought Kai had allowed those five days to occur because it was a reaction to three years of being left to emotionally wither on the vine of her marriage, never fed by Sam, never intimate in ways other than sex. In Sam's world, sex was the only expression of emotions he had available to him to give to Kai. Gil knew there was so much more than just sex. As he studied her in silence, he compressed his lips and gave her a wry look.

"It's a new chapter for us, Kai. All I want is to be there for you if you need someone." He patted his broad shoulder. "I'm good at carrying loads for others, so let me carry some of yours when they get too heavy?"

KAI LAY AWAKE in her bed that night. Her mind was racing. Her body was achy and needy. She knew what that gnawing sensation meant. Not having had sex for years was turning her into something she'd never felt before. And Gil unexpectedly dragging her into his arms, holding her… God…holding her, had just about unraveled Kai in every possible way. And he smelled so good. So familiar. She closed her eyes, her heart twinging with so many beautiful memories of Gil holding her, incredibly intimate, warm, humorous, making her laugh and allowing her to cry in his arms.

"Oh, hell," Kai muttered, sitting up in bed. She wore a soft cotton nightgown of heather color. The sheet and quilt settled around her hips as she stared at the door straight ahead of her. Across the hall was Gil's room.

Shortly after they had separated from one another's arms, Jordana had come in with her nurse and checked Gil's thigh. All was good and she was pleased, pronouncing the blood vessel had self-sealed. She'd waved her finger in Gil's face, becoming stern, ordering him to rest for the next three days. That meant no horseback riding, no walking around except in the house. The torn blood vessel needed time to heal or, she warned him darkly, it would re-open and tear again. And this time, it meant surgery.

Smiling a little, Kai crossed her legs beneath the covers, elbows on her thighs. Gil looked like a little boy getting scolded by his mother. In this case, by Jordana. Kai had stood back with Cass, both grinning like fools because they knew just how much Gil hated sitting around. Operators, by nature, were a restless breed, and they rarely sat in one place for more than a few minutes at most. Gil was officially housebound for three days and Cass hadn't let him live that down on the way home. Operators needled the hell out of their kind. To outsiders, it would look like one wolf savaging another, but that was the brotherhood and Gil took Cass's razzing in good stride, although unhappy with the three-day prison sentence handed down by jailer Jordana.

What had happened in that ER cubicle with Gil?

Rubbing her face slowly, Kai tried to sort through the mass of emotions still burning brightly in her heart. When Gil had pulled her into his arms, she'd collapsed against him, needing him so desperately, needing what he'd given her so long ago. Was it because he got her to talking about her dad? Because it had brought up a horrendous amount of anguish and feelings of being abandoned by him. She had been kicked out. No place to go. No more family except for Steve, and she couldn't even see Steve except off ranch property.

Gil had given her life back to her in Bagram. She'd felt dead inside. Dried out. Numb. The years with Sam had been stressful and the longer they were married, the more she felt bereft, unable to be nurtured or held by him. Sam had never been comfortable with Kai's emotions. And when she tried to get close to him, have him hold her after they'd made love, he'd get up and leave the bedroom, upset. Kai had cried at first, not understanding why he'd left her side. She never could until Gil had stepped into her life like sunlight after a dark, raging storm. He'd not only fed her emotionally, he'd lavished her with his tender intimacy. Oh, God, she'd craved him holding her in the ER tonight. All the dryness and all the loneliness she carried within her suddenly dissolved in that magical moment. He'd held her close, the sense of protection drizzling through her like a soft rain on the parched desert of her emotional landscape. She was the parched desert. Just talking about her father, the terrible sense of alienation since age eighteen, never seeing him again, never able to talk to him like a real father, had left her hurting in ways she'd never realized before.

Not until tonight. Not until Gil had taken her into his arms and simply held her. He didn't try to kiss her, but his hand ranged gently up and down her back, smoothing out the tension within her, his moist breath caressing her ear and hair, and it made her want to sob. He fed her heart. He shared intimacy with her. He was all the things Sam had never been. Her heart ached with pain for Sam. For herself. For Gil. It was a triad that had nothing but unhappy endings.

Kai longed to get out of bed, walk across the hall and knock on Gil's door. Wanting to lie in his arms, his strong body against hers, to absorb the touches and grazes he would give to her, his mouth on hers, the way he held her after they made love, made her ache with raw longing.

Kai recognized she had depression. She'd had it off and on for years, ever since her father had disowned her. Being in Gil's arms had lifted her out of that terrible cloud of feeling lost, feeling hopeless. Every time Gil was around her, he magically uplifted her. Silent tears slid down her cheeks. Kai closed her eyes, hiding her face in her hands. Her whole life was in chaos. And she was lost in a way she never had been before. In the Army, it was structured, it gave her stability; it had banks like a river that she could flow within. The Apache squadron was her family, and she was admired and respected. She was the go-to person when another mechanic got into trouble and couldn't figure out what to do. They always came to her.

If only her father would come to her. Kai touched her nightgown where her heart lay beneath the fabric. It had felt like a hole had been punched through it the day he disowned her. He might as well have taken a real gun and pointed it at her heart and fired. Her heart always felt lacking. Even Sam couldn't fill it.

But Gil did. Around him, Kai felt alive. Felt whole. Felt hopeful. He'd been so damned sincere tonight, asking her to turn over a new chapter in their lives. He was right: what was done in the past was done. But, after walking into her barracks, larger than life, like a sun wrapping around her heart and soul, he'd walked out on her without a word. Could she trust him a second time?

A new kind of fear niggled through Kai. Gil had given her love. Real love. She'd realized that after the dry, desert years of being married to Sam. Gil had nursed and nurtured her back to life, unafraid to show his emotions, share them with her, revel in them. Kai had never laughed so much as she had in those five days with Gil. He wasn't a mean tease like Sam had been to her. Sam didn't realize the black ops teasing was downright cruel at times and he couldn't see the difference when he teased her. She had loved her husband so much, drawn to his strength, his utter confidence and rebellious attitude toward life. Gil had never walked away and left her cold like Sam had. He was loyal to her. And if he could make it happen, he was there for Kai, a strong support, urging her to always aspire, believing in her. Sam was like her father, Kai realized belatedly. Why hadn't she seen that before? She'd been young, blind and dazzled by Sam, that was why.

She lay down, nestling her head into the goose-down pillow and pulling the sheet and quilt over her shoulders. Closing her eyes, Kai made a mental comparison of her dad and Sam. Both were unable to emote. Her father froze and tensed every time Kai, even as a young child, had run up to him, her arms open, wanting to hug his knees. He had called for his wife to come and take her away from him. Sam was similar, though not as coldhearted as her dad. He could handle anything when it came to sex. There, he was open, available and giving to her.

It was afterward that Sam couldn't stand the intimacy she craved and so desperately needed. Sex was one thing. But love, real love in Kai's heart, was about far more than just the act of sex.

Sam found it uncomfortable to hug and kiss her goodbye. Kai knew he was trying. And Sam was aware she needed more because she made it known to him. Digging back into his past, Kai eventually, after a year of marriage to him, found out that Sam's father had been a meth addict. He'd beaten Sam with a belt where it never showed. When Sam was old enough, he'd stood up to his druggie father and fought back. But it was too late by that time, Kai thought, feeling badly for her dead husband. He'd been severely abused, his mother weak and unable to protect Sam when he needed her the most. She was needy and dependent, and Kai often thought Sam confused her needs for intimacy—a simple hug, an embrace or kiss—as being like his mother. She wasn't, but she was fairly sure Sam couldn't tell the difference.

Kai knew something of Gil's growing-up years. They must have been similar in that one way, but in other ways, Gil was the opposite of Sam. And maybe that's why those two hit it off so well, like long-lost brothers. When Gil came over to their home and the men had beers, Sam was always laughing. It was the only time Kai heard her husband laugh. The rest of the time he was emotionally locked up, unavailable or unable to reach out and give her what she needed most: his vulnerable heart. That, Sam kept behind a stone fortress. And even she, as much as she tried, could never penetrate those walls around his heart.

Kai had loved him so deeply, so completely. There was goodness in Sam. He loved children, worked with several charities in Afghanistan, giving back. Helping the poor and the suffering was important to him. She wondered if he saw himself in some of these young Afghan boys. The fathers in Afghanistan, at least the ones she'd seen, brutally beat their sons. The rod was not spared in the least. Had Sam seen himself in them? By the time Sam was fourteen, he had five broken bones thanks to his violent, addicted father.

Yes, there were similarities between Sam and her dad. She remembered one time her mother telling Steve never to hit his children. That to lay a hand on a child was a mortal sin. She was Catholic and Kai had stood there, leaning against her mother, her fleshy arm around her tiny shoulders, holding her as she talked to Steve.

Steve had asked why. Her mother, Olivia, had made a sad face. She told Steve that their father, Hal, had been severely beaten as a child. He'd been the oldest in a ranching family that had created the ranch they now lived at. Hal had been the oldest. It was his job to take care of the other children. Kai remembered her mother pushing away tears, her voice trembling. Hal's younger sister, Janie, had wandered into a pen of bulls. And she'd been killed by them at six years old. Hal had been beaten badly by his grief-stricken rancher father. And from that day forward, his father had called him a murderer and no-good.

Kai lay there, eyes closed, trying to put herself in her dad's place. Both he and Sam had suffered from abusive fathers. Tragic things had happened to them, scarring them for life. She often wondered if her mother was the only warmth, the only intimacy and love that her dad had ever known. Pain filtered through her heart as she thought of Sam and herself. Had she played the same role with him that her mother had with her dad? God, the pattern was the same. *The same.*

Tears leaked from beneath her tightly shut lids for both men. Kai wanted so desperately to reach out to her dad before it was too late. Because she loved him in spite of what had happened. He was her father. And there was a different, deeper ache in her heart to connect with him. To tell him to his face that she loved him, that she forgave him because he was her father. He needed to hear that from her. But Kai didn't know how it was going to happen or if it would. Steve was grim about the prospects. Her brother knew how important it was to tell her dad these things. But Hal, as he was dying, had become an angry person that no one could stand being around. Not even Steve. And even the hospice workers refused to be around Hal for the same reasons. He was an angry, raging man striking out at everyone who got close to him.

Gil...

I need you so much...so much...and I'm so afraid you'll leave me again. Just disappear like before. Can I trust you? How can I begin to trust you again? You broke my heart. I can't stand to have it broken again. I just don't have the strength to get up off the floor a second time. First, my dad. Then Sam. And then you. I just can't risk my heart with you again as much as I want to...

CHAPTER FOURTEEN

KAI WAS IN the kitchen helping Cass with the turkey dinner that would be served today at four o'clock. Miss Gus, and Griff and Val McPherson, with their daughter, Sophie, were coming over for Sunday dinner once more. They tried to make it over at least once or twice a month, and they were always more than welcome. The kitchen was filled with wonderful smells. Gus had said she had a surprise for all of them.

Glancing into the living room, Gil was unhappily sitting in a recliner, his injured leg up and resting. Sandy was knitting a rainbow-colored afghan, half of it spread across her lap in her rocker opposite him. Cat was down on the floor petting Zeke as he lay on his large bed in the corner. Talon was in his office, doing paperwork. It was three thirty, and she was setting the trestle table when a knock came on the screen door.

"I'll get it," Cat said, jumping up, smiling. She hurried down the hall to the foyer.

Kai heard lots of greetings, laughter and chatting from the kitchen, where she finished setting the table. Rubbing her hands on the pink apron around the waist of her Levi's, she saw Cass glance up from his duties of slicing the golden-brown turkey sitting on the counter. "They're here," she said, anxious to meet Miss Gus once again. She was a legend in the valley, along with Iris Mason, who was the other matriarch of the largest ranch, the Elk Horn. These women had helped define this valley, its growth and direction. Both were in their early eighties and role models as far as Kai was concerned. She loved seeing them in action and maybe learn something she could become herself.

Kai saw Talon wander casually down the hall, a smile on his face. Sandy and Gil remained in the living room along with a very alert Zeke. "What next, Cass?" she asked coming over to the counter.

"Get all the casseroles here on the counter over to the table," he directed. "Keep the lids on them, though. If Miss Gus says she has a surprise, it might waylay dinner for a bit and I want to keep everything hot."

"Gotcha," Kai said. She pulled on two oven mitts and placed metal trivets on the table. Cass brought out the sweet potato with marshmallow casserole, the green bean casserole and a huge bowl of thick turkey gravy that smelled heavenly as she set it down and covered it. There was a huge bowl of steaming sage and chestnut stuffing that made her mouth water. Cass had spent all of Sunday morning cooking and she'd helped him. Cat had come into the kitchen and volunteered her time and hands, as well. They had been a great team.

Kai stood back and surveyed the table filled with such bounty. The fragrances were heavenly, and it made her even hungrier than she already was.

"Hey," Cat called, walking into the kitchen. "Kai? Take a time-out and go meet Miss Gus."

Kai turned and smiled at the short, thin woman with silver hair that looked like a halo around her head. Gus slowly limped into the kitchen. "Hi, Miss Gus. How are you?" She walked over and held out her hand to the elder. The woman's blue eyes sparkled with energy and warmth.

"Aren't you a pretty little thing this afternoon," Gus said, giving her a quick, warm hug of hello. "I need a whiz on mechanics." She cackled a little. "I just might swipe you from here and ask you to come over and look at some of our equipment. Good mechanics are hard to find."

Kai smiled and released her. Gus was dressed in a starched white blouse that had a red knit cape over her small shoulders. She was lean and Kai knew elderly people got cold easier than others. A dark blue set of slacks and brown leather shoes completed her wardrobe. "Well, I'll be more than happy to do that for you, Miss Gus, as long as Talon lets me." She smiled up at Talon, who stood behind the elder.

"Any weekend, Miss Gus. Kai's the best. She's gotten all our equipment, which sat in that barn for nine years without any care, up and working."

Gus patted Kai's arm. "Good. Because I've got a cantankerous old tractor that I dearly love." She looked up at Griff, who was coming into the kitchen with Val, who had Sophie in her arms. "Griff tells me to put it into the dump, but it's kinda like me— old and touchy." Her eyes sparkled with mirth as she held Griff's gaze. "As long as I can putter around, if I can get that tractor worked on, we'll both stay active and working on the Bar H."

Everyone laughed.

Cass came over, drying his hands on a small towel. "Hey, Miss Gus, nice to see you again." He was a big

man and towered over her. Cass leaned over and gave
her a gentle hug and then released her. "Your favorite for dinner this afternoon—roast turkey with all
the goodies."

Rubbing her hands, Gus said, "I could smell it
comin' up to the porch." She peered between people
into the living room. Raising her hand, she said, "Hi,
Sandy. Hi, Gil."

Sandy smiled and started to get up by putting her
afghan on the stool in front of her rocker.

"No, no, stay there," Gus called. "Don't move for a
minute. Stay there because I have something for you."

Sandy relaxed. "Okay, Gus."

Gus peered up at Griff. "Go get the basket and
bring it in."

"You bet," Griff said, grinning.

Gus looked at everyone standing in the kitchen.
"Let's all go to the living room and sit down for a
moment. I have something for Sandy and I want to
give it to her."

Val led Gus to the living room, where she sat in an
overstuffed chair next to Sandy's rocker.

Gil told everyone hello, shook hands and looked
miserable to Kai. He was not a happy camper being
tied down like this. Since getting up this morning,
Cass had wrapped that leg and given him stern orders to keep it up, to be quiet and rest. Kai felt sorry
for him and gave him a sympathetic look. Gil patted
the arm of his overstuffed chair, asking Kai to come
and sit with him. She wanted to.

Val, Cat and Talon took places on the sofa next
to where Zeke and his bed were located. They left
enough room for Griff to come and sit by his wife

and daughter when he returned. Cass sauntered in and stood behind Gil and Kai, towel in his hands, wearing his red apron.

"That's a mighty pretty apron you're wearin'," Gus told Cass, an evil grin on her mouth. "Never saw a man wear one before you came here, Cass. You give it new meaning, young man."

Cass chuckled and picked up one side of the red apron that had white ruffles around it. Being tall and muscular, the apron looked more like a postage stamp around his waist. "I kinda like it, Miss Gus. This is one of Sandy's and she told me to take my pick of them from the kitchen drawer."

Everyone chuckled.

"Well, red certainly brings out your skin tones," Gus noted, gesturing toward him.

"Thank you," Cass said, grinning wickedly.

Griff came in carrying a huge basket with a green cloth draped over it. "Gus? You want me to give it to Sandy or do you want to do the honors?"

"No," Gus said, sitting back in her chair, folding her hands in her lap. "You go ahead."

"Okay," Griff murmured, smiling as he lifted the basket and gently placed it in Sandy's lap and extended hands. He sat down next to his wife, his arm around her shoulders.

Zeke whined. Suddenly sitting up, his eyes were riveted on the basket.

Sandy said, "What did you bring me, Gus?"

"Oh," she said, arching one silver brow, "take a look and see."

Sandy pulled off the dark green cloth. She gasped. "Oh, my God!" she cried, joy in her voice.

About that time, Zeke whined long and loud.

And then, everyone saw a little golden retriever puppy pop her head up and over the basket, looking at Zeke and excitedly wagging her thin, short tail.

Sandy gathered the squirming, happy puppy that was six weeks old into her hands. The puppy whined and wildly licked at her face. "Oh, Gus! This is such a wonderful surprise!"

Everyone oohed and aahed over the wriggly puppy, whose tiny tail was going sixty miles an hour, back and forth, as Sandy took her to her breast, cuddling her gently between her hands.

Kai sighed and smiled down at Gil. He smiled up at her. Warmth went through her heart. They hadn't had time to talk since last night. She wanted to, but there were too many other things going on this morning. The puppy was so cute and tiny. Kai loved dogs.

Talon frowned and gave Zeke a firm order to remain sitting on his bed.

Zeke whined painfully, looked pleadingly at Talon and then became mesmerized by the puppy, who was no more than three feet away from him. He thumped his tail avidly, panting, wanting to leave the bed to go smell the new doggy visitor.

Sandy laughed and began to cry as she looked over at Gus. "You shouldn't have done this, Gus."

"I heard through Talon that you'd gone over to look at the breeder who had puppies, but that he wanted too much for the one you had picked out." Shrugging, Gus said, "I know you used to have a golden retriever. Val, Griff, Sophie and I thought it would be a nice coming-home gift to you." Gus waved her hand around the living room. "We want you happy and healthy. I was able to purchase your ranch back for you. I don't think buying a puppy is anything financially stressful on us." She jabbed a finger toward the puppy. "It's a female. The one the owner said you fell in love with. The runt."

Sandy nodded. "Well, the owner called her a runt. But I don't. She looks fit and healthy to me. So what if she's a little on the small side? With proper food, love and care, she'll grow up to be just as fine and beautiful as the other puppies in that litter." Sandy freed a hand to wipe her eyes. "I think I'll call her Daisy. When I saw her for the first time, I thought she was like a fresh little daisy out in a meadow."

"I like the name," Gus said, pleased. "Daisy sure likes you."

Sandy gave the puppy a fond look, touching her small, silky golden head. "She's priceless, Gus." Looking up, tears in her eyes, Sandy said, "You are such a fairy godmother to all of us. I don't know what we did to deserve you, but I'm so grateful."

Zeke whined long and loud, looking at Talon and then longingly over at Daisy. His tail was thumping so loudly at this point that everyone was looking at him.

Talon had opened his mouth to say something when, suddenly, Daisy slid off Sandy's lap and plopped down right in front of Zeke's front paws on his bed.

Kai heard Cat gasp, sitting up, fear in her face.

Talon snapped a Dutch command to Zeke.

Instantly, the Belgian Malinois froze and didn't move.

Daisy jumped playfully around on his soft bed and started pawing and playing around Zeke's legs.

Talon moved swiftly, his gaze riveted to his combat assault dog. His face was hard and tense.

Kai remembered too late that Zeke had not been around many other dogs. Talon was worried his dog would kill another dog if they got too close. Cat was sitting up, anxious as Talon closed the distance.

Talon gave Zeke another command and leaned down, scooping up the puppy.

"Why doncha let Daisy play with Zeke?" Gus demanded as Talon placed the puppy back into Sandy's lap.

Talon petted his dog, murmuring praise to him. He turned, his hand resting on Zeke's neck. "Because Zeke has not been around many other dogs, Gus. I couldn't be sure if he'd kill Daisy or not. And he could," Talon told her grimly, remaining standing between Sandy and Zeke, like a barrier.

"Oh," Gus said, brows raising. "I didn't know…"

"No one does," Cat said sympathetically, her shoulders dropping, the fear leaving her expression. "Zeke had been so highly trained for military work for three years before he ever got out in the field." She gave Talon a sympathetic look, her husband clearly upset and worried the dog might hurt Daisy. She returned her attention to Gus. "When Talon was assigned Zeke, they worked together for six months before going to Afghanistan. There, he worked with Talon taking down the enemy for three years."

"Yes," Talon said, starting to relax a little, his hand on Zeke, "he's been trained to take down a tango," he told the group. "He's highly competitive—he sees whatever comes at him as something to compete against. And he's been specially bred to want to win every time." He pointed to the puppy licking and chewing on Sandy's finger in her lap. "I was afraid he might see the pup as an enemy, a tango."

Gus snorted and shook her head. "Talon Holt, where has your common sense gone?" She wagged her finger in his direction. "You can't tell me Mother Nature can't smooth that one over? Zeke's a he. Daisy's a she. Both are dogs. Did you ever stop to think that biology might make Zeke very happy to have her around? The opposite sex?" She grinned and looked around at the riveted group, who were watching the puppy and Zeke. "It can't be lost on any of you that opposites attract. Look at all of you! It ain't no different between any species of animals, if you ask me. Zeke is not gonna rip Daisy apart! You saw him. He froze when you told him to. And if he was really that competitive, he would have chomped poor little Daisy anyways. But she's female. He's male. No way is he gonna do anything but cuddle with that cute little girl."

Talon managed an embarrassed look toward Gus. His cheeks turned ruddy. "You're probably right, Miss Gus. I'm just a little jumpy because I'm working at slowly getting Zeke out of military mode. It takes time and a lot of patience."

"*Humph.* You ask me, I'd say put those two dogs out in your front yard and let them run around like happy kids. Zeke is not gonna hurt that little pup. Look at Daisy! You see how she's pining away to get to see Zeke again? And look at Zeke. He's absolutely hypnotized by Daisy! You think Daisy is a morsel for him? Nah," She chuckled and shook her head. "She's company for that poor, lonely dog of yours."

Talon nodded. "I don't disagree with you, Miss

Gus. For right now, I want to keep them apart. Maybe tonight, if things go all right, I can introduce Daisy to Zeke and make sure he doesn't think she's food."

Gus relented, seeing Talon was seriously concerned. She knew he wanted his mother to have that puppy. "It's okay to be extra cautious," she soothed. "Maybe put Zeke in your bedroom and we can let the little puppy run around to all of us out here?"

He nodded. "Good idea. Come on, Zeke," he said, and tugged on the dog's leather collar.

It was as if Zeke understood English, heard the entire conversation. He whined and lay down, a sad look on his black-and-tan face, his gaze pinned on Daisy.

Cat laughed a little. "He's never done that before," she told Talon.

Grimacing, Talon crouched down, hand on his collar. "You're right. Maybe he's more socialized than I thought. He's never disobeyed me before."

"You ain't a little female puppy, either," Gus said pointedly, cackling.

Everyone laughed and it broke the tension in the room.

Cat said, "Just be patient with him, Talon. He really looks so happy to see another dog. Maybe he's been terribly lonely?"

Patting his dog's head, Talon said, "Yeah, from the looks of it." He gazed over at Cat. "Bring his leash to me? It's hanging around the bedpost."

"I'll get it," she said, rising off the couch.

Sandy smiled at her tense son. "It's going to be all right, Talon. If Zeke didn't snap at her when she hopped up on his bed and played between his legs, I really don't think he'll hurt her."

Grudgingly, Talon muttered, "You and Miss Gus are probably right, but I don't want to take any chances. We'll introduce them slow and easy over time."

Cat returned with the thick leather leash and handed it to Talon.

Zeke looked up and then gazed longingly at Daisy. He whined, his head sunk between his paws, his eyebrows moving up and down.

"Oh," Kai said softly, "he knows he's going to be banished."

"I swear," Sandy said, studying Zeke, "he looks like he's going to cry."

Talon snapped on the leash and stood, giving Zeke the order to stand. "He'll be okay." Instantly, the Belgian Malinois got to his feet. But his eyes never left Daisy, who was whining now and wagging her tail, looking adoringly up at Zeke.

"I think they're in love," Kai said, and sighed. "Look at them." She smiled sympathetically at Talon. "Kismet. Star-crossed lovers, maybe?"

Managing a grudging smile, Talon said, "It sure looks like it. I'll be back in a minute." He led Zeke out of the living room and down the hall to their bedroom.

Cat sighed and smiled. "Kai, I know you're right. Those two just looked at one another like long-lost lovers."

Kai twinged inwardly and she slanted a glance down at Gil. Were they star-crossed lovers, too? Last night she realized that maybe…just maybe… She swallowed hard, afraid to think it much less say it. Had she, a long time ago, started falling in love with Gil? Even though she was married to Sam? It caused so much confusion in her, not to mention guilt, that

Kai wasn't ready to go there. And she wasn't sure she ever could. But when Gil glanced up, as if sensing her looking at him, the warmth in his blue eyes for her alone, she swallowed all her questions and misgivings. Kai tried to remind herself that Gil wanted a new chapter between them, and so did she.

But where would it lead? What would be the outcome? Was it possible to fall in love twice? Looking over at Sandy, whose face was suffused with joy over Daisy in her lap, Kai recalled that Cat had told her she'd had two husbands. She'd loved both of them fully and completely. Touching the area of her heart, Kai wondered if she did. Sandy's husbands had died and neither of them had walked out and left her like Gil had. There was such a Grand Canyon between how she felt toward him and their jaded past. No matter what Gil had said, Kai could still feel the hurt, the abandonment, waking up that morning and finding his side of her bed cold, only an impression of where his body had once lain next to her. And he'd left without saying anything or leaving her a note of explanation. It played too closely to what her dad had done to her. He'd abandoned her, too.

Pain drifted through her because the look Gil exchanged with her made Kai want to melt into his arms and be held by him once again. He had always made her feel as if she were a queen to be worshipped. Her lower body gnawed at her, reminding her how long it had been since she'd had sex. Or an orgasm.

Looking away, breaking contact with Gil's gaze, Kai tried to remain immune to him. She was so unsure of herself. And of him. Kai could see he was trying to bridge that gap between them. And with just

one private look for a few seconds, he had turned
her knees to jelly and she felt shaky once again. Just
as she'd felt the first time he'd made love to her at
Bagram.

"Well," Cass said genially, waving his hand toward the kitchen. "Time to giddyap and canter to the
table to eat!"

Kai followed Cass into the kitchen to be his helper
once again. The noise level was low, but the laughter and chatting were infectious. Gil was the last to
come because he had to walk slow and easy. The set
look on his face told Kai he hated his incarceration.
Grateful that Jordana McPherson had put the fear of
God into him, threatening him with surgery, which
he clearly did not want, Kai pulled his chair out at the
table. Today, it was Miss Gus at the head of the table
and Sandy at the other end.

Talon had come back from putting Zeke in the
bedroom and he helped Sandy with Daisy. He gently
held the puppy in his large hands, found a nice, large
cardboard box and placed a small blanket in it. Talon
set the box next to his mother's chair so Daisy could
see her mistress. Then, he walked into the kitchen
and got a small bowl and filled it with water for her.
He also stole some cooled turkey from the platter.

Crouching down, he spoke quietly to Daisy, patted her tiny head and put the water in one corner of
the box. The puppy drank thirstily and then eagerly
chewed on the breast meat Talon held in his fingers.
Daisy was more than happy, her little tail thumping
rhythmically against the box. Cat was sitting next to
Sandy and she leaned down, petting Daisy.

Kai sat down at Gil's elbow. This time, she didn't

mind how close he was to her. She gave him a small
smile when he looked over at her as he passed the
bowl of stuffing her way. Their fingers met. Before
the ER last night, Kai probably would have jerked
her hand away, not wanting contact with Gil. Now,
as their fingers briefly met, she felt tiny skitters of
tingles through them. Her heart opened with longing. She tried to ignore it because the look in Gil's
attention was for her alone and it was turning her
into melted butter. It wasn't a sexual look. But it was
definitely a man who wanted his woman. The banked
tenderness she saw deep in his eyes made Kai's heartbeat pick up in anticipation.

The people around the table were hungry, and conversation ebbed and flowed between bites of savory
sage stuffing mixed with chopped chestnuts, gravy
and turkey. Everyone praised Cass and thanked him
for the delicious meal. Kai felt herself go all gooey
inside when she caught Cass with yearning in his expression for a fleeting second as his gaze alighted on
Sandy. There was no question in Kai's mind that Cass
was falling in love with her. That would be wonderful
if it happened, but Kai also wondered if Sandy had the
heart, the courage, to try to love a third time around.

She knew how much it had taken out of Sandy as
each of her husbands had died, because they'd had
conversations about it. Kai also knew that Talon felt
strongly that the loss of her second husband had sent
her into a grief spiral that shocked her body so deeply
that she'd developed breast cancer. Talon had once
told her he felt health was connected to a person's
emotional state. Kai believed him. She was at an im-
passe with Gil precisely because of her emotions.

As she ate the mouthwatering turkey and gravy, Kai wondered if she had the emotional strength to try to narrow that gap once more with Gil. Could she risk her heart again with him? It had hurt her so badly the first time he'd left. After being abandoned by her dad, Kai just didn't feel strong enough to throw caution to the wind with Gil. Maybe he was right: to just let things develop slowly and naturally between them. See what, if anything, was there.

The food was so good she ate until she felt she was going to burst. With the Holt and McPherson families surrounding her, Kai had never felt as happy as right now.

She remembered times like this when her mother was alive. The happiness between the four of them at the dinner table had been wonderful. Olivia's cooking was equally delicious to what Cass had made for all of them. The chatter. The laughter. Even her father would crack a joke every now and then. And remembering back to that time when she had memories as a six-year-old, Kai saw love in her father's eyes for her mother. It was always there. Always present. And he'd been warmer to his children at that time, too. Not anything effusive, but he had patience with them, he stopped to help them, he smiled every now and again. And sometimes, he would come in and kiss them on the brow and tell them good-night at bedtime.

Kai starkly recalled those warm, fuzzy days. Each time had been so special for her—when her father would lean over and she could smell the clean Wyoming sage and dried sweat on his skin as he kissed her good-night. He tucked her in, touching her small cheek, smiling down at her with love in his eyes for her.

Throat tightening, Kai drew in a ragged breath. She'd lost her appetite. Slowly, she pushed the blue-and-white plate away from her.

"Are you all right?" Gil asked her, snagging her gaze.

"Yeah...sure." Kai was shocked Gil had felt her shift of emotions. His gaze was penetrating without being intrusive. She saw the concern, the care, burning in his eyes as he studied her. With a half shrug, Kai whispered, "I'm just remembering the past, is all..."

CHAPTER FIFTEEN

"WOULD YOU LIKE an ice pack?" Kai asked Gil. She came to his side in the now-empty living room. It was nearly ten o'clock.

He nodded, grateful she'd asked. "Hate to admit it, but yeah. I can get it." He sat at one end of the couch, his leg resting on a stool that had a pillow on top of it.

She placed her hand on his shoulder momentarily. "No, you stay put. I noticed you looking a little stressed as the afternoon wore on. Are you in pain?"

Gil hungrily absorbed her fleeting touch, wanting more. The fact Kai had even done this for him was progress in his book. Since their talk in the ER, she'd stopped being frosty and retiring when he was around her. "A little," he hedged. Moving his hand lightly over his dark blue gym pants because the fabric was far more forgiving than jean fabric, he admitted, "I guess I didn't grasp the seriousness of my injury with the bull."

Kai's mouth curved. "Spoken like a true operator," she teased. "I'll be back in a moment."

As she passed him, Gil inhaled her scent. His body tightened. Kai had been right: as the day had worn on, he'd become tired. Jordana had told him about post shock and trauma reaction. Gil had honestly thought nothing of the brush with the bull's horn. It made him quell some of his restlessness, because there was no way he wanted anyone cutting into his leg.

The room was quiet. Miss Gus, Val, Griff and Sophie had left around seven. Daisy was with Sandy up in her bedroom, comfy, he supposed, in her box. Sandy had put an extra small towel in there for the pup to keep her warm at night. Tomorrow, Cass was taking her into town, to a pet store, so she could buy Daisy a nice dog bed, the kind that Zeke slept on.

Zeke was in the bedroom with Talon and Cat. Every night, Talon hauled the huge cedar-chip-filled dog bed in there. In the morning, he brought it out to the living room.

Gil heard Kai rooting around in the kitchen, heard the freezer door open, heard ice cubes being hauled out of the box and being placed into his big ice pack.

All evening, Kai had remained close to him, not across the living room, as before. There was still so much to discuss with her, to disarm the land mines still spread like a deadly carpet between them. Gil wished she could be in his arms tonight, in his bed, snuggled up against him. He wondered if Cass felt the same, dreaming of Sandy in his arms. Gil would bet money on it.

"Okay," Kai said, coming to his side, "here's two ibuprofen."

When her hand touched his palm, Gil stilled his reaction. "Thanks."

"And a glass of water."

He could get used to this, the constant contact with Kai. Small things, but such important steps. She didn't act as if it was stressful to help him. In fact, as she leaned over, her head near his, to hand him the glass, he inhaled her scent again, this time mingled with the subtle fragrance of oranges. Her hair gleamed burgundy and gold beneath the only lamp sitting next to the couch.

"And, last but not least," she murmured, moving around the stool where his foot rested, "your ice pack." She gently set it upon his thigh and arranged it so that it wouldn't fall off.

"Thanks," Gil told her. Noticing the smudges beneath her eyes, he said, "You're wiped."

Running her fingers through her short hair, Kai smiled a little. "Some. But it was a great day. What a wonderful surprise with Miss Gus bringing Sandy that little puppy. I just about cried."

Gil tipped his head back, tossing the ibuprofen into his mouth and then slugging down the water. He placed the emptied glass on the stand next to his chair. "It was a thoughtful gift," he agreed. He gestured to the nearby sofa. "Why don't you sit a spell?" He wanted private time with Kai. Everyone else was in bed. He saw her hesitate fractionally and then she gracefully sat down, tucking one leg beneath her. Kai had taken the other corner of the couch, shifting her arm to it, head resting on her upraised hand.

"Does Miss Gus do this often?"

"What? Be Mrs. Santa Clause?" Gil smiled a little, absorbing her nearness. There was peacefulness in her expression, her eyes half-lidded and her gray eyes dark with exhaustion.

"She's a generous woman, no question."

"So are you," Gil said quietly, holding her gaze, absorbing that soft half smile on her lips. "You helped everyone today."

Shrugging, she said, "Just my nature. I'm like you. I don't like to sit still too long."

The silence strung between them.

"Tell me more about your growing-up years, Gil?"

Gil stirred and rolled his head to the right, holding her gray gaze. "Funny, isn't it?"

"What?"

He lifted his hand off the chair arm. "Us. We've known each other for a long time but we never, really, got around to knowing much about one another personally."

Nodding, Kai shifted. She regarded him through half-closed eyes. "When Sam came home with you, both of you grabbed beers out of the fridge and went off by yourselves. All I heard were your stories as operators."

One corner of his mouth quirked. "Yeah, that's true. But I wanted to know about you."

"You could have asked."

Shaking his head, he said, "No. It wouldn't have been right. Sam might have gotten the wrong impression."

Frowning, Kai said, "What? To ask me about my background?"

"Sam was damned jealous of anyone who looked at you twice, Kai."

She frowned. "Well, he was protective, that's true."

"No, more like possessive." Gil rearranged the ice pack on his leg, some of the throbbing pain drifting away. "I just didn't want to rock the boat. Sam was my best friend, like a brother to me, but I also saw other things."

"I guess I didn't," Kai admitted. "I mean, he was

always protective of me, but I never saw him act that way with you. He really did trust you. And he was glad you could be there for me if I needed anything at Bagram when he was sent out on an op by himself."

"He did trust me." And he, of all people, should have not been trusted, because he'd been falling in love with Kai throughout the first year he'd met her. And it was a dead-end street for Gil. He roused himself, wanting to open up to her, and maybe it was a less mine-laden area by telling her about himself. "My dad was a rancher near Billings, Montana. He owned a large spread that had been handed down for a hundred years through our family. I was firstborn, so my dad, Wayne, made sure I got indoctrinated in running a ranch and being responsible for Rob, who was born two years after me. I drove my mother crazy because I was such a risk taker at a young age."

Kai smiled faintly. "Little did she know you'd end up in one of the riskiest businesses of all—being a Delta Force operator."

He snorted softly. "Yeah. Who knew?"

"Did you dream of being in the Army?"

"No, not really. My dad was grooming me to some-day take over the ranch duties." He held her sleepy gaze. "In some ways, our paths were alike, Kai. When I told my dad I wanted to join the Army at eighteen, he stripped gears. He got really angry and couldn't understand my need to travel, to see other cultures, find out how other people lived."

"At least he didn't disown you," she said sourly.

"No, he was pissed, but he always loved us," Gil agreed. "And then, when I went in, Rob followed two years later, and my dad was blown away. He thought we were both irresponsible and he couldn't understand we were young and just needed to do a little traveling and exploring. I craved adventure." Gil shook his head.

"Did he hold it against you?"

"No. When I came home from boot camp, we cried together. He forgave me and things were back to normal."

Her brows lowered. "Your dad cried?"

"Yeah, it was the first and only time. He tried to be tough but fair on us boys, but he didn't believe in lifting a hand against us. Kind of talked us into and out of things."

"Far cry from my dad."

Gil nodded, hearing the pain in her voice. He didn't want to go there with Kai tonight. "My dad always made us boys think. He'd take a piece of equipment like a carburetor apart, and tell us to figure out how it went back together. If we asked a question, he made us research it the best we could. And if we still couldn't find the answer, then he'd lead us on what we used to call a treasure hunt, dropping hints and suggestions. And in a way, he set us up to be damned good operators when we entered Delta Force." His heart contracted with missing his father.

"It sounds like he was really involved with you. Invested. What is your mom like?"

"Her name is Linda. And she was a grade school teacher. She's retired now, enjoying the big garden that her second husband built for her."

"And when you went home? How was your mom doing?"

One of the many things he loved about Kai was

her care of others, her concern genuine. "She was still coming out of the shock and grief." Gil looked up at the ceiling and then over at Kai. "I realized that the ranch was going to start breaking down if I didn't get out of the Army with a medical discharge and stay there and take over the reins of the place. She was still so devastated, in deep depression, that she wasn't even paying the bills that were overdue."

Kai whispered, "That had to be a tough decision."

"It was," Gil said. "I was planning on staying in for twenty and then getting out." He cut her a slight smile. "I found out a long time ago that life never gives you what you want."

She became pensive. "My dad was pretty good up until my mom died. Looking back on it now as an adult, it broke him. He just seemed to shrink inside himself. Steve and I both saw it and, of course, we were too young to understand what real love is and what happens when you lose the one you love."

"Yeah," Gil said quietly, searching her face. This was the Kai he knew for those five days. They had talked of so many things, although family had never came up at that time. "Love is a son of a bitch from what I can see."

"Is that why you never married?" Kai said.

His gut tightened. Wanting to admit he loved her would be a disaster. Gil was relieved Kai was relaxed and talking to him, no longer defensive. "My dad once told me that when I met the woman who was right for me, I'd fall head over heels in love with her."

"Your dad sure sounded a little bit like a romantic."

Hitching a shoulder, he said, "He would never admit it. He idolized my mother, though. Rob and

I grew up seeing two people very much in love. My dad used to kiss my mom in front of us. Sometimes, they'd dance around the kitchen, laughing and having a great time."

Sighing, Kai whispered, "That was something I so looked forward to when you came home with Sam. You weren't afraid to give me a hug. I always loved that about you, Gil. Sam was so…withdrawn. He didn't understand humans needed to touch one another."

The sadness in her tone ate at him. "Sam came out of a really bad home life. His father beat him, broke five bones in his body. He had it really tough, Kai."

"I know," she said, giving him a sad look. "I would be around you and wish that Sam would emulate you. He… I guess he just didn't know that people needed to be held sometimes… He'd never been held, so how could he know other humans needed that?"

Gil moved uncomfortably. It shed new light on those five days with Kai, how much of a toucher she was. He loved it, absorbed it hungrily, needed it, needed her. "Sam was a good man, Kai. I know he tried his best to make you happy." He saw her give him a soft look.

"He was. He wasn't mean. He never lifted a hand or voice to me. But in other ways, he was like my dad after my mom died. He just seemed to shrink inside himself and was never able to reach out to anyone again. Not even to me. It hurt a lot."

"You made him happy," Gil said. "That, I know for a fact." He saw Kai brighten a little.

"Really? He told you that?"

"Yeah, when we got drunk one night about a year

before he was killed, he told me that. He didn't usually talk about personal things or about you, but that night, he did. Sam said he'd never been happier than when he married you. He said it was the highlight of his life." Gil saw Kai's eyes grow moist, her lips part, his words, he hoped, healing to her. It looked like it, but he couldn't be sure.

"I'm glad you told me that, Gil. There were so many times I felt I was living with a cold, robotic stranger. He…he just wasn't very emotionally available. I mean, when I found out about his childhood, I didn't take it so personally. I thought it was me before finding out, but now, I don't think it was."

Gil had to physically restrain himself from standing up, pulling Kai off the couch and into his arms. And kiss her until they melted into one another. Because that was what happened the last time. And he'd never forgotten it. "It wasn't you," he said gruffly. "Don't you ever think that. You gave him so much love that he never got from that father of his. I saw many positive changes in Sam over the years and I knew it was because you were in his life." His throat tightened, his voice going low with emotions. If he didn't leave now, he was going to do something he'd be eternally sorry for. Slowly rising from the couch, he said, "I need to hit the sack."

Kai nodded and stood. They were so close. She was aching inside, her lower body a hungry animal. Her heart bled for Sam, for herself. And then she felt her heart cleave open and she suddenly moved forward, sliding her arms around Gil's neck, pushing up on her toes, her mouth barely touching his. "Thank you for telling me. I—I needed to hear that," she whispered tremulously, feeling her breasts graze his chest, feeling her nipples tighten with memory. Her whole lower body flooded with heat and a hunger so acute, she wanted to moan. Her body remembered Gil, remembered his hands, his mouth.

Gil stood very still, shocked at Kai's impulsiveness. Slowly, he raised his hands, framing her face, looking deeply into her drowsy gray eyes that glimmered with tears. Jesus, he was such a goner. Was this how Kai had looked after she'd realized he'd walked out on her? There was part devastation in her eyes and he sensed it was grief about Sam and herself. That she wasn't able to ever reach inside of him, get him to trust her enough to let down those thick, hard walls he'd built up around himself in order to survive.

Everything stilled. His hearing honed in on the sound of her wispy breath; her lips parted, begging for him to kiss her. Gil felt the birdlike beat of her heart against his own. "Kai," he growled, his whole body vibrating with need of her. "Is this what you really want?" He desperately searched her eyes.

"I..." She stumbled, holding his gaze. "I just want... I don't know what I want, Gil. When I'm around you, I feel things... You make me feel good..."

Everything was so damned tentative. Gil saw the confusion, the arousal, the need for him in her eyes. Kai had never been a woman who was able to hide what she felt. He brushed his thumbs gently against the slopes of her cheeks, which were now flushed. Her arms were still around his neck and she didn't back off. "Tell me what you want, Kai. I don't want to hurt you. And I don't want to go back to where we just came from." His voice vibrated with feelings.

His erection had sprung to life in seconds. Her belly
was barely brushing his hips but she had to know.
She had to know.

Their bodies swayed even closer toward one another and Gil lowered his head. Kai leaned upward,
stretching, wanting to meet his descending mouth.
His world anchored. It felt as if the earth were holding her breath as he lightly grazed her lips. A groan
rose in him, her lips just as soft as he remembered.
Kai smelled so good to him and he drank in her scent,
getting drunk on it.

Gil didn't want to barge in and crush her mouth
against his. He was so damned unsure of what Kai
really wanted. Maybe just to be held? Not kissed?
Did she want to make love with him? He didn't know
and it was driving him off a cliff, his body screaming to plunge into her, take her, have her scream with
pleasure as she orgasmed. Those torrid visions raced
across his closed eyes as their moist, ragged breaths
mingled, lips barely touching. Gil had to find out and
he slid his mouth a little more surely against hers,
waiting for a reaction. It came hesitantly and then he
knew Kai wasn't on solid ground with him. The urge
to take her, sweep her into his arms, carry her to his
bedroom, lay her out on her back and be on top of
her, feeling her sigh, feeling her move her hips sinu-
ously, teasing him, raced through him.

Their mouths clung together. Gil wanted to cher-
ish her, worship the sweet mouth that opened shyly
to him. Kai's arm tightened again, drawing herself
fully against him. Something old and hurting dissolved within his gut and he felt the tension bleed out

of him. Kai was trembling. Every protective mechanism within Gil reacted.

He took her mouth a third time and invited her to respond. She did. And it rocked his world, the years of need springing wildly to life within him, making him tremble as her mouth slid hungrily against his. When that lush sound of pleasure caught in her throat, Gil almost lost it. Almost got slammed back into their time together.

Kai's breath was hot and ragged. He could feel the roundedness of her belly pressing against his throbbing erection. They fit together so well. So easily. His mind was deteriorating. His heart was pounding. Her scent destroyed his thinking processes and flung open the doors to his lower body. Kai was warm, hungry and within his arms.

And if he didn't stop…

The last thing Gil wanted to do was stop kissing Kai. He could feel the warmth and wetness of her mouth sliding wetly against his, opening him more. Knowing where it would lead, he had to stop or they'd be sorry. It was too soon. Too much. Stunned by her wantonness, triggered by it, voraciously wanting every cell of her absorbed into himself, Gil had felt Kai fully surrender over to him. She would come to bed with him. What then? There was so much more from the past to be straightened out between them.

Tearing his mouth away from hers, Gil heard a low cry of protest lodge in Kai's slender throat, saw her eyes barely open, sharpened with arousal. Oh, Gil knew that look in her eyes. Kai was a hunter in the bedroom. They met and matched each other time and again. She was bold, assertive and knew what she wanted. And he more than wanted to give her everything—and even more.

He was breathing roughly, his chest rapidly rising and falling as he stared down into her glistening, lust-filled eyes. His voice was scratchy, unsteady. "Dove, we have to stop. You know that…" He hated saying those words. He saw Kai wince, saw the disappointment register in her eyes. He had called her Dove in special moments like this. Her dove-gray eyes. Gil hated himself. But he was more afraid of any future with Kai if they went beyond their kiss. His hands itched to release her face and slide down, cupping those small, pert breasts of hers.

With a moan of frustration, Kai released him. Her knees were wobbly and Gil's hands left her face and settled lightly on her shoulders to steady her. Lips tingling with the taste of his mouth, she tried to think. Tried to get the strewn, glowing parts of herself under her control once more. "God," she whispered, giving him an anguished look. "I—I'm sorry. I didn't mean—"

"Hush," Gil ordered her with a growl. "You did mean it. And so did I." Gil slid his fingers through her hair, needing to retain a connection with her in some way. Her cheeks were flushed, her gray eyes like velvet diamonds, her black pupils so large as she stared wonderingly up at him. "I'm not sorry, Kai. And you shouldn't be, either. It had to happen." His mouth curved inward. "We'd be fools to ignore our past."

She closed her eyes, her fingers gripping his upper arms for support as she weaved slightly. "Oh, Gil," she whispered in a strained tone.

Gently, he folded Kai against him. At first, she

resisted. He maintained the same pull, not increasing it, just waiting. Her eyes were a little wild with panic, but then she capitulated, allowing him to draw her against him. He didn't hold her tightly, wanting her to control the embrace. He kissed her hair, feeling the strength of the shining auburn strands beneath his lips. Gil wanted to trail a series of them down her skull to her nape, where Kai was particularly sensitive. It was an erogenous zone that sent her into a wild-woman reaction. Every woman had a particular spot that unzipped her from civilization and she became that stalking female animal who was fearless and taking what she wanted. Gil didn't dare kiss her there. Kai would come apart in his arms and he knew it. What had just happened? His mind was barely functioning. His erection ached so much he wanted to bend over and groan. She turned him on so swiftly, so completely. She always had.

Kai stood with her head against his shoulder, her arms loose around his waist as if absorbing him, appreciating him. She had no idea of the love he held for her. And as he rested his chin against her hair, Gil closed his eyes, grateful that Kai was once again in his arms. She had come to him, not the other way around. His heart grew to twice the size in his chest and Gil could barely take a breath because joy was flowing so strongly through him. Kai lifted him. She always made him feel like a man. *Always*.

Gil felt her stir and regretfully opened his arms so that she could step out of his embrace. She pushed her fingers through her hair, looking at him, looking away, scared and unsure of what had just happened. Gil knew he needed to be solid and steady right now because her eyes reflected fear, arousal, confusion and so much more. "Listen, we need to get to our rooms and catch some sleep."

Kai gave a jerky nod, nervously smoothing her tee down across her waist, fingers trembling. "Yes. Yes, that's right," she whispered.

"Come on," he said in a low voice, "I'll walk you to your room." Gil looked deep into her eyes and saw relief. Kai was just as blown apart by what had happened as he was. She was going to need time to figure it all out. And he was unsure where he fit into her life, if at all. Would Kai back away now? Run away? Too fearful of the sexual chemistry that exploded between them every time they got close to one another? Gil had no answers and that tore heavily at his vulnerable heart.

CHAPTER SIXTEEN

KAI WATCHED AS little Daisy, now chewing ardently on one of Sandy's leather shoes in the living room, whined with excitement. The puppy had been home for three days. Kai stood quietly at the kitchen entrance, having come in for lunch. She saw it was a training session in progress, which Talon tried to do three times a day, to acclimate his combat assault dog to tiny Daisy. Everyone knew to stand still and not speak.

Talon was on one knee, his hand on Zeke's leash. Zeke sat five feet away, in the center of the room, watching the golden retriever puppy whine and wiggle happily, teething the toe of Sandy's shoe.

"Okay, Mom," Talon told her. "Pick Daisy up, and I want you to hold her in your hands and bring her within three feet of Zeke."

Sandy nodded and scooped happy little Daisy up from the floor. "He's been so good, son."

Talon nodded. "I know, but you don't untrain a combat dog in one day or one week. I want Zeke to get used to you holding Daisy and walking around him with her in your arms. He has to stay put. He can't follow you."

Sandy stood and gave Cass, who had just come up to stand next to Kai, a smile of hello. He was leaning casually against the doorjamb, arms across his chest, watching the training session with interest.

Kai heard Zeke whine, but he didn't move. His tail eagerly thumped on the floor. Sandy did as she was instructed by her son.

"Okay, great, Mom," Talon praised in a low, calm tone. "Now, walk a large circle around us. I have to make sure Zeke will obey me and remain sitting, no matter where you are going with Daisy."

Sandy nodded, placed wriggling Daisy against her breast, both hands folded gently against the puppy and did a walk around.

Zeke twisted his head, his gaze trained on Daisy.

Sandy came around to the front of Zeke. "Okay?"

"Yes, good," Talon said, smiling up at his mother. "You two are doing good."

"I just think Zeke is lonely and he's dying to have Daisy around him all the time, Talon."

"You're probably right, Mom, but we have to be sure about it." Talon glanced at his watch. "It's lunch time. Let's call this training session to an end." He rose and took Zeke over to his big, round bed at the end of the couch and ordered the dog on it. Zeke complied. Talon took off the leash.

Kai smiled to herself as Sandy took Daisy, who was just a bundle of energy, to her bedroom. They couldn't allow the puppy to run freely through the house yet until Talon was sure Zeke wouldn't charge or run after the puppy. The Belgian Malinois had already proved he wouldn't bite or snap at Daisy, because the first thing Talon did was to place the puppy in his hand so that Zeke could smell her. It had only made Zeke more happy from what Kai could tell.

But Talon was being cautious and she knew he had a right to be. Zeke, when unleashed in the field, was a rocket on four legs with over four-hundred pounds per square inch of bite when he took down an enemy. And the dog wouldn't let go once he clamped his teeth around the tango until Talon arrived to give him the order to release him.

Everyone at the ranch was circumspect and supported Talon's efforts to socialize his dog. And everyone had fallen instantly in love with giddy, silly Daisy.

She felt more than heard Gil come up behind her. He stood about six inches away from her and she could feel the heat rolling off his masculine body. Her body reacted, heat flowing through her, that gnawing feeling growing intense, wanting Gil. Even her mouth tingled in memory of his searching kiss, so tentative, against hers.

Gil had been right to call a halt to it, because she was coming undone beneath his kiss. He had been the one who was thinking far more clearly than she was.

Turning her head, Kai met his warm blue gaze. "Hi," she said. Everything was changing between them. Since the kiss three days ago, they'd had no time to sit and talk privately. Gil's leg was almost back to normal, and he was past the incarceration period. Fence post replacement was a priority and he, Cass and Talon were out working all day on the long-term project. Gil was sweaty and she inhaled his scent, which was a mix of the Wyoming sage along with his own masculine scent that always drove her crazy.

"Hey, how's it going out in the barn?"

Her big project, the hay baler, was turning out to be a cantankerous job at best. "One step at a time.

I'm nowhere near done. So many parts to replace. I need to go into Ace Trucking and use their metal machine shop." She saw his brows drop, a sudden sense of protection wrapping around her. She honestly didn't know why everyone was so jumpy about Chuck Harper. He'd never given her any reason to think he was the lowlife that everyone said he was.

"When you going in?" Gil asked.

"After lunch. Why?" She gave him a teasing look. "You want to be my big, bad guard dog this time around?" Only once—plus the picnic they had gone on—had Kai skirted the rule Talon had made that she had to have a male escort when over at Harper's trucking company.

"Yeah, I'll do the duty," Gil said, and gave her a half smile. "And maybe, if we get lucky, can I buy you a cup of coffee and some apple pie at Mo's afterward? We need to talk and we're not getting much opportunity to do it around here."

Quirking her lips, Kai agreed. "Sure, I'd like that."

Gil nodded. "Talon's done. Let's go eat. I'm starving."

He moved with such powerful male grace and confidence, Kai thought as she followed him through the bright sunny kitchen. It was Cat's turn today to help Cass with food and setting the table. They all took turns and it was working out well. Cat raised her hand in hello to Kai as she brought over a stack of tuna sandwiches piled high on a wooden tray. Sandy was always served first because she was the head of the Holt household.

"I made an extra big tuna sandwich for you,

Sandy," Cass called from the kitchen. "Cat knows which one it is."

Cat grinned and offered it to Sandy. "He's on a mission to get that lost twenty pounds back on you or else."

Wrinkling her nose, Sandy picked up the special plate that had the sandwich on it. "Tell me about it. I've already regained seven pounds."

"Yes," Cat said proudly, "and it looks great on you, Sandy." She turned and stopped and allowed everyone else to pick up two or three sandwiches a piece. Placing three on Cass's plate and two on her own, she took the emptied tray back to the kitchen.

Cass came over with two huge platters of hot sweet potato fries, which brought a collective smile from everyone. He placed one in front of Sandy's plate and the other in front of Gil's plate. He'd added thick dill pickles, sliced, on the side of each person's plate. A big bowl of potato salad filled out the lunch menu for everyone. He took off his pink ruffled apron and dropped it on the counter. Coming around to his chair, he took it and sat down at the kitchen table.

"Grab a bunch," he told Sandy. "Sweet potatoes will put more weight on you faster than anything else."

Sandy smiled a little. "You're such a tough guy, Cass. What are you going to do if I don't eat ten handfuls of them?"

He gave her a grin. "Oh, that's a surprise."

Cat tittered. "Sandy, I'd watch out for him. He's always been a man of his word."

Kai saw Sandy's cheeks pink up. They did every time Cass became a little intimate with her, always chiding and teasing her into eating a little bit more. Sandy was responding wonderfully to his support. The longer Kai saw Cass working with Sandy, the more she thought that genuine care and love could pull a person out of their funk.

Cat had said Sandy suffered for years from depression, but since Talon had come home, and now with Cass caring for her, the symptoms had disappeared. Love was a powerful antidote. She risked a glimpse to her right, where Gil sat hungrily eating one of his three sandwiches.

He had shaved this morning, but already by noon, his face had darkened, giving him a more intense look. It only made him that much more appealing to her womanly side. Paying attention to her sandwich, she listened to the quiet chatter around the table. This was a happy group. And she loved watching Talon and Cat because they were so much in love. Her heart stirred. She wanted Gil. Again. Despite their past. Despite him walking away from her. Kai was glad she would have some precious private time alone with him. It just wasn't available at the ranch like she wished.

KAI SETTLED INTO the booth at Mo's. The waitress had just brought them two cups of coffee, and Gil had ordered two thick slices of apple pie with three huge dollops of vanilla ice cream. He sat opposite of her and he had set his Stetson beside him on the seat. It was two in the afternoon and the place was filled with tourists from around the world.

Maybe the tourists stared at Gil because he truly looked like an iconic cowboy from the Wild West.

He wore a blue chambray shirt, black leather vest and a red neckerchief around his strong, thick neck. Gil walked with a confidence Kai knew only an operator could carry off.

She saw a number of patrons stop eating and look up as he passed by their tables. He radiated a masculinity she had never seen so strongly in any other man. Not even Sam. She sipped her coffee, watching Gil dig into the pie and ice cream. She had one scoop of ice cream on her apple pie.

"There's no secrets to you," she said, and laughed quietly, pointing to his dish of pie.

"Hey," he murmured between bites, "I'm a happy man."

Kai could see it. Since she had kissed Gil, he'd remained completely readable to her. No more game face. No hiding. Her heart pulsed in her chest and she felt happiness thrumming through her. "I'm glad we have this time," she began, the cup warm between her hands. "So much is happening so fast, Gil."

He hesitated and wiped his mouth with the paper napkin, setting it aside. "That's what I thought. I could feel you retreating."

Kai licked her lower lip. "I got scared. I admit it. I liked kissing you, no question."

"But?" He dug into her gray gaze. He could see that tension back in her expression.

"I'm trying to untangle the past. I know you said that chapter is closed, but there's parts of it that aren't finished or closed for me."

"Like what?"

Taking a deep breath, Kai knew she had to be completely honest with Gil. "I'm afraid that if I allow my-

self to like you, you'll walk away from me again."
She saw him sit up as he digested her worry. "I know
you gave me an explanation of why you did what you
did, but it hurt, Gil. It hurt me so badly, you'll never
know how much." He frowned and she saw his eyes
grow sad.

"I could have handled that situation a lot better
than I did," he admitted, his voice low with regret.
"And I see the damage I did to you, Kai. And I understand it's no longer a matter anymore of me apologizing for my actions."

"No, it's not," she whispered, pained.

"It's about me holding myself accountable to you.
You need to see that I won't walk off and leave you
again. I get that. And I'm going to do everything in
my power to prove to you that I'm reliable. That I
would never do that to you ever again."

The gruff sincerity in his voice, the barely held
feelings in them, made Kai feel so hungry for Gil.
"I don't know why I kissed you when I did," she offered, shrugging. "It was like before. You showed up
and I just caved in to you. It's as if being around you
is like having dessert offered to me." She managed a
wan smile, holding his narrowed gaze.

"At least I'm dessert."

She grinned with him. "You always were." Sighing, she whispered, "I've been looking back to the
time Sam introduced us. Even then, I realize now,
I had been drawn to you. But I was so in love with
Sam, I just didn't get it."

"You shouldn't have, Kai. You loved Sam and that
is where your heart and focus had to be."

She tilted her head. "I always felt this warm care

coming off you when you came home and visited us. Was I imaging it, Gil?"

"No. I always cared for you, Kai."

Frowning, she asked, "Because I was Sam's wife?"

He moved uncomfortably, pushing the nearly empty pie plate aside. "If I told you it was more than that, how would you react, Kai?" he said, and somberly held her gaze.

Sitting back, Kai felt her emotions suddenly roiling within her. "I—I don't know, Gil. I always thought you cared for me because I was another operator's woman, later, his wife."

"I did," he reassured her. Shrugging, he sipped his coffee and said, "But over time, I began to like you for you. Not because you were Sam's wife. I always looked forward to coming over and I enjoyed seeing both of you, not just Sam."

Giving him a concerned look, she said, "I never realized that…"

"I couldn't tell you for obvious reasons. I loved Sam like a brother, Kai. I would never have done anything to create problems in his marriage with you."

Staring in disbelief, Kai tried to put his admittance together, remembering how warm and teasing Gil had always been with her. She had treated it as if he was a long-lost brother and she, his little sister. Sam had been fine with the relationship Gil had with her. But when she looked deep into his blue eyes, she found something else, an emotion she couldn't translate. Instinctively, she knew it had to do with her. "I guess," she admitted, "I didn't know."

"As it should have been," Gil reassured her. "Sam

loved you with everything he had. And you loved him."

"I did," Kai admitted. She took a deep breath and said, "When you came over to my barracks at Bagram, right after Rob had been killed, it was because of how you felt toward me from before?" She saw Gil's expression change and her heart thudded.

"When Rob died in that firefight, the only person I wanted to turn to was you, Kai," he admitted in a roughened tone, holding her questioning gaze.

"I thought… I thought because of our past with one another—" she opened her hands, unsure of where this conversation was headed "—that because we were friends…that was why you came over and asked me for help."

Gil grimaced. "I was a wolf in sheep's clothing, Kai. I had liked you ever since I met you. And frankly, I was in such deep grief and shock, I found myself in your barracks, in the lobby, asking for you. I was hurting so damn much I couldn't think straight. Rob was the other half of me. We grew up together, shared so much together, and when he was ripped out of my life, it broke me in a way I can't even begin to describe." Gil held her luminous gaze. "There was no one other than you that I wanted to go to."

Kai stilled, hearing the raw emotion behind his words, seeing it in his turbulent-looking gaze and feeling it through her entire body. "I still don't know what happened between us, Gil. One moment you were standing there in the lobby, and then you were holding me as if, if you let me go, you'd die."

He nodded. "That was pretty much it. You were an anchor to me, Kai. I knew you had the strength to help me. And when you pulled away and kissed me, it tore open a side to myself that I'd been hiding since the day I'd met you."

She pushed the cup aside, frowning. "I don't know why I kissed you, Gil. I felt so driven to do it—if I didn't do it, I'd die." She gave him a wry look. "Something just happened within me. And to this day I don't understand it. And nothing had ever felt so good, so right, as to step into your arms, be held and kiss you."

It had taken every ounce of courage to tell him that. His eyes widened with surprise, and then she felt an incredible joy radiating around him even though his expression remained placid, almost unreadable. But she felt his reaction. She'd always been able to feel Gil, as if they had an invisible telepathic connection strung between them.

"I hadn't come to see you thinking that you'd kiss me," Gil admitted, shaking his head. "And this isn't on you, and I'm certainly not blaming you for what happened after that."

Giving a ragged sigh, Kai whispered, "We just crashed into each other, Gil. I don't know. I've thought so much about it over the years and never come up with any good answers. I thought maybe my grief over Sam, losing him a year earlier, was the reason. Maybe because he was your best friend and I knew you…" She gave him a concerned look, felt old guilt stirring. "I just collapsed into your arms, Gil. And when you kissed me like you did, I melted. I lost my mind. It wasn't your fault, either. I'm responsible for my own actions."

"It escalated," he agreed, "and I wasn't thinking clearly, either. I was so damned hurt by Rob's loss, that when you kissed me, Kai, it felt like the single most right thing in the world to me. It was life over death. An affirmation of life."

"It did for me, too." She tinkered nervously with her cup. "And I just kissed you again, three days ago."

"You have a habit of doing that," he said, smiling a little. "But I kissed you back, too, Kai. It wasn't one-sided."

Her heart strained in her chest. She felt a need for more air, realizing she was holding her breath, waiting to see how Gil felt about her. About their kiss. "I'd be lying if I told you that I didn't like it."

"You're not a good liar anyway," Gil told her gruffly, his eyes warm. "You're an open book, Kai. You've always been that way."

Grimacing, she grinned and muttered, "Tell me about it."

"I like you the way you are," he said, his voice thick with emotion. "I always thought you were beautiful, intelligent and brazen."

"Brazen?"

His smile widened. "Yeah, brazen in all the right ways."

Kai felt heat fly up her throat and into her face. There was no question, looking into Gil's eyes, that he was remembering their wild, hungry lovemaking. And, yes, she'd been brazen, all right.

Dodging his gaze, she looked away, and watched the tourists coming to and going from Mo's busy establishment. Licking her lower lip, she knew she owed Gil her honesty. "Only around you. I've never been spontaneous like that in my life, with anyone." Her voice lowered with pain. "Not even with Sam."

Gil sat very still.

Kai felt the need to continue. "I wish I had more experience with relationships, Gil, but the truth is, until I met Sam, I'd had only one other affair. And after Sam died, I was lost. And then you crashed into my life. So I'm a little green about all of this. And I've been floundering ever since you left me. I had a disastrous affair two years ago, and it didn't work out at all."

Gil felt his heart expanding in his chest over her unsure, confused words and look. The fierceness of his love for Kai tripled. She looked so lost. He'd always known Kai was the kind of woman who wouldn't have a lot of affairs with men. She was a one-man woman, and she put her whole heart and soul into that relationship. She was not a flirt and did not purposely lead a man on. How badly he wanted to tell her that it was silent love that had held them together through all these years. Kai didn't have enough experience to know the difference between a red-hot affair in the moment and truly loving another person. Sam had been the one and only man with whom she had fallen completely in love.

Now he understood why Kai was wrestling so much with what had occurred between them. It was complicated. And because he'd had more than his fair share of affairs and relationships, he did understand what was happening. What he felt for Kai was an undying love. And it had never gone away. Never lowered in its intensity. That is what he had hidden completely from her. She was a neophyte in the world of sex, lust and love. But he wasn't. And even now, Gil couldn't admit his love to her. Kai was scared, as if on thin ice with him, wanting him, not knowing why, but it was there, nevertheless. Plus, even more damaging, there was the threat of him walking away from her.

His gut tightened. Fear ran through Gil as he said, "Look, maybe over time we can straighten all of this out between us, Kai. I'd like a chance to get to know you. This time, under less stressful circumstances. I like what we've shared before this. And I want to show you I can be a steady, reliable man in your life. You're in charge here, not me. I don't want to rush or push you into anything. But I'd at least like to know if I have a chance with you. To look at a serious relationship with you if it works out in that direction?" He saw her face crumple and moisture come to her eyes. God, she was so easily affected. But something he loved so much about her was her sensitivity and her inability to hide how she felt. Gil held his breath unconsciously, watching the softened expression come to her face.

"I'm scared, Gil. And you know why."

"Then we'll go as slow as you want. Give me a chance to prove myself to you?" Her mouth compressed and Gil knew that was a sign Kai was torn, unsure what to do. Dammit, he'd wounded her so badly and he cursed himself for his utter stupidity. He wished like hell he could do it all over again; the outcome would be very different.

"I just need time… I need to get used to the fact you're back in my life." Kai searched his eyes. "Does that make sense to you, Gil? I'm not sure about anything right now. I—I couldn't stand to give you my heart again and have it crushed a second time." She placed her hand against her chest, her voice breaking. "I just don't have the strength, or whatever it is, to risk my heart like that again with you. I wouldn't survive it."

Gil did something that could either hurt or help. He reached across the table, gently easing her hand from between her breasts, folding it into his. "I would die before I'd ever do that to you again, Kai. I won't walk away from you a second time. I promise you that." He felt her damp, cool fingers move shyly with his warm, dry ones. If only Kai would give him one last chance. Gil would not screw it up this time.

"Okay," Kai said in a low tone, her brow scrunching. "It's just so scary for me, Gil."

"We'll take it a day at a time. Your pace. Your call, Kai. All right?" He felt her unsureness, her wanting him as desperately as he wanted her. Gil saw some relief come to her eyes.

"Yes, that sounds good. Thank you for giving me the space, because I need it." She gestured with her hand. "I really need this job at the Triple H, Gil. I want to prove to Talon and Cat that I'm a great employee and worth keeping."

"I will never do anything to jeopardize your job there," Gil promised her. "What we have is private. Outside the ranch. I'm not going to do anything to put you in a position to lose your job." More relief was reflected in her eyes. Could he keep saying the right thing? To convince Kai he cared enough about her to protect her, keep what they had sacred and apart from her work life?

"Yes, because I don't want anyone to know. I really want to keep my personal life separate from my work life."

"I'll protect you, Kai." Gil saw her eyes widen and an array of emotions in them, all good. All telling him that she was drawn to him. He had never felt such a rush of relief in his entire life. He didn't have a life without her in it, but Kai couldn't know that. At least, not yet.

And they had such a long way to go to get to where he wanted them to be—together. It was going to take every vestige of his considerable patience to woo Kai slowly, with sensitivity, and Gil prayed like hell he could pull this off right this time.

Only time would tell...

CHAPTER SEVENTEEN

THE JULY FIRST sun beat down on Kai as she rode Mariah along the fence line in the southern part of the Triple H. She relished the warmth, soaking it up. Mariah plodded along, her ears moving alertly back and forth as they took a path down to the south fence. She'd finished with all her work in the green barn and had desperately wanted to be outside in the fresh air and sunshine instead of being enclosed in the equipment barn. The sway of her horse lulled her and she felt happiness flow quietly through her. The hills were lush with nearby calf-high green grass. The sky was a deep blue with high cirrus clouds that reminded her of hair blowing in the wind. Unconsciously, she touched her own growing hair. It was getting unruly and it needed to be shaped and trimmed a bit. Kai liked the feeling of longer hair, enjoying being feminine when the Army did not allow such a luxury.

A bright red cardinal was singing on a fence post, his melodic song filling the air. The soft snort of Mariah made her move even deeper into the peace she felt within her. Riding a horse was like moving into a deep meditation. The clip-clop of Mariah's dainty hooves on the soft trail of grass made her smile. Closing her eyes, Kai allowed herself to sink into the sensations of her five senses. Automatically, her heart moved to Gil. The past three weeks since their kiss, he'd hadn't made a move to touch her again. The ache in her body for him, however, was growing even more. And her heart was beginning to trust him. How she wanted to.

Her cell phone vibrated in her pocket. Unhappy at being snapped out of her reverie, she pulled it out. It was from Chuck Harper. *Again.* He'd been calling her every day for the past two weeks, wanting to get together and go on a date with her. How many ways could Kai tell him no?

"Hello?"

"Kai? This is Chuck. How are you today?"

"I'm fine, thanks."

"Hey, there's a July Fourth dance at the Armory coming up. I'd really like to take you, Kai. What do you say?"

Rolling her eyes, she said, "I can't, Chuck. I told you, I'm in a serious relationship. It wouldn't be right."

"Well," he said, somewhat amused, "I had to try. I still would like to have some kind of friendship with you, Kai."

She hated the way he manipulated her. "I'll let you know, Chuck. You'll have to excuse me, I'm at work right now." She clicked off the call and jammed the phone into her pocket, her day souring. Why couldn't Harper just leave her alone? She'd told him she was in a relationship as soon as she and Gil had made peace with each other. Moving her shoulders to dislodge an invisible weight, she crested the hill. Down below on the southwest corner of the fence line, she saw Gil working to remove a post. He had the truck and she saw all the fence and post supplies he'd need for repair purposes in the back of it.

Her heart raced as she watched him work. His chambray shirt was stained with sweat down his broad back. The sleeves were rolled up to his elbows, and she could see even the elk-skin gloves, which were thick and protective, were splotched and darkened with sweat from his hard, continuous work. Her lower body stirred as she watched his powerful shoulders tense, his muscles bunch, when he put his arms around the lower part of the post, hauling it upward out of the ground with brute strength alone. She keenly remembered his strength, the feel of his ropy muscles around her. Groaning outwardly, Kai didn't try to escape memory of their bodies fused together, absorbing his strength as they had loved one another.

She called out to Gil as she aimed Mariah down the path along the fence. Raising her hand, she saw him drop the post on the ground and raise his head. He lifted a gloved hand and then wiped his gleaming face with it as he straightened. Gil walked to the rear of the truck where they kept a large plastic water dispenser. He was pouring himself a glass when she rode up. Sweat was running down the sides of his face and neck as he lifted it to his lips. Her breasts tightened. The man was so damned sexy.

"Hey," she said, lifting her leg across the saddle and hooking it around the horn, "where's everyone else? This isn't work for just one person."

Gil finished the glass of water and wiped his mouth with the back of his hand. "Cass and Talon had to go into town to Horse Emporium. They're getting more things we need to complete this section." He gestured toward the fence. "Did you escape the barn?" he asked, grinning as he lifted his hat off his head and wiped his brow.

"I did." Kai sighed and looked around, resting her arms on her leg, feeling Mariah cock one of her legs up into a rest position, her weight on the other three. "It's so beautiful out here. I miss the sunshine. The air."

"Downside of being a good mechanic," he agreed. Gil took a break and lifted himself onto the tailgate of the truck, his legs hanging and almost brushing the grass below them. "Did you finish on the baler?"

Groaning, she said, "Yes. That's in part why I escaped. That damned piece of machinery has been my karma for far too long. I think I've got it fixed, but we're going to have to hook it up to the tractor and give it a test run."

Gil nodded. "Well, this grass is more than ready to be cut. Maybe get it out here tomorrow after lunch, after the dew has dried off it."

"Sounds good to me. I'll ride with you guys and bring my toolbox along. Just in case."

"Want some water?"

She was thirsty. "Yeah, sounds good." She sat up and dismounted. Pushing her Stetson a little higher, she pulled the reins over her mare's head and led her to the truck. After tying them to the truck, she took the glass Gil handed to her, their gloved fingers touching. Kai hungered for these moments when they happened, which wasn't often.

Gil pulled off his gloves. He ran his fingers through his damp hair, taming it into place. Hat hair was the price for wearing a Stetson. He watched Kai drink, his eyes on her slender throat. How many times had he lavished that part of her body? Knew how sensitive it was to being worshipped by him? Gil couldn't be around Kai for long before he felt himself hardening.

"Thanks," she said, handing him the emptied glass.

"Been riding around long?" he wondered, watching as she leaned her hip against the tailgate, facing him.

"About half an hour." She smiled a little and tugged off her deerskin gloves, tucking them in her back pocket. "Not long enough."

"Your hair is really growing. Looks good on you. Big change from your Army days, isn't it?"

Laughing a little shyly, she nodded, wanting to walk in between his opened thighs and kiss him. He was damp, dirt stained, but Kai didn't care. Gil was a working man, a man of the land. "Funny, I was thinking the same thing." She touched her hair. "It's nice in some ways to be out of the military. I miss the people, the teamwork, but not some of the other stuff."

Gil poured himself another glass of water from the dispenser. "I feel the same."

Kai felt incredibly happy. Being with Gil, being alone, felt wonderful. She watched him polish off the second glass, understanding how tough it was hauling a twelve-foot four-by-four out of the ground. If anyone thought wrangling was easy, it wasn't. It took someone like Gil, who relished hard work, who funneled his passion through his body, to make physical changes in a ranch like this. It wasn't always about roping a calf from a horse, branding or herding cows.

"Hey," he said, picking up her hand and pulling her toward him.

Kai absorbed the burning look in Gil's eyes and

knew what that meant. He wanted to kiss her. She knew she could have pulled her hand out of his, because he waited to see what she wanted to do. Instead, Kai moved toward him, a nonverbal response to the question in his eyes. He was starting to guide her next to him, but she resisted and moved around his opened legs and stood between his thick, hard thighs. A hunger flared to life in his eyes. She placed her hands on his thighs, looking up into his gleaming face, drowning in his darkening gaze. "I've been thinking a lot about us, Gil," she admitted, feeling his muscles tense beneath the light touch of her hands. "I'm not the greatest at communication and I don't think you are, either. I know in my case, I assumed a lot of things. And that's really bad, as I found out with Sam. And we... well...there wasn't much talking when we came together later. From this moment on, I'm going to try very hard to let you know what's on my mind, or in my heart, Gil."

Nodding, Gil smiled a little. "I know you're right. And it's a two-way street, Kai." He reached up, gently removing a few errant strands from her cheek, watching her eyes widen with pleasure over his brief touch. "And along that line—" his eyes crinkled "—I want to ask you to the Fourth of July dance at the Armory. Would you feel comfortable going with me? I don't do fast dancing, but I'm pretty good at slow dancing."

Her flesh radiated with heat where his roughened fingers had grazed the slope of her cheek, taming those strands back into place. "I'd love to go with you."

"You know that if you do, everyone here at the ranch is going to the dance and they'll know there's something going on between us? Are you ready for that?" He studied her thoughtful-looking gray eyes. "And if you don't want them to know, I'm fine with not showing up at the Armory with you. I want to make you happy, Kai. Not stress you out."

Her heart turned with fierce emotions over his low, concerned voice. How could she ever think Gil didn't care for her? He had been showing it to her in small ways nearly every day. Never touching her. Never doing anything except to let her know that he cherished her. And that was the feeling washing through her right now. She moved her hands slowly up and down his Levi's-covered thighs. "I considered that," she admitted quietly. Raising her eyes, she met his. "I'm okay with it, Gil. Are you?" She saw that male smile of his that made her lower body go hot with longing.

"It will be our first official date. And I'm not worried what anyone else thinks. All I'm concerned about is what you think."

Just the damp, nubby texture of the Levi's beneath her fingertips made Kai ultrasensitized to Gil. She could feel the tension in him as she moved her hands. It was a nervous reaction, not meant to be teasing him, but he probably didn't know that. "I don't even own a dress," she lamented.

"I don't own a suit, either."

She laughed, feeling suddenly free in a way she never had. "Well, then, it looks like I need to shop and so do you."

"Mine will be easy. A suit is a suit."

"I think I'll get Cat to go with me. She's got a good eye and she won't lie to me and tell me something looks good on me when it doesn't." Kai was beginning to melt beneath his blue gaze. Gil didn't hide how he felt about her—it was there to read. She languished between his legs, knowing it was an intimate gesture, but what she craved was this kind of easy flow between her and Gil. She hungered for it. And she was starved for him. Getting up her courage, she said, "Gil? I want to kiss you…nothing more… but kiss you."

"You were reading my mind," he growled, his smile disappearing. "Come here… I've been dreaming of kissing you, every night before I go to sleep…"

She flowed into Gil's opening arms, feeling him draw her to him, against his hard body, the tension easing out of her as she tilted her head upward to meet his descending mouth. This time, there was no hesitancy between them. This time Gil took her mouth hungrily, and she was no less starved for him. Her body became like a willow relaxing against the hard oak of him. Kai was more than aware of the erection pressing against his Levi's, her belly tingling with memory, with wanting him in every possible way. His scent flared into her nostrils as she allowed him to guide her against him, leaning fully into him, glorying in the taste of him.

It felt like the past had overlaid her present, his mouth against hers questing, asking, giving, taking. A moan rose in her throat as his tongue barely brushed each corner of her mouth. Heat scalded her lower body and she pressed herself wantonly against him, hearing a low, deep groan rumble through his chest as he crushed her mouth beneath his. Her breath went ragged, her fingers caressing his sweaty nape, tunneling up through his short, damp hair. A sense of love floated through Kai as she felt Gil ease off a bit, cherishing her lips, cherishing her, his hands supporting her head, angling her, teasing her more deeply. And when his tongue slid against hers, a faint cry lodged in her throat, and she became damp between her thighs.

As if he realized it was too much, Gil eased his mouth from her wet one, his breath shallow, his eyes narrowed and burning upon hers. Kai managed a trembly smile, sliding her hand up across his cheek, his stubble inciting tiny fires in her fingertips. Her heart ached to do so much more. It would be so easy to lie in the grass and have him take her. The ache in her entrance was turning into an almost painful throb, begging to be touched, begging for his skilled attention. Blinking slowly, dazed by the power of his kiss, she whispered, "Nothing has changed, has it?" She saw Gil give her a faint smile, his eyes glittering with hunger for her.

"Nothing's changed, Dove," he said gruffly, and cupped her cheek, drawing her forward, kissing her tenderly, not like before.

Every time Gil called her by this endearment, her heart flooded with overwhelming love for him. The word vibrated deep in his throat, like an invisible hand caressing her. Never had Kai felt more loved than in this moment, because each graze along the slope of her cheek, trailing down the side of her neck, fire erupting wherever his fingertips wandered, weakened her resolve even more. Lifting his hand, he sent his fingers through her hair, her scalp bursting with pleasure as he lightly massaged the area. Kai felt worshipped. And only Gil had ever given her this gift. Until this moment, Kai hadn't realized how much she'd missed him in her life. He treated her as if to him she were the most valuable and priceless person on the planet. His mouth was cajoling, wanting her participation, but in a slow, exploratory way. She moaned and melted helplessly against him, her head in the crook of his arm as he continued his tactics to ask her to surrender fully to him.

And then she heard a truck coming.

So did Gil, and he gently eased her up on her feet, his hand on her arm to make sure she was steady.

Giving him an apologetic look, Kai nervously smoothed her hair, looking toward the crown of the hill above them. The truck hadn't appeared yet, thank goodness. She'd have died of embarrassment if Talon and Cass had seen them kissing like this. Her whole body felt like a flame roaring out of control. She was shaking inside, her lower body feeling hot, wet dampness coating the insides of her thighs, soaking her panties. Gil turned her on like a blowtorch. Her body was highly reactive to him in every possible way.

"Dove? You might want to come over here," Gil said, and smiled a little, guiding her from between his legs, helping her stand next to Mariah after handing her the reins.

Flustered, Kai whispered, "My God, Gil…" She searched his amused-looking gaze. "What happened?"

"Us," he rumbled. "We're good together. That hasn't changed one bit." He glanced toward the hill, seeing the white ranch truck, weighted down with fence supplies, slowly cresting the top of it. Gil studied her. "To be continued after the Armory dance," he promised her in a growl.

Kai touched her lower lip, still wet from his slow

exploration of her. "Yes," she whispered, her voice sounding very far away to her. "Yes, I'd like that." She saw the pleasure burn in his eyes over her response.

"Good, because I think it's time we got a hotel room in town and took this all the way. I can't kiss you without wanting all of you, Dove. You know that."

Yes, she knew that. Glancing down at her thighs, she was afraid the material would be darker than the surrounding fabric. She felt the wet slickness between her thighs. Gil had almost brought her to orgasm with just a kiss! One kiss! Giving him a disconcerting look, she said, "That sounds good."

"I'll take care of it," he promised her, watching the truck approach. It wouldn't be lost on either one of those operators that he had one hell of a painful erection. Gil wasn't concerned. If they teased the hell out of him, he'd take it in stride because Kai had come to him of her own accord. And he sensed how close she was to orgasm. He'd wanted to slide his fingers between her legs, put just the right amount of pressure on her entrance, let her ride against his hand and watch her come. He felt so damned elated and happy he could barely control the feelings pouring through him. Even the ache of his erection took second place to the joy sweeping into his chest, grabbing his heart, giving him the one thing he wanted most with Kai: hope. Hope for a future with her. It was another step they were taking together. And she was controlling the pace, the process.

One look at her swollen lips, her flushed cheeks and her gray eyes like soft, sparkling diamonds of arousal, and Gil knew that what they would have in

bed was solid gold. And he was going to exploit that
connection with Kai as much as he could.

Kai mounted Mariah, looking like a woman who
had been more than well kissed. Gil gave her a reas-
suring look as the truck continued toward them. As
he searched her wide, luminous eyes, he no longer
saw confusion in them. Only desire. He'd been right
in allowing her to lead them. Now she was more than
ready for another important step in their growing relationship. And he could hardly wait for that Armory
dance to arrive.

"WHAT DO YOU THINK?" Kai worriedly asked Cat. They
were in a dress shop in downtown Jackson Hole. Kai
wore a summer dress, a soft green color reminding
her of newly sprouted leaves found only in the spring.
Nervously, she smoothed the silk folds of the fabric.

"Wow," Cat said, sitting up in the chair. "You look
so different, Kai."

Giving Cat a pleading look, she said, "It's that
bad?" Because she had grown up without a mother
to teach her about clothing, about how to be feminine,
all Kai knew was she liked the look of the ponte-
shaped dress with side ruching and a square neck.
The sheath was slimming and she felt pretty in it, but
Cat had more experience with girly stuff than she did.

"Amazing," Cat laughed, "and it looks so good on
you, Kai. That sheath emphasizes how beautiful you
really are. Who knew? All I ever saw you in was jeans
and a tank top." She chuckled some more. Standing,
she gently smoothed the cap sleeves on each upper
arm. "I love this neckline on you," she murmured. "It
reminds me of a trapezoid shape, but it sure empha-

sizes the length of your neck." Cat fussed some more with the ruching on the sides of her dress. "This design really emphasizes your small waist. Wish I had one that small, but it ain't gonna happen in this lifetime." She smiled into Kai's eyes and, stepping back, she said, "Slowly turn around?"

Kai did so, feeling odd in the slimming dress, the hem barely touching her knees. She didn't want a dress above her knees because she felt almost naked. But this dress, the color, the way it draped her body, felt right to her.

"Oh, I like it." Cat sighed, stopping her and running her hand down her back. "And a hidden zipper. It sure gives your dress a beautiful line, Kai. It's unbroken and it flows so nicely around your great-looking body. You sure got the right genes this time around." She smiled. "Keep turning slowly. Let me just see how it moves on you."

As she faced Cat, Kai slid her fingers down the smooth, gleaming silk. "So? You think it's okay for the Armory dance? Not too, well, you know? Tight?"

Cat stood back, hands on her hips. "With the auburn color of your hair, that green just emphasizes your face, your eyes." She gave Kai a wicked look. "I don't think Gil is gonna be able to keep his hands off you."

Kai flushed—she had told no one of their growing relationship. "Oh…well…it's just a dance. And everyone else in the family is going."

"Uh-huh," Cat murmured, grinning. "I've seen how Gil watches you when you're not looking, Kai," she said, and tittered.

Kai chewed on her lower lip, touching the soft material. "He's a good person." She knew it sounded rather lame.

"Well, you are certainly gonna set that man back on his heels, that's for sure."

Giving her a stressed look, Kai said, "Do you think this is too much? I mean, is everyone there going to be wearing Western clothes? Is this too... I don't know...citified?"

"No. I was talking to Miss Gus the other day and I was having the same worries because I like sleek-looking outfits. She said people wear any and every-thing from dress up to dress down. Some do come in Western clothes, but a lot of the richer women of the valley whose husbands own a corporation or are filthy rich wear the latest New York and Paris fash-ions. So, I think you'll fit right in."

"I just don't want to look dorky."

"Trust me, every man in that place is going to be so jealous of Gil Hanford," she promised. "Go ahead and get changed. Do you have earrings? A necklace?"

"No."

"I know," Cat said, "you were in the Army. Being girly wasn't encouraged."

Kai bought the beautiful dress. Cat took her over to the shoe department. She refused to wear high heels with pointed toes, knowing they were uncom-fortable and ruined a woman's feet over time. In-stead, Cat found a nice pair of white sandals with a low heel that suited her. In the jewelry depart-ment, Kai opted for a pair of tasteful sterling-silver earrings, which complemented her gray eyes, and a thin chain with a heart that slid back and forth on it when she moved. Cat liked her choices and Kai was so grateful to the woman, who definitely had more awareness of women's fashion than she ever did.

"Now," Cat said, leading her out of the store, "I think you should get your hair washed, shaped and a slight trim." She touched Kai's hair and smiled. "It's such a beautiful color, Kai. You're going to take Gil's breath away. Do you have a shawl or a jacket to wear over your dress? It gets cold in the evenings."

"No," she said. "I'm hopeless, huh?"

Giggling, Cat walked with her down the wooden sidewalk toward a hair dresser's studio that was located on the other block. "Not hopeless. You didn't have a mom to help you navigate the woman's world of fashions, is all. This way, we'll get your hair trimmed and then we'll go to another store I know that has nice evening wear accessories."

Kai was nervous about the dress. How she looked. She was used to being in the background, not out in front. But she wanted to look beautiful for herself and for Gil. The dress had felt incredibly comfortable to wear, not so tight she couldn't breathe or move around in it. And looking into the mirror, Kai had thought she looked even more slender in it. She was glad she wasn't short waisted. A dress like this would make a woman look like an accordion if she was. But with Cat's eye and knowledge, Kai felt she had the right clothes for the dance. And, God, it had been ages since she danced! Smiling a little, Kai knew she had to warn Gil that she wasn't exactly from *Dancing with the Stars*.

CHAPTER EIGHTEEN

GIL HAD NEVER seen Kai in anything but Army uniform or wrangler gear. He had a tough time, as he drove her in the pickup to the Armory, keeping his gaze off her. She seemed nervous when she had walked out into the living room of the ranch house and all the men whistled and gave her looks that made her blush. Cat had told the guys to cool it, placing a protective arm around Kai's shoulders.

Gil hadn't said anything, shocked at how beautiful she looked in the light green silk sheath dress. He'd never seen her with makeup on, either. Her lips were a soft pink, a hint of charcoal above her eyes, a natural blush to her cheeks.

When their eyes met for a second, Gil smiled at her, feeling his whole body tingle with anticipation. He'd been dreaming of this moment with Kai for so many years. He would have her alone, in his arms and he intended to love her until she knew to the depths of her soul how much he needed her. Knowing it was too soon to tell her, Gil was grateful she'd given him this sign of trust.

As they pulled into the packed Armory parking lot in Jackson Hole, he felt her tense a little. "Relax," he murmured, turning off the truck engine, sliding his arm across the seat and his hand closing in on the small, dark green shot-with-silver shawl that covered her shoulders. "You look incredibly beautiful, Kai."

"I'm just not used to wearing clothes like this." She picked at the hem of her dress, and then Kai gave him a wry smile, touching her lips momentarily. "I can't remember the last time I wore lipstick. I honestly can't."

"Brings out the shape of your lips," he soothed. "And it doesn't hurt to be a woman every once in a while. I think Cat did a nice job with your hair and makeup." The shyness in her eyes, the uncertainty of herself as a gorgeous woman, made his heart open even more. Realizing Kai had no mother figure to show her the feminine side of herself, Gil caught and held her gray gaze. "Dove, you're with me tonight. Okay? I'll be at your side. And if men look at you, they're damned jealous of me because you're mine."

Giving a jerky nod, Kai whispered, "Okay. Thanks… I'm just a nervous wreck, Gil. And I don't know how to dance very well." She grimaced. "I was a wallflower in high school. I was afraid of boys. And, really, none paid any attention to me, which was just fine with me."

Gil grinned and leaned over, lightly touching her mouth with his. "Their loss, my gain," he rasped, looking deep into her eyes. "And, as for dancing, I won't embarrass you, but I'm not exactly a great one on the dance floor, either. We'll just take it at our pace. Okay?"

"Okay," she said, smiling a little, drowning in the dark, burning look Gil gave her.

"Ready?"

"I think so…"

Kai walked on Gil's arm through the packed parking lot. Above them the stars hung large and heavy in the dark heavens. They were like scattered diamonds thrown across the black velvet sky, as if celebrating this night. She heard music drifting out of the opened doors of the Armory, saw many people coming from around the parking lot and walking toward the building. It was dark, but the sulphur lights in the lot allowed Kai to see what other women were wearing. Some looked incredibly elegant in floor-length gowns. Others wore pantsuits. Still others sported more Western-like dresses or skirts and blouses. She did spot a number of women who were wearing clothes similar to hers, sleek and fashionable looking. Some of her nervousness was tamped down when she realized she wouldn't stand out and look odd or different from everyone else.

Kai felt safe and protected on Gil's arm. He wore a tan Western suit, the cut showing off his broad shoulders and chest. His dark brown Stetson brought out the ebony color of his military-short hair. He smelled of sage soap and she inhaled it deeply. He had cut his stride in half for her, sometimes looking down at her, a hint of a smile on his mouth.

"I feel as if I'm Cinderella going to the ball with her prince," she admitted softly to him, holding his dark blue eyes, which clearly showed his care for her. Kai knew it was more than that but was afraid to go there. She knew what love looked like on a man's face. She'd seen it in Sam's as they'd made love. And she saw that same look in Gil's eyes. Happiness wove through her because he was able to show how he felt about her all the time, not just in bed. It was something she desperately craved and Gil was hitting all the right notes with her.

"Well," he said, amused, "I'm hardly a prince, and I don't think our truck is going to turn into a dazzling coach drawn by white horses, but I'll do my best to make you feel like you're in a fairy tale tonight that has a happy ending."

His words flowed through her, filled with promise. "You're a warrior," she said. "And I'd rather have a warrior than a prince at my side any day."

Grinning, he eased his hand from hers and slipped it around her shoulders, giving her a slight hug. "You're my princess tonight, though. You look elegant, Kai. And you're going to turn male heads, that I promise."

That sent a wave of nerves through Kai. "I'm hardly princess material," she joked. "Just a working woman who usually has grease under her fingernails." Kai was an introvert. She was shy by nature. She didn't like being stared at by men, because it made her feel unsettled and uncomfortable. The sense of protection surrounding her was coming directly from Gil. He was a tall, big man. And he commanded attention because of the quiet confidence that radiated around him like the sun itself.

"Well," Gil said to her in a low, growling voice, "you're *my* princess. Never forget that, Dove." He remembered the day Kai had told him how much she loved the mourning doves on her father's ranch. It was one of the few times they talked of the past during that torrid five days together. And his endearment for her was born out of her love of the gentle bird, but also her stunning gray eyes.

Kai didn't have time to absorb his last comment as they drew up to the doors of the Armory. The music inside was Western: several fiddles, an accordion, drums, and someone was calling a square dance. They moved into the crowd and slowly entered the huge building. As they did, Kai looked up to see huge red, white and blue banners strung across the ceiling above them. There were large, round tables in one of the festive colors along three sides of the Armory, and the venue overflowed with people. The noise, the crowd, the loud music, made her instinctively move closer to Gil. As if sensing her unease, he slid his arm around her waist, drawing her to him a little more, as though to silently tell her she was fine. It helped.

"Over there," Gil said, pointing to the right, "the Triple H table."

Craning her neck because she didn't have Gil's height, Kai glimpsed the table. Cat and Talon, Sandy and Cass, were already there and seated. Gil threaded her through the chatty crowd and brought her out of it. Now, Kai saw them clearly. Each table had patriotic-colored carnations in a slender, tall vase. She saw the look on Cass's face as he sat next to Sandy. There was clearly something sweet and good going on between them. Sandy looked beautiful in a dark blue dress with gold jewelry at her throat and on her ears. Her blond hair was up on her head, making her look young. Cass had worn a casual gray Western suit with a red tie at his throat, making him blend in with the festive crowd.

Next to them were Talon and Cat. He had his arm around his wife, talking with her. Kai's heart was suffused with happiness because the love that was in their eyes was clear for everyone to see. Cat wore a pale pink summer dress with spaghetti straps. Her black hair was long and she'd worn it up on her head, a gleaming gold barrette holding it in place. Her blue eyes sparkled as she looked up into her husband's worshipful gaze. Talon wore a black Western suit with a crisp cotton shirt and black tie. It made him look intense, and brought out his rugged good looks, Kai thought.

As Gil led her to the table, Kai went to each woman, leaned down and hugged her, telling her how beautiful she looked. And they did. Gil pulled out a chair next to where Cass sat. After seating her, he asked if she'd like some of the fruit punch or a glass of wine.

Wine would settle her nerves and Kai asked for a glass of white. Gil asked the others and he took their orders, going over to the bar area.

Kai's back was partially toward the square-dance floor crowded with over a hundred couples. She saw her four friends collectively tense and then frown. Before she could ask them what was wrong, she felt a man's large hand come to rest on her shoulder. Startled, Kai turned and looked up. Chuck Harper smiled down at her.

He was in a dark gray Western suit and Stetson. He looked polished and handsome.

"I had to come over and tell you," he said, leaning down near her ear so she could hear him, "that you're the most beautiful woman here."

Kai gulped, unsure what to do or say. "Thanks, Chuck." She felt his hand become more firm on her shoulder. She eased out from beneath it by turning toward him in her chair. "I hope you enjoy the dance tonight," she said lamely.

His expression changed, his voice lowered. "I intend to. I just wanted to come over and tell you that you're a babe compared to everyone else here." He patted her shoulder. "Have a good time. I'll touch base with you later…" He left after nodding deferentially to the rest of the table.

Kai was shaken. She clearly saw anger in Harper's eyes. The change in his voice sent a chill down her spine. It was as if he'd taken off that smiling mask he wore and she saw who he was for the first time. And it upset her. Maybe the warnings by everyone at the ranch were true? That he was manipulating her? Kai didn't like the guttural warning in his voice that he'd see her later. What was that all about? She frowned and turned around, scooting her chair up to the table. "Sorry," she told everyone. Talon looked grim as he stared after the departing Harper.

Cass said, "If there ever was a weasel in this place, it's him. You all right, Kai?"

Licking her lower lip, she nodded, her hands knotted below the table in her lap. "Yes, fine."

"He's pretty bold," Cat muttered, frowning. "Good thing Gil wasn't here."

Talon snorted. "Harper wouldn't have tried it if Gil was here."

Kai had never told any of them about her trail ride with Harper. Now, she regretted even doing it. At the time, it had seemed okay. Harper had been the perfect gentleman. He never made a move on her. Until tonight. She felt that his hand had left residue on her shoulder and she wanted to get rid of the feeling. "If you'll excuse me? I need to go to the ladies' room for a moment." She stood up, placing her green shawl on the back of her chair. "Tell Gil I'll be right back?"

KAI ASSUMED GIL knew about Harper coming over to the table. He rose from his seat as she approached them. Quickly appraising his expression, she saw nothing in it to indicate he was upset. She didn't want to bring it up and ruin the night. Her glass of wine was in front of her and she sat down, thanking him.

"Did you see how many men turned their heads to look at you?" Cat asked between songs.

Sipping the wine, Kai shook her head. She was glad Gil had placed his hand against the back of her seat. It was comforting to her. "No, I didn't."

Cat beamed. "Well, a *lot* of men did. You look so svelte and elegant in that dress. It just suits you so well, Kai."

Kai smiled weakly. "Thanks. I guess I'm just not used to this kind of attention." She felt Gil's arm a little more firmly against her back, as if to soothe her. "I feel better in a hangar fixing an Apache combat assault helicopter," she joked.

A slow song came on. Cat got up, tugging at Talon's hand.

"Come on, we can dance now!" she pleaded, smiling at her reluctant husband.

Talon grudgingly got to his feet. He gave Cass and Gil a hard look. "You two are coming with me. So let's get on it."

Kai chuckled as they obeyed their boss. When Gil took her hand, curving it warmly into his, she felt less tense and followed him out to the dance floor. It was nice to have Cass and Sandy nearby, as well as Talon and Cat. They were a family. As Gil slid his arm around her waist, his other hand taking hers, she smiled up at him. She drowned in the burning look in his blue eyes, felt sizzling heat arc through her as he drew her against him, their bodies lightly touching.

"Remember," she warned him, "I have two left feet." Gil gave her a patient smile and a slight nod of his head as his gaze moved across the area. He was an operator. He would never lose that ability.

Gil looked down at his polished brown cowboy boots. "Well, makes two of us, Dove." He smiled at her. "We'll just move nice and slow."

Kai sighed as he called her by his endearment. The sound rolled off his tongue like an invisible caress. Kai leaned her head on his chest, inhaling his scent. Gil's arms enclosed her intimately and she closed her eyes, needing this. Needing him. He moved with such boneless grace and it was easy to follow him around the floor.

Kai knew that the Holt family was probably realizing there was something indeed serious going on between herself and Gil. The music lulled her and she relished being so close to Gil, his hand light against the small of her back, his other hand tucking hers between them. It was wonderful and she felt all her nerves and tension dissolve.

Gil leaned down, his mouth near her ear.

"I've got a nice hotel room reserved for us. I think you'll like it. It has a Jacuzzi in the room."

Lifting her head, she grinned. "That sounds interesting."

Shrugging, he smiled a little. "You always liked trying new things," he reminded her.

"I think you called me brazen?"

"Indeed I did," Gil agreed, amusement in his low tone. "And it was a compliment, believe me."

Everything felt so right. Kai laid her head on his chest, the fine weave of the fabric of his coat beneath her cheek. She felt his lips press a kiss to her hair and her body hummed with anticipation. Why had she waited so long? Kai knew it was fear. There was still half of her that didn't believe they could have a lasting relationship. The past had scarred her more than she'd ever realized until Gil had come back into her life.

Their hips brushed and she could feel the bulge of his erection. It excited her and, already, Kai ached to be out of the Armory and in that bed with Gil. But good manners dictated they must stay a decent amount of time.

As they were coming off the dance floor, they met Miss Gus. She was with a gentleman her own age. Kai smiled and leaned over, hugging her.

"You look beautiful, Miss Gus," she said, releasing her.

"And you clean up darned well, too," she said, gesturing to her dress. "I think you could be on the cover of a magazine."

Laughing, Kai said, "Thanks, but you know what? I'd gladly trade this all in for my jeans, boots and a blouse." Miss Gus was dressed in a bright red dress that made her silver hair shine. Her partner was conservatively dressed, bald and had a proud look on his face as he kept his hand on the small of her back.

"I just wanted to come over and tell you how great

you look, Kai," she said. "Me and Henry need to get back to his family's table."

Kai had wondered why Miss Gus hadn't sat with them. Now she knew why. There was a devilish sparkle in her eyes for her handsome partner. "Have fun," she called after them.

Turning, she looked up at Gil. "Miss Gus is such a role model. Here she is in her mideighties and she's spunky, involved with life and loving every minute of it."

Gil's hand moved lightly down her spine, coming to rest on her hips. "That's what I see for us, Dove."

Her heart blossomed and Kai felt tears prick the backs of her eyes as she absorbed his solemn, warm expression. Gil meant every word of it. Kai hadn't even thought that far ahead, every day still tentative with him. She slid her arm around his waist and said, "Let's go back to the table."

GIL TOLD EVERYONE at the Holt table good-night before he escorted Kai out of the Armory. It was nearly ten o'clock, and some of the couples were starting to leave, but most were remaining. In this part of Wyoming, they had eight months of snow and winter, so spring and summer were short. The people of the valley loved getting out, meeting their friends and finding out how life was treating them. So, it was no wonder that rare dances like this were very popular and most of the partygoers stayed well into the early-morning hours.

Gil sensed the subtle tension amping up between them as he led Kai to the truck and opened the door for her. The air was chilly, in the forties, and he removed his jacket and placed it over her shoulders. Kai gave him a grateful look because the small green shawl, while around her shoulders, couldn't protect her against the breezy evening. She climbed in and Gil enjoyed the view. Kai had a fine butt and that dress of hers showed it off in the best of ways.

On the way through town to their hotel, Gil felt Kai retreating from him. "Tired?" he asked.

"No...just...pensive, I guess." Kai gazed over at his profile. "Where are you at?"

He drove slowly through the traffic of downtown. "Probably right where you are—remembering our five days together."

"Yes," she admitted quietly, her hands in her lap.

"I've never forgotten them," Gil told her, making a turn that would take them to the south side of the town. "Have you?" He glanced over at Kai. She looked introspective. He had a powerful intuition and could feel the longing in her matching his own.

"No...never..."

The Wyoming Inn came into view. It was one of the nice hotels in the upscale Western town. Gil parked and turned off the truck. The shadows and light played through the window, bathing Kai.

"Ready?" His heart thudded once to underscore the fear he felt that she'd say no. But he wasn't going to push her into something she didn't want as much as he did. When Kai lifted her head and gave him that soft, sweet smile of hers, his entire body flushed with fire and need. Yes, Kai was ready—he could see it in her velvet gray eyes.

"More than ready," she promised him huskily, unharnessing her seat belt.

Nodding, Gil left the cab and came around, opening the door for her. Kai put her slender hand into his.

In no time, he had them checked in. His body thrummed with anticipation. They took the elevator to the third and highest floor. When he opened the door to the large suite that had a fireplace in it, Kai made a sound of awe.

"This is beautiful, Gil," she said, walking in, handing him his suit coat.

He took the coat after closing and locking the door. "Not half as beautiful as what I'm looking at right now," he said, dropping the coat on the overstuffed, antique couch. Kai turned and smiled, opening her arms to him.

The trust she was giving him staggered Gil. More than anything, he wanted to be there for Kai. He brought her lightly against him, monitoring her, sensing where she was at. He felt like a caveman, wanting to drag his woman down and taking her with the primal lust that was flooding his body. But that wasn't going to happen tonight. Maybe later, but not the first time.

Gil wanted this introduction to allow Kai to set the pace and tell him what she needed. Judging from the arousal in her eyes, she was feeling as needy as he was.

"Tell me what you want," he rasped, kissing her hair, her temple, inhaling the scent of oranges from her recently washed hair. He felt Kai sag against him, belly against his aching erection.

"Could we take a shower first?" She looked up, sliding her hand against his shaven jaw. "I don't want to make love in there, just…well…get clean and be with you?"

"Sounds like a plan," Gil agreed. He led her to the overstuffed chair near the fireplace. It was gas fed, the flames sending dancing shadows across the low-lit room. "Let me get it started?"

Nodding, Kai sat down and slipped out of her shoes. "I'll be there in a minute."

Gil leaned over, caressing her hair, seeing the burgundy and gold highlights in the firelight. "No, I want to undress you," he said, and looked into her eyes as she lifted her chin.

"That sounds nice, too," she whispered.

Gil nodded and walked to the bathroom. The Jacuzzi, a huge round tub filled with warm, clear blue water, was in the other room. He made sure there were plenty of towels available. The glass-enclosed shower was tiled a pale green, almost the color of Kai's dress. He smiled to himself, placing a washcloth inside the shower on the tile bench. Above were two rain-shower heads. Opening the soap, he set it on the dish near the faucets. Visions of taking Kai in here danced through him, but he was going to follow her needs, not his.

When he stepped out of the bathroom, Kai had taken off her hose and it was lying next to her sandals. She looked so slender and delicate in that body-hugging dress. She had always been small against his weight and height. He saw the sudden shyness in her eyes and he halted before her, laying his hands gently across her shoulders, feeling her begin to melt a little beneath his calming movements.

"Are you protected?" he asked.

"I'm on the pill." Kai wrinkled her nose. "I don't

want you to use a condom tonight, Gil. I remember how good it was with you without one last time." She lifted her hand, smoothing it across the crisp white shirt, his muscles tensing beneath her exploring fingertips.

Gil slid his hands up her slender neck and framed her face, leaning down, moving his mouth tenderly across her parting lips. "How long has it been for you?" Because he wasn't the average man and Gil did not want to hurt Kai even accidentally. He felt her respond, her lush lips pressing against his. Her scent flooded him.

"Two years," she admitted, pulling away, giving him an ironic look.

"Okay," he rasped, taking her mouth more surely, easing his hands down to her shoulders, following her strong, supple spine. He eased his fingers upward, feeling her flow against his body, trusting him utterly with herself. Finding that hidden zipper, he drew it down to the small of her back. Pulling away from her lips, Gil skimmed his hands beneath the material, bringing it off her shoulders, then kissing each one, lavishing her with small kisses, a nip against her neck, hearing a sound catch in her throat, feeling her hands grip his shoulders in response. He drowned in her mouth, opening her, tasting her, absorbing her.

Not wanting to leave her mouth but knowing he must, Gil broke the kiss that was sending shock waves through his body. He'd waited for what felt like a lifetime for this moment, but he was in no hurry. There was another kind of pleasure in slowly undressing Kai, pulling the cap sleeves down her long arms and slender fingers.

He allowed the dress to pool around her perfect, small feet and helped her step out of it. Gazing down at her, he saw that she wore a lacy black bra and panties. Kai looked exquisite to him as he leaned around her, unsnapping the bra. Her small breasts were high, the nipples pink and tight beneath his hungry gaze. His mouth watered. How badly he wanted to taste them, but he forced himself to wait. Sliding his fingers beneath the elastic material around her hips, he saw her eyes shutter closed as he lightly stroked her flesh, a soft catch in her throat. Smiling into her eyes, Gil helped her step out of them.

"My turn," he growled, devouring her with his gaze. Kai had always been petite. But she was perfectly balanced with small breasts, a slender waist and soft, flaring hips. His gaze pinned on her belly and he thought that she'd be able to carry a baby. The sizzling thought that she could carry his baby careened through him like a shock wave. Yes, he loved her. Gil would marry her in a split second if he thought Kai would say yes.

As she helped him unbutton his shirt, spreading it open with her hands, her cool fingertips brushing against his dark-haired chest, he tensed and closed his eyes, his hands resting on her shoulders. Her touch felt so damned good to him.

In no time, she had the shirt off him. He saw the impish quality in her eyes as she deliberately slid her fingers beneath the waistband of his trousers, watching his reaction, her other hand firmly brushing against his erection, which was killing him. Groaning, he rasped, "I'm almost there, Dove…don't…" Gil wanted to come within her small, tight, welcoming body. Where he belonged.

With a softened laughter, she said, "Okay, I won't mercilessly tease you." She unbuckled the belt, unsnapped his trousers and pulled down the zipper, brushing against the thick erection just beneath his boxer shorts. She smiled and said, "I see you haven't changed, Hanford. At all..." Kai pulled his trousers down to his ankles. He stepped out of them.

"You make me this way," Gil rasped, grazing her breasts, not touching her nipples, watching her eyes shutter half-closed with arousal and gray fire. Kai was still just as responsive and he felt her heat, her need of him.

Moving her fingers around the elastic band, she nodded. "I think we have that effect on one another." She pulled his shorts down, his erection making her smile even more.

Gil knew he was going to throw her on that bed behind them if they didn't get to the shower in a hurry. He moved her in front of him, watching the sweet sway of her hips, her cheeks a special focus of his. "Let's go," he urged. He heard her laugh and, suddenly, he felt the last of his worries, his tensions, dissolve. Kai was committed. Completely. She'd placed whatever else she might feel about them—or him—aside for this night.

CHAPTER NINETEEN

THE MOMENT THE twin rain showers soaked Kai's hair, she lifted her face to the soft streams, closing her eyes, allowing the warm water to sluice in rivulets down her body. Gil lathered up his hands and approached her, water flowing across his powerful shoulders and down his dark-haired chest. Placing her hands near his heart, she could feel it pounding beneath her palms. His eyes glittered with hunger—for her. The same look she'd seen before. It made Kai feel shaky with need for him.

She felt Gil's hands begin at her neck, the sensation of his callused hands sending wild, teasing shocks downward. Her breasts tightened as his hands moved slowly across her shoulders. Wordlessly, Kai allowed her brow to touch his chest, lost in the feel of his hands upon her once more. It had been so long…so long…

And as he gently wrapped his hands around her arms, sliding them down to her elbows, she sighed, the trembling sound lost in the shower.

"Feel good?" he rumbled near her ear.

"Yes," she whispered, barely nodding her head. His hands left and, moments later, there was more lather as he slid his hands in slow, circular motions across her shoulders and began to work down. Her body tightened as his fingers followed the flare of her hips. More than anything, she wanted Gil to cup her cheeks, bring her against him, his erection pressed deep against her belly. She arched into his touch. He did not disappoint, his long fingers following the curve of each of her cheeks, bringing a moan of anticipation from within her.

Gil drew her against his hips and she slipped her arms around his torso, holding him tightly, lips against the hair on his chest. He smelled so good to her. So stable. Rock solid. Kai could hear the heavy thud of his heart against her ear, water running down either side of her cheek. Kai didn't care if she drowned as Gil held her against him. There was no terrible, life-threatening urgency as there had been years earlier in their lives. It was a quieter time now, in some respects. Her heart blossomed with such fierce love for Gil that she buried her face against his wet flesh, never wanting to let go of him again.

Slowly, Gil opened her thighs, dragging his fingers inward, following the curve of her body between her thighs. A cry of yearning tore from her, more haunting than anything, echoing in the mist and steam gathering within the enclosure. She felt his lips caressing the shell of her ear and then his tongue moving to the sensitive area behind it. Kai shuddered, her knees weakening as he stroked her folds, teasing her wet entrance. Each time, she cried out, clinging to him, afraid of collapsing from the pleasure of him merely stroking her, teasing the knot that was so swollen and throbbing, his fingers finding her more than ready for him.

"You're hot, like thick honey, Dove," he growled,

easing his hand from between her legs. "I want you. All of you. But not here. I want you in bed where I can see your face, look into your eyes, hear your sweet songs…"

She felt his arm go around her waist, as if sensing she was on the verge of not being able to stand from the pleasure he'd just given her. Gil had never been selfish or taking. He'd given generously to her. Always. And it was happening again. Kai barely lifted her chin, meeting his narrowed eyes that gleamed with arousal. "Then," she whispered, "let's hurry. I—I can't wait, Gil… It's been so long…so long…"

His smile was so very male and yet incredibly tender. He nodded, kissed the tip of her nose and continued to soap her body down, taking his time, as if reacquainting himself with every inch of her flesh. By the time he was finished, she couldn't stand and had to sit down on the wet, warm tile bench and watch as he washed himself.

Kai had always thought Gil was beautiful in a masculine sort of way. He was built tall and strong, but he wasn't overly muscled, more ropy and solid. His flesh glistened with the water and she was mesmerized by the smooth flow of muscles contracting and relaxing as he moved the washcloth languidly across his body.

Kai knew he was a hunter. And he had hunted her in the most delicious and satisfying of ways. The first time they had made love, he had been trembling with the need for release, but he'd focused on her needs before his own. She knew it would be no different this time.

Kai wondered if the reason for his approach to loving a woman was because of his solid, loving family background. Sam had always been in a hurry. His needs overrode hers. He used her as a release, she felt, more than anything else. If he wasn't too exhausted after climaxing, he would then tend to her needs, but it didn't happen as often as she wished. With Gil, every time, he had placed Kai first. It didn't matter how badly he wanted to climax, she was the object of his affection. Completely. Fully.

Gil turned off the showers and moved outside the stall and grabbed two towels. He eased Kai to her feet, wrapping one bath towel around her body. She held on to his upper arm, unsteady, as he pulled his around his waist and tucked it in. And then he growled, "Come here," and lifted her into his arms as if she weighed nothing.

With a gasp of surprise, Kai's arms flew around his thick, solid shoulders as he carried her out from the bathroom into the bedroom.

"What?" Gil teased, giving her a warm look. "You didn't expect me to sweep you off your feet?"

Smiling, Kai drowned in his stormy-looking blue eyes. "You always surprise me, Hanford."

Taking her over to the king-size bed, he gently laid her down on one side of it. Her towel had come loose, the material barely draping across her breasts as she stared up at him. Gil sat down, his hip next to hers. She saw the hunger in his expression yet felt nothing but gentleness as he eased his fingers through her damp hair. Shards of fire leaped across her scalp, down her neck and tightened her nipples hidden beneath the fluffy towel. Now even the fabric aroused her as it moved across them.

"I've been dreaming of this day for so long," he

confided, allowing his fingers to move to the back of her skull, gently massaging it. "Right here. Like this. Wet, your skin glistening, your eyes sultry looking and seeing your skin turn to goose bumps wherever I touch you…"

Her lashes shuttered closed and Kai reached out, sliding her hand down his chest, feeling the hard wall of muscle beneath the dark, damp hair. "Touch me anywhere…everywhere… I love it all, Gil…please…" She heard that low, animal growl and she quivered, knowing he was going to be so thorough that she could barely wait to have those callused fingers drifting to the next part of her wildly sensitive body. The warmth and stickiness increased between her thighs. He could turn her on with just a look, never mind the slow, massaging movement of his fingers that made her melt into the bed beneath her.

But if he thought for a moment she wasn't going to be a partner in this reunion, he was mistaken. Opening her eyes, Kai allowed her hand to drift down across his heavily muscled chest, feeling his skin grow taught as she grazed him. Gil reached out, capturing her hand, moving it above her head, leaving her open to him, his eyes part amusement, part the hunter he was. A fierce yearning bolted through her as he leaned down, his mouth a bare inch from hers.

"I'm so close to coming, Dove, that normally, I'd want you all over me." One corner of his mouth crooked as he held her sultry gaze. "This one time? Let me set the pace for us?"

She nodded and flexed the wrist he held captive. Gil released her, allowing her to frame his face, which was so close to hers. "This one time, but I'm wanting you right now, too." Her lips drew upward and she saw the joy and fire burning in his narrowing blue eyes. It was as if they were back with each other from so long ago, as if they were merely picking up where they had left off.

Kai didn't want to think of the heartbreak of Gil leaving her without a word, a note. She pushed it all away, wanting to believe he would never do that to her again. The way he looked at her, as if she were something beautiful and sacred being held his hands, made her heart throb with possibility. His hand ranged downward from her neck, across her collarbone, eliciting tiny licks and flames in the wake of his trailing fingers.

He slowly released the towel, exposing her breasts to his gaze. Kai saw the change in his face, the satisfaction that he was going to suckle them. Her breasts tightened beneath his searing look as he pulled the towel free so that she lay naked beside him.

"I've never met a woman like you," he told her thickly, dragging his fingers upward from her hip, across her torso and curving around her breast that fitted within his palm. "I feel like a man that's been given a second chance, Kai. I'm not going to waste the opportunity." Gil took her mouth gently, asking her participation, celebrating their being together once more.

The moment his mouth met hers, he brushed a thumb lazily across the peak of her breast and Kai jerked upward, the pleasure so intense, a cry echoing in her throat as he deepened their kiss. Jolting shocks raced down, gathering in her lower body. His tongue moved against hers and her breath jammed with exquisite pleasure.

Kai rolled to her side, pressing her hips against his, silently asking him to come inside her. She felt desperate, beyond starving and he seemed to read her mind, because he eased from her mouth, looking deep into her half-closed eyes. His breath was ragged and she felt tension in every line of his body. The moment was excruciating as Kai gave him a pleading stare.

Rising, Gil pulled the towel away from his waist.

Her gaze moved to his powerful erection, thick and more than ready. She felt a flood of heat pool deep within her. She watched as he turned off the light, just the faint illumination from the nearly closed bathroom door giving her enough to see him approach her. Gil walked with such male grace. It had always turned Kai on even though she'd never told him.

As he moved to the other side of the bed, his knee making a deep indent in the mattress, he pulled her onto her side so that she could stroke and slide her hand down across his torso to his narrow hips.

"Hurry," she whimpered as his hand lay on her hip and then moved slowly down her curved thigh as he watched her reactions. His scent entered her nostrils and Kai saw him give a bare nod, watching her intently. As he pulled her thigh up and over his leg, leaving her utterly exposed to his coming exploration, Kai surrendered to him, her head coming to rest on his shoulder, her hand stilling across his waist, waiting. Just waiting. *Please touch me. Touch me...*

His fingers followed the curve of her cheek, trailing downward, and she moaned, pressing her breasts against his chest. Her nipples tangled in his damp hair, further sending tiny jolts through her. And just as his fingers met her wetness, he plundered her mouth, her cry drowning in him as he stroked her, absorbed her within his ravishing mouth. Her fingers curved into his hard flesh and she arched into his fingers sliding through the folds, teasing her, testing her, making sure she was more than ready for him. Somewhere in the boiling haze of her mind, Kai knew Gil was always concerned because she was smaller than he was, that he never wanted to enter her unless she was more than slick and swollen.

Right now, Kai didn't care, her whole body contracting into a throbbing ache as he slid one finger into her, beginning to lavish that swollen knot at her entrance.

He plunged his tongue deep into her mouth, emulating the rhythm of sex between them, his second finger sliding into her, massaging her, making her mewl, her entire body tensing as she felt the boiling fire build. Mindless, wanting, she thrust against his fingers, beyond starving and needing an orgasm, her lower body only wanting relief. As he lifted his mouth from hers, his lips settled on one puckered nipple and captured it. She felt herself flying apart. And as he suckled her strongly, she felt her body bloom with searing heat, the orgasm ripping through her. Kai screamed, clinging to Gil, her senses flooded and overwhelmed with the most violent orgasm she'd ever experienced. The searing intensity swept through her in a rush, leaving her gasping, crying out, unable to move as he continued to stroke her, drawing every last vestige of pleasure he could give her from her own body.

Hurled into heat and light, stars exploded behind her eyelids and all she could do was sob as relief began to follow in the wake of the massive release still rippling through her, ever expanding outward, giving her even more keen satisfaction.

As Gil eased his fingers from her and released her nipple, she moaned and suddenly fell apart in his arms, lost within the inner world of gratification reverberating through her body and blinding light behind her eyes. Only vaguely aware of Gil gathering her next to him, his hand brushed down the full length of her spine, cupping her cheek, holding her tightly against his erection, and he caught her dazed attention. His lips caressed her temple, her cheek and, finally, moving slowly, deeply, across her parted, wet lips. It felt so good to bury herself within his strong, cradling embrace, his mouth worshipping hers, growing gentle, not as intense or teasing. Kai lost track of time, only aware of the cherishing caresses of his hand along her damp, fulfilled body. She knew he would give her time to fully absorb the orgasm still flickering hotly within her. He understood a woman needed time between them.

GIL FELT HIS heart open powerfully as he held Kai, a faint smile touching her lips, burning satisfaction evident in her drowsy, barely opened eyes. As she looked up, met and held his gaze, the love he had for her nearly spilled out of his mouth. He held such secrets from this woman who had artlessly and trustingly given herself without reservation to him once more. He felt the chaffing guilt of having left her, knowing Kai didn't have to be here with him right now or try, once more to make a relationship burgeon between them. He'd felt like a man consigned to life imprisonment until this moment.

So much hope tunneled through Gil as he studied her soft gray eyes, her pupils huge and black as she looked wonderingly up at him. Gil knew that expression. He'd pleased her. All he lived for was to do exactly that. It was more than sex with Kai. It always had been so much more. Gil could not separate his emotions from the act itself where she was concerned. She just naturally drew his heart out of hiding, twined her soft, giving body around him and captured it within her small, slender fingers.

Kai sighed and weakly reached up, touching his temple. "That felt so good..."

"Yes, it did. And there's more to come..." He smiled at her, continuing to kiss and lavish her slender throat, moving his tongue to behind her ear, which was so sensitive to his siege, to bring her satisfaction once more. The moment he licked the area, she reacted and made a happy sound. Then he drew her fully against him, positioning her so that he could easily reach her nape, one of the primary erogenous zones in her body. Her soft hair brushed his nose and cheek. He hungrily inhaled her scent, his erection throbbing. And as he lightly used his teeth to graze the sensitive area, he felt Kai fly apart in his arms, her cry startled and throaty, her body restless and demanding against him.

She gripped him, her arm going around his waist, drawing him as tightly as she could, his thickness jammed hotly between them. As he licked the area, raked it lightly with his teeth again, he felt her shudder from her toes, upward, knowing the searing pleasure it was bringing her. And as he eased her onto her back, he slid his fingers between her thighs, feeling her. She was so wet her entire inner thighs were coated and damp. Kai was more than ready and he lifted off her, using his knee to open her wider, settling between her sweet, curved thighs.

Every nerve in his body was taut and screaming as Gil eased over her, covering her, keeping most of his weight on his knees and his elbows positioned near her shoulders. She was breathing raggedly, her eyes half-closed, the diamond-like sparkle in them telling Gil she was more than ready for him to enter her. And as he nudged her entrance, they both groaned, the sensations acute, scorching, and she gripped his hips, offering herself fully to him, lifting her hips, pleading in her eyes to consume her.

He wanted to thrust hard and deep into her, but damn, it had been two years for her and Gil knew she would be so tight that she'd need time to accommodate him. Still, he framed her face with his large hands, taking her mouth, plundering it as he eased just inside her. The tightness instantly surrounded him and he groaned deeply, feeling the heat, the sweetness that was only Kai. Only her. His mind was obliterated as she thrust wantonly upward, swallowing more of him. He heard her moan softly, felt her walls grip him, and he tore his mouth from hers, growling her name. Her body relaxed and he flowed more deeply into her, seeking her heat, her honey sweetness surrounding him. His whole body trembled as she lifted her hips, beginning to establish a slow, teasing rhythm designed to allow him fully into her.

He made a dark sound of frustration, pressing his damp brow against hers. "Dove... I can't hold it much longer..."

She laughed softly, thrusting her hips upward. "Then fill me," she whispered into his ear. Her voice grew low and gritty. "Give me all of you..."

His hands knotted into the bedspread on either side of her head and he pumped into her, hearing her cry. But it was a cry of welcome, her slender, strong fingers clasping his hips, holding him in place, not allowing him to leave the confines of her. Losing his mind to the sensations blistering through him, feeling the overwhelming blaze building swiftly, she egged him on with her sinuous body twisting and thrusting, causing him to lose his steel control over himself.

The moment she turned her head, her mouth hungrily taking his, thrusting her tongue against his, an explosion ripped down his spine, scorching him, making him freeze, their hips joined, fused together. Lifting his mouth from hers, he clenched his teeth, eyes tightly shut as the searing fire tunneled down through his lower body, slamming through him, spilling into her welcoming body. Dizziness assailed him as Gil lay taut above her, unable to move, caught in the webs of singeing heat erupting throughout his lower body.

Gil had no idea how long his climax went on and on, but it felt like forever. The intense, almost painful pleasure fired through him, sending him rocketing into another dimension. All he was aware of was collapsing against Kai's warm, damp body, him sliding his arms beneath her shoulders, his head pressed against hers, gasping raggedly for air, weakness totaling him in the best of ways.

He dragged in her womanly fragrance, the scent of their sex, the cool, silky strands of her hair against his sweaty face. The boiling heat kept rolling through him and he savored being so deep within her, melting into her, holding her tightly, never wanting to ever let her go again. Kai was his. His heart was wide-open, love spilling fiercely out of him for only her. And as her slender arms wrapped around his neck, drawing him to her completely, he sank fully against her for a moment, relishing their contact, their breathing, their hearts pounding against one another.

KAI SLOWLY CAME AWAKE. It was still dark and she sleepily turned her head on Gil's shoulder to look at the clock. It was three in the morning.

Groaning inwardly, she didn't want to leave the circle of his arms, their bodies pressed sweetly together. He was sleeping deeply and she closed her eyes, languishing in remembering, once again, the angles, the hardness of his male body against her more rounded, softer one. Her head lay in the crook of his shoulder, his arm possessively wrapped around her waist, keeping her against him even in sleep. His other arm had curved beneath her shoulders. Never had she felt so loved, so protected and happy.

Her drowsy mind fled back to the first time they'd made love, and she could see no difference in his fierce emotions toward loving her then and now. Whatever Gil felt for her, it had not changed. He was a considerate lover, tender as well as ravishing, depending upon where she was at. More than anything, he knew her, he knew her body intimately on a level no other man ever had.

Closing her eyes, Kai relaxed in his arms, absorbing this moment because she felt worshipped and fiercely loved. She knew neither of them had said those words. It was far too soon, but Kai swore what she saw in Gil's eyes was love for her.

And, yet, their future was so tenuous, so uncharted, and she didn't even try to figure out what was happening between them except that it felt so damned good and satisfying. Kai had never felt the happiness that was bubbling through her right now. She had come to the conclusion that her feelings for Gil had always been there, latent and subconscious. And because she was married to Sam, Gil never once gave her any signal that might make her think of him as anything other than a friend to her.

Moving her cheek against his shoulder, Kai delighted in his male scent, the power of his muscles. His protection was overwhelming and Kai had never felt as loved as she did right now. Her heart whispered she could have this every night. To sleep with Gil. To love him when they felt the urge. To feel his male warmth radiating from around him like the sun itself. Her fingers moved softly across his chest, tunneling through the dark, silky strands, adoring his strength, his passion and that it all belonged to her once more.

But for how long? Kai's palm rested over his slow, thudding heart. Most of her fear of him leaving her had dissolved. But the memory... God, the memory of waking up that morning and finding him gone without a word—that had shattered her heart. And it had taken her two years to get over his actions. She remembered the timbre of Gil's voice earlier, the solemn look in his blue gaze, promising her he'd never do that to her again. Not ever. Most of her heart believed him. Her head was wary, however, wanting time to prove to her that it was really true.

Nuzzling his shoulder, she closed her eyes, reminding herself that Gil had made no such promise to her before. He'd always been a man of his word at every turn. And he'd never gone back on whatever he said he'd do for Sam, for her or for his Delta Force team. A little part of her, the worried part, dissolved. Gil had made a verbal commitment to her this time. He hadn't done that before. This was different. Her heart felt how different it really was. And she gloried in the contentment that what they'd just shared was only the beginning, not an end.

Her heart expanded powerfully within her chest and Kai allowed herself, for the first time, those scintillating colors of hope, allowing herself to dream of having Gil permanently in her life. Could it happen? Is that where he was going with her? Is that what he wanted? Kai was unsure, knowing they had so much to sort out and to explore. She had never entertained, until this moment, the possibility of sharing the rest of her life with him. Was it at all possible? She understood clearly the operator's mind and how it functioned. Gil was a man of few words, and fewer thoughts ever left his mind to be spoken out loud.

In some ways, Gil was like Sam. But Sam had never opened up to her and Gil already had on so many different levels. He wasn't her dead husband, and she would never compare him to Sam in that way.

Gil stood alone, like a beacon to her wounded heart that was crying out for her to allow him fully and completely into her life once again. Kai wasn't sure she could do it because of the past hurt. The fear of him leaving. Yet, Gil had given his word to her and she'd never felt or heard him as serious as he was when he had spoken those words.

Sleep began to claim her once again, like soft raindrops falling around her mind that nettled and chewed on such things. Kai allowed her feelings to rule her, to lull her to sleep in Gil's arms. There was such peace, solidity and pleasure to be wrapped within his embrace once more. Until this night, Kai had not known just how much she needed Gil in her life.

CHAPTER TWENTY

"I DON'T WANT to go to work," Kai mumbled, sliding her arms around Gil's neck as they prepared to leave the inn. She saw his mouth quirk, the look in his eyes reflecting her feelings. Leaning against him, feeling his arms around her, made her incredibly happy. Her body glowed from their recent lovemaking. Nothing had ever felt so right to Kai.

"We'll survive…barely," Gil chuckled, tightening his embrace, kissing her hair and then her temple, inhaling her womanly fragrance, which always set him on fire.

Lifting her face, Kai turned her head, meeting his mouth, drowning in the kiss he branded her with. It was a man claiming his woman. Nothing less. And as his other hand slid down across her hip, pinning her against his pelvis, feeling his erection, she moaned, wanting him all over again. Already. It was as if they were trying to make up for so much lost time. Kai felt like a whining beggar. Time was too short! She had just spent the most wonderful night of her life with Gil and she didn't want it to end. Her body craved him, his touches, his inflaming kisses that left her breathless and needy.

As his mouth eased from hers, she absorbed the burning look of arousal in his eyes.

In a roughened tone, he said, "We'll figure this all out, Dove. For now, we have responsibilities and commitments to others."

Giving him a pouty look, Kai understood and stepped reluctantly out of his arms. It was six o'clock, and he'd just shaved. Before that, he'd taken her in the shower and Kai was still reeling from the impact of orgasms he'd coaxed out of her in the hot, steamy water coursing around them.

The power of Gil as a man, her heart entwined with his whether she said the word *love* or not, was real. And beautiful. "I know," she whispered, her fingers trailing down his arm, catching his hand, feeling his fingers wrap warmly around hers.

Kai studied him in the silence of the room, the early-morning light coming through the windows. "Gil? I know you promised you would never leave me again like you did." She saw his brows move down, concern coming to his eyes. Gathering her courage, her voice broke with emotion and she managed, "Before, it was just words to me and I didn't fully trust you. Now—" she clung to his gaze "—I believe you, Gil. I really do believe you." Kai tightened her fingers around his. "Whatever we have, it's always been there. It never went away. And I don't want to lose it again. I want a real chance to pursue a long-term relationship with you. Are you game?"

Her heart was pounding with fear of possible rejection from him. Gil looked stunned for a moment and then a slow grin tugged at his mouth. He reached out and smoothed several strands back into place against her temple. "That's what I want, too, Kai. Nothing less. All right? I'm here to stay in your life until—or if—you tell me to leave." He dug into her gaze, his voice low with barely withheld emotions.

Giving him a look of relief, she whispered, "Yes… yes, that's what I want, too… But I don't know where this is going, Gil."

He shrugged. "A day at a time, Dove. This is a new chapter in our lives. We're the ones writing it. It's up to us to define it." Framing her face, holding her close to him, he kissed her mouth tenderly. As he lifted away from her lips, Gil rasped, "We have the time now. There's nothing urgent pulling or pushing us anymore. We have steady jobs at the ranch. It's quiet in comparison to our former lives when we were in the military. I'm in this with you for the long haul, Kai. And I want to be able to have every minute I can spend with you outside of work. We'll keep our relationship out of ranch activities."

Nodding, her lips tingling with his last kiss, Kai whispered, "I'd like that." Then, looking around the hotel room, she gestured and added, "But this cost a lot of money, Gil. Neither of us has that to spend every time we want privacy and alone time with one another."

He smiled a little, bringing her into his arms, kissing the top of her head. "I have plans, Dove. I'm in the process of leasing a condo around Jackson Hole. I need a place of my own. I'm going to work at the ranch, but come home every night." Gil pulled her away just enough to see the reaction in her expression. It was a widening of her gray eyes, hope shining in them along with surprise over his admittance. "Are you game? You can come and go to my condo anytime you like. If you'd rather stay out at the ranch, that's all right, too."

Kai became pensive, mulling over the information. "I like the idea, Gil. I really do." Her voice changed, more emotional. "When I feel like it? I can come home with you?" Her heart fluttered with possibilities.

"That's the idea, Dove. No pressure from me, either. I know we have a jaded past and I have a lot to make up for. It's going to take time for you to trust me fully again. I get that."

She moved her hands up and down his lower arms. "My heart is already there, Gil. It's my head," she said, and gave him an apologetic look.

"We have the time," Gil urged her quietly. "I'm okay with whatever feels most comfortable for you. You have nothing to apologize for, Kai. I'm the one who wounded you, not the other way around."

She closed her eyes and took a deep breath. "That sounds wonderful, Gil."

"Okay, let's saddle up." He patted her rear, a very delicious part of her anatomy and then released Kai. "I'll be moving into my condo two days from now."

"It's part of our new chapter in our lives," Kai said, picking up her purse. She had brought a change of clothes so she wouldn't have to wear her beautiful green silk dress back to the ranch. Gil had done the same and was now in a chambray shirt, jeans and boots, settling the Stetson on his head. "I'm ready..."

THE TWO-LANE HIGHWAY to the Triple H was clear of traffic at this time of morning. Gil felt a widening joy in his heart. It suffused him and he'd never been

happier. The windows were down, the cold air brac-
ing and Kai was relaxed, her elbow on the window
frame. He'd never seen her look so happy, either. He
loved her. Gil had almost said the words to her in the
inn before they left. Almost. He had to wait. Kai was
trusting him now more than ever. She'd had the courage to speak up, to tell him what she really wanted
with him: a long-term relationship. Nothing less.

He wasn't sure if Kai wanted to move into the
condo with him or not. Gil would leave that up to her.
He didn't want to push her and make her uncomfortable. Having a choice would allow her to enter into
a deeper relationship with him on her own terms.
Now the control was in her hands, unlike the other
time. His heart had soared wildly when she'd asked
to be in a serious relationship with him. Gil had to
keep his face carefully arranged so as not to let on
how much it meant to him, to the dreams he'd always
held for them.

The highway entered the mountainous area. Glancing at the hundred-foot rocky cliff that led down to
the boiling Snake River below, his gaze moving to
the thousand-foot rocky cliff on his right, he enjoyed
this particular part of the drive. The low guardrail
wasn't much of a barrier between the highway and the
mighty Snake. The gray-green water churned, white
foam in the rapids of the deep, powerful river. Above,
the sky was a light blue, and he could see sunlight just
touching the tips of the evergreens on the cliff to his
right. He felt Kai rest her hand on his long thigh and
he took one hand off the steering wheel for a moment
to cover hers and squeeze it, letting Kai know silently
how much he loved her.

In a split second, he saw an old, rusted dump truck suddenly looming in his rearview mirror. It was traveling at too high a rate of speed! And it was going to smash into them!

"Brace!" he yelled at Kai, gripping the wheel, tensing as the massive grill of the fifty-four-ton tandem-axle truck hurtled toward them. A truck like they drove was only fifteen tons. Gil took evasive action, but there wasn't much he could do. He was pinned between the cliff and the guardrail. He heard Kai gasp, suddenly reaching out for the dashboard, her hands braced against it.

The powerful collision between the pickup and the hurtling dump truck roared around Gil. The pickup lurched drunkenly sideways. He heard Kai scream. He corrected. All air bags deployed simultaneously, blinding Gil.

The dump truck roared down on them again.

Gil cursed. *What the hell!* The driver was deliberately trying to run them off the road! He sucked in a breath as the second hit occurred.

The pickup spun wildly, coming up on two wheels, careening toward the guardrail. The odor of burning rubber filled the cab. Gil heard the smashing and tearing of metal. The air bags blocked his vision and he couldn't see anything! From his rearview mirror, Gil saw the dump truck come at them a third time, pushing the pickup right into the guardrail.

No!

He knew this wasn't an accident. It wasn't a dump truck that had lost its brakes. This was someone trying to kill them!

Too late!

The guardrail snapped and the pickup went sailing into the air, heading straight toward the Snake River a hundred feet below. The pickup landed on the passenger side, crashing into the rocks, metal tearing and shrieking. It stopped sliding only feet away from the river's small, muddy bank. The force of the landing jerked Gil's whole body. The safety harness bit deep into his shoulder and chest. He heard Kai scream again. And then her cry was cut short. The pickup suddenly moved and skidded into the river.

Cold water bubbled and rushed into the cab. Gil was semiconscious. He blindly reached over, jerking the seat belt off Kai. She was unconscious, slumping toward him as the cab tilted in Gil's direction. She was unresponsive as the water surged into the cabin. They had seconds to escape!

Gil fumbled and opened his harness, jamming his arm upward to push the deflating air bag away from his face. Sliding his arm around Kai's shoulders, he felt the truck suddenly get whisked out into the center of the dominating river current.

Taking a breath, he shoved Kai across him and pushed her out the opened window. Nearly filled with water, the pickup turned slowly around in the center of the river. Gil shoved himself out the window, keeping a hand on Kai's ankle so that she wouldn't be torn away from him by the current.

Get her air! The words screamed in Gil's mind as he grabbed Kai, who floated unconscious in front of him. The water was shockingly cold. Kicking hard, he surged toward her, lifting her by her waist, thrusting her head up above the water.

He popped to the surface, the current carrying them swiftly around the bend.

Gil's whole life, his whole focus, was on keeping Kai's head up and out of the water. He brought her to him so her head rested on his shoulder, his arm tight around her waist so the river couldn't pull her away from him.

The Snake was at least sixty feet wide and right now, they were in the center of it. Gil shook off his own dizziness, feeling warm blood running down the left side of his face. Kai's face was white, her lips parted. She hung like a broken rag doll beneath his arm, limp and unresponsive.

Gil knew how to work away from a strong current. Delta Force training was going to get them to shore. He maneuvered in the current, pushing his legs out in front of him, his boots pointed downstream. He wanted to assess Kai. She couldn't be dead! Using his free hand to plow through the water, drawing them inches at a time closer and closer toward the left bank, he couldn't take her pulse at the base of her neck.

Gil knew he didn't have the time he wanted. The water was glacier fed, near freezing. Hypothermia would kill them in a matter of minutes if he didn't get them to the safety of shore. He felt pain in his back and hip and ignored it, keeping Kai safe against him, her cheek resting on his shoulder.

Within two minutes, Gil had maneuvered them close to the rocky embankment. Once his boots struck the slippery bottom beneath them, he hauled Kai up and over his shoulder, getting her out of the icy grip of the water as soon as possible.

Gil labored, slipped and nearly fell several times

as he fought the surge of the current wanting to pull him back out toward the center. No! Adrenaline was fueling him now, giving him the superstrength he knew he'd need to get out of this deadly river alive.

He looked up, surveying where they were at. Trees were thick along the bank, making an almost impenetrable barrier in front of them. He saw they had floated around the mountain, at least a mile from where the pickup had fallen into the river.

Relief tunneled through him that they'd gotten to land. Whoever had pushed them over and into the river, had done it on purpose. He had no pistol on him. Just a Buck knife. And his cell phone was not working because it had been flooded with water.

They were on their own.

Mouth grim, Gil positioned Kai across his shoulders in a fireman's carry, holding on to her arm and ankle as he slogged and slipped through the knee-deep water. With every step, it brought them closer to the shore. *Hurry! Hurry!* His breath was exploding out of his mouth. The air was cool and he could feel himself already trembling and shaking from hypothermia. Kai! He had to tend to Kai!

God, let her be alive. Let her live!

His knees were shaking badly as he hauled them up the rocky six-foot embankment and onto a small, oval area of rich green grass. Gently, he eased Kai down onto it, laying her on her back, tipping her neck to keep her air passage open and then straightening out her legs. There was a gash along the left side of her head, the blood running swiftly, covering her temple and neck, dripping and soaking into the ground beneath her.

Kneeling beside her, Gil placed trembling fingers

against her slender neck, willing her to give him a pulse. His fear amped up. She looked dead.

There!

Relief sizzled through him. Kai was alive! But the feel of her pulse was weak and thready. *Son of a bitch!* Gil lifted his fingers away, quickly assessing Kai, looking for more injuries, broken bones or worse. Delta operators had EMT-level training and he quickly used all his knowledge. More relief rushed through him as he found no broken bones. It was a head injury.

Worried, Gil pushed the blood away for a moment to see the depth of the cut on her brow. It had gone to the bone of her skull. That wasn't good, but it could have been worse. It could have cracked her skull, leaving her brain exposed to serious, deadly damage.

"Kai?" he growled, "stay with me. You hear me? Stay with me. Don't you dare leave me! Fight. Fight to stay with me!"

Gil had worn his jacket. He jerked off the wet material and wrapped it up, placing it beneath Kai's neck. It was absolutely imperative that her airway be kept open. If she shifted, it could close the airway and she'd suffocate. Even though he was doing an assessment, his hearing was keyed to everything around them. Had the driver of the dump truck stopped? Had he followed them down that cliff? Was he hunting them right now? The urgency to get Kai out of sight pushed him into moving quickly.

Gil looked toward the dark barrier of fir and pine. The back of his neck prickled. It was a sign of coming danger. Coming at *them*.

Cursing softly, he picked Kai up, her head loll-

ing against his chest. Hurrying into the tree line, Gil
found an old fir that had been uprooted. The root
ball was massive, at least ten feet in diameter, the
roots sticking up in all directions like a wheel on its
side. Beneath it, he saw the hole and slid down into
it. Settling Kai so her air passage remained open, Gil
quickly climbed out of it, heading back to where he'd
left his rolled-up jacket next to the bank of the river. If
he left it in plain sight, whoever was following them
would find it and know they were in the vicinity. He
had to retrieve it now!

His neck prickled again. Mouth thinning, Gil
leaned down and picked up a fallen branch. It was
a good four-foot-long club that could be used as a
weapon. He hefted it into his hand.

Slowing, Gil hung back, crouching behind two
firs growing close together. The trunks provided him
good protection.

His heart was still thudding with adrenaline. He
sensed an enemy. He'd been an operator far too long
and had an extraordinary sense of when danger was
coming his way. Slipping down on his belly, hidden
by the darkness of the forest, as well as behind the
huge trunk of the tree, he saw a man about six feet
tall, a pistol in hand, slowly walking along the bank.

He was looking for them.

And dammit, his jacket was about ten feet away
from him. He'd spot it in a minute.

Rage flowed through Gil. The man was Cauca-
sian, wearing sunglasses, a baseball cap. It had to
be the driver of the dump truck. And he was a pro.
Gil could tell by the way the man walked and moved
as he slowly gazed around the area that he was a hit

man. Probably former black ops because he had a military bearing.

Gil wanted to take this bastard alive. Find out who had paid him to kill them. Excitement thrummed through him as he spotted a cell phone on the killer. It could get Kai to a hospital quickly if he could only get his hands on it.

Stealth and silence were a Delta Force specialty and Gil waited until the hit man had passed him by about six feet. The man suddenly halted, spotting the rolled-up jacket. *Perfect!*

Gil surged silently to his feet as the killer leaned down, hand extended to pick up the jacket. As he did, Gil moved behind him and lifted the club he carried, bringing it down on the man's right hand carrying the pistol.

The wood smashed into the man's lower arm.

Bone crunched. The man gave a scream as the pistol dropped from his nerveless hand.

All of Gil's rage funneled into a narrow focus as the man staggered, grabbing for his broken lower arm. He whirled to meet his attacker, and Gil was waiting for him. He closed the distance, hand curling into a fist, arcing out at the man's face. The impact of his hand into the man's face made satisfaction roar through him. Flesh met bone. Gil felt the man's cheekbone shatter beneath the power of his assault.

The man screamed, knocked off his feet, flung backward. He landed on his back.

Gil advanced upon him with the club. "Stay down!" he snarled.

The man's lips lifted in a snarl, blood running out of his nose and across his chin. He jerked a hunting knife from the sheath on his waist, staggering to his feet.

"You're dead," he muttered, lunging toward Gil, his right arm dangling uselessly at his side.

Gil dodged the slicing motion. He understood this hit man was going to either live or die. And he wasn't going to stand down.

With a grunt, Gil brought down the limb on the side of the man's neck with all the force he could bring. There was no way he was leaving Kai unprotected. He would do whatever it took to give her a chance to survive the crash.

The man gave a gurgling cry as the limb snapped his neck. His eyes widened. And then, he fell bonelessly to the grass, dead. The knife clattered to the ground beside him, released out of his fingers.

Breathing raggedly, Gil stepped forward, limb raised in a defensive position as he leaned down, pressing fingers to the man's exposed neck.

No pulse. He was dead.

Dropping the limb, Gil quickly grabbed the cell phone from the man's back pocket. Hands shaking, he quickly punched in 911. Looking back toward where he'd left Kai in the forest, his whole world, his heart, centered on her. How bad was her injury? He knew brain trauma, had seen it in too many others, and seen it wreck lives forever.

Trying to steady his breathing, he connected with 911, his heart constricted with terror. He loved Kai. She couldn't die on him! Not now!

GIL NEVER LEFT Kai's side after the helicopter from the Jackson Hole hospital picked them up and delivered them back to civilization. They'd placed her, unconscious, on a gurney and quickly wheeled her into the ER, where he met Dr. Jordana McPherson.

Her face was grim and as Gil walked swiftly with her to an available cubicle, he told her his assessment on Kai. It was a special hell to be with Kai as he waited for results from the MRI they'd given her.

He'd called the ranch earlier, letting Talon Holt know what had happened. Right now, Cat and Talon were on their way to the hospital. Cass and Sandy would remain at the ranch.

Because this was a hit, Gil warned his black-ops boss that more attacks might be coming their way. No one had any way of knowing whether there was more than one hit man and whether they might attack the ranch or one of them. Talon grimly agreed, carrying not only a pistol on him but a rifle on a rack in the cab of his truck. Cass would take similar defensive measures at the ranch to protect Sandy.

The nurses had gotten Kai out of her wet clothing, into a blue cotton gown and she was covered with warm, thick blankets to raise her near-hypothermic temperature.

Gil was grateful for the swift professionalism of everyone involved. He stood in his wet clothes, keeping guard over Kai, watchful, the curtains open so he could see anyone coming toward them from the side door or from the huge sliding glass doors down at the end of the room. Who had done this? Why? His mind wrenched one way and then the other with no forthcoming answers.

Sheriff's deputy Cade Garner entered the ER, his face grim as he made eye contact with Gil.

Gil remained with Kai, his hand on hers, warming it up. She looked a little better, not as waxen, but still it scared the hell out of him.

About that time, Talon and Cat came rushing through the doors, spotting him and Kai immediately, their expressions stricken.

Jordana came into the cubicle, catching Gil's look. "She's going to be all right," she told him immediately, her hand going to his upper arm. "The MRI sees no brain trauma. She's taken a hard hit on the head and it's a level-three concussion," she said, going to Kai, briefly touching her damp red hair. "She should be coming around soon, Gil. The good news is her blood pressure is normal. Her pulse is a little high, but that's to be expected considering all that she's just gone through. Stay with Kai. She's going to be disoriented when she becomes conscious. Call me the minute she opens her eyes."

A lump formed in Gil's throat. "That's good news," he choked out, lifting his hand to Talon and Cat, who stood nearby, hearing Jordana's diagnosis. Relief was etched sharply in their faces, too. Cade Garner, who stood at the foot of the gurney, looked relieved. Gil wanted to cry with sheer relief, too, but forced back the reaction. His gaze went to Kai's smooth, clear face. Jordana had put the butterfly bandages across the gash, closing it without stitches.

Kai looked like she was sleeping, more angel than human to him. She was so damned delicate. Now, she was fragile, too.

Jordana looked around the cubicle at all of them. "Cat? Why don't you stay with Kai?" She looked at the grim-faced men. "You three? Take your discussion outside where you have some privacy. I don't want all this going on around Kai. People who are unconscious or in a coma hear people speaking around them. She doesn't need this extra stress right now. Okay?"

Cat came over, her hand protective on Kai's shoulder. "Sounds good. Guys? Take off. I'll let you know if Kai becomes conscious."

Gil didn't want to leave, but he knew Cade was in a hurry to talk to him and find out what had happened. Talon remained grim, his gaze flicking between him and Cade. "Good idea," he told Cat.

Gil leaned down, kissing Kai's slack, cool lips. Gil wanted them all to know what Kai meant to him. He wasn't going to hide it from now on. Not after what had just happened. When he lifted his head, he saw them all grin, happiness gleaming in their eyes. They got it. Besides, they'd have been well aware they hadn't come back to the ranch last night and put it together.

Gil followed Cade out. Talon walked beside him. They left the hospital premises and halted near the brick wall where they could be more or less unseen, and have the privacy they wanted. Gil told Cade everything. The deputy was writing it all down on an iPad. At one point, he got on his radio, ordering another deputy to go to the crash site and find the license plate on the truck. The driver of it had been brought in earlier on the helo flight with Kai and Gil.

The medical examiner had already taken fingerprints from the dead man and they were being run through a national system to try to identify him. Gil had searched the hit man earlier and found no information on him. None. He'd taken the gun, and Cade would get the ballistics at the sheriff's office. He'd noticed immediately that the number had been filed off so it couldn't be traced. It wouldn't help them to track the man's name or who he'd bought the weapon from. That avenue was closed to them.

Talon rubbed his face after Gil and Cade were finished discussing the attack. "What do you think, Cade? Who's behind this?"

Cade gave them a grim look. "Gut hunch? Chuck Harper." He looked over at Gil. "It's a slender thread, I'll admit. Harper is known to be obsessive about a woman he puts in his sights," he warned them.

"But," Gil muttered, "all because she was over at his repair shop? Is this what triggered his response, you think?"

Shrugging, Cade said, "I don't know. We need to get Kai conscious. We need to find out more from her about Harper possibly approaching her at Ace Trucking. What did Harper do when she was there? Did he accost her? Try to touch her? Hell, we don't know."

"If Harper did, Kai has never said anything to me about it," Gil admitted, frowning. "Plus, she always had one of us escort her there when she needed to use the equipment."

Talon snorted. "Do you honestly think Kai would tell you anything? If something did happen, she'd be afraid you'd go over and pound the shit out of him. Kai had already been warned by Cat weeks ago that he was a major regional drug dealer. She's not dumb."

"What?" Gil growled. "Kai was afraid if she told me what happened that I'd confront Harper?" When he'd arrived back at the table at the Armory and Kai was in the restroom, Talon had told him about Harper approaching Kai. It had made Gil burn, and he didn't like what Harper had done, but he wasn't going to accost him at the Armory last night, either. Harper hadn't tried to talk with Kai after that. Gil had kept an eye on the bastard, but Harper had disappeared into the crowd, not to be seen again. Every particle of him wanted to find Harper, slam the bastard up against a wall and tell him to never touch Kai or approach her again. But he hadn't. He didn't want to upset Kai, and he desperately needed the time to connect with her. Gil had planned to drive over to see Harper at Ace Trucking and set the record straight with him. He was going to warn the bastard to never touch Kai again, that she was his.

"She may have been afraid of reprisal," Cade said, nodding his head. "You're the foreman. It's your responsibility to protect her. And I'll bet if something did happen, she was afraid she might get fired by you, Gil."

Talon blew out a breath of air. "Hell, this may or may not be Harper at all. We just don't know yet. The fact that Harper went over to our ranch's table last night, put his hand on Kai's shoulder and talked to her is suspicious. But it's not out of character for Harper. You know when he stakes a claim on a woman he hassles her and he stalks her."

Gil glared at the deputy. "If Harper did something to her, his ass is mine."

Holding up his hand, Cade warned, "Look, it's too early to go there. Let's all take a deep breath and stand down until we get more information. I just hope Kai regains consciousness soon so I can find out the rest of the story."

Restless, angry, wanting to punch something, Gil snarled, "If we're done, I'm going back in to be with Kai. You'll find me there." He stalked off, turned at the corner of the building and disappeared.

Cade shook his head, giving Talon a worried look. "You should stay with him. I don't need Gil going after Harper."

"Yeah," Talon breathed, "I'll hang close to him. Don't worry, okay?" He slapped Cade's shoulder. "As soon as Kai awakens, his whole focus is going to be her, anyway."

"Well, keep it there. Until we have some answers, I don't want him going off half-cocked."

CHAPTER TWENTY-ONE

KAI SLOWLY OPENED her eyes. Everything blurred and then came back into focus. Her joints ached and she felt stiff.

The first person she saw was Gil standing near her, his eyes narrowed and intense upon her. She felt his roughened hand, warm and firm, around her fingers. Her mind spun with questions and then she closed her eyes, feeling dizzy and seeing blips of a crash. Gil grazed her cheek and Kai lifted her lashes. Everything was such a huge effort and she felt weak.

"You're at the Jackson Hole hospital and you're going to be okay," he told her quietly. Cat stood on the other side of the gurney with Talon and she brushed Kai's other hand. "How are you feeling, Kai?"

It hurt to think. "Rough," she managed, her voice barely a hoarse whisper. She felt bruised to her core.

"You have a cut on your brow and you have a concussion, Dove…"

Kai frowned, but her head ached when she moved it. The crash all came rushing back to her…about something big hitting them from behind and being shoved across the narrow highway and into the guardrail.

She swallowed, watching Gil's expression. Kai saw the worry in his blue gaze, terror and relief. More than anything, his love for her. Movement snagged her attention and she slowly turned her head to the right. Cat gave her a kind smile.

"Welcome back, Kai. Just lie there and get your bearings. You're going to be fine…"

Kai saw Talon near her shoulder and he was looking concerned. Needing Gil, she focused her attention on him, his hand on hers, the way he gently touched her hair. "W-we were hit from behind…"

Gil nodded. Slowly, so Kai could retain what he said, he told her a shortened version of the crash.

"B-but why?" Kai asked, giving him a stressed look. "Why did that guy hit us? I never heard a horn being honked. He could have warned us, tried to pass around us…"

Gil nodded. "There's more to this, Kai, but look, you're really tired and I just want you to rest. We can cover it when you're feeling better. The most important thing is that you're safe and you're going to have a full recovery."

Kai saw Jordana McPherson slip in between the curtains and enter the cubicle. The doctor beamed at her. Gil released her hand and stepped back so the doctor could get to her side.

"Hey, how you doing, Kai?" Jordana asked, pulling out her small penlight from the white lab coat she wore. She slowly moved it across her eyes two times.

"Rugged… My mind…it's not working right…"

Jordana said, "You have a level-three concussion, Kai. It really shakes a person's brain up for a while. Now that you're awake, we're going to move you to a private room where Gil can keep an eye on you." She gently patted Kai's arm. "It will take you about forty-eight hours to really come back from the crash. Until then, you're not going to be feeling very chipper. The good news is that your pupils are equal and responsive, so that tells me your brain has not been traumatized." She gestured to Gil. "And this big guy will be at your side the whole time."

Nothing had felt better to Kai than hearing that. She noticed Gil had a head wound that had been sutured up. Her mind just wasn't cooperating and she remembered bits and pieces. "Okay, that sounds really good," she told Jordana wearily. "Thank you…"

It was near evening when Kai awoke again. The new room she had been placed in earlier was semidark, weak light filtering in around the window where the blinds were drawn shut. She still had an IV in her arm and she heard the soft beeps of nearby equipment. A chair squeaked and snagged her attention. Kai slowly turned her head and looked to her right. Gil rose stiffly out of the plastic chair.

"Hey," Kai whispered, putting out her hand toward him. "How are you?" He looked exhausted.

"Better than you," Gil teased quietly, taking Kai's hand and leaning over, gently taking her mouth, brushing his lips against hers, feeling her return his kiss.

Just the touch of Gil's mouth fed Kai strength and grounded her. As he eased away, his dark blue eyes hooded, he intently assessed her. "I'm better. The dizziness seems to be gone."

"Your eyes look cleaner. Brighter." Gil's mouth hooked upward. "Like somebody's home this time," he said, and caressed her cheek. "Even some color here, too. I think you're coming back to life, Dove."

The endearment flowed quietly through Kai, her heart opening wide to Gil. She felt cherished. Loved. And there was no longer mistaking that she saw love in his eyes for her.

"You give me life," she said tremulously, searching his eyes, feeling protection radiating off him and embracing her. It made Kai feel safe and she didn't know why she felt so threatened. There was danger and she could sense it. Maybe because of the accident and her bruised brain?

He rasped, "You *are* my life. You always have been." Gil halted, not wanting to say more right now. He saw her eyes go liquid with love for him. It was so clear and unmistakable. That realization lifted him as nothing else ever could. "Are you hungry? Thirsty?"

"Thirsty," Kai admitted.

"Water okay? Or do you want something else to drink?"

"No, water's fine." Kai watched him pour a glass from the nearby tray. He brought up the bed so she was in a comfortable, semireclining position. Sliding his arms around her shoulders, Gil brought her into his embrace and held the glass to her lips.

Kai hadn't realized how thirsty she really was until she'd completely drained the glass. "Thanks," she said ruefully, wiping her mouth afterward. "Call me a camel." Gil smiled a little and sat on the edge of the bed, facing her, their hips barely touching. "Jordana said you would be thirsty for a while. Any headache?"

"No." Kai sighed and reached out as he offered his hand to her, fingers meeting and tangling. "I'm just glad you're here."

"Do you feel up to hearing the rest of what happened to us?" Gil asked her gravely.

Kai felt a catch in her throat, increasing that fear and threat she'd felt around her earlier. Gil's face was unreadable, that operator's mask partly in place so she couldn't decipher his expression. "What happened, Gil?"

He told her about the events that transpired after the crash. Kai remembered nothing after the pickup slammed into the rocks near the river's edge when she lost consciousness. Gil watched her eyes grow wide with shock. And when he told her about the man he had to kill, she gasped, her hand flying to her mouth. She stared at him, stunned.

"But—who was he? And why was he hunting us?" she asked, shaken.

"That's what we're trying to piece together," Gil said, smoothing his fingers across the back of her hand. "Cade thinks Chuck Harper is behind it, but he's not sure just yet."

Kai stared at him. "Chuck?"

Nodding, Gil said, "Cade told us earlier, after we got you here to the hospital, that when Chuck finds a woman he wants, he obsesses over her until he gets her. Anyone who snubs his advances ends up missing. That's happened twice, as far as Cade knows. But none of it can be legally proved. The other two women he wanted and who spurned his advances just disappeared. Never seen or heard from again, Kai. He thinks Harper either had them murdered or they ended up sold to a sex-slave ring, most likely sent to Eastern Europe. He said Harper is forging a sex-slave trade in this region and women are being sent over there."

"Oh, God," Kai muttered, touching her brow. She swallowed hard and looked away. "I—I didn't know... Cat had told me a while back that Harper was obsessive toward a woman he wanted. She told me to stay away from him," she began lamely.

"We all should have been blunt with you about Harper from the beginning, and we weren't," Gil admitted. "I asked everyone not to tell you this. I didn't want you scared of going over to Harper's repair shop. We all figured if you were always escorted over there by one of us, Harper would leave you alone and everything would be okay."

Giving Gil a look of apology, Kai said, "I didn't help matters, then. About a month after I was hired, Chuck asked me to go on a trail ride with him on a Saturday." She winced, seeing Gil's eyes suddenly narrow, felt the tension rise in him. "I did go and we spent half a day riding the Lupine Trail in the Tetons. All we did was share a lunch and we talked about stuff, but that was all. Nothing went on and nothing happened." She felt like a traitor to Gil.

Kai could see the hurt in his eyes. "Look," she added hoarsely, "this was long before there was anything between us, Gil. I was lonely, if you want the truth. You and I were not getting along at all, so I couldn't ask you to go on a trail ride with me. After that, though, Chuck started calling me every day, asking me to go out with him again. I kept telling him no, but he wouldn't leave me alone. Then, he'd switch tactics and suggest I go to lunch with him or go to dinner. I turned him down every time. He made my skin crawl. I felt like he was stalking me." Kai wrapped her arms around herself, giving Gil a worried look.

"And then he approached me at the Armory in front of everyone. You were busy getting drinks and didn't see it happen."

"Talon told me about it later. I was going to see Harper at his business next week and tell him to never touch you again, that you were mine." Gil folded his hands, scowling. "It sounds like Cade is right—Harper was obsessing on you, Kai." His voice lowered and gentled. He picked up Kai's hand, now cool and damp feeling. "Look, I'm not angry with you. I understand why you did it. You just didn't know how much of a predator he really is. And I'm at fault for not telling you everything about Harper. I was trying to protect you because we needed that repair shop of his. Plus, we all thought if someone escorted you over there, things would be fine."

Tears jammed into her eyes and her voice became raspy. "I didn't know, Gil. I swear to God, I didn't. I—I was working so hard, long hours, and I just wanted a day off to relax. I love riding trails." Lifting her chin, warm tears fell down her cheeks. "I'm so sorry. I didn't mean to hurt you in any way. I really didn't—"

"Hush," he rasped, releasing her hand. Gil got up and sat closer, slipping his arms around Kai's shoulders and drawing her gently against him. "Don't cry over this, Dove. You couldn't have possibly known everything about this bastard. I didn't know the full extent, either. Only Cade knew he formed obsessions and we just found that out today. Everyone was more or less in the dark."

Gil kissed her hair and slid his hand reassuringly up and down her back. "You did nothing wrong. Nothing. So, let's let it rest between us, okay? I'm just glad you're alive. It scared the hell out of me…" His voice cracked with emotion. Gil didn't want to squeeze Kai too hard; she was as bruised and battered as he was. He kept his embrace gentle. More than anything else, he didn't want Kai feeling badly about choices she'd made regarding Harper. Kai was right: at that time they were on tenterhooks with one another. And he was sure she was stressed-out by it. A ride in the Tetons would soothe anyone's soul. But no one realized Harper's real intentions behind the invitation. He could have raped her, drugged or killed her out there alone in the mountains. That sent a frisson of galvanizing fear through Gil. He was at fault in this, too. He bore responsibility for what happened, as well.

Giving a slight nod, Kai pulled away, self-consciously wiping tears from her cheeks. "Harper just kept pursuing me. When you and I started to heal things between us, Gil, I told him I was in a relationship with you and to stop calling me."

Taking a deep breath, Gil said, "He was obsessed with you, that's why he kept after you, Kai. Do you feel up to talking to Cade? I think he'll want to know about this."

"Sure," she muttered. "But what will it prove?"

"I'm not sure. But it is evidence about his continued behavior toward you. Also, Cade can get proof of it via your cell phone. His number is going to show up and show how many times he called you."

Gil said nothing as Cade came to the room and listened to Kai's story about Harper. He could see the deputy sheriff's face turning more grim. It was near dinnertime when Kai finished her story. She looked tired again. This was a helluva stress on her, and Gil wished he could have protected her from it.

"Did Harper do this?" Kai asked the deputy.

"We can't prove it. At least, not yet." Cade gave her a kind look and said, "I wished I'd have told you about his other behavior, Kai. I'm sorry I didn't. I thought if you knew he was being watched for drug dealing, that would be enough to warn you off. This was my fault. I should have asked Gil or Talon to tell you everything about him."

Kai grimaced. "I just didn't feel concerned about what I was told by Talon because one of the guys from the ranch always went in with me to Ace Trucking's machine shop, with the exception of two times. And I was only in a shop where three other men were working."

"Harper's smart and he's careful," Cade warned them, standing. "We'll just have to wait until we get more info in and put the pieces together."

"Nothing on the hit man?" Gil asked.

"He's a criminal," Cade said. "His fingerprints brought up his entire record. Tony Fausterman just got out of prison about six months ago. No ties to Harper that we can prove yet. The truck had no license plate on it. We're tracking the VIN number on it right now."

"So many little pieces to check," Kai said, folding her hands in her lap, giving the deputy a grateful look.

"Well, until we can put a picture together on this, Kai, I want Gil with you. Go nowhere alone. Okay?"

"I promise," she said solemnly.

"And there's no way to track the pistol Fausterman was using, either," Gil said, frowning.

"No," Cade agreed. He pushed the notepad into his pocket and buttoned it.

"Talon was concerned about another hit man who might still be around," Gil said. "What do you think?"

Cade grimaced. "No way of telling. My gut tells me Harper was after Kai. I don't think he wants a war with the Holt ranch. If anything, Harper likes to play it quiet on the surface and try his damnedest not to raise law enforcement's attention. So I think Harper got pissed that Kai had offed him for you. And he probably hired Fausterman out of New York, paid him in cash, got this dump truck from somewhere and told the hit man to kill both of you. It's Harper's way of getting even. At least—" he shrugged "—that's my own personal theory of what went down. The problem is proving it. With Fausterman dead, he can't turn over evidence. The pistol's numbers have been filed off. The dump truck has no license plate. I'm hoping for a hit via motor vehicles on the VIN number. But it's a slim thread."

"Then," Kai said wearily, "if Harper is behind this, he'll probably never be found out. Right?"

Cade sighed. "Yeah, that's about it. After I get the VIN number info, I may go over to Harper and talk to him. But he's a cagey bastard and won't tell me anything."

"Send me over," Gil growled, giving the deputy a hard look. "I'll get information out of him."

"No way," Cade said. "I'll end up having to put you in jail, too, and I don't want to do that, Gil. Besides, look at it this way—if we can't prove he was behind this and I don't go over, he'll think he got away with it. Criminals get bolder when they think they've outsmarted us. And it gives us information about his tactics that we can use later if he tries to go after another woman."

Gil gave him a hard look but said nothing.

Kai frowned. "Then...if he is behind this, and there's no proof, Cade, he'll get away with it. Worse, he'll go after me again? Or another woman? My God."

"Anything is possible," Cade said gently. "No one's more frustrated about this than me. We continue to search for those two missing women. We've found nothing. We're working with regional states, APBs, photos of them to all law enforcement, and the FBI is involved, as well. But we've come up empty so far."

Kai gulped. "Then, I'm not really safe?"

"You're safe," Gil growled, glaring over at Cade. "He'll never get near you again." His voice vibrated with barely held rage.

Holding up his hands, Cade said, "If this is Harper's work, I very seriously doubt he'll try to harm you again, Kai. He hates being in the focus of law enforcement. Besides, this is premature. We have to have proof. We can't do anything without it. I'll be back in touch with you as soon as I learn anything." His eyes gentled as he held Kai's distraught gaze. "Two things. First, do not ever use Ace Trucking's machine shop again."

"No," she whispered, "I won't. I'll drive to Idaho Falls to do my work, instead, if I need to."

"Good. Secondly——" Cade glanced over at Gil, whose face was hard and unreadable, his eyes stormy looking "——you go nowhere without one of the men of the Triple H with you. At least until we can try and get this sorted out."

"Don't worry," Kai said, "I don't want to go anywhere alone."

"Okay," Cade breathed, giving her a tight smile, "that's what I need to hear."

Kai drew in a shaky breath after Cade left. A nurse came in, smiled and removed her IV, asking if she'd like dinner. Kai was going to say no, but Gil interceded and said yes. When the nurse left, she looked over at him. His face was completely unreadable, but she felt the controlled anger pulsating off him. "You think Harper did it?"

"No question." Gil flexed his fist and watched as she slowly pulled off the cover, revealing her long legs. The blue gown was hitched up to around her knees. Wincing inwardly, he saw all the bruises on them, and more anger tunneled through him. And more fear that she could have died. "What are you doing?"

"Getting out of this bed." She gave him a faint smile. "I hate being bed-bound." She held out her hand to him. "Help me?"

Gil walked over, grasping her left elbow. "Take it slow."

Kai wanted to feel in control again. Gil's fingers were warm and firm, not hurting. Her bare feet met the cool tiles of the floor. Straightening, she kept her other hand on the bed, waiting to see if the dizziness assailed her. It did not. "I'm going to walk to the bathroom," she said, gesturing toward the opened door. To her surprise, her legs were steady. They were sore as hell and she got the first look at all the colorful bruises over them as she walked slowly to the entrance.

"Hey," she murmured, risking a smile up at him, "not bad, huh?"

"Don't get too frisky," Gil rumbled, releasing her elbow. "Jordana said forty-eight hours."

Kai saw the rage he held disappear from his eyes. Gil was good at hiding things he didn't want her to see, but that was the operator coming out in him. Instead, he gave her a tender look, one corner of his mouth crooking. Her heart swelled with such love for him. If only they could go home right now to his condo, but she knew he had two days before he could move into it. And she'd move in with him, no question.

When she emerged later, Gil got up and walked over, cupping her elbow. "I'm okay," she assured him. "Do I have any clothes here, Gil?"

"Yes," he said, moving to the small closet. "Cat brought you a fresh set of clothes and your leather shoes."

"Bless her heart," Kai murmured, walking over to it. Gil opened it and handed her the clothing, a pair of jeans, a red tank top, socks, a bra and panties.

"I can dress you if you want?" Gil said with a slow smile, holding her gaze.

Heat flooded her, feeling wonderful, dissolving the fear inside her. She held the clothes in her hands and said, "I'll use the bathroom. I'm in no shape to do much of anything."

He reached out, caressing her cheek. "I know that, Dove. Just trying to make you feel a little better, letting you know you look beautiful to me."

Heat spread from her neck up into her face as she

held his dark, hungry gaze. "Oh, sure," she joked lamely. "I'm so bruised up, I look awful."

"Bruises go away," he rasped. He patted her butt. "Go get dressed. Your tray of food will probably arrive soon."

By the time she was dressed, Kai felt much better. She didn't like hospitals. At all. And sure enough, there was the dinner tray on the rolling table waiting for her. She sat on one edge of the bed and Gil on the other side of it. There were some thick slabs of beef pot roast with gravy, mashed potatoes and green beans. There was chocolate pudding for dessert.

Gil had cut up the meat and handed her the fork. He used the spoon and they ate in silence, quickly wolfing down all the food. When they finished, Jordana dropped in.

"Hey, you're looking surprisingly good," she told Kai. "I was coming in to see how you were and if you were doing well, I was going to release you from the hospital."

Kai smiled a little and touched her jeans. "I'm already dressed to leave, believe me."

Jordana grinned as Gil pushed the tray aside so she could check Kai out. "Yes, well, I don't know anyone who loves coming to a hospital. Not on anyone's list of top ten things to do," she said, and chuckled as she took the stethoscope from around her neck and listened to Kai's heart and then her lungs. And one more look into her eyes to insure her pupils were still equal, which they were.

"Okay," she said, "you're free to go. I do want to see you in two days at my clinic. I'll have my receptionist ring you for an appointment."

"Great," Kai said, relief obvious in her voice. "Thanks for everything, Jordana." She reached out, squeezing her hand.

"You're more than welcome. Now, take it easy the next couple of days. No heavy lifting. No nothing but sitting, maybe washing some dishes or cooking, but *light* work."

"Light, it is," Kai promised. "I'm so stiff and bruised up I really don't want to be twisting around like a pretzel."

Jordana laughed and opened the door. "Okay, see you two later…"

Gil had gotten the small suitcase Cat had brought earlier and put what few things Kai had into it. "Ready to go to the ranch?"

Was she ever. Sliding off the bed and waiting to see if dizziness struck, she whispered, "I sure wish you had your condo, Gil."

He lifted his head and nodded. "Makes two of us, Dove."

"I'm going to wish I could be in your arms tonight." Because it would make her feel safe. She would have drowned if not for his quick rescue of her.

Gil closed the suitcase. "I know. But two days from now, you'll be where you belong—with me, in bed."

CHAPTER TWENTY-TWO

CHUCK HARPER JERKED AWAKE. Momentarily disoriented because he was sleeping so deeply, his heart pounded violently in his chest, as if he was under attack. Lying on his back, he quickly rose on his elbows, looking around his large master bedroom. It was new-moon time and it was utterly dark. As his eyes adjusted, his heart thudding heavily in his chest, he saw nothing. Yet, he felt under attack. He started to sit up, but something had pinned his legs down.

What the hell?

Reaching for the lamp on the bed stand, he turned it on, scowling. Looking at where his legs were positioned beneath the covers, he gasped. There, between his legs a large hunting knife was buried to its hilt, capturing all the blankets and sheet, pinning his legs so he couldn't move easily. Jerking his legs up, scrambling toward the headboard, his eyes widened with shock.

There, beneath the knife was a note kept in place because the blade had pierced it. Confused, suddenly terrorized, he jerked a look around his room. Instantly, he opened the door to the bed stand, hauling out his Glock 19, cocking it, holding it up, afraid that the intruder who had done this was still in his room.

Everything was quiet.

Nothing moved.

Breathing raggedly, Chuck leaped out of bed, dressed only in a pair of pajama bottoms. Now, he was scared. His gaze shot to the two windows in the room. They were closed. He went to the door of his bedroom and it was closed. He never locked it at night. Warily, he jerked it open, the Glock up and ready to fire. The hallway was dark and quiet. His heart felt as if it was going to leap out of his chest.

He didn't dare call the police. No, he didn't want anything to do with them. He knew he was under their scrutiny because he had certain trucks at certain times carrying drugs on board them.

Shit!

What the hell was going on? He flipped on the light. The hall was empty. All he could hear was a faint rush of wind outside the windows from time to time. Shakily wiping his mouth, he knew he had to check every room in the condo. The person who did this could still be here, waiting for him. His fingers were damp and slipping around the grip of the Glock as he tiptoed down the hall. His hearing was keyed for the slightest noise that was out of place. Sweat had popped out on his deeply wrinkled brow. He could feel it trailing down his temples as he cleared one room after the other. All were empty on the second floor where his bedroom was.

He moved as silently as he could on his bare feet to the top of the wooden stairs that led to the first floor. He turned on the light so it flooded the open-concept living room and kitchen. Glock in both hands, Chuck tried to ferret out the intruder, who might be below.

Nothing.

Dammit! Now Harper wished he had an assault rifle on hand. They were all hidden at the trucking terminal where no one could find them. Breathing as if he'd run miles, he slowly crept down the stairs, tense and frightened. Forcing himself, he took the creaking stairs slowly. As he reached the bottom of the stairs, he quickly tried the front door, which was always locked at night.

The door opened!

Gasping, Chuck hauled the door open. Someone had slipped into his condo through this door! Now he wanted to call the police, but he didn't dare.

Wiping his mouth, the cold air rushing past him, he noticed the porch light, which was always on, was out. Aggravated, he flipped the switch from the inside once again. It wouldn't work! Upon closer inspection, he found the bulb had been broken. Looking down at the walk, he saw shards of glitter beneath the light flooding out into the yard.

Frightened, he slammed the door and locked it.

He had to investigate the first floor and he quickly did that, finding no one in the house. Further, the alarm system, which was massive, had been disabled in the pantry where it was located. Shakily, he set the Glock on the granite island, pushing his hands through his sweaty hair. Feeling like a primitive animal that was being watched by a bigger predator he couldn't find, he grabbed a drink of water from the sink, his mind whirling with questions.

Who had done this?

Taking the stairs two at a time, Chuck ran back down the hall to his bedroom. The light clearly showed the huge hunting knife stuck into his bed, the note around it.

Staring at it, Chuck wondered why the hell he hadn't heard anything. The intruder had jimmied the front door, come up the stairs, slipped unheard into his room and had put that paper on the bed between his legs as he slept. Not only that, the unknown assailant had pushed the heavy knife through all the bedding and through that paper and deep into the mattress.

Between his damned legs as he slept!

"Jesus," Harper breathed. He hesitated, wondering if there were fingerprints on the knife. What good would it do him? If he called the cops, there would be an investigation. And then that would give them full access, without a search warrant, to go to the trucking terminal. No. He couldn't do that. Right now, he knew how badly law enforcement wanted any excuse to get inside that terminal and bring in drug-sniffing dogs and find out where he was hiding the marijuana, heroine and cocaine. No friggin' way.

Growling a curse, Chuck jerked the huge knife free from the mattress. Grabbing the paper, he saw that it had something typed in small, ten-point type, obviously from a printer. Barely able to read it, he sat down, gripping the paper, dampening it with his sweat.

Leave the people of the Triple H and Bar H alone. If you don't, my face will be the last one you see.

Harper's heart leaped. His mouth grew grim as he stared blackly at the threat.
What the hell!

And then real terror began to leak through him. Who had found out he was behind the hit on Gil Hanford and that bitch, Kai Tiernan? Chuck had already found out through other sources that the hit man he'd carefully hired had been killed by Hanford after the crash. Even worse, Hanford and Tiernan had survived it.

Cursing richly, Chuck threw the paper on the floor. It floated down near his bare feet. He savagely kicked it away. Rubbing his face, he felt real terror deep down, crawling around in his belly. He didn't like being threatened. Who had done this? His mind whirled. Harper knew that Talon Holt, Cass Reynolds and Hanford had all been in military black ops. They knew how to move without being heard. They were lethal killers.

He looked around the room, feeling violated. Unsafe. One of them had done this! He was sure of it. And he was also sure that they would be careful not to leave any fingerprints or evidence that they'd been here, either. They weren't black ops for nothing. His hand curved into a fist as rage and fright twined within his aching gut. Harper was used to scaring other people. He never expected anyone to come and threaten him. *Son of a bitch!*

Glaring around the quiet room, he realized one of those bastards had done this to him. They'd stood over his bed. They knew how to use a knife to kill, without thinking twice. A shiver of dread skittered through Harper as he thought about the intruder standing there, looking at him, the knife in his hand while he slept. He could have slit his throat.

But he hadn't.

Shakily, Chuck rubbed his throat, gulping hard.
What scared him more was that he knew enough
about black ops military men to know you didn't
screw with them. That they had the training and ca-
pability to steal like a silent shadow anywhere they
wanted. And one of them had come in here.

Completely shaken, Harper got up, needing a
drink of whiskey to calm his shattered nerves. He
walked into his huge closet, jerking down a set of
clean clothes and getting dressed. Heading down-
stairs, the Glock still in hand, he went first to check
the front door. It was still locked.

A little frisson of relief went through him.

It wasn't lost on him, as he poured the whiskey into
a tumbler on the granite island, that Hanford knew he
was the one behind the failed attack on him and Kai.
Dragging the glass to his full lips, he threw his head
back, drinking all of it at once. The whiskey burned
on its way down to his tightened stomach. Somehow,
Hanford had figured it out. Harper had been very,
very careful about hiring the hit man, who was an
ex-Ranger who had been in black ops for a decade.
He had been a hit man at-large, well-known for his
lethality and getting a job done right. This time, he'd
failed. Miserably.

Sitting down on a padded black leather stool at
the island, Harper poured another slosh of whiskey into the tumbler, feeling his taut nerves settling
down. Harper had had the entire agreement done by
third-party Russian mafia contacts he had on the East
Coast. None of it could ever be traced back to him.
Further, the rusted dump truck had come out of a Star
Valley auto-wrecking service and bought by the ex-

Ranger who had used a fake name. Again, a dead end. Nothing would lead back to him to suggest he was behind ordering the hit on Hanford and Kai.

He sat there sipping the whiskey, his mind going at light speed, looking at the angles, the possibilities. Harper would bet his life that it was Hanford who had done this. But if he hadn't, he had two buddies, one a former SEAL and one a former Special Forces operator, who could have done it for him. Scratching his head nervously, Chuck knew that one of them had figured out he was behind the hit.

The good news was that law enforcement couldn't do a friggin' thing about it because there was no evidence suggesting he had instituted the hit in the first place.

Chuck grinned a little, feeling a bit better. And then his grin slipped as he realized that if he didn't leave those people at those two ranches completely alone that the intruder would be back. And this time, he'd slit Chuck's throat while he slept. His dark brows slashed downward and he chugged the rest of the whiskey, feeling vulnerable, terrified of dying.

Getting up, Harper moved to his office on the first floor. He would do exactly as the note read: leave those who worked for or owned the Triple H and Bar H to hell alone. He had wanted to get even with Kai for leaving him in favor of that bastard, Hanford. Revenge was a way of life for him and he enjoyed exacting it on anyone who snubbed him. The other two women who had were now somewhere in Eastern Europe, sold to the highest bidder. They would remain sex slaves for the rest of their lives until someone got tired of them and either sold them as used goods to someone else or put a bullet through their heads if they dared to fight back or tried to escape their owner.

He smiled mirthlessly over that thought. In Kai Tiernan's case, he wanted to just outright kill the bitch and her boyfriend.

And the plan had completely backfired on him.

He wasn't used to being outfoxed. Garcia, the Latin drug lord, had chosen him specifically to take over for the murdered Curt Downing, to continue to quietly and carefully run the regional drug business. He used his trucks to haul goods all across the Western states. There were special compartments where drugs were placed and they, too, were distributed by certain drivers who were part of the drug business. He had employees who were drivers who had no clue as to what was going on.

His special drivers were all under Garcia's command. They were his foot soldiers. All Chuck did was give them the drugs and they would then take them to a drop house or person waiting for them in another town or city, and collect the money.

As badly as he wanted Kai Tiernan, Harper mentally removed her from his revenge list. Life was too short. There were plenty of other damn good-looking women around Jackson Hole he could find and then make his. *Screw her.* She wasn't worth dying over. Harper would make sure to never approach her again in any way, shape or form. She was off-limits. Just like the Holt and McPherson families on those two ranches were. No, he'd leave them to hell alone. *Forever.*

* * *

"WELL?" GIL ASKED Kai as he brought her to his newly leased condo for the first time, "what do you think?" The condo was completely furnished with all the furniture he had stored away in a rental when he'd first come to Jackson Hole. She stood beneath his arm and he relished having bodily contact with her.

Two days at the Triple H, unable to sleep together, had been rough on both of them. He glanced down at her clean profile. Today, her hair was mussed from the windy conditions midafternoon and she looked edible in her clinging pink tee that outlined those small, beautiful breasts of hers he was aching to hold and suckle again. Her jeans outlined her long, long legs that he took such delight in running his hand up and down.

Today she seemed to have come out of the shock of what had happened to her. Nearly dying always changed a person. Gil was glad she wanted to come and live with him. They would drive out to the Triple H every morning but then return here each night. It made his heart pound with relief and joy.

"Oh," Kai whispered, giving him a quick smile, "I love the decor!" She slipped from beneath his arm and walked into the open-concept living room and kitchen. She ran her fingertips across the burnt-orange corduroy couch. There were two overstuffed chairs of the same material gathered around a colorful stained-glass oval coffee table. Over the stained glass, to protect it, was another sheet of smooth glass. The furniture was rustic and made of natural blond oak. The oval rug beneath the coffee table was a dark green, reminding her of the leaves on an evergreen tree. Beneath it was a blond bamboo hardwood floor, which gave the place tons of light. The fireplace was made of flagstone rocks, floor to ceiling. The cinnamon, red and cream stones blended with the decor. It would be wonderful to sit in front of it on the many freezing, wintery nights that this part of Wyoming had.

"What do you think of the kitchen?" Gil asked her, shutting the door and watching her expression. Her gray eyes were shining with life in them, and his lower body automatically tightened with need. If nothing else since the crash, it had brought home to Gil that he loved Kai more than his life. As he watched her walk into the large, bright kitchen, some of his happiness was shaded with a keen desire to kill Chuck Harper.

He wished he could have seen Harper's face when he woke up and found that knife with the note positioned between his legs. Gil hoped it would put the fear of death into the bastard, to let him know he could not bother anyone on the Triple H or the Bar H ever again. Satisfaction flowed deeply through Gil. He figured Harper was a smart enough bastard to get the message in spades. How badly he'd wanted to slice open Harper's throat and end it all right there. But Gil didn't. Not because he didn't want to. He did. But if Harper was found dead, there would be an investigation. Gil understood he would become the number-one suspect in the case.

He loved Kai and wanted a life with her, not a criminal investigation against him. He wanted what was left of his life with Kai. And Harper was a smart enough drug runner to know that he would be good for his word if he in any way ever approached Kai again. And Gil would make sure no one could ever pin the murder on him. He was too good in black ops to ever be discovered. But he would be a suspect and it would be stressful on Kai, so he wasn't going there unless Harper was stupid and approached her again. Then? All bets were off. He'd deal with an investigation, but no one would ever know that Harper had been taken down by him.

"Wow," Kai said, turning around in the kitchen, grinning, "I just love the earth tones in the granite counters." She gestured toward the huge window above the two steel sinks, feminine white curtains around them. "I love the light, Gil." She walked over to the Wolf gas stove, beaming. "And this is perfect! I love to cook and this is just the best stove to use. You have good taste." She gave him a teasing look.

He smiled and wandered into the kitchen, where he leaned against the large rectangular island. There were four wooden stools with thick brown leather padding on each of them around one side of it. "The fridge is full, too. We can have our first dinner here tonight. Or, I can take you out to eat if you'd like?" Because for the past two days Kai had truly been taking it easy. Miss Gus had come over and been like a virtual grandmother hen, fussing over Kai, cooking up her world-famous chicken soup in a huge pot and remaining in the guest bedroom those two days. Gil had been grateful to the elder, who gave Kai a combination of tough love and mothering.

He couldn't hold Kai or be affectionate with her at the ranch, although everyone knew that they would live together at his condo. Miss Gus had come in like a pinch hitter and made the difference. Kai had responded quickly to Miss Gus's care of her.

Today, the third day after the crash, Kai looked almost normal to most people except for the bruise around the healing cut on her brow.

"No, I'd love to cook for us tonight." Kai gave him a pleading look, running her fingers across the stainless-steel stove, appreciation in her expression.

"Sure," he said, opening up the fridge, showing her how huge it was, well stocked and with a lot of food choices for her. He'd come over here earlier to make sure the movers put everything in the places he'd chosen. The look of happiness in Kai's face made his efforts all worthwhile. Gil could see the heat in her eyes when she looked at him. That yearning he could feel from his heart straight down to his lower body. She wanted him just as much as he wanted her.

Nosing around inside the fridge, Kai pulled out two elk steaks and placed them where they would be easy to reach later. "Elk steaks, potatoes au gratin, a nice salad and toasted garlic bread. What do you think?" Kai twisted a look as he stood holding the door open for her.

"Sounds good," he rumbled. And then he added with a grin, "As long as I can have you for dessert?"

Laughing softly, Kai stepped aside and allowed him to shut the fridge. "Oh, believe me, you're *my* dessert once we go to bed."

"Yes, you are," Gil murmured, lifting his hand and gently caressing her hair, watching the sunlight lance through the kitchen window, touching the strands, making them gleam gold, burgundy and red beneath the slats. "Come on, let's see the rest of our condo."

It felt so good to say *our*. He drowned in the softness coming to her gray eyes. He'd nearly lost Kai. That shook Gil as nothing else ever would. In time, the deep cut on her brow would heal. A small scar would always remain to remind him how close he'd come to losing her. Inwardly, Gil swore he would never take one day with her for granted. Not ever.

KAI NEVER WANTED anything more than what she had right now—she was naked in bed with Gil. The huge king-size bed made it easy to snuggle into his waiting arms, and when she did, he eased her onto her back. The bedroom door was open, enough illumination spilling in from the hallway night-light. She gazed upward, seeing the love shining in his eyes. Sliding her hand across his muscled upper arm and then his shoulder, she whispered, "I think it's time I told you something."

"What?" he growled, leaning down, kissing her brow. He inhaled her scent, the jasmine soap she loved to use in the shower they'd shared just now. His body vibrated with need to be within her. If she wasn't getting over a concussion, Gil would have hoisted her into his arms, wrapped her long legs around his waist, gently placed her back against the warm, wet wall of the shower and taken her there.

Trailing her fingers down the hard line of his jaw, his stubble sending prickles up them, Kai gave him a tender look. "That I love you, Gil."

The words hung sweetly between them.

Kai saw his blue eyes narrow, saw the words turn his hard face soft. She saw the way his mouth flexed. "I've been wanting to tell you this for a while, but I kept holding back because it was too soon. I didn't want to rush anything between us, Gil. I was trusting you like I had before, and I was afraid." Kai looked away for a moment and then returned her gaze to him. "But the crash… God… I would have died if you hadn't rescued me. And then, you protected me against that hit man. I know I don't remember any of it, but it doesn't diminish how scared I felt after I woke up. The more you told me about what had happened, the more alarmed, the more scared I got."

"Scared of what, Dove?" he asked, his voice low with emotion.

"Scared of never telling you that I loved you. That it was stupid to wait because none of us know how long we have on this earth. You could be gone in a split second and I began to realize you needed to know now." Kai gave him a tremulous smile, absorbing the light and shadow across his hard face. To someone else, she knew Gil looked threatening. He had a rugged face hewn out of hard times and harsh weather conditions, and military training backing it all up. Cupping his jaw, she whispered brokenly, "I love you, Gil. I never want to be anywhere else but here, in your arms, a part of your life for as long as you'll have me…"

Gil shoved back tears burning in the backs of his eyes. He leaned down, kissing Kai gently, her mouth eager and warm beneath his. His emotions threatened to cascade through him as he eased away. "Listen to me," he said roughly, skimming her flushed cheek, "You need to know that the first time I saw you with Sam, I was powerfully drawn to you, Kai. It shook me to my soul." He saw her eyes widen with shock. "Hear me out," Gil pleaded. "I felt as if someone slammed me in the head and I was left spinning when Sam introduced me to you. I can't explain it to this day, Kai. As time went on, the more I saw of you, listened to you, the more I found myself starved to know everything about you. And yes, I knew Sam and you loved one another. I did not want to intrude upon that in any way, Kai. I love Sam like a brother to this day and I was his best friend. I wasn't about to let you know how I personally felt toward you."

Kai gasped softly and sat up, the covers pooling around her waist as she stared down at him. "You... loved me even then, Gil?" she choked out, her fingers going to her throat.

He winced, hearing the emotional break in her voice, seeing the stunned realization in her gray eyes. He shrugged and shook his head. "Yes, I did. I tried to explain it to myself. Told myself at first it was lust, not love. That I was lonely and maybe jealous of Sam on some level, although I honestly never felt that way about him or you. And as time went on, it was a secret pleasure to see you again, just to be around you. I couldn't get you out of my heart, Kai, no matter how hard I tried. After a few years, I just accepted that you were the woman that I wanted to spend my life with and I never would." His mouth quirked. "When Sam was killed, I had to contend with the grief of his loss, as well as the guilt of secretly wishing you were mine." He slanted a look up at her, realizing she'd gone pale once more. Gil sat up, arranging the covers around his hips, sliding his hand into hers. "None of this was your fault, Kai. It was all on me. Sam never knew how I felt about you. It was my secret and I was more than willing to go to the grave with it."

Kai stared up at him, absorbing the sadness and guilt in his eyes. "Were…were you ever going to tell me after Sam died that you loved me?" She saw a tortured look come to Gil's expression, felt his fingers tightening some around hers.

"Yes, I was planning on it. But I needed to give you time to grieve for the loss of Sam. I figured in three or four years, whenever you were coming out of his loss, that I'd try approaching you, Kai. It wasn't like I was going to tell you any of this. I didn't ever want to let you know what really happened…

"But…a year later I needed you. I needed just to be near you after Rob got killed. I came to your barracks with the idea of just asking you to sit in the lounge and let me talk. Cry, maybe. I always knew you had a tender heart. I saw how you had drawn Sam out of that damned hard shell he lived within. I saw him bloom beneath your love. I wanted… I needed you, Kai. I loved you even though you didn't know about it. I was hurting so much you were the only person I wanted to turn to for comfort."

"God," Kai whispered brokenly, pressing her fingers against her eyes for a moment. "I didn't know… I didn't realize this, Gil…" Lifting her head, Kai saw the apology, the regret in his blue gaze. Tears leaked out of her eyes.

Tenderly, Gil took his thumbs and removed them, holding her wavering gaze filled with regret. "No, you didn't know. I wasn't going to tell you, Dove. All I wanted…at least I thought I wanted, was to sit down, talk to you and hope like hell you could give me some peace from how I was feeling. I was so torn up..."

She rested her cheek against his rough, opened palm, closing her eyes. "And I kissed you..."

"Yes," he rasped heavily, watching as her moist eyes opened. "It changed everything for me in that second. And I kissed you back. I gave you the most desperate, longing kiss I had inside me. I was carrying so many secrets, so much grief, in shock and not in control like I wished I'd have been."

She took his palm between her own, kissing the back of his hand. "You're human, Gil." And then Kai added softly, "And I found out how human I was when I kissed you."

Gil studied her in the silence between them. "Why did you kiss me, Kai? Was it because you were just trying to ease my pain? Because you felt sorry for me? Why?" Because that was the one question he'd asked himself a million times and had no answer. And it was the one that had gnawed like a wild animal at his heart until this very day. Gil tried to brace and prepare himself internally for her answer.

Kai licked her lower lip, looked away, took a deep breath and turned, meeting his gaze. "No...none of those reasons. I guess we all carry secrets. I—" She choked out, "I had always been drawn to you since the first time I met you two."

Stunned, Gil's lips parted for a moment over her admission. He saw guilt in Kai's expression. "Then? We were both drawn to one another? But we didn't let the other know about it?"

"Right," she said, and sighed, giving him a look of apology. "I loved Sam. I loved him the best I knew how, but he never let me in, Gil. When I met you, I felt my heart open in a way it never had with anyone else, not even Sam. At first, I couldn't understand it, but in the three years I lived with Sam, always fighting a silent battle with him to let me in, he never did. I wanted him to give me intimacy, to share the love I knew he had locked inside himself with me. When you visited, you let your game face drop away. I saw the real you, how open you were and unafraid to show your emotions to me, unlike Sam. I began to realize over time just how emotionally wounded Sam was. You can't know how many times I cried myself asleep when he was out on a mission, blaming myself, that there was something wrong with me that I couldn't get him to open up and emotionally trust me like I trusted him."

"Jesus," Gil muttered, leaning against the headboard, retaining his hand around hers. "Sam was happier than I'd ever seen him, Kai, after he met and married you. He suddenly started living life more fully and I knew it was because of your love, your influence on him."

"Yes," she said sadly, "but it never translated any deeper than that, Gil. Sam couldn't open up like you do. He was afraid of being vulnerable. I know it came from his childhood. I knew that. But I couldn't get him to trust me enough and that hurt me more than anything. It didn't lessen the love I held for him. But I was giving, and he was taking. Those three years I felt like a plant that was slowly being starved to death, not receiving the water or emotions I needed from Sam." She pulled her hand from his, pressing them to her eyes for a moment. Allowing them to drop into her lap, she said hoarsely, "Two weeks before Sam was killed, I had made up my mind to ask him for a divorce when he got off that mission."

Gil blinked, the words slamming into him. His brows fell. He saw the devastation and guilt in Kai's face. "Did he know?"

"No, thank God. I was trying to time it such that he would be rotated stateside for six months. I was planning on telling him then. There was no way I would tell him while he was over in Afghanistan and cause him to get killed. I would never do that."

For a moment, all Gil could do was feel the twist and shock of emotions filtering through him. "What a mess," he muttered, shaking his head.

"Isn't it?" Kai said unsteadily, wiping tears from her eyes. "From the moment you and I met, we were falling in love with one another whether we knew it or not. Whether we acknowledged it consciously or not. I always felt, when you came for a visit, you breathed new life into me, Gil. You were the diametric opposite of Sam in so many ways. You could laugh, tease, had a sense of humor, and Sam couldn't do any of those things. At least, not with me. I felt I was living half a life with him. I was emotionally dying around him, and no matter what I did, he couldn't take that step and open up and share himself with me. That's what I so desperately needed with him," she said, her voice strained and scratchy.

"Come here," Gil urged, pulling Kai into his arms, tucking her alongside him, her head resting on his shoulder so that he could look into her glistening eyes, the tears silently falling down her cheeks. Smoothing her velvet cheek with his thumb, he rasped, "You loved him the best you could, Kai. Sam was so damned wounded by his childhood he just couldn't span that trust to you. It wasn't your fault. I saw how you tried. But know this—" he looked deeply into her dark gray eyes torn with grief "—you made Sam happy. You gave him the best three years of his sorry-assed life. And you did make a difference, Dove. Sam was as happy as I'd ever seen him. So don't gig yourself on what happened. That's what you need to embrace. You gave him something no other human being had ever given him—real love. And that was the greatest gift one person could ever give another. And just another reason why I love you so damned much…"

CHAPTER TWENTY-THREE

"WE'VE GOT A surprise for you, Kai," Gus said, pointing at the birthday cake she'd made for her at the Triple H. "Come and sit."

Kai smiled and leaned down, gently embracing Miss Gus. "You didn't have to do this for me. Thank you."

Everyone else in the household came and sat at the table. Outside, fat, thick snowflakes were lazily twirling out of the gunmetal-gray sky that covered the area. It was only October and already winter was setting in for good. It was Saturday and Kai had known the Holts were going to throw her a birthday party. She suspected strongly that Gil had something to do with it, but he didn't own up to it, just grinned proudly at her, instead. Miss Gus was an unofficial grandmother to all of them as they sat down at the trestle table.

The cake was three layers of chocolate, white frosting with pink roses and green leaves decorated across it. Today, she was thirty years old.

The laughter and chatting was high in the warmth of the kitchen. Gil sat at one end of the table, Kai at his elbow. Cass pulled out the chair at the other end for Miss Gus to sit in.

As Kai gazed around the table of happy faces, she

had never felt more at peace and joyful than right now. The months living with Gil had helped to heal both their wounds in so many ways. Thanks to him, Kai had finally released the guilt she'd carried over Sam's death. They'd had so many long, deep talks about that time in their lives, the decisions they'd made, the secrets they'd kept from one another, and why they had.

As Kai glanced over at Gil, who looked incredibly handsome in a dark red cowboy shirt, a blue neckerchief around his thick neck, the look of love in his eyes for her alone, she smiled shyly over at him. He smiled back and she saw the tenderness burning in his eyes. The months after the crash were remarkable and memorable. Beautiful. Dreams coming true. The fierce love she held for Gil took her breath away. Her body still glowed from this morning's lovemaking with him.

He had left midmorning, saying he had things to do out at the Triple H. Little did she know he was helping the Holt family set things up for her birthday party. Kai never knew she could love one person so deeply and widely as she did Gil. Her heart blossomed fiercely for him. She had never felt this kind of love for Sam, now understanding, with Gil's insights and help, that there were many kinds of love, not just one type. And that all of them were sincere and genuine.

Sandy, who had helped Miss Gus make the birthday cake, held up her hand. Everyone quieted. She gave Cass a look that clearly would be interpreted by everyone as a look of love, but no one said anything about it because, as they'd grown closer, it was obvious to everyone.

"Kai, this is a very special birthday party for you."

Her eyes grew warm with tears. "And I think Gil has a gift for you. Gil?"

Kai turned, smiling at him. "What did you do? Get me that copper teakettle I was drooling over at the hardware store in town?" Because she loved copper in all forms. She had excitedly told Gil two weeks earlier about the beautiful hand-beaten copper teakettle. That it would be a wonderful addition sitting on top of the elegant Wolf stove in his condo.

"Well," Gil murmured, moving to one side and drawing something out of his pocket, "not exactly. But I thought you might like this even better."

He brought out a small green velvet box and opened it up in front of her. Inside was a set of wedding rings. "Will you marry me, Kai? Be my wife? My best friend? My lover?" His voice faltered with emotion as he held her widening, stunned gaze.

The table completely quieted, all eyes on Kai as she stared in shock at the glittering diamond solitaire engagement ring and plain gold band wedding ring. She pressed her hand to her lips, staring at Gil, tears running down across her fingers. He gave her an understanding smile, taking her hand away, holding it.

"Just tell me yes?" he teased, tears glittering in his eyes.

Sobbing, Kai nodded. "Y-yes. I'll marry you. You know I will!" She pulled her hand out of his, stood and threw her arms around his broad shoulders, holding him as hard as she could with her woman's strength.

The table broke out in cheers and clapping as Gil released her, pushed back the chair and stood up. He held Kai against him, their heads buried against one another.

Gus cackled. "This is one birthday Kai is never gonna forget." She beamed at the happy couple standing at the other end. "Put the ring on her finger, Gil, before she changes her mind!"

Laughter rang in the warm kitchen.

Gil gave Miss Gus a grin and picked up the engagement ring. Kai extended her left hand, her eyes moist and only on him. He slipped it on her left finger and it fit perfectly. "Now," he said unsteadily, "it's official." He took her into his arms, kissing her tenderly amidst more cheers and clapping.

As they eased apart, Gil sat down and guided Kai between his legs and she sat on his long, hard thigh.

As she slipped her arm around Gil's shoulders, holding him close, her head resting against his, she saw Cass stand up. He pulled the chair aside and he looked at everyone, a softened expression coming to his face.

"Well, we're going to make this a *very* special day," he told everyone. Turning, he knelt down on one knee in front of Sandy and produced a red velvet box. Swallowing hard, Cass held her look of surprise. "Sandy, I know you aren't expecting this," he began, showing her the box, "but I can't see my life without you in it." He opened the box, producing a set of wedding rings. "These belonged to my grandmother, who has now passed. She gave them to me before she died and told me when I found a woman who made me wake up in the morning smiling and going to bed at night smiling, I should ask her to marry me." He searched Sandy's stricken expression. "Will you marry me, Sandy Holt?" he said, and he offered her the box of rings.

Giving a cry, Sandy burst out into tears.

Everyone made sounds of sympathy.

Cass set the rings on the table, rose and slid his arms around her shaking shoulders, drawing Sandy gently against him. He patted her back and soothed her with words against her ear. When she finally got a hold of her escaping emotions, she sat up, embarrassed, wiping her tears away until Miss Gus offered her an embroidered linen handkerchief she always carried in her pocket.

Sandy thickly thanked her, gripping the handkerchief in her lap as Cass brought the ring box over to her to look at the very old-fashioned diamond ring set. She gave Cass such a loving look, reached out and touched his cheek. "You know I'll marry you. You always did." She managed a slight laugh that mingled with his proud, burgeoning smile.

In no time, Cass had slipped the diamond engagement ring on her slender finger. "Well," he warned her good-naturedly, "I'm your *last* husband, dear woman. You're stuck with me for the rest of our lives."

Everyone broke out in laughter and nodded.

Cass leaned forward, sealing the deal with a kiss that showed just how much he loved this brave woman warrior who had fought cancer twice and survived it.

KAI SIGHED, CONTENT to be in Gil's arms as they sat on the sofa at their condo. She lay across his lap, in the curve of his arm, her head resting on the couch behind them. Gazing fondly over at him, she admitted, "I'll never forget this day as long as I live, Gil Hanford. You were such a sneak, taking off midmorning. You didn't have business in town, you were busy helping them with my birthday party at the Triple H."

"Guilty," he admitted, sliding his fingers down her arm, feeling the nubby warmth of the black velvet tee she wore. The color made her hair, now brushing her shoulders, stand out. He enclosed her left hand, looking at the ring gleaming on her finger. "But it was a white lie for a good cause."

She smiled. "And did Cass tell everyone he was going to propose to Sandy beforehand?"

Nodding, he said, "Yeah. We all knew."

"Except for me and Sandy."

Giving her a wry look, Gil lifted her hand, placing a kiss in the palm of it. "You ladies were the object of our affection. We wanted to surprise you."

Laughing softly, Kai stroked his cheek. "Oh, we were both surprised, no question."

Gil settled his hand on her hip. "When do you want to get married? Or have you thought that far ahead, Dove?"

"I was thinking next June." Wrinkling her nose, Kai said, "I don't want a winter wedding like Cass and Sandy do. I want sunshine, wildflowers blooming, warmth..."

"You can have it," Gil assured her, squeezing her.

"I don't know who I'm happier for," Kai admitted softly, trailing her fingers across his cheek. "Us or Sandy and Cass."

"Her doctors gave her a good bill of health," Gil said. "And personally? I think because Cass is so damned strong, gentle and concerned with Sandy, it's going to give her the break and support she emotionally needs to really get well."

"Love is the greatest healer of them all," Kai whispered, closing her eyes, her brow against his head. "I predict Sandy and Cass are going to live to a grand old age, silver haired, just like Miss Gus."

Gil chuckled and slid his hand over her shoulder and down her curved back. "Cass is going to be a solid foundation for Sandy. She's come so far since he arrived at the Triple H. And I feel she's going to continue to improve under his love and care."

"Love makes even the worst and darkest days bearable, Gil."

He met her half-opened eyes that swam with love for him. "I know you did for me. Those five days you gave me put me back together in ways I can't ever put into words. But it was your heart, your care—" Gil drew her closer, kissing her lips "—and your love which neither of us had ever spoken about to one another, that healed me."

"They were beautiful days," she agreed in a choked tone, her lips an inch from his. "I'll never forget them. I never wanted to forget them, Gil. You had loved me so well, was so vulnerable and sharing with me, that I'd felt reborn with you."

"Now," Gil rasped, holding Kai's glistening gaze, "we have the rest of our lives with each other..."

* * * * *

*In February, don't miss OUT RIDER,
Lindsay McKenna's next story of
love set in Wyoming!*

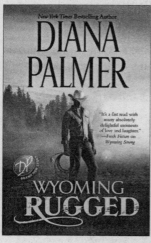

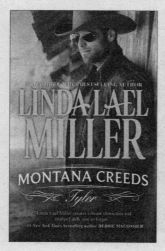

REQUEST YOUR FREE BOOKS!

2 FREE NOVELS
FROM THE ROMANCE COLLECTION
PLUS 2 FREE GIFTS!

YES! Please send me 2 FREE novels from the Romance Collection and my 2 FREE gifts (gifts are worth about $10). After receiving them, if I don't wish to receive any more books, I can return the shipping statement marked "cancel." If I don't cancel, I will receive 4 brand-new novels every month and be billed just $6.49 per book in the U.S. or $6.99 per book in Canada. That's a savings of at least 19% off the cover price. It's quite a bargain! Shipping and handling is just 50¢ per book in the U.S. and 75¢ per book in Canada.* I understand that accepting the 2 free books and gifts places me under no obligation to buy anything. I can always return a shipment and cancel at any time. Even if I never buy another book, the two free books and gifts are mine to keep forever.

194/394 MDN GH4D

Name _____ (PLEASE PRINT) _____

Address _____ Apt. # _____

City _____ State/Prov. _____ Zip/Postal Code _____

Signature (if under 18, a parent or guardian must sign)

Mail to the **Reader Service**:
IN U.S.A.: P.O. Box 1867, Buffalo, NY 14240-1867
IN CANADA: P.O. Box 609, Fort Erie, Ontario L2A 5X3

Want to try two free books from another line?
Call 1-800-873-8635 or visit www.ReaderService.com.

* Terms and prices subject to change without notice. Prices do not include applicable taxes. Sales tax applicable in N.Y. Canadian residents will be charged applicable taxes. Offer not valid in Quebec. This offer is limited to one order per household. Not valid for current subscribers to the Romance Collection or the Romance/Suspense Collection. All orders subject to credit approval. Credit or debit balances in a customer's account(s) may be offset by any other outstanding balance owed by or to the customer. Please allow 4 to 6 weeks for delivery. Offer available while quantities last.

Your Privacy—The Reader Service is committed to protecting your privacy. Our Privacy Policy is available online at www.ReaderService.com or upon request from the Reader Service.

We make a portion of our mailing list available to reputable third parties that offer products we believe may interest you. If you prefer that we not exchange your name with third parties, or if you wish to clarify or modify your communication preferences, please visit us at www.ReaderService.com/consumerschoice or write to us at Reader Service Preference Service, P.O. Box 9062, Buffalo, NY 14240-9062. Include your complete name and address.

LINDSAY McKENNA

77851   HIGH COUNTRY REBEL   ___ $7.99 U.S.   ___$8.99 CAN.

(limited quantities available)

TOTAL AMOUNT	$ _____
POSTAGE & HANDLING	$ _____
($1.00 FOR 1 BOOK, 50¢ for each additional)	
APPLICABLE TAXES*	$ _____
TOTAL PAYABLE	$ _____

(check or money order—please do not send cash)

To order, complete this form and send it, along with a check or money order for the total above, payable to HQN Books, to: **In the U.S.:** 3010 Walden Avenue, P.O. Box 9077, Buffalo, NY 14269-9077; **In Canada:** P.O. Box 636, Fort Erie, Ontario, L2A 5X3.

Name: _____

Address: _____ City: _____

State/Prov.: _____ Zip/Postal Code: _____

Account Number (if applicable): _____

075 CSAS

*New York residents remit applicable sales taxes.
*Canadian residents remit applicable GST and provincial taxes.

HQN™

www.HQNBooks.com

PHLM1215BL